WHAT
BOYS
ARE
MADE
OF

Book 1 of the Saint Flaherty Series

WHAT BOYS ARE MADE OF

A novel by
S. Hunter
Nisbet

~

Badapple Press

BadApple Press

WHAT BOYS ARE MADE OF

Printed in the United States of America
Published by Badapple Press

First Printing, 2016
ISBN 978-0692635193
S. Hunter Nisbet
Athens, OH 45701

www.shunternisbet.com

Cover design © 2016 by Stephanie Hunter
Editing by Jennifer Zaczek, Cypress Editing
Author photo © 2016 C. Zob

To those who didn't make it.

Simon

Erin

~~Art~~

TAYLOR

Grace

1

Simon

My opponent is some hick from across the river they put in shorts and called a contender. They got him ten feet away from me, surrounded by the guys who set up this match. They're probably telling him he's gonna win.

Yeah, no, ain't gonna happen. The crowd filling this alley didn't come for him.

Chris Hopkins stands on his toes to shout in my ear. "Got some big bets on you, boy!"

Art pushes him back into the crowd. "We're busy, piss off."

"Oh come on, Artie, I gave you good odds. Gimme a tip at least."

"My boy Simon's gonna win, that's your tip."

My opponent's people are moving, the coach stepping out. Art meets him in the open space between our two crowds to shake hands, knuckles white. No refs in a street match, no. The only rules here are no eye gouging and no fishhooks, and the Market guards have already been paid off. Ain't no one gonna stop this fight; we'll go until one of us can't swing no more.

I take one last drink from my water bottle before sliding my mouth guard in. Check the laces on my boots, 'cause there's too much broken glass to fight barefoot. Across from me, my opponent's taking off his shirt to show knife scars, with muscles underneath.

That's okay. I got muscles too.

The coaches nod, the noise ramps up, and it's time to get started. Ain't no homework in this alley, no teachers, no nagging, just me and my fists and a thousand ways to win. Art takes my coat, and I strip down to my shorts, waiting, waiting, breath white in the air of All Saints' Day. I'm ready for this, bouncing on the balls of my feet, taking a few practice jabs. Warmed up, taped up, let's get this started.

Art leans in so close it's like his voice is inside my head. "Fuck him up, Saint Flaherty."

I stride forward, touch knuckles with my opponent. He's big like me, got a reach like mine, exactly like we heard beforehand. If there's a difference, it ain't much.

Let's do this.

I punch once, feint back. Land a hit on his shoulder that he don't block in time. He tries a right straight but puts too much power in and I dump him on his ass. Twenty seconds in and I'm winning by a mile. Seriously? This guy's supposed to be a contender?

His people hiss, like it's my fault their guy's shit.

"Don't get cocky!"

That's Art, and he knows what he's talking about. I'm gonna win this not 'cause this guy's bad but 'cause I'm good. I'm better.

The other guy's up and swinging, and I'm on him quick, going for the gut. He fetches me a clip on the temple and I feel the impact, but it's not enough to even make me pause. A kick to the leg distracts him enough for me to smash his nose.

He reels back, blood running down his chin. What the hell just happened there? I shouldn't have been able to get that hit in this early. This is a fucking joke, a slaughter. Anyone can see he's losing hard, standing there panting with his people flooding around, putting a towel to his face and—

A knife in his hands.

Holy shit. No way, there's no fucking way.

I back up, 'cause the match goes until one of us can't. Period.

What do I do now? That'll cut my knuckle protection to ribbons, take a finger off if I don't watch it. I fall, he'll fucking stab me. Probably I could kick the knife out of his hands. Probably. Or...

I could be a legend, exactly like we practiced. I don't do knives, ain't never learned 'em, 'cause it takes time, but enough assholes pull 'em when they get cornered that we came up with a defense. It's short and it's quick and it'll make people lose their minds.

I get my hand behind me, feel Art's brush mine as he passes over the baseball bat. I'll win 'cause I'm the best.

My opponent lunges in. The blade gouges deep in the wood, but I hold, knock him back. He slashes across this time. I jump aside, but his knife glides across my chest like my skin's butter and I don't feel it now but I know I will. This ain't a game no more.

If I fuck up, I could die. Holy shit.

"C'mon, Saint Flaherty."

I ain't gonna die. I'm gonna win.

I catch his elbow on the downswing, hear him hiss in pain, good, but still he circles, swinging wildly now, like he's crazy. Maybe he's on something. Maybe they found a madman and set him on me. He's gonna take off my fingers if he gets the chance, and that still won't stop this fight.

"Take him out, Simon!" Art yells behind me, and I know, I know I gotta get my opponent before he gets me. I gotta knock him out, gotta end it now.

He closes in, teeth bared, knife aiming for my side in a wild attack, but I'm ready for this, and as he comes 'round, I put the bat up and *swing*.

It sounds like a boiled egg being smashed.

He hits the wall and slides down it in slow motion, like he's just lying down to take a rest, only you don't take a rest when your head looks like that.

Oh God.

Oh my God.

I can't move. There's a ringing in my ears, like someone's boxed 'em. That guy should be getting up any second now, any second. Or moving. Or someone should at least be coming to check on him. Someone should check to see that he ain't—

A hand touches my shoulder, icy fingers freezing my hot skin. "Put it down, Simon," Art says.

Down. It. The bat that I hit the other boy with.

I drop it, wipe my hands on my chest to get the feel of the wood off. Only, my chest is slick with blood. My blood, bright red and sticky even in the alley shadows. Art pushes a towel in my hands, and they're shaking, shaking from my heart beating so hard in my ears, ringing with the noise of that guy's head hitting the wall. He looks so wrong. He should've moved by now, he should've—

"Get it together, Simon." Art's fingers dig into my chin, jerk my head around until he's straight in front of me, blocking out the screaming crowd, screaming at the blood, so much blood. "Simon, c'mon, *look* at me."

The other coach kneels next to the guy I fought. He picks up a wrist, feels around for a pulse. Shakes his head and stands back up.

No, no no no. The baseball bat was for show. I didn't really just...I couldn't've...

I try to force my lips to move, but I can't. They feel like old rubber bands, not real, none of this is real.

The coach wipes his hands on his pants. "He's dead."

Art nods back. "Yeah. He is."

"But..." They both look at me. My mouth won't connect with my thoughts as I hear myself say, "I didn't even swing that hard."

Art's grip on my chin goes slack. For once he don't got nothing to say. Good, 'cause I just...oh my fucking God. His brains are on the wall and now the ground is heaving up 'cause there's blood on my hands and everyone saw and I...and I...

Art hits me across the face. I stagger back, gasping for breath as he drapes my coat over my shoulders, hissing, "Don't you dare pass out here, Simon, not in front of the fans." He turns me around, gives me a shove so finally I can't see the body no more. "Let's go."

Chris is still here, standing in the crowd collecting money, all those bets on what would happen. Bets on what I'd do to that guy.

Did they bet I'd kill him?

Kill him. I killed him. It echoes back and forth until it's all I can hear with the sound of his head as it broke. I can't seem to breathe right, but I can't pass out here, so I look around for something, anything.

There, turning the corner ahead of us, is my dad.

He saw it all.

Art turns back long enough to clamp his fingers around my wrist and drag me along. "Come on, kiddo, let's get you home."

2

Erin

The look, the lost look on Simon's face when he comes through the back door: a thousand yards long and going nowhere at all. It shows, don't it just? Yeah, I know what happened. Just because this ain't the kind of town to bother about another body don't change what's going on in his head. Blood on his hands, blood on his heart.

I strip him down to his boxers right there in the kitchen, set his fight gear to soak in a tub while I set about stitching the cut on his chest. It's maybe three inches below the collarbone, a clean wound at least, easy to pull back together. I smear on the numbing gel before I put the needle in, but I'm pretty sure he wouldn't notice even without the gel, not with the way he is right now. I know shock when I see it.

He needs to wash the blood off, that's the important part. He might never feel clean again, but stains of the soul shouldn't show on the skin. I slap a sponge in his hand, and it's like he's eleven years old all over again, shown up in my backyard, digging through my compost heap for scraps as the peace treaties were being signed in Washington. Back then he was a foot shorter and hella skinnier, nothing but a war kid with no family to speak of. I dewormed him like a stray dog, cleaned him up and found that he shined underneath. A good kid. A sweet kid. And I kept him for my own.

And now the only sound in my kitchen is Simon behind the curtain in the corner, washing off blood into a basin careful-like so he don't mess up the bandage, careful like he always is. I swear, it's been five years since he came to me, but some days it's been all my life.

Art stands in a corner and don't say a word. Too late to say anything. Too late to take things back. Drones change course, but the bombs have already dropped. Ain't nobody gonna come to arrest Simon, but that don't make what happened right, and even Art understands that. He and I both have our share of bodies in our wake, but there's killing because you have to, and there's this.

Not that a little difference like that stopped Art from collecting the prize money, of course, grimy paper notes that dirty my kitchen table. That was the point of the fight after all. Art ain't got principles, but he does have priorities.

An hour to opening time at my bar, Art finally gets the hint, slamming the back door behind him. From behind the curtain, Simon emerges with a damp shirt and blank stare. The table's set with a plate of stew and a measure of cutthroat gin to cut the pain he'll be feeling any minute now from those stitches.

The stiches, yeah. Inside his head, from his heart, from every bit of his soul that's screaming out for what he's done. I know, I know. Gotta numb that pain before it takes over.

"I'm going to hell," he whispers.

We ain't going down that path. "It was a fight."

"But it weren't supposed to be like...like this."

His eyes, oh his eyes. Blue, so familiar in a million ways too many. My boy, my kid brother. My charge and ally against this harsh world.

I put my hands on my hips, wait for him to sputter to a stop. "What was it supposed to be like, exactly?"

"I...I don't know. He just pulled a knife. Art and I had practiced—"

"Simon." I stop him right there. "Now you listen, and you listen good. He pulled a knife?"

"Yeah."

"And then you pulled one?"

"A baseball bat."

"Jesus. Fine. A baseball bat." Good God, Art, what have you done. Simon's staring at his bowl like he's waiting for the dead to rise, and I can't tell him it ain't his fault, but I can tell him why it don't matter. "Point is—and you listen to me—point is, he pulled first. He upped the ante, not you. Do you understand?"

"But I—"

"I said, do you understand me?"

"But I walked into that fight. I touched his knuckles. And I—" He stops himself, runs his fingers through his hair as the sunset catches on it so it shines red like the blood I wiped from his face. The gin disappears in one shuddering gulp. Simon, boy-o, I won't tell no one if you cry, I swear I won't.

But men don't cry, and Simon ain't a boy no more. You don't get to kill people and stay a child, not even in this town.

Especially in this town.

"I'm going to hell."

"No more than the rest of us." On the other side of Buchell a bell begins to ring. Five o'clock. Just another night in a town what don't care about another body, so long as it don't block the door to the bar. "C'mon, Simon, it's opening time. Let's get this place moving."

3

Art

They buried the cholera dead in the old park four, five years back, the spring the river flooded people's wells. The Market guards piled the bodies in the sunken skate park, 'cause concrete doesn't leak too quick, and filled it over with rubble from the bombed-out houses near the center of town. Since then, the rest of Buchell's left this place alone. People think it's haunted, think ghosts will stalk them if they set foot on hallowed ground. That suits me just fine. I been training Simon here for four years now, storing our gear in the crumbling shelter house, and no one's bothered us yet, even though we meet every morning these days and most afternoons.

Simon shows up just after dawn, blank-faced and distant. We go about stretching, then I outline the drill, something simple, strike and defend. I put up my arms and take a stance, leg back. Simon stares somewhere past my right ear and takes his.

"Start when you're ready," I say.

A bird calls nearby, and bare branches scrape in the wind. I wait. He knows what he's doing.

Simon strikes without warning. I block it too easily. "Come on, kiddo, put some oomph into it."

No reply. Big surprise. He didn't talk after the fight yesterday, either. I half wondered if I'd broken his mind.

The next punch is weak, the third's off target, and he's yet to meet my eyes. What a freaking joke. I flex my fists and take a new position.

"Come on, Simon, this is pathetic. Unless you seriously hurt your hands, you better start taking this seriously. Try again."

Simon mutters something that I don't catch.

"Excuse me? What was that? Something you wanna say?"

He talks to his feet, but his fingers curl into fists, so maybe I'm getting through. "No."

"No. Right. Why are you flinching?"

"Don't matter."

"Don't give me that crap. Is this about yesterday? That why you're acting weird today?"

"Shut up."

Now we're getting somewhere. I sneer, cruel to be kind. "Why should I? This is training. You're here to get better, and how are you supposed to do that if you're not willing to give a hundred percent?"

"Then I don't wanna train today!" The words seem to echo through the clearing.

Gotta lance a boil, not let it fester. "Why? 'Cause you think killing someone means you don't have to work hard anymore? Is that it? You're too good for this now, huh?"

Simon freezes for all of a fraction of a second as rage writes itself all over his face. Then he leaps at me.

I kick the muscles in his thigh to knock him down, but he's straight back up, murder in his eyes, and it's a real fight now. I'm still blocking him, but only barely, and if I don't start hitting back, he'll have me down. I swing and miss, and he uses my momentum to grab onto my shirt and come around with a hook that stops just short of my jaw.

He's not looking at me. He's staring at his fist, at what he was about to do. We both are. Jesus Christ, he weighs twenty pounds more than I do, and it's time to end this before he actually does kill me. He's out of control, totally out of control.

Palm meets knife, knife meets the hollow under Simon's ear, pressing just hard enough to get his attention. We stare at each other for long seconds, his fist still hanging in the air. His pupils are huge, dilated with fear. Fear of my blade, or of himself?

Get it together, Simon. Come on, kiddo.

He blinks and drops his fist. I lower my hand and touch my cheek where he was gonna hit. I don't let on, but my heart's beating fast. That could've broken my jaw, and there would've been nothing to stop him after that. Jesus Christ.

Simon snatches the knife from my hand and sticks it in his pocket. It's the switchblade I stole off the dead boy after the fight when no one was looking. Wonder if Simon recognizes it?

"No," he growls.

"What?"

His voice doesn't catch or anything, but his jaw is clenched. "No, it don't mean anything," he grinds out. "Killing that guy don't mean a goddamned thing."

And it doesn't, not really, not in this godforsaken world. One more man dead, and who will notice or care?

But firsts break barriers. First kiss, first fuck, first kill. You can't go back, and you can't stop once you start, because if you've done it once, you can do it again.

I shoulder my bag. I've been meaning to do this for a while, but maybe today's the day. "Come on, kiddo. We got someone to see. About time you learned how to use a knife."

"What, baseball bat not make 'em dead enough?"

Christ, that was bitter. "No, because that trick only really works once before they figure it out, and you've done it. Bunny's out of the hat. Time to learn a new one, should they wanna try it again."

"So you're gonna learn me."

I glance at him. He scowls back, shoulders hunched. A tear runs down his face.

Oh Simon, oh kiddo, you're all guff and tough guy, but a week ago you were only fifteen, and don't look at me like that, please don't look at me like that.

I take him in my arms, muffle his face against my shoulder. He doesn't cry, and I don't hear him as the sun rises over the old park where only weeds grow and boys turn into men the hard way.

Fear has to be met head-on, and there's only one way to do that. I give him five minutes' grace, time enough for him to wipe his nose on his sleeve before we set out. I can't teach him knives, but I know a guy who can.

After both militaries cleared out of the foothills, Mick Perry dumped his uniform in a ditch, stole a truck full of ammo, and drove back here to set up shop in his old family home, a two-story that opens straight onto the street. The sign on the front of his place says it's a pawnshop, but what Mick deals is arms.

He also headlined the first knife tournament Buchell ever had.

I bang on the door as we enter, bell ringing above our heads. Mick's hunched over his counter, staring into a cup of coffee. His eyebrows go up when he sees who it is.

"Hey lookie, if it isn't the new angel of death and his handler." He gives a whistle between his teeth that I could kill him for. "What are you doing in my humble little establishment, Saint Flaherty?"

"I got a boy here who needs to stay alive next time someone pulls a knife."

"So you thought of your good friend Mick, huh? Knew you'd come by sooner or later. It'll cost you a pretty penny, but yeah, I'll give your boy knife lessons. That is why you're here, isn't it?"

Simon looks to me and I grin. "Mick and I go way back. We fought together, played high school football together."

"Haven't seen you in a long while, Artie. Must've been, what, couple months? Forget where I live?"

"Yeah, well, I been busy getting Simon here into winning shape."

Mick looks Simon up and down, theatrical to a fault, taking in everything from the enormous old army boots to the T-shirt stretched tight across his shoulders. "Jesus, you sure have. And now you wanna arm him?"

"Can you do it?"

He moves before I'm even finished with the sentence, the knife coming out of nowhere. Steel flashes for a brief second and then gleams, stopped mid-plunge as Simon's biceps strain. Eyes lock, will against will, as he slowly pushes Mick's weapon away from his heart.

Simon doesn't see the second knife until it's up against his neck.

Mick grins like a wolverine before stepping back and dusting his hands off. Who knows what Simon's thinking. If he thinks.

"Always wanted to try that. Not half-bad reflexes, good strength.

Yeah, I can do it. Get him over here every day, and don't let him fight for at least a month, regulation or otherwise, not until I've got him in shape to defend himself. Has he got a knife?"

Simon begins to shake his head, then pulls out the dead boy's jackknife that he took from me. Not that he knows what it is. "Yeah. I do." It's the first thing he's said since we left the park.

"Then bring yourself and that here when you're done with—you're still in school, yeah? Yeah, knew I'd heard something like that. Three o'clock, be here. Now scram, Artie and I gotta talk." Mick watches him go. "Hell of a boy there."

"Yeah."

"Sixteen?"

"As of five days ago."

"And you've never brought him to learn in all these years because...?"

I stare at the white-shirted figure outside, tramping over the broken sidewalk, going home to clean up before class. He barely fits in the desks anymore, but still he goes.

"'Cause I didn't think it'd come to killing so soon."

"Hey now, just because you can use a knife—"

"Save it, Mick. I'll see you this afternoon, alright?"

He grins, almost leers. "What, you don't trust me and your little pet alone?"

"Course not. He's already killed one man this week. Wouldn't want to make it two, now would we?"

4

Simon

We used to go down to see the soldiers, all us kids. They was called the old soldiers 'cause they still wore their uniforms, tan, green, or dark brown, three different colors for three different sides: Pro-DC, Anti, and the Second South. I mean, most of the men around here fought, and a lot of the women, but then the war was over and they all got jobs and weren't nobody gonna talk about it. But the old soldiers, they would. Three of them, sitting on the porch in the cul-de-sac with their shotguns and their chaw, drinking until they fell asleep without their fingers ever leaving the triggers.

Erin didn't like them. She said they was disgusting, but they let me drink from their cups of homemade and told stories without leaving anything out. Sometimes they'd even give us kids our own cup if we'd run errands for them, like go get more tobacco or weed or something. We'd share one of them cups between two or three of us and stumble home, and I used to wonder how those old men could drink so much and still keep things straight.

Older I get, the less I wonder.

After enough time's passed to make it look to Erin like I went to school, I go home to change and head back to Mick's shop. He shakes my hand and leads me to the pole barn out back of his property. It's got a fancy solar generator, 'cause the guy who owns this town, Petrowski, he supported the Anti and won't let the government come in to put up new wires. When Mick flips the switch, the barn lights up like the gym at school does, only the gym don't got a dirt floor and crates of ammo all piled up in the back.

"Art say much about me?" he asks.

"No, just said you were the best. At knives."

"You see the scars on my face?"

I peer closer. He smells like polished metal. "No?"

"Course you don't; I don't have any. And if you want to keep your pretty little face intact, you'll do as I say. Strip down and stretch."

Once a soldier, always a soldier, Erin says. But what she don't say is there's two types of soldier. There's them like Art, like Mick, clean shaven with buzzed hair 'cause it's what they know and what they like, or anyways, what they're comfortable with.

And then there's the old men. It's like what they learned in the war just erased everything else, and once there weren't no new orders to follow, they just shut down. Thinking hurt too much, so they lived to drink. Drank to live.

Mick takes off his shirt, and there's the scars, ridged lines crisscrossing, tic-tac-toe, and another on his wrist what's gnarled and puckered. He's put a tattoo over that one, but even the ink don't seem to like it.

"Is that from a fight?"

"Almost." He holds it out for me to look at, to touch.

The door bangs open and there stands Art, glaring and trying not to show it. "Sorry I'm late. Hope I didn't miss anything."

"Not at all. Simon was just admiring my last scar."

"Was he, now."

Art's got a twitch in his jaw. Him and Mick, they got the same military stance and the same bark when they give orders, but they're nothing alike, and they ain't really friends. I've only known Mick for two minutes, but already I can see that.

I pull out the knife what I stole from Art, press the button. Open, it looks the same as the one from yesterday. Exactly the same.

I can smell blood and brains and sweat. The alley walls are closing around me, cold red brick and wet asphalt and a crowd of people screaming for death. I started fighting 'cause it made me sleep dreamless, 'cause hitting stuff felt better than being helpless, but for the first time since I was a kid, the nightmares was back. I almost woke up screaming at dawn, praying yesterday had been some sort of god-awful dream and it weren't real and I didn't kill—

Mick knocks into my shoulder as he turns. He's watching my face, careful-like. Does he know? "Ready, Simon?"

He was a soldier, but he's the kind who moves on.

What kind of man will I be?

5

Erin

Somewhere along the time he started fighting in the official tournaments, Simon figured out that if he scowls constantly, no one asks him questions. It's a man's way of lying, not with words, but with actions, because his fists had made him a celebrity around here. He weren't just Erin's kid no more, no, he was the teenager with a one-hit KO. So to people who don't know him, he probably looks the same today as he did two days ago.

He ain't. God, but he ain't.

He's still glaring, but it ain't to hide from the world, no; he's hiding from himself. He's gone back to that same place in his head from when he was a just a kid screaming from nightmares every night. Had them for months, blank-faced all day, and then at night I'd hear him crying in his sleep. At first I thought it was just war stuff he was afraid of, but no, it was memories, fire and death and a jump from a window that his mom didn't quite make but he did. When I held him close, I could feel the dent in his skull what proved it, healed lumpy beneath the hair just above his ear. First four months I had him, he woke from terror more often than he didn't.

And then one day Art taught Simon how to punch straight, and I never heard his nightmares again. He smiled sometimes, and he was fine. Maybe that's why I didn't try to stop him training, back when I could've.

If only I'd have known. I should've seen, and I didn't, and now he's got that look like he's dying inside, and I swear to God I woke up at dawn wondering why he weren't knocking on my door asking why nothing was okay anymore. Passed his little room on my way to the outhouse and swear I heard him holding his breath, hoping that I'd go away so's he could get on with grieving in peace.

Peace. He'll never have peace again, and who's to blame for that?

"You took him *where*?"

Art and I are in the cellar after the bar's closed for the night, me sorting supplies, him holding the lamp and looking shifty.

"Mick was the best, back when. He'll teach Simon right."

I glare at him. "The man's dangerous."

"So are you."

I damn well nearly stick my finger up his nose, pointing it so fast. "That's not the same, and you know it. I run a business based on my reputation. He runs his on blood."

Art lays his hand on my arm and I shake it off. "C'mon, Erin, don't be like that. I'm gonna be paying him, and he'll keep his word. Guys like Mick live by their reputation. He won't break his promise."

"And what," I bite out, "is that, exactly?"

"Simon isn't gonna get hurt."

"The man's teaching him dueling! Of course he's gonna get hurt!"

"Well, he did fine this afternoon. And yeah, Mick was taking it easy, but not by much. Simon'll learn how to survive another knife fight, in regulation or on the street, and hopefully without having to kill."

And that's just it, isn't it? There will be another fight, because Simon likes them in a way he don't like school. I had to use every threat I know to keep him from dropping out last summer. I went to high school, so did Art and most everyone else our age and times were different then, but they haven't changed so much that dropping out at fifteen's a smart thing to do. Simon's going to high school, and then he'll, well, he'll do something more than working for the local cartel. Boy's got a brain. He's not stupid, just slow. Solid.

"Simon don't have time for knives. He has to study, and right now he does that after school. He hasn't done his homework yet today, thanks very much."

"We'll still train in the morning, and school's only, what, five hours a day?"

"I have a bar to run, and I need his help."

"Get Burkes in full-time," he suggests. "I know he's only doing weekends now, but he's looking for more hours, I know he is. He could start tomorrow."

"I already pay someone to be here full-time. His name's Simon and he gets room, board, and school fees, and I put up with your meddling to boot."

Art has the good grace to look abashed, at least.

Things used to be so simple. Temp school was a trial for all the fights Simon got in, but they stopped altogether when he hit that growth spurt at fourteen. In just a couple of months, he went from being the one everyone wanted to fight to being the kid nobody wanted to mess with. That should've been the end of trouble, but no, because Art had seen the potential. *Potential*, ha, yes. He stepped up the occasional self-defense lesson to weekly training sessions. And then twice a week. And then every day.

Then had come the day that Simon came to me and said he'd be fifteen and a half soon. He wanted to enter the official tournaments, and Art said he was ready, and wasn't that wonderful?

I'd never been so mad in my life. Used to be you'd learn to drive at that age, but now you can enter regulation matches and get the shit beat out of you, ain't that just special.

"We made a deal, Art. Simon don't quit school, and in exchange, I let him fight. I don't like regulation, and I really don't like street matches, but I let it slide because he loves it. And then he walked in yesterday saying he was going to hell because he damn well *killed* someone. Can you look at Simon's face today and say this is still okay?"

Like Art gives a shit. "I've killed people, and so have you. He'll be fine, give him a couple of days. Think of the purses, Erin. That's why you let him fight before, isn't it?"

He's not wrong. It eats away at me; I sold Simon's soul for cash. Brightened up the place, put in a good solar generator and a pump and a composting toilet, stopped having to bring men home...

"Erin, if Simon starts winning knife matches, he'll more than make up for what you'll lose on paying someone else to wait tables for you. Do you know what kind of prize money they give out for the duels?"

I stare at him, long and hard. "Are you saying that Simon should kill for money? Is that what you're saying?"

"They don't do that in regulation and you know it."

"Ain't nobody supposed to die in street matches neither, but tell that to the boy yesterday."

"Dueling's first cut, not knock 'em down. If anything, it's safer."

"Can you actually hear yourself, Art?" He takes a step toward me. The air down here's getting close. "Because there's two of them in the ring, in case you forgot, and I don't care what they say about no kills in regulation, it's happened and you've seen it!"

"That," whispers Art, "is why I hired Mick. Because you don't have to play the odds when you can narrow them, darling." The lamplight's making his eyes gleam, and suddenly I can hear my heart thudding in my ears. "Erin, you know I just want you to be happy."

His hand is on my arm again, and my back's against the shelves, can't back away no more, and now there's no air in the room at all because he's leaning in.

"Knock, knock," Simon deadpans from the top of the stairs. My mouth closes with a snap. Art steps back quickly, and I freeze where I am, hands up in front of me. Safe. "Front room's all locked up."

"Good. Art here was just going."

"I—" His face closes, jaw tightens. "Yeah, sure. Just going." And he does, climbing up until Simon steps aside to let him past, then slamming the back door behind him.

Simon is standing in the middle of the kitchen when I get up there, arms crossed. This is what he does for fun, for money: squares off and measures up. Something crackles in the air as I set my load on the table, and it feels like a fight.

"Your homework done?"

"Yeah."

There's a long pause. The fluorescent lights give us both a strange, ghostly appearance. "You wanna talk about something, then?" I snap. Art got on my nerves.

His eyes flicker. "I was gonna ask you that."

"What exactly is this about, Simon? If it's yesterday—"

"It's not that."

"Then what?"

He draws in a breath, rubs his face with one hand, looking almost too tired to stand. Then he locks eyes with me for the first time all day.

He knows.

"Simon—"

"How long you been pregnant for?"

The words are flung across the room hard enough to make me take a step back. "Excuse me?"

Simon glares. "I'm the one who swills the outhouse down. It don't take a genius to smell puke every morning for the last couple of weeks, or hear you running out the door soon as you get up."

"I—"

"I'm not stupid, Erin, okay?"

"I never—"

"Do you even know who the dad is?"

I can't speak, can barely even breathe except in big, shuddering gulps. Simon hasn't moved, hasn't changed his expression. I feel like I've been slapped. I thought the argument he was squaring up for would be about that boy what he'd killed, or maybe even Art, but no, not this, not ever.

Simon stalks toward me, looming taller than life in the darkness, and I can hear the resentment in his voice. "Did you think I wouldn't find out, was that it?" I need to run, get away, but he's closing in on me, his body blocking out what light there is. "Well? Am I right?"

He touches my stomach. I flinch.

All at once, Simon shrinks down until he's only himself and not some terrifying shadow come after me for all my sins.

"I—" He hesitates and looks away. "I ain't gonna hurt you, Erin."

I close my eyes, feel him move past me to the door. Too much has been said already, but I have to get this out.

"Don't go telling Art, okay?"

Simon keeps walking. "Wasn't gonna."

6

Art

Simon isn't pulling his punches this fine morning. If I get hit right now, I'm going down in a permanent way. Did he and Erin have words after I left? Did she tell him to stop fighting?

He goes in for a high kick and I dodge just in time, but this is getting out of hand. "Time out, kiddo."

"Why?"

"Because I said so, that's why," I retort, harder than I meant to.

"'Cause you're losing, you mean?"

I look up to find him watching me closely. "Yeah," I reply, "it is. Because right now you aren't practicing. You wanna fight for real? Fine. Say the word. But don't you get an attitude like I just kicked your dog. Try acting like an adult instead."

"'Acting like'? What, I ain't killed enough people to actually be a grown-up yet?"

"Grown-up? You? Don't make me laugh. Hitting someone with a baseball bat don't make you a man."

For the second time this week, Simon lunges at me.

I armed him yesterday, gave him a knife and a lesson in how to use it, but even so, there's no way he'll beat me. Simon's strong, raw muscle and guts, but I haven't exactly been slacking off these last few years. Training Simon's been an education in itself. I know his every trick, and he doesn't know all of mine.

He hits me full force, and I let him take me down so he lands on top with his weight on my chest, but he left my hands free, and that's a mistake, because this isn't regulation. I box his ears.

It works. He rolls off me and stares at the sky, eyes screwed shut. That hurts, I know it does, but maybe now he'll actually listen instead of just sulking. "Are you pissed about Mick?"

"Why the hell would I be pissed about him?"

"You don't remember?"

"Remember what? Erin freaking out? I was eleven and who gives a shit."

"Hey, we're just watching out for you. Because, for whatever reason that I can't think of right now, we care about your sorry ass."

He shrugs. Only Simon could shrug at something like that. "I didn't ask you to."

"You all but begged me to train you, back when those kids kept beating you up at school."

"Shut. Up."

Erin said it was kid stuff, to leave it alone. Then Simon came home one day with a broken finger, and I couldn't pretend I didn't see anything. What's the point of knowing shit if you can't change anything? It wasn't a big deal at first, just a throw or two, the right way to make a fist so he wouldn't break his hands. Hardly anything, really. Pissed Erin off like hell, but from that day on, Simon couldn't get enough.

I try again. "Is this about the kid you killed—"

"Look, can we not talk about that?"

"Can you stop trying to kill me?"

"Sure. Fine."

"Alright. Then let's get back to practice."

We do, and he starts acting his age, and I don't let my guard down for a single second. Watch his every move, don't turn my back, because something's changed. Between us, between Simon and the world, something is so very different.

Simon's a kid. Except, now he isn't, and why wasn't he before?

Fact is, I might be his coach, but I don't know why the boy with the knife was the first to end up dead at Simon's feet. I taught him all these years to hurt people, yeah, but I never taught him mercy. And I don't know where he learned it, or even, really, if he has.

And that scares me, just a little. Just enough. Erin's worried about him; wonder if she ever worries about me.

7

Simon

At age eleven I was learning to sling hash, which is what Erin called waiting tables. She worked from morning to night to keep her bar going, and after she took me in, I worked too, staying up later than ever before, getting up early to start the day all over again. Mick was a regular back then, same as Art, and Erin didn't like him for reasons she wouldn't say, but he tipped good, so she let him in.

One night he was bragging about his knife collection to anyone who'd listen. I'd been there for maybe a week at that point and was still figuring out how things worked. When I came up to take a drink order, he leaned in and caught my wrist. "Hey, kid—what's your name again?"

"Simon."

"That's cute. Like Simple Simon met a pieman." The guy next to him sniggered. "Well, Simon. How'd you like a treat sometime tomorrow?" He pulled me close in a too-tight hug, beery breath all in my face. I wasn't scared or nothing, but I didn't really know what to do. Like, I didn't know if that was okay. I mean, guys hugged Erin all the time. Was I supposed to hug them too?

I looked at Erin, and she saw what was happening, and she *freaked*. Like, came after him with a shoe, yelling and cussing and telling him to keep his filthy hands to himself. He let me go, and she shoved me back toward the kitchen, then she screamed at him to get out, stay out, never fucking come back again, her who don't ever swear.

Later, I asked what the problem was. "Can't be having with that," was all she said. "He's a coward, a filthy coward," whatever that was supposed to mean.

It was Erin who gave me my first lesson in keeping away "anyone I didn't like the look of." It involved my beat-up sneaker and a lot of words Erin would normally swat me for saying. And then Art started coaching me and I learned better ways of doing things, smarter ways, harder. Learned it good and I can't unlearn it, can't unsee. Don't think Mick meant harm that night, but that's what Erin saw when he hugged me, 'cause it's what she knows and she can't ever unsee that.

I killed a guy. The world can't unsee what I done. I get into class for the first time since the fight, 'cause I skipped yesterday, and the teacher's smile don't reach her eyes when she says good morning. I hold out my homework.

"Leave it on the desk."

She won't even risk touching my fingers, like killing's a disease and it's catching. All day long, not a single person in my class so much as bumps into me at lunch or in the halls. Someone's told them all what happened Sunday. Erin thought it'd take a few days for word to get 'round. It didn't.

I get home in time to scrub up before work, and she stops me with two fingers hovering just above my wrist. Even Erin won't get too close. "Taylor Burkes is gonna take over your job."

"Why?"

"Art says you got lessons in the afternoon. You'll do your homework at night now." She turns away, moving quick. "Can't have you falling behind at school."

Can't have me falling behind in the fights. Gotta bring home the money, and we'll need it more than ever if she's having a baby. Bringing a life into the world to replace the one I took out, until the day Art sells me for the wrong fight and it's me who hits the wall brains-first.

She points me to my desk in the front room where I study on nights we ain't that busy, tucked under the stairs by the side door where the customers can't see but she can. She can keep an eye on me. Can make sure I don't kill nobody else.

Until Art says so, of course, and ain't that a comforting thought.

8

Erin

Turns out Art was right. My weekend waiter, Taylor Burkes, was only too happy to take over Simon's position full-time when I threw in room and board. He's young, though even as I say that, I realize he's only four years younger than me. He quit fighting last May when Simon pulled a one-hit on Taylor's head and started waiting tables instead. He and Simon get along okay despite that, and everything would be fine around here if it wasn't for that scumbag Mick. I got a sign on my door:

NO CONCEALED WEAPONS
NO HARD DRUGS
NO MICK PERRY

I'm chatting with Nathaniel Greene about this and that when the room goes silent, and I mean dead silent. I look up, glass in hand, and there he is, Mick Perry, standing in my bar what he's been banned from these last five years.

"The hell—" is all I get out before he holds up a hand.

"Erin."

I blink. "That'd be me."

"Look." He shuffles his feet a bit, and I don't like that his other hand is hidden behind his back. I try to signal to Taylor, but he's got his mouth hanging open, damn him. "I—well, I came here to say what I should've said years ago. I'm sorry. I shouldn't have done what I did.

I was out of line, and I feel bad about it. I never meant to cause you any trouble or offense, nor Simon, for that matter."

Are you...are you shitting me? My mouth's open, and I think half the mouths in here have dropped with it. And Mick's just standing there looking repentant. Mick Perry, sorry.

"Anyway, it's been quite some time since I was here, and I know you were pretty pissed about what I did, but I brought this in hopes that it'll mend a few fences."

He steps forward and holds out a bottle. In the dim lights it gleams amber, and there's wax over the cork. Imported whiskey.

"You're kidding."

"No joke." He leans in so only I can hear him over the sound of whispered exclamations. "I hope you won't mind my not saying where I got it, but I've got a few more like it in the truck outside that I'd be happy to sell to you, at cost. First on the house."

"Who'd you get it from?"

"Not Petrowski." He gives me a sharp look, sharper than I'd like. "Connections up the road, friend of a friend. It's the real stuff, honest to Christmas, yours if you want it."

Back when he was coming here, I was still serving bad beer and bathtub gin I made myself. He must know how much good stuff like this will mean for business, considering how hard it is to get spirits through the checkpoints down here. I mean, of course he does, and I know that this is just a bribe and there ain't no honesty in Mick Perry, but even so. Real whiskey.

I nod, a jerk of my head that lets my customers know it's okay to relax. "Apology accepted. I'll take the sign down under the assumption that you won't try it again. Though," I add, unable to resist, "considering how the times have changed, I'd be interested to see what'd happen if you did."

Laughter from all sides, and even from Mick in front of me, though his is edged in steel. Already I'm surrounded by men wanting to buy shots, asking me how much. By the time I have a moment to breathe, Mick's nowhere to be seen and someone is organizing a toast.

"To peace!"

"And booze worth drinking!" someone adds to much laughter all around.

I raise my shot glass, down the miniscule amount I poured. It evaporates in my mouth.

A movement in the corner catches my eye. Simon's desk is there, behind the stairs where he can keep an eye on the side door and no one in the bar can get a good look at him without going over there. Mick's bent over the desk, handing a second bottle to Simon, who nods and takes it.

I catch Mick's eye. He just smiles and holds up the glass one of the regulars handed him. Simon is drinking something too, sixteen years old if a day, but he throws it back like a professional, and why does that feel so wrong? Everything's wrong. The bar's doing great, I'm turning out fry and fritters like they ain't the same thing I been serving for years past, things have never been better—and here I am, waiting for the catch, holding my breath until I hit the ground.

The smell of frying onions sticks in my nose and makes me gag for a moment, nausea rising despite my empty stomach. I cover my mouth with a hand, smile even though it hurts. Puking every morning's bad enough without adding nights to the list of everything that's gone down the drain, straight down it.

Maybe I'm not waiting for the ground after all. Maybe it's already hit, and I'm just waiting for the shock to wear off and the pain to really set in. There's worse things than this life I'm living, but right now I couldn't name a one.

9

Art

Chris Hopkins sidles up to me outside the depot as I'm heading off shift at dawn. Got a smile on his face like he's got something for me, tired and pissed as I am right now, needing breakfast and a drink like you wouldn't believe. What a night. Four detours due to deliberate obstructions and a bandit attack at four AM to top it off. I have earned that damn drink and sure as hell don't deserve Chris instead.

"Got some news for you, Art."

"Yeah?" You're moving far, far away? You've grown a brain? "Like what?"

"Heard you were getting your boy into knives, right? A spot's opened up in the next tournament last minute. Ainsley Miazga was found in a ditch yesterday afternoon. Apparently he double-crossed Petrowski on some bets."

"Fucking moron." Nobody smart does business with that guy, and nobody in their right mind crosses him. "It's a quick turnaround."

"You telling me Saint Flaherty won't be up to scratch in time? I don't believe it." Chris is watching me. His mouth is too wide, and the way he holds his upper lip sets my teeth on edge. "They're getting the posters printed this morning. If you want in, now's the time."

"Who was Miazga fighting?"

"Hall."

Well, this might be a good day after all. Last August, Simon beat

Connor Hall in the ring in front of the whole town, first round, just absolutely whaled on him. Got him so bad Connor stopped fighting with his fists...

...and got into knives.

"This'll be his debut, then," I realize.

"Yeah, and wouldn't it be nice if it were both of them?"

Grudge match. I like it. There's a certain sort of justice to it, 'cause Connor lost that fight and, in revenge, started going out of his way to make Simon's school life hell. Not that Simon said a word, but Erin likes to tell the world who she's pissed off at and why.

"Hey, by the way, Mick was in the bar last night," Chris adds.

"Good, I gotta talk to him."

"Yeah, but that means—Art, hey, listen. Erin took down her sign. Like, that's news. Have breakfast with me and I'll tell you about it."

It's six in the morning, I've been driving for the past ten hours, give or take, and I've got Simon to train in an hour. Between then and now I need to find food and make it the two miles from the depot to Mick's shop and then to the park, and then fit talking to officials in there somewhere. Are you kidding me?

"Some other time. Thanks for the tip, Chris. I'll talk to him."

But when I get to Mick's shop and rattle the door, the only person who turns up is a brick-faced woman who could probably smuggle half a shipment under her shirt, and probably has.

"Mick ain't here."

"Well, where is he?"

"He went to Erin Livingston's bar. Took a truckload of whiskey for her."

"What?"

"Are you hard of hearing?"

"No, I..." Chris's final words sink in.

Erin took her sign down.

Erin let Mick Perry into her bar when he took her something far too expensive. A gift, something Erin couldn't refuse. Simon's getting training, and she'll be grateful, and he hasn't come home yet, even though it's nearly dawn...

Erin hasn't been talking to me much lately, Simon is pissed, and

Mick is a fucking gentleman when he wants something, and what does he want more in this world than a leg up over the rest of us? Nothing, that's damn well what. I'm jumping to conclusions, but I'm gonna kill that son of a bitch, gonna kill him with my bare hands.

He's standing on the sidewalk behind me, with a crumpled shirt and tousled hair and a smile on his face. Smirk, not smile. "Art, fancy seeing you here. Late night for both of us. What's up?"

"Heard you were at Erin's place last night."

He stretches and yawns. "What? Oh yeah. Figured if I was going to be spending time with her boy, I might as well be able to get a drink after. You know?"

"No, I don't know." Fucking Mick. Keep it cool, Artie, play it off. "Anyway, I thought Erin hated your guts."

"That's 'cause she's a frigid bitch."

"And maybe you can shut the fuck up right now before I shove my fist down your throat." I am seriously about three seconds from ripping him a new one.

Mick holds up his hands. "Whoa, back down. Okay, sorry, Art. Didn't mean to hit a nerve there or anything. I just don't like Erin. We don't get along, but I didn't know there was actually something between the two of you."

"There isn't. Erin's a friend, and I look out for her."

"Right. And I literally just sold her some stuff so she'd take down that fucking sign, so cool it. Had breakfast yet?"

"No, I just got off shift."

"There's a place down the street that does a good fix-up, my treat." He slings an arm around my shoulders. I can still smell the beer on his breath and all the weed he must've smoked. "Sorry if I offended your 'friendly relations' with Erin."

I kick his feet from under him so he hits the concrete hard, straight on his tailbone. If I've pissed him off half as much as he's pissed me off, then mission accomplished.

"What the hell, Art?"

"I don't like you hanging around Erin, you get it? So tell me what really happened."

He glares up, I glare down. I win when he leans over and spits.

"Nothing happened, Jesus. I'd rather sleep with a raccoon in heat. No disrespect, but not my type." He climbs to his feet and cocks his head. "Of course, I couldn't say the same for your boy Taylor Burkes. You know, the one you recommended? He's got a hell of a crush on her. Could smell it a mile away."

I start toward him and he laughs, catches me by the shoulder, and pushes me along. "Breakfast, Art. You and I got lots to talk about. C'mon."

Mick's such a dick. It's his best quality and his worst, because he might be obnoxious, but people like him, people listen to him.

"Hey, Mick, you think Simon'll be ready for the tournaments by the end of the month?"

"I think he'll be ready for the special forces by then. Why?"

"No reason."

Simon's been getting quieter and quieter, and angrier and angrier, until yesterday afternoon, when he was fucking silent. I don't think he said two words the entire time. Didn't look me in the eye neither, so maybe I got through to him in the morning session.

Now he'll win again, and maybe the world will become a safer place in his mind. A quick bite, and then I'll arrange it all, no problem.

Simon's not gonna believe his eyes.

10

Erin

I shove open the door from the outhouse and step into the morning air with a shiver. A cloud of softness envelopes me, strong arms wrapping a blanket tight around my shoulders and holding it there. Calloused hands stroke my neck, wiping the sweat away. Is this the feeling that's made generations of women give up dreams and rights, just for this moment of feeling utterly safe? I never do feel safe, never have. Not in so many years, so many, and now, between the bar and the baby and the fights...

Oh God, I'm crying, huge shuddering sobs that muffle themselves in Simon's shoulder. And he just lets me, stroking my hair and making shushing noises in my ear so gently it makes me cry even harder.

He's speaking, mumbling into my hair. "...and I'll take care of you and the baby, I'll stop fighting, get a job doing something and quit school, and you won't have to have anyone over if you don't want them, and you can tell them the baby's whoever's you like, even mine. I'll back you up, and it'll be okay, 'cause I ain't never gonna leave you, Erin. So don't cry, it's okay..."

Simon, Simon, oh boy-o, oh love, you don't know what you're talking about. Not a thing. And if you knew the truth...

I'm so tired I can barely move, even as he's saying these things what I never wanted, never asked for, but he thinks somewhere in his sixteen-year-old mind might make things better. Like anything could make better the things I done. They weigh me down like chains, and I just can't seem to stop weeping. Always been a waterworks, me, never been able to help it. Oh, Simon. What have I done, what have I done, all my sins repaid, what have I done...

Simon is leading me across the yard to the house, but I stumble badly. Instead of putting me on my feet, he picks me up, carries me up the stairs into the kitchen, and sets me on a chair, pushes a dishcloth in my hands while he bangs around the stove making breakfast. I need to get myself under control, get up and help him, do it myself. Can't rely on anyone, not me. Only I always rely on Simon. He brings in purses and bounces drunks, and maybe he's still a kid, but this morning, I'm not sure, and I don't know how it got this way.

When did life stop being hand to mouth, and my place go from a hole-in-the-wall to an establishment? When did I start letting scumbags like Mick back in my bar? When did I stop whoring and become a kept woman?

Simon starts frying eggs for the two of us, hunched over the stove. Muscles ripple under his undershirt when he moves.

When did Simon grow up? But no, that ain't the right question, is it? When did Simon decide he's a man, is more like it. I look up. "What do you mean, I mean more to you than fighting?"

Simon goes stock-still for a moment, then flips an egg. "You always have."

"Don't lie."

"Ain't lying."

He tips the eggs out onto two plates, sets one in front of me. He's already shoving food in his mouth. I stare at my plate, and it stares back. Give it a sniff and push it away.

"Eat up."

"I'm not hungry."

"Yeah?" Simon pauses, looks at my plate. "When'd you last eat?"

"I'm fine."

His hand hits the table so hard I jump, and suddenly he's glaring at me. "No, you're not! You're sick morning and night, and the last time I saw you eat anything was two days ago. You have to eat! What about the baby?"

I'm crying again, great heaving sobs. "Stop it!"

"No! You gotta eat!"

"I'm not hungry!"

He lunges, and I close my eyes. His arms close around me, as gentle as probably he knows how, lifting me out of my chair.

"Put me down."

"No."

"Put me down right now or I'll—"

"You'll what? Puke on me?"

"No, I'll...I'll..." We're in the front room, heading to the door. "Where are you taking me?"

"Doctor."

Panic floods my veins. Doctors mean people knowing, and I can't afford that. Fear makes my voice go low. "You put me down right now or I'll scream and Taylor will come running."

"And?" he asks, but stops anyway. Stubborn as a rock.

"And"—I swallow—"you won't never get the answers you're looking for."

I look up and he looks down and our eyes meet for a long, hard minute. Something's going on behind his face, and from here it looks like an argument. Do what he thinks is right and make me mad, or do as I say and satisfy curiosity?

"You gotta eat," he says. Curiosity wins, and I knew it would.

I sigh. "I've been doing oatmeal gruel and that's been okay. Just nothing strong."

"And if I don't take you to the doctor, you'll tell me a few things?"

"One or two."

"Three." His voice is hard, and I know that's the best I'm gonna get out of him.

"Fine. Three. Now put me down."

"And no lies."

"Fine!"

He nods, a jerk of his chin that makes the muscles in his neck stand out. God, I'm so small compared to him. Hell, most people are bigger than me, but I'm half his size, probably literally. Big like his dad, never mind his mom, who I've never heard him speak of even once.

I can feel his gaze, watching me, watching my face, so careful. Always careful, always kind. To me, anyway.

Simon kisses me on the cheek, right next to my mouth.

"Simon? You okay?"

His skin is soft as a child's as he presses his forehead to mine. Shoulders shake, and I am not so much held as cradled, his hot tears mixing with my cold ones.

Any minute now Art will come to see why Simon is late to training and Taylor will walk down the stairs to get breakfast and a thousand other things will happen, but for these few minutes, as the shadows turn from black to gray, there is nothing but his eyelashes against my skin, his breath in my ear, and the words he whispers there:

"I'm going to hell..."

11

Simon

Erin used to kick me out of the house when she had a guy over, and I'd go to run with whatever neighborhood kids hadn't decided I was their mortal enemy that week. We'd go listen to the soldiers, listen to their stories, wide-eyed and waiting, 'cause the best thing about the stuff they said was that it was true, every word. We could tell somehow, even though we didn't know what *blitzed* really meant. They never lied neither. Not about going to war or saving their buddies or shooting until all their ammo was gone in hopes that someone out there was gonna save them. Especially not about that.

This one day, when we all went down there, the oldest guy, Sarge, had me go fetch him a can of chaw down at the corner. When I came back, he poured us big cups of their homemade. All us kids shared them out, choking on the taste but swallowing it down, except for Jordan Peters, who threw up all over her bare feet, which made the old guys laugh. And then, as we was sitting there, drunk and dizzy, Sarge told this gruesome story about how he lost three fingers to an IED and how he'd dragged his dead buddy's body through the streets all night looking for a medic. He didn't finish the story neither, just went silent toward the end until Ryan Jesser asked, "And then what?"

"And then he found one," Mr. Nowak growled. "Now get!" He swung his shotgun and we ran, chasing each other out of the cul-de-sac and up the street, too tipsy to run straight. I lost the others and ended up back on Erin's front porch.

I fumbled with the latch, let myself in, and wandered over to the griddle where Erin was frying eggs and beans at the same time, chatting with customers. She glanced up and dropped her spatula, grabbing me in a hug so her long hair pressed against my cheeks.

"There you are! I thought you were lost, I was that worried." She rubbed my hair. "You smell like booze. Don't tell me you were down with those dirty old men again."

"They gave me a cup."

"A what?"

"To drink. From the cup."

"Drink what."

"The stuff Mr. Nowak says puts hair on your back."

"You're *drunk*?"

I opened my mouth, then shut it. "Maybe?"

She grabbed my chin, made me look her in the eye, dead serious. "Simon, you listen to me. Don't you *ever* go around those streets drunk again. You hear me? There's a lot of things that can happen out there, and I don't want you mixed up in none of it. Okay? Promise me. *Promise* me you won't."

I stared into her eyes, brown and fierce, and all at once I realized that she was only angry 'cause she was scared. Scared for me and whatever the hell she imagined might happen. "Promise," I croaked, 'cause what else can you say when someone's like that?

She kissed me on the forehead, sent me to deliver a plate to a customer, and then gave me a cup of strong black coffee. It was that night I realized Erin loved me, though now I wonder if she even knew it.

Me, I've loved Erin since, well, since forever, maybe. Washed dishes for her, helped out, was around when she needed me and left the house when she didn't, though didn't that begin to rub after a while, just.

Wasn't until I was fourteen and just into high school that anything changed, though. I was getting tall and finding muscles where I'd never known I'd had them before, and one night a drunk started mouthing off at Erin about half an hour before closing. Erin didn't do nothing, 'cause she's heard it all a thousand times and didn't really care no more, but I was pissed off. Side effect of the growth spurt: all of the sudden I had this massive fucking temper, like it hurt or something. The guy was being an asshole and nobody liked it much, but nobody was saying nothing.

And then he reached across the bar and grabbed Erin's wrist, and I put down the pint of beer I was delivering, walked over, and broke his arm. Just did it, like snapping my fingers, like it was nothing. He screamed and I shoved him out the door and that was that. I was the bouncer.

Wouldn't have mattered, I mean, 'cause who cares about some dickhead drunk getting what's coming? Except, somewhere in my haze of fury, I'd stopped remembering that the dickhead drunk also happened to be my math teacher.

Yeah.

He didn't tell nobody what had happened. No, didn't need to, now did he? Connor had seen it. Next day in school, my teacher didn't say boo to me, but by lunch, everyone knew. Oh, did they, knew I'd done it and how and weren't they pissed, just. Never mind they didn't like the guy or he'd deserved it, or at least deserved *something* for being an asshole. I wasn't no kind of hero, just some stupid animal who'd beat you up soon as look at you. Ha.

And didn't I prove them right? Ryan Jesser thought he was so hard, so tough. Seventeen, three years older than me, used to be friends but weren't no more. He came into the bar a week later, drank enough to make him brave, grabbed Erin's waist as she walked by, and smirked.

I didn't get mad that time. Didn't need to get mad, not after the week I'd had, 'cause I was already there, coiled like a trigger. Erin asked him to let go, and he said no while looking at me. She bashed him across the face with the glass she was holding and took his wallet while he recovered. And then, while she counted out the money he now owed her, I hauled him out front and beat him into the sidewalk. The blood filled the cracks in the pavement until he didn't fight back no more, just cried for me to stop. I did, eventually.

Ryan Jesser ain't come back, and my math teacher still don't look me in the eye, and I don't bounce drunks that hard, mostly 'cause it's bad for business. That was the week I started training serious. And what does it say about me that beating some guy until he begged ain't the worst thing I ever done? Not by a long shot. Not by a million and one.

12

TAYLOR

Art said he could get me a gig waiting tables, and I went for it even before I knew I'd be working with Simon Flaherty. And it's funny, but after weeks of working weekends here and a couple days of even living in the same house as that guy, I don't think I know a thing more than I did before. He's got a mean right hook that isn't so good for the old IQ, yeah, I know that from the ring, but what else? Nothing, that's what.

I work, I sleep in the room Erin gave me, and when I wake up I do it again. Not like we have time to talk. Right now it's six in the morning, predawn, and it's time for the day to start again. Pants up, boots on, gun belt buckled and I'm ready to go.

Flaherty sits on the kitchen table, blanket under his arm.

"Morning."

He nods and says nothing back. I open my mouth, close it, leave by the back door. What was Flaherty doing? Why a blanket? Was he waiting for Erin?

Now, Erin, on the other hand, I know plenty about her. Everyone knows about her. Five years back or so, right after the war had officially ended and everything was right on the edge of famine because it was still early spring and nothing was growing yet but rations were suddenly cut off, a few nutjobs at the Church of Eternal something-something cooked up a plot. Not enough food to go around, right? So what did the idiots do? They started poisoning wells. Less mouths, more food, right? Starvation makes you crazy.

Most of them got caught in a couple of days, but a few dozen people died, and more than that got sick, real sick, and more wells were going bad when the story says that one of the terrorists went after Erin's well right there in her yard. She caught him around the neck with a cleaver and then got some guys to drag the body down the streets until his head ripped clean off. After that, someone went and stuck it on a damn pole in what passed for the Market back then, and Jeff Petrowski went and gunned down the whole church, men, women, and children. It solved the problem, so. Everyone knows Erin.

And, I mean, she's hot. That's a pretty good reason to know who she is too. Long black hair, eyes that aren't quite kosher, if you know what I mean, and a way of walking that just about sets the ground on fire. Point is, everyone and their dog knows Erin, knows what she looks like.

So when I'm standing at the Market gate checking for weapons, troublemakers, and anyone the Market Authority's decided to ban, and a woman tries to slip past me by covering her face with a hoodie? I know it's her from the walk alone. But no one gets in the Market with their faces covered, not even her. I grab her arm quick and tug the hood back.

The arm is skinny, but it yanks itself out of my grip to fly to her lips. Too late, I've already seen it. Someone's caught her one across the mouth but good. Mary, Mother of God, did Simon do that?

"What happened to you?"

"None of your business, Taylor Burkes."

"Yeah, but..."

"I tripped on the stairs. Now, can I do my shopping, or you gonna stare at me all day?"

Sticks and stones, but I pull my hands back, put them up. "Go on. They're doing a special on red peppers down the third lane. You could..."

She's gone. The noon bell rings, and I move to the guard hut, turn in my badge and vest, punch out. What the hell happened to her?

There's only one way to find out, because Art will wanna know. He got me this job, and I guess I gotta keep up my end of the bargain.

She's easy enough to find, because she's stopped at the announcement board where the tournament poster is just going up for the month's fights. Perfect timing for me. I don't fight after that knock to the head made me lose a couple of IQ points, but watching, well, that's another thing.

No wrestling this month, but it looks like a good mix of mixed martial arts and knife duels. Kenny Ritchie's fighting Sky-High Volkes, yeah, Kid Kwan's got a fight and...

Nobody told me Flaherty was doing knives, but there's his name in red and black letters three inches high: SIMON "SAINT" FLAHERTY, 6'2", 185 LBS., VERSUS "ABLE" CONNOR HALL, 6'4", 185 LBS.

Mary, Mother of God. That'll be a good fight. Like, that'll be fight-of-the-century good, shit, and I know I'm not the only one who thinks so, because everyone's talking and pointing, and someone's even making a call on a satellite phone. Who wouldn't wanna see this fight?

Erin's shoulders bump my chest as she sways backward. She jumps, then looks at me, and her face is actually white. Whoa.

"You okay?" I murmur, leaning down low.

"Connor Hall." Her voice is barely audible above the noise of the hawkers and shoppers.

"Yeah?"

"He's the class president."

"What?"

"At Simon's school. They had a vote. Connor's class president. Simon voted for him." She sucks a breath between her teeth. "He ate his birthday dinner in my own front room. And Simon's gonna kill him."

She's taking this way too seriously. "He's not gonna kill him. This is regulation, they disqualify you if you do that."

"He's gonna kill him."

"He's not—"

She looks about ready to spit in my eye. "How long did you fight for, boy?" she hisses. "You watch! If they draw or Simon wins—and he will, because he's good—Connor will want a rematch in some dark alley where only one of them will walk out. Because Connor hates Simon."

"I thought you said—"

"Simon don't care one way or another. But Connor's a nasty little shit with a grudge, and he's gonna die." She's breathing hard, eyes unfocused, voice hardly above a whisper. "He's gonna die, and my boy's gonna kill him."

But then she snaps to, looks me in the eye, and I feel like I'm missing something here but don't know what. "Come on, Taylor. You know where Art lives, right?"

"Um, yeah? I mean, I guess..."

"Good. 'Cause we're gonna go see him."

"Why?"

"Because I'm gonna kill the son of a bitch myself."

"Why?"

"Because this isn't worth it." She says it to herself, but I catch the words anyway. "Not anymore."

13

Erin

In all the years since he came back from the war, I never asked Art where he lived. Didn't want to know; knew if I did, he'd start asking why I wasn't over there, start thinking I wanted what I don't. Don't need a man. Don't want one. Not that *want* has ever been what you'd call a determining factor, but it's always counted with him, for all he won't quit trying.

The place Taylor leads me to has paint peeling off the porch in long strips, though the front door's new enough. Those who don't protect what they've got, lose it. I stare at the house as Taylor looms behind me, ogling my bum. Boy's so transparent you could use him for a window. Boy. Ha. Twenty-two years old and a boy, 'cause I'm such an old woman. My stomach rolls. Old, and getting older every day.

I knock. Wait, knock again. Footsteps inside, then the door opens wide enough to show old eyes peering through the crack the chain bolt allows. "You looking for Art?"

I don't ask how she knows; I'm well-enough known myself. "Yeah."

"Well, he's not here. Ain't come home from work yet."

Odd. This time of day he should be asleep. "When'll he be back?"

"Don't know. Come back later."

Taylor gets his boot in the door before the landlady can slam it closed. Good on him. I lick my lips, grit my teeth. I'm about ready to start spitting tacks because Art is a dead man and if I don't get my hands on him *now*, heads are gonna roll.

"Let me in. I'll leave a note for Art in his room, and then I'll be gone. Alright?" I pause, and realize that I never gave an alternative. "Or my bully boy here rips your door off and don't give it back."

There's a couple clicks and the sound of metal sliding on metal before the door swings open all the way. Inside is an old woman huddling against the wall and pointing upstairs. Old, yeah. She's maybe fifty, sixty, though that is old around here anymore.

"Key."

She don't like it, but she hands it over with a scowl that's half-resentment and half-fear. Yeah, she knows who I am alright, knows who's got my back. "Upstairs, second on the left. And don't steal nothing!"

I don't think she's in any position to bargain, but I nod anyway and gesture to Taylor to stay. Typical man, he follows me up the creaking stairs anyway. Our shoes nearly squish on the rotting carpet, mildew and cat piss clogging my nose strong enough to make me gag, actually gag. A hand props my elbow up while I catch my breath, and then it's onward and upward until we reach the hallway.

I stare at the second door to the left for long seconds before using my shirttail to open it. There's a bed in the corner, clean enough as far as I can see. An old table next to it, with a wind-up alarm and the type of magazine I know Simon hides under his mattress. Crumpled towel on the floor, clothing in a small pile in the corner too close to an unlit kerosene heater, and hanging from the ceiling...

I back right into Taylor. His fingers close around my arms and squeeze. Hanging from the ceiling are braids of hair with a patch of what looks like dried leather attached to each. The hair gleams in this dim room, long and short, red, brown, black, blond, and one faded pink, each one neat as you please. Oh my fucking God, please tell me they ain't what they look like, though I don't know what the fuck else they could be.

"Are those...?" Taylor starts to ask. His voice cracks, and he tries again. "Are those scalps?"

It happened later in the war when things were going from civil to absolute panic, if ever they were really civil to begin with. Both sides did it, men gone mad with fighting trying to make this war end any way they thought might work. Something like that, anyway.

The dirty old men a couple streets away used to have a few. One of them, the one with the nasty tobacco-stained mustache, he kept his on his belt. Took 'em himself and proud of it, and damn if I'll ever understand why Simon liked to hear their stories, not what with knowing what those were. Human scalps, like the Indians used to take hundreds of years ago. The ultimate war trophies. Avenge, revenge, and rebirth.

I'm gonna puke for real.

"We're done here," I hear myself say.

"What about the note?"

"No." I give one last glance to the scalps, then turn. "No note."

A hand on my shoulder stops me, and Taylor has yet to let go of my other arm. He leans in. I can smell him even over the odor from the hallway, sweat and leather boots and aftershave, a man's smell. His eyes are intense.

"You okay, Erin?" Taylor whispers, voice husky as he touches my cheek.

Disgust hits me in a wave, like bile rising. He's trying to hit on me at this time, in this place.

I duck, twist, and wrench myself out of his clammy grip. He don't like that, no, not at all, reaches out for me again. I haul back and slap him across the face so hard that my hand buzzes with pain.

Taylor clutches his jaw. "The hell did you—"

My finger's already in his face as adrenaline clenches my gut. "Don't you ever try that again. You hear me? You wanna work for me, you do as I say, and you don't touch me, not ever! Do it again and I won't just hit you, you'll get your legs ripped off! Do you understand?"

"But earlier in the kitchen—"

The adrenaline is flowing, though, and I can't be stopped. "I don't care what you saw, I don't care what you heard. You don't touch me and we'll get along just fine. Now I'm leaving, and you ain't gonna follow me out, got it?" I spin around and glare at the landlady. "And neither do you! Not a fucking step!"

I all but run down the stairs, and they squelch beneath my feet. My heart is thudding in my chest. I'm taking big gulps of air, like it won't ever be enough. Art's out there somewhere, and I never knew he took scalps. All these years and I never knew, and this shouldn't shock me, but it does, God, it does.

I need to talk to Art now if not sooner. Enough is enough.

14

Art

Simon's signed up for his fight, the posters are going up, the news is out—a few early side bets laid—and it's finally time for me to hit the sack so I don't run my truck into a ditch tonight. I turn down the alley shortcut toward my place, feet heavy on the pavement. My eyes are killing me. Used to be I could stay up all night, now I'm thirty and suddenly—

A hand yanks the back of my shirt. I stumble, start to turn, going for my piece, and something pricks me in the kidneys.

A moment ago my world was fuzzy around the edges from lack of sleep, but now I'm awake, sharp as a tack. Behind me in the gloom, between some trash cans where no one can see, someone's got a knife to my side.

"Just tell me straight out, and don't you try to lie, Art Weber, or I'll have your guts for garters, and you know I could. Was it you who got Connor Hall paired up with Simon at the end of the month?"

Ah, yeah, I know that voice.

But I don't relax too much, because Erin can gut me like a pig if she wants, and from the way she's hissing at me, I'd put money on *want* being about three seconds away from *happen*. I go to take a deep breath, then rethink that and just let the words come out. "Yes. Yes, I registered him."

"And the scalps in your room, did you take those?"

Fuck. "Erin, I—"

"Yes or no, Art. The answer is yes or no."

She wasn't supposed to see those. "But..."

"Ain't gonna ask again."

No one was supposed to see those. "...yes."

"Why."

"*Why?* Fuck, Erin, it was a war, but I'm not like that now!" Keep your voice down, Artie, keep it down. "I'm not going after yours, if that's what you wanna know. I don't do that *now*."

The world has narrowed to this point in time: her breathing in my ear, the sting of the knife, and me counting all my sins in the long seconds it takes her to respond.

Her voice is hard as nails. "Ain't no now, Art. Ain't no then. There's only is and is not, and all the excuses that lie between. A man who'd take a scalp then would take a scalp now."

"Erin, just listen."

"To what? Some bullshit excuse about the 'horrors of war'? Because I was in the middle of it, Art, and don't you forget it."

"The middle? *You?*" The word hisses between my teeth because I can't contain it. I wish I could see her face. "If by 'middle of it' you mean looting by day and whoring by night, then yeah. But you didn't fight."

"I was there. And I didn't take no scalps."

I'm still breathing shallow as I can, but my right hand's itching and I'm seeing red. "You had a home, not a uniform, and no one gave you orders to block the exits before setting fire to buildings, and you've never stabbed anyone with a bayonet—"

"*Oh yes I did.*"

Silence, filled only with ordinary street sounds. I'd forgotten where we are, for a moment.

"You never."

"I did." I can feel the heat of her hand next to my skin, the edge of her voice, designed to cut. "He was gonna scalp me. I stabbed him, and then I bandaged it up so his wound didn't rot."

I'd never known that. All these years, and I'd never known that. And how many did you save, Artie?

I ignore that thought, focus on the small body behind me, the knife that hasn't moved, the accusations being thrown like candy at a parade.

"Sometimes," I say, "you do what you have to do. And I had friends. I had a unit. We stuck together, and now there's only me and Mick left of the people I used to know. So yeah, I took scalps, and you would've too, because you would've wanted the ones who died to have done the same. Anything to make it end."

When I take a deep breath, the knife moves with me rather than sinking in. I lay a hand over hers, softly, gently, keeping the blade in place.

"You can stab me right now if I lie, Erin. I'll help you do it, even. But truly, you would've done the same."

She tries to move, but I've got a good grip on her fingers. How dare she assume I'd been some sort of prize taker, the kind who killed for fun and gore. How dare she think that of me, Erin, who knows me as well as anyone in this world.

Doesn't she?

What the hell did she have to go to my room for?

I can feel her bones scraping together. I turn and glare at her, the knife between us now, her face red. Embarrassed much?

"And while we're at it," I bite the words out, "the fuck did you let Mick in your place for?"

"You think you have a right to tell me how to run my business?"

There's ice in her voice, sharp as needles, sharp as the knife in her hand, and, fuck, she's not embarrassed; she's about three seconds away from clawing my eyes out.

"I'll tell you something, Art, and you listen to me good. You don't know what I did during the war, and you never will, 'cause it's none of your damn business. And you're right, I weren't a soldier, nowhere near. But I'll tell you something for free: you don't tell me what I feel, you don't tell me what I think, and you sure as hell don't tell me how to run my bar. And if you don't let go of me in the next two seconds, I'll scream bloody murder until the whole town comes running, you got that?"

"Got what?"

"One."

"You're just pissed 'cause of the knife thing, is that it?"

"Two."

"If that's the problem, then just come out and—"

Her mouth opens wide, drawing in breath.

"Okay, okay! Fine." I fling her hand back, watch her tuck the knife in her pocket with a curl of her lip that says just because she's putting it away doesn't mean she trusts me anymore than a minute ago.

Yeah, well, she's not the only one who's reached the end of her rope. "What do you want from me, Erin? You're right, I took scalps and I'd do it again if it came to that, because it worked, didn't it? The war ended. Take a scalp, spit on a grave, live to see another day, it *worked*. So what the fuck do you want from me?"

"You got Simon up against Connor Hall."

"You're damn right I did."

"They're at school together! You had no right—"

"I had every right—"

"He's gonna get killed!"

I've had it up to here with this bullshit. "No, he's not! Simon's not gonna die, though maybe Connor will and the world will be a better place for it. And before you say something like you never wanted this to happen, it's a little too late for that. You could have said no. Back before he started in the tournaments, you could've said it, but you didn't, and it's way too fucking late to start now."

"Like I ever had a choice."

My hand shoots out before I can even think about it, dragging her nose-to-nose.

"Don't give me that shit, Erin. You had every choice. Every choice in the world. Take some fucking responsibility for once in your life." She tries to pull away, but I'm not done, because I am purely poison angry. "I never invited you to my place. You just had to pry, didn't you? And now you don't like what you found? Now, whose fault is that?"

I shove her away, and a small part of me is satisfied to see her stumble and almost fall, face a mask of shock. I thought she knew me.

I thought she understood. Shows how much I know.

15

Simon

When they started up the temp schools, back when they was really temporary, back when people thought that seeing as the war was over, things were gonna go back to how they'd been before, I hated school. Absolutely, one-hundred-percent-plus-one hated it, 'cause I sucked at it.

I could do math okay, yeah, and science weren't so bad, but goddamn if reading wasn't the worst thing I ever done. Letters seemed to change shape when I wasn't looking, and when I'd finally get one word right, there'd be the next one and it'd start all over. None of it made any sense to me, and Connor Hall knew it and dug it in, and made me purely wanna kill him just for existing. Got everyone in on it, couldn't leave me alone, Simple Simon's too dumb to read, fuck you too, whatever. It sucked, but it was fine.

Then I beat him fair and square in the ring last August. I beat him hard and everyone knew it and Connor didn't smirk no more. He told everyone at school I was dangerous. Crazy, even, would come and get them in the night.

Second day of class, the girl who sat next to me asked the teacher if she could move, like I was contagious. Like I really was unstable and if something pissed me off in class I might just haul off and belt her one. Connor started smirking again, 'cause he's always gotta win.

Today it's some stupid third grader who runs in the room shouting the news that me and Connor are facing off again. Connor throws his head back and laughs. When I turn to look, the teacher gasps, like she believes I might kill him right there.

They all believe it.

And maybe it's true. Under his desk where the teacher couldn't see, Connor had his knife out. Maybe he ain't saying shit just to be a jerk. Maybe he really does believe I'm nothing but a wild animal, and I am 'cause when I saw his knife I wanted to tear his throat out and feed it to him, and nothing but the thought of how that'd mean he was right kept me in my seat. When the bell rings, I'm out the door before anyone else, lest they call me back and I do what I want so badly to.

I all but run to Mick's shop. He jerks a thumb back to his pole barn and I follow, wait until the door closes before launching the words what have burned their way into my head.

"Why him?"

"Connor Hall, you mean?"

"Of course I fucking do! Of anyone, why him?" I swallow, turn away. "They said you were there, you helped Art change the lists. I already beat him, so I wanna know. Why him again?"

Mick ain't the type to give straight answers. "If you're going to fight, Simon, sooner or later you're going to fight someone you know."

"Then maybe I don't wanna fight anymore!"

"Then don't."

"I have to!" The words rip out, and I can't take 'em back, can only pray he don't ask. Please don't ask, please don't anybody.

He don't.

Instead, Mick turns his back to me the way nobody's done in days, in months. Does he *know*?

"A long time ago," he begins, speaking slowly, "back when the war was really hot, I joined up. Got the training, because they were still doing training at that point, and a gun and a pack and a uniform, and got sent out with the rest of my unit.

"Thing about a civil war is that you're fighting everyone. Anyone. Uniforms aren't compulsory, which is a shame, because uniforms make things easy on a soldier, you know? It's easy to kill a figure wearing the wrong color. It's a lot harder to kill a face." His back's still to me, but his hands are moving, fidgeting with his sleeves. "My first skirmish, I was down this back alley and this guy jumped out at me with a crowbar. That's a hell of a nasty thing to have swung at your head, a crowbar. I shot him, of course. Took him about three seconds to die, 'cause I did it right, but his face..."

Just for a moment, I see the old men sitting on their porch, telling us the worst stories in the world.

"Thing is, I'd been imagining some faceless opponent, like a cartoon or something. But the guy I killed was real. And I think that's what's really bothering you, isn't it? You killed that guy in your last fight and saw him die. Now you're up against a boy you've seen almost every day, and he doesn't just have a face, he has a history. He's real. Sure, he's not supposed to die, but neither was the last guy. It's not a game anymore."

No. No, it's not.

The silence seems to echo after his words, and it echoes in my mind. "How old were you, when you went to war?"

"Eighteen."

"And before you joined...?"

"I was in high school. Signed up three days after graduating."

"I've got two years before I graduate." I look at the ceiling not to look at him. "It's not fair."

If he asks, I'd swear to God I'm not scared. But I am, and he don't ask, 'cause I think he knows.

Mick shakes his head. "You aren't going to kill the next guy."

"I never meant to kill the first one." My voice cracks. "I thought I'd just hit him and he'd be knocked out. I never thought—never wanted that to happen." The words seem to pull themselves out. "Now someone's gonna do it to me unless I get them first, 'cause all that needs to happen is one wrong move and I kill him, or he gets lucky and it's me dead instead, and I don't graduate school or get a job, and I ain't never even kissed a girl..."

And I don't got anybody to tell who will listen except him. Because no one else seems to care. They think I'm an animal. Maybe he does too, but he ain't flinched away yet. Even Erin won't turn her back to me anymore.

"Simon, what happened that last fight was a fluke, and it's not going to happen again because you're not working with baseball bats anymore, right? You're learning to use a knife and use it well. The next time you kill someone, if you kill someone, it will not be an accident, and if that's not a comfort, then you're in the wrong sport."

"What if I die instead?" I ask, and wait for him to say I won't, I won't die, don't worry, I won't *let* you die.

But he won't.

"I don't have a map of every fight. Maybe there will be someone and you will die. But I'll tell you this for sure, Simon. Connor's being trained by Tom Keats, and if you're going to die, he won't be the one to kill you. Yeah, you're raw now and he's got a head start, but give me a month and no one'll be able to touch you. If some new guy shows up, we'll see, because dark horses are what we gotta watch for, but you aren't going to die soon. Certainly not before Erin has that baby of hers."

No.

Oh fuck, oh no...

"But it's not yours," he adds.

I open my mouth, but he presses a finger to my lips. "You said it yourself. You never kissed a girl; you most definitely didn't knock one up. Especially not Erin. And I *do* know that for a fact."

He drops his hand, moves away. Doesn't smirk like the kids at school would, or get angry like Art, or look scared like Erin does anymore. "Oh come on, don't act surprised. You got mad when Erin drank last night, and when she was in the middle of cooking, she left to go dry heave in the outhouse. You followed her out there to check on her and keep the customers away. It's not hard to extrapolate from there."

It's all there. He knows everything, and I didn't tell him, but he's watching me careful-like, gray eyes following my hands as I hug myself tight, trying to keep my brain together. Want to deny it and can't. It's all fucking true and I can't tell anyone.

"She won't tell me whose it is. She says it won't help."

"Come on, Simon, you're the one that lives with her. She got a boyfriend or what?"

"There's no one. She stopped having to do that when I started bringing money in." My voice won't work right. "That's *why* I'm bringing money in."

I meet his eyes square, and we stare at each other for a moment. Then his widen. "Oh shit. Tell me, Simon, is Erin acting like normal?"

"Normal?"

"Happy."

"I mean...no. But she's always been serious. Why?"

He shakes his head. "Erin's been turning tricks since forever. She knows how nature works. Simon, if she's doesn't want a kid, then why's she having one? Think."

'Cause she got careless, 'cause she was drunk, 'cause she forgot, 'cause...

I don't know, and she wouldn't tell me if I asked.

Only, maybe no one asked her.

Erin's plenty good at putting shitheads in their place. So who's the one person in the town she couldn't say no to? Who runs the cartel what controls the checkpoints? Who owns the land the Market's built on and the trucks the guards patrol in? Who owns everything, everyone, and no one in Buchell says no to him, 'cause if you say no, you don't say anything ever again?

"Petrowski."

Mick meets my eyes, and for the first time, he looks afraid. Not of me—for me.

"Yeah," he says. "Petrowski."

You don't say no to Petrowski. I known that since the day he killed my mom in cold blood.

Oh shit, oh shit, this is all my fault.

16

Erin

I am in a purely foul mood tonight. The customers don't know that, of course, because it wouldn't do to be grumpy in front of them, but the first man to give me lip is getting his ass handed to him in a paper sack before being tossed out on the sidewalk, and that is a fact. Taylor's doing his job, Simon's out avoiding his homework, and I'm not taking shit tonight.

The side door opens. I don't stop my frying, just switch hands so that I can reach my paring knife with the other one. No one uses that door except me and Simon; customers needing the outhouse go outside and around. Maybe someone made a mistake, though. Maybe.

In the gloom, the figure in the door looks to be around Simon's height, but it ain't Simon, I can see that from here. Mick?

He beckons, holding out a full cloth bag. What the hell is Mick giving me now? I don't know why—maybe curiosity, maybe just a death wish—but I give the food on the griddle one last stir and go over, paring knife still in hand, to take his offering. It's heavy, like it's full of books or something. I undo the tie and look inside.

It *is* full of books, actually, a couple of library paperbacks and a hardback or two. The hell is Mick going and giving me books for? Mick, of all people. I give him a weird look. He shrugs. I pull one out.

Son of a bitch.

"I think you're mistaken," is all I say, doing my level best to look amused and puzzled rather than, say, shocked and horrified. The book is about pregnancy.

"Really?" His voice is as even as mine, pitched low under the conversations going on ten feet away. "I don't think so."

I laugh, and it don't sound false to even my ears. "You finally knock up a girl or something?"

"No, I didn't." He stares at me, a faint smile on his face what don't reach his eyes. "Little bird told me these would be just up your alley, in fact."

"Did it?" *Did it?* Shit, shit, shit. No, he's bluffing. He must be. "Well, little birds have a habit of being wrong. Why don't you give these to the right bird and come have a drink, Mick. I don't generally let customers use my side door."

He don't budge, just looks at me, like that's gonna do anything. Tougher than you have tried worse, and a little stunt like this ain't gonna make me sweat.

He's the first to blink. "I really don't think I can disappoint Simon like that."

"Seriously, Mick, you've had your fun. Joke's over. Come have a drink, or leave."

"Says you throw up every morning," he continues steadily in a whisper, as if I didn't say anything at all. "Sounds familiar."

"Right. Next thing you're gonna be saying is my supposed baby is Simon's."

"No, I'm not. He said he didn't do it, and I believe him, just like I believe that if I walked out into that room right now and started guessing names, that I'd get the right man on the first try."

"You're being ridiculous."

"Who cut your lip between today and yesterday, Erin?"

This is so stupid. If I really wasn't pregnant, I'd be in big trouble right about now, but seeing as I am, well, actually—no, no, it couldn't get much worse, I'm pretty sure of that. Rock and a hard place. I'm stuck and Mick's got me but good. Lord, I hate him so much. Hate all those assholes with power who use it like it makes them better than us who don't got none, assholes like Mick, like...

I do the only thing I can do. I give him a puzzled look and say, "I slipped on wet leaves. Look, if you're gonna be pushy about it, you can put these in the kitchen." I shove the bag into his hands, and he reluctantly takes it. "By the way, you seen Simon today? He's not been back since this morning."

"Course. He came by after school. We didn't do much, though; someone'd already told him about the upcoming fight, and he was pretty worked up about it. Didn't like it one bit, if you get my drift." Mick's expression is neutral.

"I bet." Oh, do I ever. Of course he wouldn't, and if he'd heard it before he got to Mick's, that meant he'd gotten the news at school. That'd be enough to ruin anyone's day. After all, it'd ruined mine. Ruined a lot of things. Fuck Art, just fuck him.

Mick heads into the kitchen. I don't like him being back there alone, but I don't want him out front without me to supervise him. Who's he gonna tell back there, the stove?

"Erin!" Taylor's voice from the bar jolts me back to real life, and I turn to see that if I don't give the griddle a quick stir-up, I'm gonna be serving charcoal. There's glasses to be filled, drinks to be poured, and dammit, somehow he managed to leave a book on Simon's desk. I grab it before anyone can see the title. Damn you, Mick.

The bell over the door jingles, more customers, more orders, coming right up, paste a smile on my face and look up in time to...

...meet Simon's too-blue eyes. He's back.

Noise ramps up, everyone calling out, asking about the fight, him and Connor, gonna do knives, gonna beat him, yeah? Yeah? Darryl Hensley grabs his sleeve, and Simon shrugs him off, keeps coming across the bar, watching me all the while. He knows what a sinner I am; I know it in my soul like I've never known anything before as he comes around the bar and takes the book from my hand before I can hide it, and for one second I know he's gonna hit me across the face right here and now with all the world's eyes on me.

Simon pulls me tight against his chest, squeezing until I can barely breathe.

And just like that, he's two feet away, slinging his backpack down by his desk, like it never happened, and what the hell just did happen?

"Simon!" someone calls.

"Yeah?" It's like he just realized there's other people in the room, frowning with confusion. What's going through your head, Simon?

"You and Connor," Seth Williams says, like that means anything.

"What about us?"

"The fight. Whatcha gonna do?"

The room goes quiet at that, the kind of silence that could go either way. I hold my breath, like that'll help. Then Simon smiles, only it's not his real one, it's the smile he only uses in the ring when the scent of blood's in the air. "I'm gonna fuck him up, yeah?"

Someone whistles, another beckons. He shrugs and goes to them. All's well in his world, it seems.

Then my eyes fall on the book. The book, oh God, the book Simon took from my hands and put on the counter, the book about pregnancy what Mick left on the desk. It's sitting there and Nathaniel Greene's picking it up and reading the cover, oh God…

He's already looking at me with a question on his face. I reach for it, but he pulls it back, and now Seth's leaning over to see what the fuss is about, and it's way too late now. Oh God. Oh God.

The beer jug next to me is empty. I need to run downstairs and fetch up more. Anything to leave this room right now, anything to get away from the pair of them now staring at me like I've grown two heads. I pick up the jug and flee.

The darkness of the kitchen is a relief. I cover my mouth with a hand to stifle the panic that's rising like bile. God, oh God, this is bad, this is bad, bad, bad. The world knows, and the world wasn't supposed to know, though I don't know for how long I could have kept it a secret, but I was gonna try, somehow…somehow…and they'll tell *him*.

"It's Jeff Petrowski again, isn't it? It's his kid."

It's Mick, sitting there at my kitchen table. Mick, who probably remembers, because you don't forget that sort of thing.

I shake my head anyway. Maybe if I never say it, it won't be true. It'll all go away if only nobody ever speaks it aloud.

"Simon's figured out it's him."

No, no, no. He can't have. How could he? I've been so careful, as careful as I've been in my life. I can't move, lest I throw up. Lest I scream for real this time. I've wanted to so much, all day long.

"You didn't trust Simon enough to tell him, but he's not dumb, you know. Young, headstrong, but not stupid. You could've trusted him. Of all people, you could've told him. Hell, you could've told me, but you should've told him."

I'm gasping for breath. The world is spinning.

"I always wondered, seeing as your mom's dead, is Petrowski still legally your stepdad?"

Hand over my mouth, I stumble to the sink and puke, heaving until nothing comes up. I'm sure the front room is loud as usual, but back here the only sound is me, sliding down until I'm crouched on the floor.

Mick hasn't moved. "Simon scares you, doesn't he? Deep in your bones, where you won't admit it to yourself, Simon's started to scare you, but you can't tell him to stay away because you need to be seen having a steady man about the place."

Maybe if I close my eyes it'll be over faster, but Mick is still talking.

"And anyway, Simon keeps Art away, two birds with one stone, right? Only now he's a liability too."

"No," I whisper. "No, it's not like that."

"Then what's it like?"

I can't answer, don't know if there is an answer. It's everything, it's nothing, nothing at all, just like I am nothing. Nothing, worth nothing.

Silence suffocates me, and the longer it goes on, the more I can't even begin to speak.

The chair scrapes back. Footsteps cross the room to pause next to me. Someone pumps water into the sink, washing the mess down the drain. I'm hyperventilating. I take the towel I'm handed and hug it close, hold it over my mouth until my breathing is somewhere close to under control. Right now, nothing else is.

The kitchen door opens and closes again. A body leans against the counter next to me, bringing the smell of soap and sweat and that fresh scent that is Simon, and over that, a hint of beer. Men, always alcohol, it's their scent. Always.

Arms around my shoulders. Time to get up. Life goes on. On and on and on.

17

TAYLOR

Everyone's finally gone, the front room empty for the night. Erin's in the back washing dishes, and I start stacking the last of the glasses. Only seven hours until work in the morning. I mean, I like this job, but the schedule might kill me. She and I just about bump into each other in front of the kitchen door, next to the desk where Flaherty's doing his homework.

"Sorry!"

"You're fine." She takes the glasses and nods to the clock. "Wipe the tables, stack the chairs, and then you're done for the night."

"Thanks." Her hand brushes mine.

"Something wrong with my shirt?"

I'm staring at her stomach. "No, no, nothing, sorry. I'll just be getting things finished."

The door swings shut behind her, and I find a rag. I didn't mean to stare. I just saw that book being passed around, and I wondered if she really was...

Flaherty's looming next to me.

"Uh, you need something?"

"I saw the way you was looking at Erin."

The last time I saw his eyes like that, I took a punch that ended my fighting career. I take a step back.

He follows. Oh shit. "So? I'm just looking."

Another step back for me, another step forward for him. My shoulders touch the wall. Double shit.

Flaherty leans in so our faces are about six inches too close. I try to slide away, but he gets his fist in the front of my shirt. Oh, I'm going to die.

"You can look if you wanna, but touch her and you'll wish you were dead. I mean it."

"Why do you care?"

"Don't worry what I care about, worry what Erin thinks. You lay a finger on her and I'll personally rip it off." He lets me go, and my heels touch the ground. "No hard feelings, yeah?"

Like that made anything better. Why the fuck does he care so much?

Unless...

He heads to his desk and goes back to his homework. No, not his homework, his guard duty. He's guarding the kitchen door. Mother of God, her ass is better protected than the pope's. She's ten years older than him. It's sick. No hard feelings, my ass. Wouldn't have tried if I'd have known, now would I?

You wanna set your baby daddy on me, Erin? Go ahead and do it. Just go ahead. But I saw that book and saw your face when you realized we'd all seen it. I put the dots together, and if you think I'm keeping my mouth shut, you got another thing coming.

Dawn can't come soon enough. I open my eyes with one thought on my mind. Pants up, belt and holster, and I'm going to be a few minutes late for work 'cause guess who's telling Art the news? Let no one say that I don't pay back favors.

The depot's teeming, just like it always is, but it's not hard to spot Art. I just look for the red hair—well, orange, really—and wave him over. "How was your shift?"

"Fine." He's annoyed about something. "Whaddya want?"

I've got valuable stuff, even if he doesn't know it yet. I can afford to take my time. "Got some news for you, straight off the press."

"That so."

"Big stuff, you might say."

"You gonna stand there gabbing, or you gonna get to the point?"

Art starts to walk, but I don't bother to move. "You might wanna stick around, Art, because I think you wanna know this. Trust me."

That gets his attention, if only for a moment. He stops and pretends to be interested. "Yeah? And why is that?"

"You asked me to tell you if Erin had a guy. Well, I found out last night"—and considering all his big words about making her his woman, I shouldn't smile, but some things are too ironic not to find funny—"that your boy Simon's going to be a father."

I pause to let the news sink in. Art stares at me, apparently struck dumb. Way too ironic.

"And Erin Livingston's the mom. I know, right? Kids these days, but everyone knows that Erin's such a who—"

WHAM.

Pain explodes in my jaw, and lights dance in front of my eyes. I stagger back from the blow. "The fuck was that for?"

Like a bull, Art rushes me. Oh fuck. I duck, weave to the right, catch him in the stomach with an elbow. He slams me against a wall, but I get a foot up and connect.

As he stumbles back, I manage to get out, "The hell d'you think you're pulling, Art? I didn't say I slept with her, said it was Simon!"

He twists out of my grip, grabs my neck, punches one, two, three times. There's a ringing in my ears, blood running into my eyes. Art's face is twisted up as he screams in my ear between hits, "Don't you ever talk about Erin like that again!"

Blood runs down my throat, and I'm down. Fucking hell, he's trying to kill me.

Arms yank me back, hands pin me down. More men are dragging Art away. There's blood all over the concrete, all down my shirt. My head feels like it's going to fall off. I'm not going to make it to work on time, I guess. Not today. And I have to buy myself a new shirt now, 'cause I only have four, and now I only have three, 'cause this one is shot. Not shot really, of course, but the blood isn't coming off, no way, ha, ha, ha...

Someone's talking to me. I know it's me they want, 'cause they say, "Taylor Burkes." And that's me.

Hands wave in front of my face. "How many fingers am I holding up?"

The hand—hands?—double and weave. "Five?" Cloth is pressed

against my nose. The world spins. "Where's za bastard?" I ask.

"Art?" They've got me surrounded, five or six of them or more—I can't tell, 'cause the world's swinging around like anything. "He's gone home, okay? And you should too."

"Got work."

I stumble and someone props me up. The voices around me are louder, then quiet again. "No, I don't think you do. Look, we'll have Cooper here run down and tell them you're out for the count. You guard at the Market, right?"

"'M late."

"It's okay, it's okay. And look, we'll take you back to your lodgings, right? Erin's place, yeah?" A low snigger goes around.

"I don't think so." The voice rings out loud and clear, even when everything else is so hazy. Everyone swivels to look, like dogs on leashes. I look too, or try, though the world wobbles like it's underwater.

There's a tall man in a dark suit, slick-looking like most people around here aren't. Taller and taller, walking toward me. I hit the ground shoulder-first.

"Take him to my place on Eden Boulevard. Joe, find the doctor."

The black-suited man bends down and lays a hand on my shoulder. He looks familiar, somehow. Like I should know his name, because I definitely know his face. Can't think where from, though.

"Don't you worry, Taylor. You're under my protection now."

18

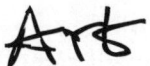

I'm sitting on the last swing in the park when Simon arrives. Still the same boy he was yesterday, sullen and silent. Doesn't look like anyone's dad, which, of course, he isn't. Has Erin been telling him tales about what a terrible bully I am? Well, it was her who said I could teach him fighting, and if she doesn't like what happened, then that's just too bad.

"What happened to you?" he asks. It seems we're talking today.

"What?"

"Your shirt. It's got blood all down it."

I glance down. "It sure does. Let's get started."

He doesn't move. "What happened?"

"Shit. Doesn't matter, it's not my blood."

"Whose is it, then?"

The way he asks, I don't like that much. "What is this, twenty questions? Taylor Burkes's, if you must know."

"Thought you two was friends."

"And who says we aren't still? I take it you heard about this month's fight?"

Simon's fairly hard to read, but from what I can see, he isn't exactly happy. "I heard it at school."

Ah. That would do it. I suck in air between my teeth. "Sorry about that. That must've sucked." Another shrug from him. "What'd Erin say about it?"

Simon thinks over the answer. He's trying to find something diplomatic to say, I can tell. "I don't think she was happy about it. She didn't really say much."

"She didn't? Really? 'Cause she sure as hell gave me an earful over it."

"Other things to talk about."

"Yeah, I heard about that."

He looks up, wary. "You did?"

"Yeah," I say carefully, watching his face. "Taylor mentioned you two talked. You getting to be friends?"

"Not really." He's uncomfortable. Taylor's face rises in my mind, smirking, laughing at me. But no, it couldn't be true. "Look, what'd he tell you?"

"Not much, really."

Definitely uncomfortable. Almost...guilty? No. No way.

"It's just that he was prying into things. Shit just happened." He squares his shoulders, looks me in the eye. Suspicion becomes certainty. Here it comes. "Erin is—"

"Shut the fuck up right now."

He stops mid-sentence, mouth open.

"If you keep talking," I continue, breathing heavy, because I am that angry right now, that downright furious. "If you keep talking, I...I'll..."

"If you're gonna hit me," Simon finally says, "then do it."

There's something about the way he says it. I look at him, and he looks at me, and I can't.

Can't hit him. Can't call him a liar. Can't yell, can't be angry, can't be anything. Not with him looking like he knows he deserves it, knows what I'm thinking, every bit of it. Is sorry for it, even.

"So you and Erin," I say slowly, carefully, "are gonna have a baby, then."

Simon takes a deep breath, nods. "Yeah. Seven months, give or take a week."

Give or take a week. It's a slap right to my face. Means it wasn't just once, no, more than that, maybe every night, and the morning too, and don't tell Art, he'll never know, never guess.

And who could? Simon, who cried in his sleep at age eleven after Erin found him eating from her compost heap, and it wasn't that long ago I was listening to his troubles with bullies. He's not grown up. Hell, he's probably still growing, if it comes to that. Fights like he's never gonna stop, killed a man when I handed him a bat, never talks much about most things, and never, ever talks about his past.

"So you're gonna be a good dad, then?"

He shrugs. "Gonna try."

"Better than yours?"

Simon stops, freezes, really. Opens his mouth, shuts it again.

Never talks about his past, never says much of anything, really. Speaks when spoken to, polite, follows the rules laid down, got an attitude lately from somewhere, but he's a teenage boy and that sort of thing happens. Fights like he means it. Never been taught how not to kill. Two months ago he was still fifteen, a child, really, and this kid's supposed to have had sex with Erin? Give me a fucking break. No. There's no way.

He takes a deep breath. "As far as you know, I will be."

And isn't that a smart-ass answer.

I spread my arms wide. "Well, that's just wonderful. I'm happy for you, real happy."

He isn't smirking or smiling. Not proud of himself for getting one up on me, no. Simple Simon, who I've watched out for like my own. And he went and betrayed me, every bit.

I reach down, pick up the baseball bat from among the stuff I bring every day. Weigh it in my hands. A blunt weapon, with blood dried on in spots, because I forgot to wash it off. It's heavy, got a good swing. Does its duty without anything fancy.

I toss it to Simon, who catches it one-handed. His eyes say he's wary. His stance says he's ready for anything. Not ready enough, though.

"How are you feeling about the next fight?"

He doesn't smile back. "Fight's a fight. We'd have been matched up sooner or later."

"What if you have to kill Connor?"

"You can't kill in regulation. They ban you for that."

And this is what's gonna tell. I smile, smile big, humorless. "I can arrange something alternative, if you'd like."

"No thanks."

"And what if I do it anyway?"

"Then I say no."

Isn't that the trick of it, though. "You know Petrowski's boys don't like it when you do that."

"They can deal with it. And you can deal with me."

We face each other. All gloves are off. First to blink loses, maybe forever.

Simon breaks the silence. "Erin said you took scalps." A pause, long as the last one. "If I don't do what you tell me, you gonna take mine?"

More than one way to skin a cat, more than one way to kill a man. There's hate in his eyes aimed straight at me, and I don't know why. I only ever tried to do my best by Simon. Only ever wanted the best for him. He's the best, and I made him that way.

Never taught him not to kill. Never taught him not to hurt beyond what he had to.

Maybe someone else already did that.

"That depends, Simon."

"On what?"

"If you lose, are you gonna take mine?"

He seems to think for a moment, then in one big sweep swings the bat at the rusting jungle-gym frame.

The wood breaks, splinters everywhere. Simon throws down the worthless remains and grabs the metal, silencing its ringing cry. A shiver goes down my spine.

"No."

That's all he says. That's all he needs to say.

We train.

19

TAYLOR

The blinds let stripes of light into the office, otherwise dark and dingy with unnamed grime. It's got orange carpet old enough for there to be a path worn down to the concrete. The guard by the door all but screams "don't touch" by simply existing, not that I would anyway. I value my fingers.

My head throbs, and so does my jaw. I've got a molar loose now, and it hurts in more than one way. Fucking bastard Art.

The side door opens, swinging inward with hardly a sound, and the guy in the suit from earlier walks in.

It's Jeff Petrowski himself. Oh...fuck.

Oh shit. Oh hell, I knew he looked familiar. Jeff Petrowski runs this town, if you believe the rumors, or Art, at any rate, and he's a pretty damn good source of information somehow. Walk in this man's office and you'll never walk out.

I'm going to die.

Mr. Petrowski stops in front of me and doesn't smile—he only smiles when he's going to kill someone, don'tcha know?—just holds out his hand for me to shake. Shake hands with the devil, boys, step right up. Does anyone even know I'm here? Will I just disappear?

"Taylor Burkes," he says, his grip firm as he shakes my hand.

"Mr. Petrowski."

He's a big guy, taller than me, built like a door. Going gray on top, but the hair on his wrists is black and thick. I've only just got chest hair in the past couple of years, and my fingers hurt from that handshake. I'm not offered a seat. Even if I was, I'm not sure I could sit, my knees are so stiff.

"You're working at Erin's bar."

He starts the conversation, cutting to the chase just like I've heard he does. No small talk for the man pulling the strings, no how-d'you-dos, nope. I'm going to die and they're not going to find my body...

"Yessir," I manage to say.

"Don't piss her off."

A warning, not that I need it. "Yessir."

I do my best to stand up even straighter, avoid his eyes like I've heard guys say you should do, because Jeff Petrowski can read thoughts. Well, not read, but see them there and have his guards come for you before you even reach for a knife, not that I have one with me right now. Not that I'm stupid enough to even try.

Mr. Petrowski's looking out the window, and why the hell am I here, in this office, on this carpet that is only still orange because they haul people outside before they shoot them, if you believe the stories. Mr. Petrowski looks at me, and I believe. I really do.

"You're living over the bar, working with Simon Flaherty."

My heart skips a beat, and I do my damn best to keep it off my face. One of the Market guys says Petrowski was at Flaherty's last fight, betting against him. Or for him? I can't remember, and it doesn't change the facts.

"Yessir, I am."

Sweat is trickling down my back under my shirt, little drops. What does he want with me? Why did he bring that up?

Mr. Petrowski studies my face like he's memorizing it.

"The kid's mine."

What? "Do...you mean...Simon?"

Mr. Petrowski just stares at me like I'm stupid, like I'm a bug he's waiting to squash once I'm no longer valuable. I can feel myself trying to shrink into my shoes and have to fight the urge to duck.

"Erin is having my son."

My blood about freezes in my veins. Mr. Petrowski is Erin's lover? What the fuck? I thought he was her stepdad.

Art never mentioned this, no one ever mentioned this. How

could...? And anyway, Simon said the kid was his, or, well, didn't say it, but with the way he was acting...

Who the hell acts like that if it's not theirs?

Mr. Petrowski breaks through my thoughts. "Put the word out."

I meet his eyes, blue as ice, and try to think of something to say that won't get me killed. Nothing comes to mind, nothing at all.

He lays a hand on my shoulder, heavy as a cinderblock. Doesn't smile, because Jeff Petrowski never smiles, not ever, not unless he's going to kill you, so I guess his scowl's a good thing. It sure as hell doesn't feel like one.

"Her mother left a few years back. Erin needs a man to look after her." The weight of his hand makes my shoulders want to hunch over. Mr. Petrowski's eyes are so blue, piercing. Have I...seen them before? "Help her out around the house, make sure no one bothers her. I can count on you."

"What about Flaherty?" I say, because apparently my brain wants me to die. "He said..."

Mr. Petrowski doesn't so much as bat an eyelash. "Just put out the word, like I told you."

I stop myself from meeting his eyes again. "Yessir."

"Don't disappoint me."

"Yessir."

He starts to leave, then turns back. I haven't moved an inch. "Touch Erin again and I'll have your legs ripped off."

That's the exact same threat Erin used on me yesterday. Apparently it wasn't empty.

Oh shit.

20

Simon

"You'll be needing a new knife before we get to the ring," is the first thing Mick says when I get in his pole barn for practice.

"Why?"

"Yours folds. It won't do."

"Why?" I flip it over and catch it. "They use butterfly knives in the ring. What's wrong with a switchblade?"

He looks way more serious than the situation warrants. "Because once you start carrying a weapon, you need to consider that you might end up using it in a situation you don't mean to, and every second you spend switching something open is a second the other guy'll be using against you. You need a fighting knife, not a tactical one."

I flip the knife again just to get on his nerves. I'm not a kid. "Who says I'd go for a knife and not a gun if that happened?"

"Who says you'd have time for anything at all?"

The knife leaves my hand again, up into the air. He slams me against the sheet metal wall so hard the whole side of the barn shakes before I have time to move. Hand on my face, fingers pressing against my eyes until colors dance. I open my mouth, but there's cold steel on my neck. He's got me pinned. I try to shift, but he presses harder until I can feel the edge of the blade on my skin, and I know what it can do, dammit. Sweat trickles down my back as I pray his feet don't slip.

His voice is low and nasty. "The difference between what you've been doing with your fists and what you're learning here with me is that all you have to do is fuck up once for everything to be over, forever, and there's no one in this world who can save you from a slit throat. You don't *get* a second chance. On the mats, it's first blood." Mick's eyes bore into mine. "On the street, it's whoever can walk away. So when I tell you something, you goddamn listen to me instead of just assuming you know best, got it?"

He lets me go and backs away. I pick up my knife, my pride, but don't turn my back on him.

Mick's still watching. "What you've been learning up until now is fighting, and the risk that entails doesn't change much with the location, because it takes a while to beat a man to death, wherever you are. But what I am trying to teach you, Simon, when I tell you to hold your knife one way and not another, or to move your feet more, or the exact amount of pressure you need to be using to cut shallow and not deep, is dueling. They call it a fight, but fights don't stop for a drop of blood, and this does. First blood and it's done. And that's what I'm teaching you."

"So what the hell did you just do?"

"That was assassination." My head jerks up, but Mick's studying the wall. "And if you ever need to do it, you do it like I did now. Hand to the face, no warning, slit the throat as quick as you can and run for it, because the Market Authority doesn't approve of murder for money."

"Why would I need to know how to assassinate?"

"Why wouldn't you?"

I wish I could lay him flat for that, right here, right now. "'Cause I don't do that! I don't do that shit, okay? And I don't see why you and everyone else in Buchell thinks that's my fucking goal in life to go around killing people for money in a cartel, like it's some kind of joke or something."

And the worst part is, he's surprised. "But you're not just any boy, you're Simon Flaherty, boy wonder at sixteen. Erin's boy." It's like it never even crossed his mind. "What did you expect when you started fighting? Pretty girls and kisses in the sunshine?"

And for just that second, he sounds like Art. I take a step forward, then another. He sounds like Art, and Art's scared of me. They're *all* scared of me. Won't get close no more.

But Mick stands his ground, doesn't back away, lets me get near. We're the same height, exactly, but he could beat me here and now. He just proved that. No reason for him to be scared of me, even though he knows what I can do.

Maybe he understands that *can* and *will* ain't the same thing.

"What did you expect," he asks, "from the people who can't see past next week, who don't understand the reasons they fought a war, let alone why you fight in a ring? What did you think you'd get, mercy?" He turns away, turns his back. "Sometimes we don't choose the life we live, Simon."

No. "There's always a choice."

"And sometimes that choice is kill or die, or is that still considered a choice at all?"

Does he believe what he's saying?

"Sooner or later," he says, "someone's gonna give you cash and you're gonna have cold blood on your hands. Don't make a career of it if you don't want to, but that ship's already sailed. It left when you went to a back-alley fight knowing how to swing a baseball bat to kill."

"I didn't mean to." It comes out too high.

He's almost gentle. "You still think that matters? Words don't mean a thing when you already did it. If you want out, then run away, and run fast and don't ever come back. But if you want to live in this town, better sit up and take notice. 'Didn't mean to' doesn't mean shit."

But I didn't, and I swear I didn't, didn't mean to hit that hard, didn't mean to kill him, didn't mean to hurt Erin or punch Art. Everything's out of control, *I'm* out of control, and ain't no one gonna stop me, no, they're gonna cheer louder until the day they decide they don't love me no more, and what do I do then?

Maybe it's not the killing thing that's the problem. Maybe it's the part where I have to live with it after.

Mick takes a stance, nods to me. "Time to practice. Come on. Feet apart, bend your knees more. Let's do this."

Maybe Mick gets that. He might not get *me*, but he gets that one thing. And that's more than anyone else.

"On my count. One. Two."

I can do this.

"Three."

21

TAYLOR

In the hours between meeting Mr. Petrowski and starting my evening shift at Erin's bar, I told everyone I knew at the Market exactly what he told me to say. Nearly stood on the rooftops and shouted it, because Mr. Petrowski told me to and I don't wanna wake up six feet under concrete. Then I went back to his headquarters to tell him I'd done it, and he gave me a wad of cash and orders to take the money to Chuck Farley's knife shop and put in a special order to be delivered to Mick Perry's pawnshop for Flaherty. So I did that too.

And, no, I don't know why Petrowski's buying Flaherty a knife, though when I stopped by the guard hut and asked the guys about it, they mentioned that Petrowski always puts his money on the Saint come betting time. So maybe he's sponsoring him now?

But why?

I don't know, I don't know, I don't want to know. I'm just doing what he tells me because that seems a better strategy for survival than *not* doing it.

And that's fine and good and well, until I walk back into Erin's place to get ready for work and realize just where that leaves me.

Erin's cooking something on her big iron range, and I'm sorry I tried anything with her, Jesus. She ought to put out a warning sign: "Do not touch if you value your nuts." And I do value them, but I have orders.

Everyone, he said, tell everyone. And I'm guessing everyone includes her.

Flaherty's backpack's on the kitchen table, but he's nowhere to be seen. This might be my only chance to talk to Erin without him squashing me to a pulp the way I'm sure he wants to. With the day I've had, it's a miracle I haven't up and left town yet. Mother Mary, my head hurts.

I clear my throat. She doesn't notice. Try again, and this time she turns.

"Taylor Burkes, what the hell happened to your face?"

Art happened, that's what, and let me tell you, we aren't friends anymore, job or not. I've got two black eyes and a broken nose because of that bastard. But that's not what's at stake here.

I clear my throat for the third time. "Sorry to bother you, but I got a message from Jeff Petrowski. For you."

Erin doesn't move, and I look away. "Yeah?"

"Well, it's not really a message, but I think you should know."

"Spit it out."

Oh hell, here I go.

"He says that I'm to help you out and make sure you're okay every day because it's his son you're having. And he's telling everyone that, like, the whole town. About you having his son, I mean." Oh Mary, I can't take my eyes off the floor lest I see her face. "And I'm really sorry I bothered you, and I won't ever touch you again, I swear..."

She hasn't told me to shut up or thrown anything yet, and I have to look.

Erin's got a dazed expression, like someone's just hit her upside the head, shoulders heaving up and down. Is she okay?

"You'd better touch me, Taylor Burkes," she says.

"What?"

"'Cause I'm gonna faint."

Behind me, the door opens. Erin starts to fall. A hand pulls me back by the face, mashing my broken nose. My back hits the wall as Flaherty shoves past. My nose, my *nose*, Mary, Mother of God, that fucking hurt, and it's bleeding again, all down the front of my new shirt. I feel around for something to put over it, anything, a dishcloth, whatever, damn it all.

By the time I stop seeing stars, get the bleeding under control, find another shirt in my room, and get back down downstairs, Flaherty's been yelling for five minutes straight.

"...the hell didn't you go to a doctor yet, Erin? Ain't like we don't got money for that! Not like it's a secret now, so why ain't you gone today?"

Erin's on the floor drinking a glass of water, glaring like there's no tomorrow. "I've been busy."

"Busy!" Simon slams his hand on the table and I jump. "You been chopping cabbage! I could've done that, Burkes, anyone. And now you're passing out? What do you think you're doing, Erin?"

"Running a business, I'd thank you to remember." She struggles to her feet, every movement saying it hurts. Did he catch her? I don't remember, and Petrowski's going to have me on the scaffold if she's hurt, I know it. "You should be doing homework right now, not telling me how to run my life."

"Fuck that."

The silence that follows those two words is dangerous, nearly crackling with anger. I step around him toward the stove as Erin's eyes narrow.

"Excuse me?" she says.

Flaherty stands his ground. "I. Said. Fuck. That. Fuck school. Fuck homework. It's a waste of money and time, and you know it. I suck at reading, and I'm stupid to boot. Ain't nobody gonna care I went to high school, not for the jobs I'll be doing."

Erin strides up to him so they're nose-to-nose, and I can't look away. It's like one of those movies they project on the buildings downtown in summer, him and her yelling at each other for all they're worth. "You ain't stupid, boy-o, not by a long shot, but you're sure as hell acting it right now. What exactly do you think you'll be doing when you finish high school, huh?"

"I'll be shooting people for the cartels, and you fucking know it!"

She slaps him across the face, and he lets her. *Lets* her, and I know it's deliberate because I've fought Saint Flaherty, I've tried it and it don't work. He stands there and takes it, and while the mark's still bright white on his cheek, he hugs her tightly. It's all too fucked up. Is she sleeping with him *and* Petrowski? Bet he won't like that.

But maybe Flaherty just hasn't heard the news. Mr. Petrowski said to spread the word, and who am I to disobey?

"Hey, y'all, I'm still here."

Flaherty doesn't even look. "Ain't keeping you."

I'm not scared of him. "Got a message for you, Simon. Erin's already heard it, but I figured I'd let you know."

"Then say it already."

I savor the moment, watching Erin. She'll regret making a fool of me, and from the look of it, she's already repenting. "It's from Jeff Petrowski. You know, Erin's dad? He says I'm to take care of her."

The temperature seems to drop about five degrees, but I pretend not to notice.

"Since when are you in Petrowski's pocket?"

"Did I say I was? He asked a favor, and I didn't mind helping out."

"Well, ain't that nice for you. And you can tell him—"

"I'm not done, and before you tell me to go shove it, you'll wanna hear this next bit." Flaherty's rolling his eyes, probably counting the seconds before he can get back to mooning over her. Ha. Well, I got news for him. "Mr. Petrowski, being a paternal sort of man, also wants me to look after his kid. Make sure no harm comes to him."

Bull's-eye.

Erin's staring at me wide-eyed, fear written all over her face in fucking permanent marker. Guilty as charged, cheating or whatever, sleeping with her stepdad. And Flaherty, he's turning slowly, turning until he's looking me in the eye like he's trying to read my soul, though having already seen that look once today from Petrowski, it isn't that...

Wait. No.

Shit.

Fucking hell and shit, Mary, Mother of God, and every saint my mother ever prayed to.

Blue eyes, blue as ice, and a stare that pins you to the wall. It clicks, oh hell does it click.

Simon Flaherty is Jeff Petrowski's kid. It's as plain as day, now that I know what to look for. The eyes, the face shape, the way he sets his chin. I know it, and staring at Simon, I can tell he knows I just made the connection. Knows it, and knows what I wanted to do with Erin, and he's going to kill me, oh fuck...

I take a step back. "You're—"

"Shut the fuck up right now." He lets go of her.

"But he's your—"

"Shut up."

"I never heard anything—"

"Burkes, I swear to God."

"You're Petrowski's kid!" I scream it out far louder than I ever meant, but now that I've said it, I can't seem to stop talking. "You are, aren't you. You got the same eyes, and that look, I know it! I know you are!"

Silence. Erin still looks shocked. Did she know? Holy shit. Does Petrowski know? He's got to.

The knife. Oh yeah, he knows.

"That's right," Flaherty finally says flatly, and I haven't earned any favors from him. "Congratulations. What's your point?"

"I—" I finally remember it and swallow. Right, my point. The thing I was going to say. Oh hell. "He didn't mean you." Oh shit. I'm going to die. He's figured it out. "He meant Erin's baby. 'Cause that's his son too."

We both look at Erin.

"Taylor?" she says.

"Yeah?"

"You're fired."

I don't need telling twice. I'm out the door, and not a moment too soon.

22

Art

I bike to Mick's shop before work, having slept like the dead. Do the dead sleep? Never really wondered, but I suppose they do, if that's what we say. The brick-faced woman lets me through to the pole barn, where Mick sits at a folding table, a disassembled rifle in front of him.

"Figured you'd come. Take a seat."

No reason not to. I open a chair, straddle it backward, keep my hands where he can see them, just to be nice. "We need to talk strategy."

Mick snaps a piece into place and finally looks up. "Yes, we do. Got a few questions for you, Artie."

"Fire away."

"Why doesn't Simon have any friends his age?"

The hell? "I wouldn't know. Ask him."

That don't seem to satisfy. Another piece of the gun clicks into place.

"Anyway," I say, "we need to be doing damage control. When word gets around that Erin's pregnant, Simon's gonna become a target."

"Why?" Mick's getting the fuck on my nerves, not even looking at me, and I'm sure he knows it, but I try not to give him the satisfaction. "Not that it's my business," he adds. "I just teach him knives."

And how not to kill?

We stare at each other, Mick and I, over the table, all pretending gone.

"Seeing," he finally says, "as we're both stubborn bastards, I suggest we get a few things straight so we're not working against each other."

"Like what?"

"Like what the hell is Simon still doing in school?"

Who cares? "That's Erin's thing. She wants him to graduate, so he goes."

"You'd rather he didn't?"

"I just don't see it as necessary."

"So that brings us back to the original question." Mick curls his lip like a dog. "Why doesn't Simon have any friends? He's a bit shook up right now, but besides that, he seems perfectly nice."

"Nice?" That comes out sour, but I've had it up to here. "We are talking about Simon Flaherty, yeah? That kid couldn't have been more of a brat recently if he tried."

"He's a teenager."

"He's an asshole."

"It happens. Could be worse, he could be Connor Hall."

"Oh Jesus fucking Christ. They used to be friends, you know."

"I know." The rifle's assembled, and Mick's hands go still. "Simon seems pretty worked up about the fight."

"No shit. He's been using training as an excuse to take potshots at me. I think he blames me for that boy dying." Mick doesn't comment, but his expression says it all. "Look, I put him in that alley, but how the hell should I have known what they were planning? He shouldn't have gone for a headshot."

"You should never have given him a bat."

"Oh, because he'd rather have been stabbed?"

"You're such a fucking child, Art. You're his coach; he trusts you. He trusted you that day to tell him the right thing to do to get him out of there alive, and you dropped the fucking ball!"

Give me a break. "What would you know about it? You went and got yourself shot in the wrist and that was it for your career. You've never been a coach, and you haven't been training Simon half his goddamned life only to have him show up one morning and say he got a girl pregnant, thanks so fucking much, now fuck off!"

Mick narrows his eyes like he used to when we were doing all that urban fighting and someone would come back with scalps. He's pissed, oh he's pissed, and self-righteous to boot. "Well then, won't you be pleased to know that Simon was lying."

What?

"The baby is Petrowski's. And he's claiming it outright this time."

Petrowski's. Jeff Petrowski's. There's a tone in my ears, high and loud, drowning everything out but the fact that the father of Erin's baby is Jeff Petrowski.

Again.

I'd rather it was Simon's.

"I bet you do."

Did I say that out loud? "Fucking incest."

"Not technically, they're not blood related. Don't think Petrowski cares, either way."

My mouth keeps going, though I'm not the one controlling it anymore. "Is he gonna take care of it, or what?"

"He's not saying, just that it's his."

"And how do you know?"

"Your little friend Burkes came knocking on my door an hour ago. Guess he found a new friend, if you know what I mean."

Petrowski, friend? More like master. Nobody's friends with Petrowski. Nobody in the world.

My brain's trying to swim through mud. Not angry, not sad, just...like if I think about it for too long, it'll begin to mean something. The world is blurring around me, Mick's face fading out of view, replaced by a thousand regrets, for Erin, for Simon, for me and every wish I ever had, hanging out in her kitchen late at night and now they're gone, gone, gone.

Petrowski has no friends, only those under his thumb. And Erin's having his kid. Again.

"Hey, you'd know, Art. What happened to her first kid?"

Five years ago, when I got back to Buchell, I heard that Erin's was the place in town to get something to eat. She'd cook your rations, and if you were lucky, she'd keep you warm after. Erin who? Erin Livingston.

The only Erin Livingston I knew had been pregnant when I left, and I wanted to meet her kid, so I went knocking on her door. It'd been a few years after all.

But the boy who answered wasn't some black-haired six-year-old, no. It was Simon. Same Erin Livingston, different kid.

"She never said."

Mick stares at the wall. "Cuckoo's nest or coincidence?"

"I don't know."

All I know is, history's repeating itself, and just like last time, it's too late for me to change a fucking thing.

23

Erin

The bar is closed, front room cleaned up, and all that's left to do are the dishes. The feel of hot water on my hands is soothing somehow after the rush of running this place by myself, and on a Friday night, no less. It was bedlam. I need someone new, and I need them quick. Tomorrow is Saturday, hair-washing day for me while Simon's out training, though maybe I should turn the compost heap first...

Here I am, baby on the way, boy doing his best to get himself killed, and I'm wondering about the compost heap. Life goes on, don't it just, and we might all die, but in the meantime, the chickens need feeding, and what's for dinner tomorrow?

And Simon. What to do about Simon.

I knew who his dad was the minute I laid eyes on him. Some things you can't miss. But some things we don't get a choice in, and when I saw him elbows deep in my compost heap, I knew this was one of them.

Soldiers find religion on a battlefield, but boys lose it fast when grown-ups are the bad guys and praying don't make the bombs stop falling. I don't know what he did in the two months between his mom dying and getting here; I don't know why he stayed with me. Maybe he thought I was an angel for feeding him, but a boy like him should've known better. Ain't no angels on earth. Just all us sinners, paying for what we done, though what I done to deserve this life, I don't rightly know.

The side door opens and shuts, and someone drops the bar across it, pushes the desk and chair against the wood after. I don't bother to look. If it's an intruder, I die, so what. At this point, I'm not sure I even care.

"Erin?"

Just Simon. Nope, not gonna die. Not from him. I dunk the plate I'm holding into the rinse bucket and prop it up in the drainer.

"What is it, boy-o?"

Hesitant steps. Lord, save me from boys who think they know better.

"How long you known about Petrowski being my dad?"

Of all the damn questions he could have picked.

"It's a long story," is what I finally settle on, putting another dish in the drainer.

"I need to know."

"No, you don't. You just want to, and that's a world a difference."

"Fine. I want to. You said you'd tell the truth about three things."

It's time to get things straight, because I ran out of patience sometime a few hours back when he yelled at me about going to the doctor, as if what I do to my body has anything to do with him. All the words I been wanting to say all day, as I stood and served every drunken louse this town can hold, who *love* me, *love* Erin, who serves the drinks with a smile and makes them feel oh-so-*good* before they go whisper in the corner about my personal business.

Simon's standing there like the world owes him the truth, like I owe him more than I've already given, reminding me of all my sins, every goddamned one, and he thinks he'll get it?

"No," is what I say, with the soap running down my arms. "No, I won't tell you, and I don't give a shit what I promised. And before you shoot your mouth off about 'having to,' why don't you use that brain I'm spending so much tuition money on and figure out what you're gonna do when I say that you can deal with it or make me? Because anything you do to me, I can tell you right now's been done worse than you have in you. You got that?"

He looks shocked, about two inches from panic, and a part of me is glad to see it.

"Learn to think before you speak, Simon Flaherty."

I wash another plate, concentrating on getting it absolutely clean. Behind me, I can nearly hear him thinking, the wheels in his head turning in their slow way. I don't believe Simon's stupid, I really don't, but slow, lord, that boy's a sloth when the thinking gets tough.

"When did Petrowski marry your mom?"

Ah, that is *not* common knowledge. If he's fishing for answers, he didn't start in bad waters. "I was ten. My brother was fifteen."

"Didn't know you had a brother."

"That ain't common knowledge, either."

He mulls this over, and I begin wiping out a frying pan with a new rag, wondering how many dots he's connected. Not stupid, my boy, not stupid at all.

"What happened to him?"

"He died," I reply, and swallow the bile down. "Petrowski shot him."

"Why?"

Why am I answering these questions? What do I want him to find out? Simon is walking into the trap that is my past, my future, my life. Sinking in until he's swallowed up and drowned, just like everyone else. My business can only hurt people. I always tried to keep him at arm's length for just that reason.

Failed at that, same as everything else.

My silence stretches, and I think Simon's realized I'm not gonna answer, because he shifts his weight.

"Okay, then. Then when did Petrowski start raping you?"

My hand keeps moving somehow, which is funny, because my arms have gone numb. I can feel my heart speeding up.

"Or is the answer to one of those questions the answer to the other?"

I switch hands, keep cleaning. "No."

"'No' what?"

"He didn't rape me." Silence meets my words, collides with them and shatters as silently as snow. "I seduced him."

"Bullshit."

"My mother was so angry."

"Bullshit!"

"Her daughter seduced her husband, thirteen years old and a slut already."

"Erin—"

"What a humiliation, what a shame. Everyone knew—"

"Stop it, Erin!" Simon's fingers dig into my shoulders as he yanks me around to face him, and I can't understand the expression on his face. For the first time in so long, I can't understand what's going on behind those goddamned blue eyes. "How'd she find out? How'd your mom know?"

"Isn't it obvious?" He's searching my face, but the answer is right in front of him, plain as the nose on his face, familiar as anything. "The same way you found out this time, boy-o. I get morning sickness something awful."

He stops breathing. I can't read his face, but I can feel understanding come to him in the loosening of his hands, the jerk of his fingers. He can see me now, see who I am, what I am.

"You had a kid?"

"That's right," I say, flat as I can make it. "He'd be about four years younger than you."

His world looks to be collapsing about him. "And your brother...?"

"Tried to get me an abortion."

"And Petrowski killed him?" he asks in a voice no louder than a whisper.

"Two shots to the stomach," I clarify. "My mom had had two daughters with him, and Petrowski wanted a son. Another son, I guess. Some things don't change."

He's staring at his hands like they're burned, looking to me and back again, thoughts crossing his face again like clouds. He's trying to think, fucking hell, he's trying to think of a way around the problem like I never could, like no one ever did. Trying to beat the devil, when just to fight is to let him win.

"Erin..."

"Stop it."

"I'm gonna stop him."

"By doing what?" The words scream out of my throat before I can stop them. "You're sixteen goddamned years old! Do you think others didn't try? Do you think my brother didn't? You think *I* didn't?"

"No! Don't you see, you can't just let him do this!"

"Let? *Let* him? How dare you—"

"I dare! Dammit, I dare because don't you see we have to stand up to him? We have to!"

"We can't!" If I scream any louder, I'll start laughing and never stop. I'm gasping for breath, and still I go on, because if I stop now, I'll die. "You want me to stand up to him? You think I *like* this? I was trying to think of a way to get an abortion or something without him finding out, and then you went and told the whole motherfucking world! Like it has *anything* to do with you!"

"It has everything to do with me!" Simon's eyes burn too bright, his face all in a rage. "You think I don't know Petrowski? You think I don't know what he does, that he's never tried to get me to join his business? You don't know anything! You don't know what he done to me, to my mom—"

The word rings in the air, the word he never says, and Simon stops dead in his tracks. His mom, who I don't even know the name of, who he saw die and he don't never, ever talk about.

His voice is low, and somehow I know that what he's saying now, he won't ever say again. "My mom tried to run, tried to take me with her, and he killed her. He fucking killed her. He locked her in the attic during an airstrike and the place caught fire and she died, and weren't nothing I could do about it." A shaky breath, about two seconds from breakdown, keeping it together with string. "If he kills you, I don't care to live. So just let me try."

If I say yes, will the world end? Will he win, or will Jeff, who tells me he loves me each and every time?

I believe Simon thinks he can stop him. I believe he believes it. But I know for a fact that Petrowski can follow through with every threat he's ever made, and I can't do that to my boy. Not this time.

Not again. I can't live through that.

I shake my head, the tiniest of movements. I'm so sorry, Simon, so sorry.

For a second, his face goes oddly blank. Then he turns and punches a cabinet.

His fist goes straight through the cheap plywood. Blood drips down from a dozen cuts, gleaming in the electric light. Just for a moment the shadows turn his face into another, and what has only been apparent in bits and pieces is now all too clear. I back up until I'm against the sink. If I ever had a doubt who Simon's father is, I don't anymore.

"I'm sorry," I whisper, though to who I don't know.

The blood drips and his eyes glitter too blue, too much like the ones that watch me even in my dreams, and his voice is low with rage all the more familiar. "You keep acting like I'm stupid, but maybe, just maybe, Erin, you could try believing in me. What do you have to lose?"

There are no words left to say.

He stalks out of the kitchen and yanks his desk away from the door so hard his chair hits the floor. There's a crunch as he picks it up and hurls it across the bar. Glass shatters. I close my eyes.

"If you leave now," I say, no louder than I need to, "don't you ever come back."

The only reply is the slam of the door, and I am all alone. Maybe it's better this way.

24

Art

Simon beats me to the park. He's sitting on one of the rusted swings, feet dragging in the dust, arms wrapped around the chains. The rising sun catches his hair, turning him into some sort of bastard angel, until I get close enough to see the dried blood coating his arm and smeared across one cheek. Something's happened, something bad, and how bad that might be I won't know until I ask.

"Bit early to be drinking," is what I settle for, nodding to the bottle at his feet. Not that he looks like he's slept, but what the hell. There's scuffs in the dirt what I don't remember seeing yesterday. What exactly has he been doing? "Are you drunk?"

He peers at me through narrow eyes. "No."

"How much did you drink?"

"It's sassafras."

I almost laugh. Only Simon would drink sassafras on a cold morning. Only him. My breath puffs out, adding to the fog. "What happened?"

No answer, just a shifting of his position and another gulp.

"Come on, don't be like that. You're covered in blood. What was it? Someone try something?"

If looks could kill, I'd be dead a thousand times over, but who wouldn't be? Simon's standing up now, draining the bottle and smashing it against a rock in one swift movement, glass spraying like diamonds. "You knew."

"Knew what?" I ask. A dozen scenes flick through my head, a dozen secrets I've never told. Angel to demon in one step. What has he discovered?

"You knew Erin. You and her lived on the same street, back when you was kids. You always said."

There's something about his eyes, something that reaches into the base of my skull and makes me wanna run. Predatorial, if that's a word. Terrifying. He hasn't sprung the trap yet, but it won't be long. I watch my words. "That's right. She was four years younger, but I was friends with her brother, Trey."

As soon as I say it, I know I've stepped wrong.

"There's those words again." He should be shouting, but instead he's whispering, which is somehow worse. "Her brother. Erin had a brother, and I never knew. Lived with her for five years, knew about her two half sisters, *my* sisters, but I only found out there was a brother last night. And he was killed, and no one ever told me why. Like it wouldn't matter to me. Like it has nothing to do with me. Like that's not my fucking stepbrother we're talking about. Him and my half brother."

Jesus Christ, when he puts it like that. I know what this is about, I know where this is going like someone painted a red X on it. I know, and how many of us are left who do?

Trey was dead and Erin was having a baby, too soon, way too soon, and everybody said it was a shame she was such a slut, but I knew who'd done it to her. The words Trey whispered in my ear the day before graduation, that Erin was pregnant and it was their stepdad's and he'd known something was off, known it, and he figured the police wouldn't do shit about it, not with the nighttime blackouts and the curfews, so he was gonna do something himself, and did I know where he could get a gun? Just for an hour, just for a day, to borrow. Just borrow.

"It seemed crazy then. Erin, pregnant. She was thirteen, and that seemed so young. Trey wanted to get her out of town, and he asked me to help. And I said no, but he came to my house at night, and I ended up going with him to Mick's house, 'cause Mick's dad kept guns." Old metal pistols that I can still smell now. We weighed them in our hands with adrenaline pumping through our skulls. First gun I ever held, I'd held knowing I was maybe gonna use it for the ultimate crime, and as Mick drove us over there in his beat-up sedan, dammit if it didn't feel right. Justice, Christ savior, *justice*, because he was her stepdad and that just wasn't right. She wasn't even my sister, but there's some things you just don't do.

I still remember the address of the clinic we were taking Erin, the way her shirt had stretched over her still-flat stomach, how she kept begging us to go because Petrowski would find out, always found out. "Erin was scared, but Trey kept saying it was gonna be okay, their stepdad was out for the evening. But she thought he was watching her. 'Please,' she said, 'hurry and run before he kills us all.' We told her to shush."

Still remember the sound she made when she started to weep, trying to stay quiet, and how many nights had she done that for?

Can't forget the sound of the shotgun as Petrowski racked in a round behind us.

"He got Trey in the stomach before Erin jumped on his gun and screamed 'run.' Three days later, Mick and I were joined up, on our way out of town." We were ready to sell our souls if it would save us from the madman who'd aimed to kill and managed it. War seemed a small price to pay in return. "I don't even know if she had the kid. For all I know, he beat it out of her."

Some days, I'd hoped he had. We all heard the stories about what was happening in Buchell.

"But you knew she was pregnant." Simon steps forward, so like his dad it's uncanny. "You knew that much."

"Yeah, but—"

"And you didn't think to tell me."

"I didn't know it'd happened again!" I explode, beyond all rage and guilt and grief. "I didn't know he was still after her! She didn't say she needed help, and I didn't know she was pregnant until you went and shot your mouth off in front of Mick, and Taylor told me—"

His punch actually lifts me off my feet, sending me crashing into the weeds. I paw at my jaw desperately, running fingers over unbroken skin, searching for the bones and teeth I'm sure are broken, but no, nothing, nothing. My head is spinning and my face hurts like fucking hell, but the only blood is from the briars stabbing into my arms and neck.

By the time I'm back on my feet, the clearing is deserted. Not a soul in the park except for me and the graves: the war dead, the cholera dead, and Trey Livingston under the slide where we used to have a fort, as deep a grave as Mick and I could dig, the night the sirens first went off.

25

Erin

No one's home to hear me retch at the bottom of the garden, sick again in the morning light. No one's here to care.

I feel almost too tired to stand, in this dark little room I've grown to hate so much. Composting toilet or not, the only reason it don't stink to high heaven is that there's frost outside, and I'm just so tired...

My head cracks against the seat and I jerk awake. Damn. Drag myself up, open the door, face the day for better or for worse. Drink water, force it down, really, wash the glass while the world sways around me, up and down, like I'm on some damn boat. No noise from the rest of the house. Taylor's gone now, and Simon...

Can't think about Simon, can't prod that bruise, it's still too fresh. Can't do nothing but wipe the counters, make things spick and span. Pull an old pair of overalls straight over my pajamas for warmth. Sweater. Boots. Gotta turn that damn compost heap, like it or not.

Every step feels like lead weights have been tied to my feet. The stairs seem to heave, up and down, back and forth. I pause halfway to the bottom, clutch my stomach as it rises, clench my eyes shut. Breathe. Just breathe. It's okay. Keep breathing. In. Out. In.

The side door opens. I left it unbarred after I came in. My hands go for the holster I forgot on the bedside table as too-familiar footsteps clomp across the front room. Only two men in the world walk like that, with that confident thud that scuffs when it goes down and makes the floors vibrate. I memorized that tread years ago, and never forgot.

I close my eyes, hardly breathing. I could let go of the banister and it would all be over. Fall down, end it all. Ha, fall down. After all these years, my old excuse would finally be true.

"Erin? You home?" a voice calls.

My eyes fly open. "Simon?"

And there he is. "You're up, then."

"Course I am," I say, too relieved not to reply. But... "I thought I told you to go."

"You did. And I came back."

"Told you not to."

"So you did." His eyes flicker, but he's not budging. "I brung someone I want you to meet. Come on down."

Is that all there is to it? Everything I said, swept aside like that? I say "don't come back" and he does anyway, end of story?

I look at him, really look at him, because truth is, I'm spooked. He's so grown up now, such a man. Just barely sixteen and an adult already, that's him. Short-cut hair, red where his father's is black, ears that go pink when he's embarrassed, the beginning hints of sideburns and stubble. The scar on his shoulder just showing around his gaping shirt collar. My boy. Always been my boy, and not my boy at all.

He's giving me a funny look now. "Come on, Erin."

"I'm coming, fine."

Take a step, take another. The floor rocks like a truck on a gravel road. Simon reaches out a steadying hand and I ignore it, make my own way into the kitchen, where I find myself staring at the back of a woman in a brown coat sitting at my kitchen table. It's a shock, I don't mind saying. Been years since there's been any woman in this room but me.

She stands and turns. "Erin Livingston. Do you remember me?"

You gotta be kidding.

A face flashes across my mind, blonde, smiling with too-white teeth, blotting out the person in front of me. It's been thirteen years. She's older now, hair streaked gray, lines all around her eyes. Do I remember her?

"Dr. Avery." The words are forced. "Of course."

Couldn't forget it if I tried. Allison Avery, MD, OB/GYN. I'm thirteen again, trapped like a rat with nowhere to run.

"You said you didn't wanna go to the doctor, so I brung her here." Simon logic. Lord, save us all.

"I don't need a doctor, no offense," I say, and move to the pantry to fetch the egg basket. It's time I got collecting, 'cause that's hella better than staying in this kitchen right now. "Sorry to waste your time."

Simon strides over, pries the basket from my shaking hands, and turns me around to face the good doctor. "She needs help. She's sick every morning, and she's losing weight." Every word is an earnest accusation, ringing in my ears. That's me, Erin, screwup of the century. And Dr. Avery is taking it all in without changing expression. "Please, Doctor, she needs—"

A hand held up to dam the torrent, and it works, amazingly. I can almost feel the words building up behind his lips, ready to bust out.

Dr. Avery looks directly at me. "I'm not going to see a patient who doesn't want to be seen. Do you feel you are in need of medical assistance, Ms. Livingston? It is still Livingston, isn't it?"

Ms. Livingston, always been Ms. Livingston, because Dr. Avery said that if I was old enough to be having babies, I was old enough to be a Ms., not a Miss. She who told Jeff Petrowski, right to his face, that he'd stay in the waiting room while she saw me or that she would personally call the police and somehow, *somehow* get a DNA test done and put him in jail for the next ten years. I wouldn't say he did it, was far too terrified to say, but she looked at me being dragged in by him and knew anyway. Dr. Avery, who I both despised and worshipped and now is standing in front of me, waiting patiently for my answer.

Anyone else, and I would order them to get out.

"Yeah, it's still Livingston." We lock eyes. "Can you see me here? Not at your office, like."

"That's fine. I don't have an ultrasound anymore, anyway. This will be just a general health checkup on you."

"We can go up to my bedroom. I got chairs in there."

I lead the way, keeping my back straight because I don't quite trust my face to say nothing. It's okay. I'm in control of the situation. I am not thirteen. Not this time.

"So," I say, trying not to rush from nerves when we've settled ourselves in my tiny bedroom, "what has my boy told you?"

Dr. Avery raises her eyebrows back. "What hasn't he told me?" That sounds like him. "Simon, yes?"

"Simon Flaherty, yeah."

"Not your son."

"No."

"Where is Jacob?"

She don't mean to be cruel, I know she don't, and I can see she's trying to ask nice, but there's nothing nice about any of this. Nothing nice about babies or doctor visits or questions like that. Never was, never will be.

I force the words to come out, and myself not to stumble on them. "My mom took him with her when she left with my half sisters, back when it looked like this place was gonna get overrun by the Pro-DC forces. He would've been about three then." His face streaks across my mind, sharp chin and blue eyes, more vivid than I've seen it in years. "I've not heard from them since."

Silence, the heavy kind. I can't bring myself to look Dr. Avery in the eye, she who brought that boy into this world and soothed me all the way through it when I thought I'd about go crazy from it all. Sunlight streams in through a window, and I focus on the bright square it makes on my carpet, quiet and beautiful, so much better than thinking of anything else.

Dr. Avery's voice has gone quiet, choked. "Simon says it's your stepfather's again."

"Don't call him that."

"What?"

There's a ringing in my ears. "Don't call Petrowski my stepfather. If my mom's dead, and I'm pretty sure she is, seeing as *he* came back here, then he ain't family no more and I'd thank you not to call him as such."

I glare at her, and what on earth, she has tears running down her cheeks. Actual tears. Dr. Avery, who never looked anything but in control, crying in my bedroom. What? I don't get it. I mean, sure, what I said wasn't nothing nice, I guess, but it ain't really her problem.

"If she's dead, then...I...I'm so sorry," she whispers. "I've failed you. We've all failed you."

She seems to be expecting me to do something, but I got a tight feeling in my chest because I don't know what's going on here, what's gone wrong. "What?"

"I did try, Erin. Grown women don't get pregnant by themselves, let alone teenage girls, and I knew when you came to me exactly what I was dealing with, but I let you down anyway." Her eyes are earnest, hands clutching her elbows, looking almost in pain. She takes a deep breath. "I should have just refused to let him take you home, but you wouldn't say anything and legally my hands were tied, and back then I still thought that mattered. I...I tried to get someone in to see you, I swear I did, but what with the airstrikes starting right then, everyone's attention was so focused on staying alive..."

Another tear runs down her cheek. This is unreal.

"We failed you, Erin. I did, your teachers did, your family. You were a child, and you should've been kept safe, and you weren't. I'm so sorry, Erin. I swore if I saw you again, I'd tell you that."

Dr. Avery, woman of steel, is begging my pardon with tears pouring down her face, and I don't know what to do.

"Weren't your problem," I mutter, groping for words, reduced to being a child again. "It was my fault anyway."

Those who don't protect what's theirs don't keep it; I learned that early on. That don't seem to satisfy Dr. Avery, though, because she's staring at me with her mouth open. I try again.

"I learned a lot from it. Got through the war, didn't I?" Still no connection. "Gotta do something to stay alive. And anyway, I got him out of here eventually, didn't I?"

She sniffs. I have a wild urge to hold a handkerchief up to her face and tell her to blow. "Petrowski?"

"Well, yeah. I mean, you don't see him in this room, now do you?"

"Well, no..."

"That's because I made him leave. So. I learned from the war. Learned from having a kid. It's nothing to cry about."

"But I—"

"I said it's nothing!" I burst out, harsher than I meant to, but I can't take it back, and I don't want to.

We both stare at each other, her shocked out of her tears, and me boiling mad, madder than I been in a long time, though what about I couldn't tell you.

She tries again, whispered words, the pleading too obvious. "I'm not saying you haven't done well for yourself. All I'm saying is, I am sorry for what I could not do."

There's something tight in my chest, a hot knot in my stomach. Not like I'm gonna be sick, and not like I'm gonna cry. I can barely breathe. All I can see is her face, the words she wants me to say, the forgiveness what I don't want to give. Nothing to forgive, 'cause if I do, that'd mean everything up until now's been wrong. Everything, half my life, all wrong, and that just can't be. Regret nothing. Never, never ever.

I take a deep breath, set my jaw, look at that square of sunlight once again. "Let's get this visit over with, okay? I got stuff to do today, and I'm sure you do too."

A long moment passes, one where I'm not sure if she's gonna press it or drop it.

She draws a deep breath. "Of course. Let me just get my stethoscope out."

Dropped, thank God. I sigh, and it feels good. Safe for now.

Safe?

"Now breathe evenly while I check your heart rate. In...and now out. Good. And again. In..."

Since when have I ever been safe?

"And out again. Once more. In..."

Oh, right. When I've been all alone.

"...and then out again."

26

TAYLOR

Fired is just fine by me. A relief, actually. I don't care what Art said about Erin's bar being safe, or the good pay, or the room and board. This shit is not fucking worth it. No way. Not with Erin hating me like she does. Huh, that's a tree not worth barking up. Jeff Petrowski's fuck-puppet, oh hell no. My guard job will tide me over until I find a new place.

I'm working patrol this morning, checking the fences to make sure no one's breaking them or whatever else those fuckers think it's fun to do. Knock two teenagers on the head when they try to give me trouble, find someone trying to make off with a live chicken. Just another day on the job. Thank the saints. After not showing up yesterday, I'm grateful to still have it, though I think that's Petrowski's doing rather than my years of service.

As I'm passing the fried-food stalls, a hand spins me around, derailing my train of thought. Art his own self is glaring at me from two feet away.

"Get your mitts off me," I growl, knocking them away. His thin lips don't budge, or his narrowed eyes. Yeah, so you're tough. I'm so impressed. Yeah, right. My swollen nose throbs in remembrance, though, and I check my tongue before it sets him off again. "What do you want?"

"You got some nerve," Art about spits.

I just give him a cool stare. "Yeah? How's that?"

"Taking the job I gave you and turning it into some fucking cash crop, that's how."

"The job you gave me? What, waiting tables? For your information," I hiss, taking pleasure in every word, "I'm fired. Yesterday afternoon."

He stares. "You what?"

"Got fired."

"You never."

"It just saved me having to quit. It wasn't worth it. You never said what a bitch Erin is."

"That's because she isn't. You're just a dumbfuck."

I don't have to take this. I'm leaving.

Art yanks me around by the straps on my vest. "I'm sorry, did I say I was finished? Because I don't think I did. Now you listen, and you listen good."

"I'll take over from here."

Art draws back, and I almost laugh until I realize that voice belongs to Flaherty. He pulls me around with that blank look that means someone's about to get their front teeth and about ten IQ points knocked out.

"Do you," he asks quietly, "or do you not work for Jeffrey Petrowski?"

Oh hell. Bad, bad, this is bad. "I—" I stop. Loophole, think fast. "What exactly do you mean by 'work'?" We're getting an audience now. Market dispute, that's boring stuff, but this? Now, this is interesting. A guard facing off with a prizefighter. Shit.

Flaherty's expression doesn't budge. "No. None of that. It's a simple question. Do you, or do you not, work for Jeffrey Petrowski?"

I suck my breath in, hear people near me in the Market go quiet. Everyone knows that between the leases and the bribes, Mr. Petrowski's got the Market Authority in his pocket, not to mention the checkpoints out of town, but that doesn't make it healthy to talk about in broad daylight. And now the whole world's listening, waiting for my answer.

But I believe Petrowski has his own graveyard, I truly do, and no matter how much Simon can make it hurt, Mother Mary, I don't wanna die. I know this now, with all my soul, more than I've ever known before. Saint Flaherty's scary, but his father—and fuck me, that's still a crazy thought—is fucking terrifying.

I do believe in spooks.

I muster up my courage, look him in the eye, raise my voice, and up the ante. "That's right, Flaherty. I work for your dad. I work for Petrowski. He asked me to help Erin out, personal-like. You got a problem with what he wants?"

The world holds its breath.

"Yeah," says Simon. "I fucking well do."

Simon doesn't look left or right, just twists my arm up behind my back and takes my stun gun before I even know what he's doing and pushes me ahead of him, all but knocking people over, steering me through the shoppers with my own weapon pressed against my neck. It doesn't look good to have a Market guard frog-marched through the place, but what can I do?

At least he hasn't killed me yet, and that's a relief, ha. Yet. Ha, ha, this isn't fucking funny anymore, it really isn't. "Where the hell are you—"

Art elbows me in the eye, and stars dance in front of my face. Goddamn that bastard, that total *bastard*. I thought we were friends, but no, no way, not anymore. My black eye throbs, and I squeeze them both shut, will the nausea away. I won't throw up, I won't throw up.

By the time I open them again, we're out of the Market and Art's beginning to laugh and Flaherty's pressing the stun gun prongs deep into my flesh as we turn down some back alley. I'm not going to throw up, but maybe, just maybe I'm going to die today.

27

Simon

First day of school, they didn't have paper. Had desks, 'cause plastic don't rot, but paper do. They was supposed to get shipments of books and tablets and stuff, but the bandits ambushed the trucks and the school had to do without to begin with.

I remember that day, 'cause they put all us kids in a room and told us to read what the teacher wrote on the board, like we could. I think she about cried before the first hour was out.

She was old, Mrs. Graham was, and talked like she was high class, and couldn't control any of us. For the first hour, she stood at the front of the class, and us kids, who'd been dragged in there by every authority what could lay hands on us, we was having a blast. Throwing shit, talking, fighting.

I don't remember who it was who called Mrs. Graham a bitch, but I remember what happened. And who could forget it? She got real quiet, and her face got hard. She went up to the desk at the front of the classroom and pulled out a metal ruler about a foot and a half long.

"The next person to cause trouble is going to get paddled," she said. "Now pay attention."

It was Jordan Peters who laughed first.

For an old lady, she moved fast. Grabbed Jordan out of her seat by the wrist, held Jordan's hand out, palm up, and smacked it with the ruler. Jordan howled, and we all laughed, so Mrs. Graham smacked her again and again. Maybe ten times Jordan got whacked. I saw her hands later. They was red and swollen, and looked like they hurt. Jordan didn't cry, but the lesson was learned.

We didn't cause so much trouble after that. We understood the message that Mrs. Graham was saying: appropriate force. It made sense then and it makes it now. You hurt me, I'll hurt you back. In a classroom or outside it, that's how the world works.

Only, Taylor don't seem to know that.

We're in Mick's pole barn. Mick is leaning against the door, waiting, watching.

Art takes off his belt and straps Taylor's hands behind his back before shoving him in a chair and smiling at me. "Floor's all yours, Simon."

That suits me just fine. "What exactly did you tell Petrowski?"

Taylor's eyes show white all the way around. "Nothing."

"Then what'd he tell you?" I ask.

He don't answer for a while, trying to find a way out of things. Looking from face to face until I lose my patience. "I said—"

"I heard you the first time. What's in it for me, if I tell?"

Art starts to laugh. "Wait, lemme get this. Are you trying to bargain?"

"I'm not trying, I'm doing—"

"Just answer the question," I shut them both up. "Now."

"Well..." Taylor draws it out, trying to watch Art as he starts pacing. "He didn't say I was supposed to keep it a secret, so I guess I can tell you. But it's not much. Said he was the father of the baby Erin's having, and I was to help her out around the house, like, like you're doing now, and that's it. Nothing interesting for you." Then he scowls and kicks the chair leg.

I run my fingers through my hair. I know all that shit already.

Mick leans forward. "Taylor, why don't you tell Simon who gave you the money for that good knife from Farley's? The one you put the order in for yesterday. Can you recall that for us, possibly?"

Huh? "What money—" I start, but Mick cuts me off.

"This knife." Mick reaches into his pocket, pulls out a blade six inches long from tip to tip. It looks sharp even from here. "Mr. Farley from the knife shop vouches to Taylor's visit yesterday afternoon, and I think we all know you don't keep that sort of cash on your person, let alone wanna make a nice gift of it to our boy Simon here. Why did Petrowski give you the money for it?"

Petrowski bought a knife for me? That don't make any sense.

Taylor's pressing his back against the chair. "I...now wait just a moment."

Mick don't have any expression at all. He passes the knife over to me. It's a fullered blade, lightweight. Carbon, maybe? Expensive. Not a custom job, don't have my name on the hilt, but I seen knives like this before. It's for fighting, and it'll do the job nicely. Sharp, yeah. Metal don't get much sharper than this.

Why the hell would Petrowski buy it for me?

For two months after school began, Mrs. Graham wouldn't let me quit writing my letters over and over again because she said I was better than ignorance, that we were all better than that. Even Jordan Peters.

Taylor's watching me now, watching the knife as I pass it from hand to hand. Good weight, good balance. Strong. Durable. Gonna keep its edge for ages.

I walk up to Taylor, feet heavy. His eyes widen. Sweat drips down his face as I hold the knife up. My face reflects on that blade, blue eyes and all. I know who I look like as I reach out and rest the tip of it on his nose.

Taylor pisses himself, right there in that chair. I can smell it.

I can't move.

A couple months into the school year, Jordan and a bunch of other kids banded together and took over the classroom. Strapped Mrs. Graham to her chair and smacked her hands until they bled all over. None of the kids she'd paddled had ever cried, but Mrs. Graham did.

"Let her go," I said, and Jordan laughed.

"Let her go now," Connor said, and the laughing only got louder.

That day in the classroom, I snatched up the ruler and found out just how much damage a dull blade can do.

How about a sharp one? Taylor's tied up. It'd be nice and easy.

Mick's watching me, watching my hands. Watching to see what

I'll do. What Art will let me do and Taylor can't stop me from doing. Will Mick stop me? Will anyone stop me from becoming what the world wants me to be? What my dad wants me to be?

What did I expect, mercy?

Toe-to-toe with Taylor's shaking shoes, I've got a choice. I got the knife, but that don't mean I have to use it, does it? It's what Petrowski wants, what Art wants.

Do I want it?

I could kill him right now by leaning forward three inches.

Mick shoves me back with a hand on my stomach so I nearly fall backward. Didn't even hear him move, but he's here now, between me and Taylor. Oh my God, oh my God, for a second I thought if I blinked I really might...

Mick's speaking. "We won't tell anyone what you said to us. And you won't either, because if you do, you won't live long enough to be killed by Petrowski's boys. See Art here? He'll take your scalp and hang it on his ceiling, next to all the other ones." He pauses, lets it sink in. "Do I make myself clear? Say 'Yes, Mick.'"

"Yes, Mick."

"And who will you be telling that Simon's knife was bought by the local crime lord? Say 'No one, Mick.'"

"No one, Mick."

"And who will you be telling about this meeting? Say—"

"No one, I swear!"

"Good boy."

Art undoes the belt and shoves Taylor to the ground. "Don't you ever come near any of us again. And that includes Erin. You're a traitor, Burkes, and I don't ever forgive those. You can bet your ugly face on it. Now go. Get! Get out!"

Art follows him to the door, laughing his head off, and me, I'm staring at the chair, new knife still in my hand. I could've done it, and Art would've thought it was funny.

I think the day I hit Jordan Peters was the day Connor turned his gang against me. I was just supposed to be the dumb muscle—he didn't like me thinking for myself.

Well, I'm still thinking. I told my dad no, I weren't gonna work for him, yet I'm holding his knife anyway.

Mick's hand squeezes my shoulder. "Get it together, Simon."

"I almost..."

"I know." And he does, gray eyes watching me every day as he teaches me how to cut, not kill. He's the only one teaching me not to kill. "But you didn't."

And can it be as simple as that?

28

Erin

The house seems emptier than ever when Dr. Avery leaves. My hands clutch the bottle she gave me, vitamin supplements and anti-nausea meds, same as last time. I always did get morning sickness something awful.

Beyond that, everything is "going well." I have a "viable pregnancy." It's proceeding "as expected," even with my "minor nutritional deficit." Lord.

At least I'm not dehydrated this time. I learned my lesson on that one. Takes it out of a person, puking does.

There's things to be done now. Chores, preparations. Today's another workday, just like the last, but somehow I seem to have lost the urgency. I drift from room to room, feet treading on floorboards older than I am. They saw my baby steps, and they saw my baby's steps, and someday, they will see this baby's steps too. My life is stamped on this house, on the walls, in the air that I breathe, and in the shadows that don't leave the corners, and haven't since the power grid went down some eight, ten years ago, never to come back on, 'cause Jeff says we're better off without them who caused the war invading our space with their regulations, and I don't know enough either way to say if he's wrong or not. For all I know, he's been right about everything he's ever said.

Here is my room where I sleep now, where my little sisters slept years ago. Big windows in the front, curtains with daisies on them. Walls still pink, never mind the water stains. Down the hallway is my mother's old bedroom, the room she shared with so many men, more than I'll ever know about or remember. When I was a kid, it seemed like there was a new one every month, and I knew them by their smells: alcohol and aftershave, sweat and pot and vape smoke of every type. And then she'd married, and it'd been their room. *His* room.

And then I'd needed food and money and was desperate, and it looked the part with its big bed and the dark curtains, and it'd become my room too. Mine and a hundred men.

For all I've laid in that bed, I swear I've never slept in it.

Finally one last door, open and empty. The room what should've been Simon's, but he wouldn't take it because he could keep watch better downstairs. So Simon lives in the little room off the kitchen where once upon a time my brother slept after our half sisters took over my room at the front of the house. I'd gotten his old room next to Mom's, because she didn't want me too far away from her where I could get into trouble. Better that I was upstairs, with them. Weren't three nights in there neither before *he* came in and caused it anyway.

Time to get busy. Vegetables to chop. Eggs to boil. Soup bones to stew over my old woodstove what I fished out of the neighbor's basement when the gas lines stopped working. My feet move down the stairs by themselves, over the wood I've treaded grooves in, I've walked so many...

The side door is closed and barred from the inside, and I didn't do that.

My hand goes for the gun I keep in my pocket—which is still on my goddamned stupid bedside table where I left it this morning. Stupid, *stupid*. Them who don't protect what they have, lose it.

If I don't make noise, I can get back upstairs and grab it. Probably it's just Art, or Taylor come back for his things; they're both quiet. Yeah. Probably. Nothing to worry about, just need to arm myself to be on the safe side, and everything will be okay. Everything will be fine.

Floorboards squeak, and I turn automatically. Framed in the sunlight, like a thousand horror stories all rolled into one, stands Jeff.

Don't have to see his face to know his shape. Don't have to hear his words to know what he wants. Here. Now. In my house.

"It ain't Tuesday yet," I say.

"I know that."

"This ain't Eden Boulevard."

He steps forward, away from the doorframe, so I can see him better. "I wanted to see you, Erin."

I take a step backward without being able to help it. "We have a deal. Once a week."

He closes the distance. "Tuesday wasn't soon enough."

"A deal," I repeat, well aware that if I take another step backward, he'll have me pinned against the wall. "I'll be there Tuesday."

"We're here now."

"And I'm busy."

"You've been busy a lot lately, haven't you, Erin?"

I don't quite meet his eyes. Don't never look him in the eye. If I can just make it to the stairs... "That's none of your business."

"You're always my business."

I make to sidestep him. Get upstairs, a room with a lock, a gun, a window. "Well, this ain't—"

He grabs my wrist, twists it until I cry out, presses me against the wall and breathes into my ear. I can almost hear the blood in his veins and the roaches in the dry rot.

"I didn't like learning about our baby from some idiot at the depot, Erin."

"I know," I whisper.

"I wanted to hear it from you myself." His lips are opening to form words I don't want to hear. Oh God, I don't want this, please stop...

"You know I love you, Erin."

"I know." It comes out as a whimper. "I'm sorry. I'm sorry..."

"Shh, shh. I forgive you, Erin. Don't worry, sweetie. I'll always forgive you."

29

TAYLOR

You don't find Mr. Petrowski. Mr. Petrowski finds you.

If I'm not going to do what he said and watch over Erin—and Art made it pretty clear that that would be a fatal decision, having quit or not—then my worth is pretty much gone. Also, I didn't check out at the Market station after shift today, so I can kiss that paycheck goodbye. All in all, my life's been flushed down the drain. My best bet is to sign on as a convoy guard and jump ship once I get far enough away, and who knows how far that'll have to be. But I'll do it. Mother Mary, I'll do it.

"Going somewhere, Burkes?"

A man leans against the depot gate. Shaved head, shoulders showing even in this weather, heart and cross tattoo with a wolf's head on his left bicep. Mary, Mother of God, he has Petrowski's mark.

I swallow and try to stand up straight. "I'm going to visit my mother."

"Really? Boss didn't mention that you'd be allowed to leave town."

"I'm a free man," I say. "My mother is ill."

"What a shame. And here I was, thinking your mother was dead." He grins at me, and my throat goes dry. "Mr. Petrowski wants to see you, and we don't want to keep him waiting, now do we?"

He strides toward me. I nod, reaching a hand around casually for the gun behind my back.

"I wouldn't do that if I was you, Burkes." From God-knows-where, the man pulls out a sawed-off shotgun. Mary, Mother of God. "Wouldn't do that at all. Now come on."

I take one step forward, then another. The guy pokes me in the ribs with a finger and grins, showing white teeth. "Aw, come on, don't be like that. It'll be fun. You'll see."

"I'm going to die." The words pop out of my mouth.

He laughs. "If you do something stupid, yeah. But come on, you ain't dead yet. Why you think he's gonna kill you now?"

"Erin fired me."

"Forget about that, it's old news. I'm Ryan Jesser. Call me Ryan. You'll be fine if you stick with me. We're the winning side. Trust me."

30

Simon

Sometime in the fall, just after I started at temp school, word got around to us that one of the old soldiers was dead and the funeral would be tomorrow. It wasn't a shock, you know, what with knowing how they lived, but it was a startle. It was Lambert Nowak, and he'd died drunk.

Erin and I went down to the cemetery where someone, probably Sarge, had dug a grave. Not many showed up, and around noon or so, Sarge and Evan Farley carried in a coffin they'd knocked together out of plywood and lowered it down in the hole. A minister said a few words and Sarge crossed himself, and that'd been it. Them who'd come murmured words and shuffled off, until it was just Sarge, Evan, Erin, and me.

Evan picked up a shovel, but Erin took it out of his hands and gave it to me. So I shoveled dirt onto the box below while Erin took Evan aside and said low words. The sound of dirt clods hitting the coffin was hollow at first, and then quieter. All the time I was shoveling, Erin was murmuring to Evan as he stared at his feet, blank-faced. Sarge stood next to me and sobbed.

I couldn't understand it. Why cry? Others had died. My mom had died, the kids next door had died. Millions of people had died. Sarge had killed a lot of people, and I bet he hadn't cried for them, but he cried for Mr. Nowak, who'd drowned in his own drink. I didn't get it. Maybe I was just too young.

A few months later, Sarge shot himself in the head.

Fear turns to depression, depression to hopelessness. Hopelessness goes to lifelessness. That's what Erin said. You get scared for too long and then it all goes from there, 'cause once you're truly scared, really terrified in your bones, you'll never feel safe again. That, she said, was why Sarge and Mr. Nowak died. Dead before they stopped breathing, that's what she said.

We buried Sarge in a plywood coffin next to Mr. Nowak, whose grave was already beginning to sink down. That's when Evan Farley closed down their still, left the house they'd lived in, and moved to the center of town to work for the newspaper. Erin said he'd had a couple of sisters and the oldest one had been a friend of hers, though she wouldn't tell me what happened to her. There's still a little sister around somewhere. Evan sometimes gets drunk at the bar and tries to talk to Erin, but she tells me to throw him out when that happens, and he won't tell me nothing.

And that's all there is to it. I used to go down to see the soldiers—all us kids did—but now we can't and we don't, and in the end it don't really make much difference. Past don't trump future. Pain don't win over everyday life. We go on, always. Or we die, I guess.

31

Grace

My mama never takes guff from anyone, and she taught me the same. She always says that if you let men run over you, they'll hound you until they're blue in the face and then ask what's for dinner. And who needs that?

Erin opens the front door with a potato peeler in her hand. I hold out one of the slips I tore off the work advertisement.

"Miss Erin, my name's Grace Farley. I heard you be looking for someone to help out around here."

"That's right. Come on in." She heads toward a table under the window where a bowl of carrots and another of scraps already rests. "You look familiar. You related to Evan Farley?"

"That's right. I'm Chuck Farley's youngest. We go to the same church."

Erin sizes me up, shrewd as anyone. Anyone who lasts in this town, that is. "You looking for room and board, or just a job?"

"I'm moving out on my own for a bit."

"Right." She picks up a carrot and starts peeling. "And you can read, of course."

"I can."

"Schooling?"

"My sister tutored me before the soldiers got her. I was in the temps for a year."

Erin clicks her tongue, at my age or the mention of Abby, I don't know. One of my earliest memories is of those two together doing hand claps in the backyard, though I'm sure she wouldn't have a clue if I mentioned it. We might go to the same church—or used to, anyway—but it's a big church.

"So then, Grace. Since you're here, I assume you cook, as per advertised."

"I do."

"What's your best dish?"

"I do good pies."

"I don't do a lot of baking."

"Well," I say, and hope I'm not biting off more than I can chew, "I thought since you were asking for cooking *and* serving skills that maybe you were looking to expand, 'cause I heard your last guy just waited tables."

Her eyebrows shoot up. They're delicate and plucked, just like my mama's. Men like a nice face, my mama always says. Makes it easier to keep them happy. Erin seems to know that too.

"How are you with a frying pan?"

"I can do that as well."

"Scrubbing floors?"

"That's fine."

"How do you tell a good fish from a bad one?"

"The ones my brother catches is good. Market's mostly bad. If it smells, don't eat it."

She smiles to herself. "Probably why I don't serve a lot of them, but good. Got any experience in a job?"

"Been cooking three meals a day for my family since my mama started her breakfast place a couple years back. Besides that, I've sanded more knife handles than I care to count and cleaned a few houses around town. I also keep a garden and do canning for myself and a few others."

That perks her right up. "You do jellies?"

"Pickles and preserves too."

That has weight; most people don't know how to do that. Get it wrong and you're puking your guts out come time to eat, but my grandma taught me and my sister right when we were kids.

Erin taps a finger on the table. "We get a lot of drunks, but not a lot of trouble. It's Simon's job to bounce, but what would you do if someone grabbed you while you were waiting tables?"

"Bend their fingers back until they let go."

A long pause, where she peels a carrot and I try not to fidget. "One last question. You probably heard about me, or will do soon enough, yeah?"

"I heard some," I say cautiously. Not really sure what I'm being asked, if it's about her family or having a baby or Simon Flaherty or what, but a general agreement can't go wrong. "Everybody's heard something. You can't help it, Buchell's not that big."

"Right. You got any problems with it? Anything you need to bring up now?"

She's still peeling, looking for all the world like that's all she has on her mind, and is that all she's thinking about?

I make a survey of the table, and of Erin herself, with her apron over old overalls, long hair in braids. My daddy said she's mixed race like me, but while I got medium skin and difficult hair from my mama, the only thing that keeps Erin from passing is almond eyes. Right now, they look so lost and lonely it near takes my breath away.

I don't know if I'm about to do the right thing, but I say the words that have laid heavy on my heart. Gotta say them sometime. Might as well say them now. I've heard the gossip. "My mama doesn't hold with men who pester women, and I don't either. I don't mind smiling at customers, but I don't put up with nonsense. I don't get drunk and I don't sleep around. I like cooking, and my mama taught me to wait tables, and that's what I'd like to do. I like to be useful."

There's a moment where I don't know what's going to happen, and then she smiles, offers a hand to shake. I let out the breath I was holding.

"Then I think you're exactly who I'm looking for, Grace."

"I hope so." I smile back. "I do aim to please."

She stands, picking up the bowls. No rest for the weary. "When can you start?"

"I'm free now."

"Got an apron?"

"In my bag."

"Then let me show you around. You just come with me." Quiet as a cat, she pads off to the kitchen, and I follow along, tying my apron as I go. There's work to be done. My mama says there always is; you just have to hold out your hands and it'll fall in. My mama always does have good advice. And when my daddy told me to keep an eye on things, well, he has good advice too, so I will do that for him. Watch Erin, and watch myself, 'cause nobody has to tell me to be careful in this house. I figured that out myself, when Simon Flaherty tore the notice off the pole and brought it straight to my daddy, begged him to help, please help, somebody help Erin, 'cause she won't help herself. He knows my daddy's always watched out for her since she was a kid clapping hands with Abby when people still thought we'd win the war.

Daddy said I should do it. Mama said it'd be good for me. My brother shrugged his shoulders, and me, I'll help Erin, and not just 'cause Simon asked us to help, or 'cause she did the family a favor way back when, or 'cause I feel sorry for her. It's all those reasons, and it's more than that. I tore off a slip and brought it here so she'll know that nobody sent me; I came on my own. Before she died, Abby said you gotta help them who need help in this world.

And Erin needs help—can't anyone see it but me?

And Simon, of course.

32

Art

"Erin?"

"I'm around back!" is the faint reply. I've been giving her a good long while to cool off, but it's time to see where things stand, patch them up. I go around the side of the house, and sure enough, there she is, shoveling chicken manure into a bucket. She pauses when she sees me, swiping an arm across her forehead. "Whaddya want, Art?"

"Well, seeing as I lost you your last waiter, I figured I'd let you know I've found a replacement."

She gives me a dead stare over the scarf wrapped around the lower half of her face. "Replacement what?"

"Replacement waiter." When she doesn't move, I keep going. "For your front room. To serve. You know, to replace Taylor Burkes."

"Oh, that? You're too late." She jerks her chin toward the kitchen, expression never changing. "You're too late by nearly a week. Ain't Simon told you yet?"

I look to the kitchen, then back to Erin. "No? Told me what?"

Erin goes back to shoveling. "Older girl, 'bout eighteen or so. Named Grace."

"Grace...?"

"That's right." Another shovelful. "Grace."

"Grace what?"

Erin pauses and leans the shovel against the chicken shed before turning to me. "If you want to know so bad, why don't you go ask around?"

So much for the job I promised Walker. He won't be happy about that. Still, it's Erin's business and all that. Erin picks up the bucket and starts walking.

"So...," I start.

"You'll have to speak up, Art," she says over her shoulder. "Can't hear you when you mumble."

I give up until we hit the compost pile at the end of the garden. This is the first we've talked since she made a go of spearing my kidneys, and what I have to say isn't something I want to shout to the neighborhood exactly. Don't really want it to involve chicken shit either, but that's life for you.

"You admiring the view or got something to say?"

Time to quit putting it off and man up to the conversation I've been rehearsing most of the week. I resist the urge to put my hands in my pockets, but only barely.

"You gonna avoid me forever, Erin?"

The look she gives me is rock hard, and I wonder what's going on behind the scarf, with only her eyes visible. "That's not up to me."

My eyes narrow. "What do you mean by that?"

"You come here, Art. I don't go to you. Never have."

Except that she did, which is what messed everything up in the first place. This has gone on long enough. "You're avoiding me right now."

"I'm going in. It's cold."

"You just turned away in the middle of a conversation!"

"So keep up, then. I'm not your nanny."

"Dammit, Erin! I'm trying to talk with you!" I grab her arm, pull her around. "Will you have a conversation like an adult?"

She yanks her arm back and pulls the scarf down so I can finally see all of her face, every inch of it covered in rage.

"I'm sorry, Art, can you not hear me when I open my mouth and speak? I am acting like an adult and not going where I ain't asked. I don't need your help running my bar, and I sure as hell don't need it running my life. If you got something to say, then you can damn well spit it out while I do my work, because right now you are wasting my time, time I do not have for this. And if that's all, I will see you later."

With that, she turns and walks away. Again. My fists shake with fury, but I hold back and follow her one more time.

"No, that's not all! And if you'd quit cutting me off, I'd tell you what I'm here for."

"Then talk and walk." She won't even look at me.

"Let's sit down."

"No."

"I'm not gonna say this out here!"

"Then go away."

She heads through the back door and into the house with me trailing like a starving dog, forced to follow her in.

A thin black girl is kneading dough at the table, her hair in tiny braids. She looks up at Erin, then me, then Erin, before going back to the work in front of her.

"Grace, this is Art Weber. Art, this is Grace." Erin disappears into the cellar.

Grace nods to me and gives a little wave with a doughy hand. A Farley if ever I saw one. "Hi."

I nod back and don't break stride. "Hey. Erin..."

She's taking down jars from a shelf, her back to me. "What?"

"About last week."

"What about it?"

"About my room."

"Yeah?"

Her arms are full, and I block the stairs, 'cause I am gonna say this, somehow.

"Look, you weren't supposed to see that."

"That all you gotta say?"

"I...no. You weren't supposed to see those. No one is anymore. Even Simon didn't know they exist."

"So...what?"

I take a deep breath. "So you'd have never known about them if you hadn't gone there. I knew that you wouldn't like them, and I'm sorry you saw them. Not exactly like I brag about them anymore or anything."

"Anymore." Erin repeats the word, rolls it out of her mouth like a battle flag. "Anymore. You don't brag about them—anymore. Right. Wonderful. 'Cause that's exactly the problem here. Good job, Art."

The sarcasm is expected. That's how Erin reacts to things, like some teenager who hasn't got her way. I keep on. "What I'm saying is, I'm sorry you saw those. I won't bring it up again if you won't."

"And ain't that just wonderful of you." She tips her head to the side, looks at me through half-lowered eyelids. "Now if you'll excuse me, I got gravy to make."

"So you understand what I'm saying, then?"

"I understand a lot of things, Art."

"But you know what I mean."

"I surely do."

She climbs back to the kitchen and ties on an apron. I'm dismissed, from this house, from this world of domestic work where once I was welcomed at the table with a smile and a nod. Erin murmurs something to Grace, and I feel like red-hot coals have been dropped down the back of my shirt.

"So you agree?" I try one last time, hanging onto my temper with both hands.

"That you should get out? Yep."

There's no getting through to some people, not when they've made up their minds to be contrary. I'd like to start shouting, and I'd bet anything that Erin knows that, sure as night and day. I stare around, looking for something to say that won't have us leaving in a fight, because damn it all to hell, this has gone on long enough and one of us has to act our age.

Fresh wood catches my eye. "What'd you get a new cabinet for?"

"Because the old one broke. Duh."

I leave, because right now that ain't all that's broke. I'll just have to give her time, that's all.

33

Grace

I'm chopping vegetables when Simon gets in from whatever he does all day, about half an hour to opening.

"Hey," he mutters. It's funny, but I've been living here a few days now and barely said anything to him. He comes and goes to school and back, training and back, but I don't think a week of sleeping ten feet from his room has told me any more than I already knew. Who'd have thunk it. He peers out the back window. "What's Erin doing out there?"

"Turning the compost heap."

"What?"

No mistaking an annoyed man, all pouts and frowns. He starts for the door, but I block his path. "Nah, leave her be. I already offered."

His forehead stays furrowed. "She's gonna have a baby, you know. She can't be doing stuff like that."

"I know she's pregnant," I say, patiently as I can. "She knows that too. But you'd be amazed what you can do when you still won't be having a baby for another six or seven months. You can do all sorts and be fine. Babies don't turn you to glass."

That seems to be news to him, and he mulls it over with a lip stuck out. I start chopping again. He'll get there when he gets there without any help from me.

"But the compost's heavy. It's hard to move."

"Does Erin know that?"

"Well, yeah. I mean, she's done it before."

"Then I expect she don't mind. If you wanna keep busy, you can help me in here. I could use an extra pair of hands about now."

I can see Simon opening his mouth to argue. Then he folds, shaking his head to settle his thoughts just like my aunt's horses do. "Okay. Fine. What you want me to do?"

Actually, I'm about done, but extra help is not to be sneezed at, in the words of my mama. "Go get the heater going up front and pull back the curtains."

The look on his face is priceless. I wanna roll it up and stick it in my pocket. "We have curtains?"

"Do now, so go pull them back."

"Yes, ma'am," he grunts and does as he's told. But the glance I seen from him, that wasn't annoyance, or even tolerance. That was respect. You can't buy that.

Let's see. Glasses are out, plates, what else?

Simon stomps back in the kitchen, and I nearly pounce on him. "Do you like the curtains?"

He shrugs that way he does, shoulders coming up one at a time in a roll. "Don't really see the point."

"They're to be making it look less bare."

"Oh." Simon thinks for a moment. "They're okay. Erin likes blue, anyway."

"Well, good. Glad they're okay by you, 'cause I'm rather fond of them myself." I smile at him, and just for a moment, for the first time that I seen, he smiles back. "Get those dishes out of the oven and up front while I carry plates. It's nearly five o'clock."

Someone knocks on the front door. Out the front window, I can see a stranger standing on the porch.

"We're not open yet!" I call.

The man looks around, then spots me in the window and beckons. He's got a knit cap low over his eyes and a cigarette dangling from his fingers. "I need to speak to someone. Open up."

Simon's in the doorway to the kitchen, watching. He'll keep me safe, I guess. I nod to him before answering. "Yes? What is it then?"

The man's voice is low, perfectly friendly. "Tell whoever put up the curtains to take them down again."

"*Excuse me?* And just who are you?"

"That's none of your business. Take 'em down. Orders from the boss."

"The boss, is that so? Well, *my* boss said no such thing. This is a private business, and if the owner likes those curtains, they're staying up."

"I said, take 'em down. They're not allowed." He says it like he's explaining something simple to a two-year-old.

Enough is enough. Who the hell does he think he is? The back door slams just in time. "Erin! There's some lunatic here saying we can't be having curtains!"

Erin hurries through. She's got dirt streaked down her cheek, and her overalls are filthy. Lucky she's taken her boots off, or I'd be sweeping for a week. "Grace, what on earth—oh. You."

The man shifts and bobs his head, almost in respect. "Boss says you can't have curtains. Either you take them down or I do."

Erin blinks, as blank-faced as Simon's ever been. "Grace, take the curtains down."

"What?"

"Just do it." She glares at the man. "You son of a bitch." Then she yanks the door out of my hand and slams it closed hard enough the house shakes.

"Who was that?" I ask. Erin stalks upstairs without answering. I turn to Simon. "Seriously, who was that? What in heaven's name just happened here?"

He regards me for a long moment. "What do you think, Grace? Curtains block the view. Take 'em down."

Block the view? The view from *where*, across the street?

That man's now standing in the road, watching the house. The glow of his cigarette flares and dies. He flicks it away and waves at me.

Curtains block the view. Oh my lord.

I take them down, and at five o'clock I flip over the sign. Simon goes out the back door muttering about finding a frog, and Erin squeezes my wrist before taking her place at the bar. My curtains lie in a heap in the corner. I can't even look at them. My stomach is still tying itself in knots when the first customers walk in.

My mama once said that men and women are just the same, only with different rules, and my daddy said no, not quite, 'cause we are the skins we live in, and men and women have such different skins. Men have muscles to think with, and women have eyes to see all that men think, and all of us have secrets we wear on our sleeves if only others will think to look. I think Simon's secret is that he's sensitive. Not as rough as he seems, as scary as he tries to be, as violent as they'd like him to become. He's got an air about him, like he pretends not to care only to cover up that he cares too much.

And Erin? Her secret, oh, that's much easier to see. It stares out at you like a fat lip, like the bruises on her shoulders she tries to hide but I seen anyway 'cause I knew to look. It leaves trails in the air from fingers that shake sometimes, hands that jerk mid-action.

She got an air about her as well, Erin does. Like she says she cares only to cover up that really, really, she doesn't. Not about herself. Not about Simon. Not about anything. She's like my brother in that way, thinking fool's thoughts: that maybe, just maybe if she makes herself try to care, it'll hurt less. Got wounds too big for any bandage, pain too much for any medicine. Trying to mop up the ocean with an old bed sheet. But life don't work like that. Love don't work like that. We care or we don't—and she doesn't.

I was called to this house, and at first I didn't know why, but I think I'm beginning to understand.

34

Erin

The front room opens when the sign flips over. That's the signal, always has been, always will be. Within ten minutes, the first customers begin to straggle in. It's time to get working, as if I haven't been all day.

Grace is shaping up well. Quiet, quick in a way that Taylor wasn't. Smiles at the customers, but doesn't take nonsense. Besides, I think the men like having another woman around the place. There's still more of them than us around here, and there's maybe a thousand reasons why, but I always thought it was because women put down roots quicker. The war went so long that by the time it was safe to come back here, they'd probably already settled elsewhere. Too many rough men around here to bother coming back, and me, serving them. Some days it seems that's all I've spent my life doing: serving men. Would you like some more? Oh yes, please.

I look up from my cooking as Grace leans over the bar. "Two servings for the corner table, and they want soup too."

"Got it." I add the extra ingredients to the cooktop as she goes around to pour two glasses of the low-grade beer. "Window table order's ready."

She takes the plates I hand her without comment, all efficiency and empty smiles. I like her for it. Stuff gets done with Grace around, as I'm finding out quick. And Art don't like her neither. That's a point in her favor.

Simon slams in at about nine, just as the first wave of drunks starts heading for the door, the kind what get up early and work day hours. The afternoon-shift men are still eating, not quite down to the business of getting legless yet, though they're working on it. He helps those who need it to find their way home, or at least off my porch, and the serious drinkers order bathtub gin while the good old boys keep pouring the hops down.

When he's finished with chores, Simon stops back at the bar to pick up his dinner from me, flapjacks and bean soup and a glass of the ginger ale I buy for him so he can look like he's drinking too without really having to, him being on duty. He eats steady, shoving it in like a robot, the muscles on his arms showing even with these small movements. God, the hairs on his chin are actually forming a beard, and since when did that happen?

"Homework done?"

"Yeah. Got a science project to work on due next week, though."

"What on?"

He shrugs, cheeks bulging. "Frogs. Yeah, frogs or tadpoles or something like that. Their life cycle. Gotta get some paper and do a couple pictures for it."

"Don't think I've seen you draw in years."

"Yeah, well, it's just frogs. Eggs and stuff."

He goes back to chewing, and I realize I don't have much else to say. Simon used to tell me his school troubles every day, talking on and on about every which worry on his mind. Hasn't done it in years. Hardly talks at all now, unless it's schoolwork or bar work or training. Always training.

"How'd it go tonight?" I try again.

"Okay."

That's all I get out of him until the last drunks go to drift out the door. He's on the sidewalk, and I've got my hand on the lock when someone dashes out of the shadows.

Faster than I can follow, Simon's got the man in a choke hold, knife to his neck, daring him to make one move. The man squeaks as he's dragged onto the porch.

It's Chris Hopkins, longtime bookie, sometimes-customer, shaking and stammering. "Don't hurt me, Simon! I...it's me, Chris!

You know me!"

Simon lets him go, and it could be the light, but was that a sneer on his face?

Chris is trying to smile and failing, but that don't stop him from turning to me. "Look, I didn't mean to startle anyone, but I'm in a bit of a hurry. I got a letter. For you, Erin."

I step down, mindful that for all I know this is some sort of bizarre trap. "Why don't you wanna be seen?"

He shifts, rubbing his arm, that scared smile still on his face. "It's from Taylor Burkes. He said—he asked me to give this to you. And he said he knows that Art said to stay away, but he feels badly about how things went. He didn't want me to be seen, though, 'cause if they knew he'd wrote to you, they might think this was too much and it would go over badly for him, and for me, too, 'cause I'm a friend of Art's, but Taylor and I, we go way back. I knew him from when he first started fighting..."

Chris trails off as I glare at him. Simon pointedly doesn't put his knife away, damn that boy. The man seems to get the idea and gets on with it. "Anyway. Here it is. I'm sorry to have bothered you and all that, but he asked me as a favor, and I couldn't say no to him. You know. Anyway."

He holds out the note to me, but Simon snatches it up. Chris backs away. "Right. Well. I'll tell him you got it. Sorry to bother you both. 'Night!"

That's my cue to go back in, 'cause Chris runs off and Simon watches him go like a cat hunting a beetle, not following me in 'til his prey's gone. "I don't like it, him delivering stuff for Burkes. He ain't supposed to contact you again, Art said."

"What, 'cause that jumped-up ass thinks he has a say in how my life runs? And neither do you, for that matter. I don't need a nursemaid. Now kindly hand me that note and grab a broom."

But he doesn't. He just stands there, scowling at the floor, that closed look on his face. Can't bring himself to obey, can't quite make himself ignore an order. I give him space, lock the front door and put the chairs up. He'll come around; he always does. All I need to do is let him make the first move.

And he does, one step and another until he's in front of me. I don't look up, just let him do what he needs to satisfy his pride. I don't interfere with men's pride. It don't serve, and Simon is getting to be a man, more and more, more's the pity, though I love him so.

The note drops on the counter in front of me. Time to see what all the fuss was about.

Cheap paper, looking to be torn from a newspaper or advertisement. Blue ink in a scribble I immediately recognize. I manage not to freeze, but it's a struggle.

Chris didn't deliver this because him and Taylor go way back. He did it because there's some people you just don't say no to. Not ever.

Tuesday 2:00 Eden Blvd.

No signature. Doesn't need a signature. Doesn't need the place even, because I know, I know, I always know, can't forget, can't breathe, God, can't breathe at all. Close your eyes, Erin. Take a deep breath. He's just doing this to gloat. You're okay.

No, I'm...

You're okay.

And I am. I know I am. I am fine, and I will always be fine. No one will ever hurt me. Not me, Erin Livingston, safest woman in this god-fucking-damned town. No one could be more safe than me.

"Erin?"

"What?"

"You okay?"

"What? Yeah, I'm fine. Surprised, though. Didn't know the boy had it in him to say thank you. Not the type, you know."

The note is gone from my hand. I stare at my fingers. I was just holding it and then—

I lunge, and Simon does what tall men do and holds it over his head.

"Give it back. Goddammit, Simon, give it back right now!"

His lips are moving and he doesn't reply. He's reading it. He's reading it, all my sins and shame.

I haul my hand back to slap him, and he catches it without looking, holding me there, reading on.

"Goddammit, Simon! I said stop that right now. That ain't your business. Don't you dare read that! Don't you dare! You give that back right now or I'll—"

"Is there a problem here?"

The kitchen door bangs against the wall, and there stands Grace holding my giant meat cleaver. Oh my God.

"I said," Grace repeats, louder, "is there a problem?"

"No." I scowl at Simon. "Not a problem, but thank you for your concern."

She don't move, eyes flicking from me to Simon. "Really? 'Cause it looks like someone was causing a problem."

I stare at her. "I said, no problem."

She takes one step forward, and it ain't me she's talking to. "Well, that's good. 'Cause my mama always said men who cause problems isn't worth the bother to help."

Simon's eyes snap to me, then back to Grace. Finally, he lowers his hand and gives me the paper back. Too fucking late for that, but Grace don't know that, and she nods to me. "Sorry to disturb you, then, Erin. I just was worried is all. Thought maybe a drunk had got back in."

"No, it's fine out here. Just fine. I'll finish the dishes. You go ahead and get some sleep, Grace."

"Alrighty, then."

She disappears into the kitchen, taking the cleaver with her, and I glare at Simon. He's still staring at where she was.

"You happy?" I spit. "I don't need you to cause scenes, I got trouble enough of my own without borrowing it. The note is nonsense. I don't know why Chris wanted me to have it."

His eyes finally cut back to me, looking at me sidelong. "Petrowski's got a place down Eden Boulevard."

"And so do a lot of other folk, including the butcher. Your point?"

"It's from him, ain't it."

"No."

"Yes, it is." Simon turns. "It's from Petrowski. Why's he want you?"

"Why do you think?" The words taste bitter, coming out with

more force than I meant. "Use your brain, Simon, and that expensive education of yours."

"He's still..."

"No, I just got pregnant because the Holy Spirit asked nicely."

"And you're gonna go to him, just like that."

I can't meet his eyes, can't do it. Not those blue eyes. Crumple up the paper instead and throw it away. "You don't know anything about it."

"Enough."

"You don't know a damn thing."

"I know some things."

I turn away, the fight going out of me all at once. "No. No, Simon, you don't. You know how to fight and win and be big and strong and fast. You don't know anything about this, and I wish you'd stop trying, 'cause you never, ever will."

Arms go around my shoulders, pull me to him, hold me quiet, but this time the tears don't come. It ain't so bad. I'll live through it. No need to cry about life. No need to cry that Simon will never know what it's like to be helpless. No, no tears for that.

We stand in silence for a few minutes, just like that, his heart thudding against my ear, our breaths not quite in sync. A hesitant hand reaches up and strokes my hair.

I dig my fingers into his wrist. "Don't."

"I'm just trying to—"

"I don't need that from you."

"Why?"

"Because your father always does that."

Simon stops breathing.

I step back until I can brace myself against the counter while my heartbeat slows down. Simon stands where I left him, staring at something I can't see, eyes wide.

I have no comfort to offer. My boy ain't turning into a stranger, no. These days, he's more familiar than ever, and ain't that the cruelest part of it.

35

Simon

After Mrs. Graham left teaching—and she was gone the day after I sent Jordan to the hospital—we got a new teacher who told us we could pay attention or leave, 'cause if we wanted to stay ignorant, that weren't his problem. Mr. Martins was a big man, hairy as a bear, didn't take shit from anyone. Found out later he'd been a bomber in the war, but I didn't know it back then, which was probably for the best.

He made us into military order, and that was something most kids respected, them what stayed. Stand up to speak. Clean your fingernails. We had to call him "Sir," and he mostly called us "Mister" or "Miss," except if you fucked up, then he'd call you stupid. Stupid if you couldn't read. Stupid if you mixed up letters. Stupid if you didn't know history or science or government or division. Stupid, stupid.

Connor loved him. Shining pupil, right there. Perfect, perfect, that was Connor. We all knew what he did to live, and probably Mr. Martins did too, but Connor could learn everything there was to learn in about two seconds, and Mr. Martins loved him for it. But he hated me 'cause I'm stupid. Weak.

My paper jolts as fingers rap my desk in the front room of the bar. "Simon."

"What?" I snap and look up.

Shit, it's Mick. He raises an eyebrow. Didn't know it was him. Does he think I'm stupid too?

"I'm going out drinking with some buddies tonight, just friends from around town. Join us?" he asks.

"Drinking?"

"Yeah, sure. You're old enough. Or look it, anyway, same thing around here." Mick winks. "I won't let you get stupid drunk, and it'll relax you. You're wound too tight."

Shit, I really am, snapping at him. Any amount of drunk sounds good. People in the bar, they always look like it's the best thing in the world, not being able to see straight. Maybe I'd like that too. It's Saturday night after all. "I gotta ask Erin."

"Ask her."

"And finish this book report."

"I'll help you. Go ask."

Like it's that simple. And maybe it is.

Erin gives me a hell of a look, and then spends a minute glaring at Mick, but in the end she just says, "You gotta stick around to bounce the drunks, but you go do what you need to."

Do I need to go drinking? I don't know. Maybe I do. Maybe I am wound too tight. It's just...it's Connor being an ass at school, it's Art and his fucking agenda at training, it's book reports I spend three hours on only to get a D minus 'cause I know my letters, yeah, know the sounds them's supposed to make, but when I try to write a word, it's never right, and it's like the world can smell it, zoom in on it. Hold it up to show and watch as I cringe, 'cause that's what it does when someone's got a weakness. Between adults and kids, I don't see much difference besides what side of the playground fence they stand on to piss, and on the playground, the best kid to go for ain't the dirtiest one; it's the one who tries to hide the dirt. That kid's got something to be ashamed of, got a weakness. You can hurt someone with a weakness. You can hurt someone with something to lose.

The first fight I had—the first real fight, after Art had given me a couple lessons and I knew a little bit about what I was doing—was with Connor on one of those days when the whole world was pissing on me. We was let out for lunch, or break, at least, for the kids who didn't have no food, and I was chewing my sandwich when Connor came over. He was a hungry kid, skinny as hell and pissed off about it. He didn't have a lunch that day, and he made a good try to spit on mine. And, well, I couldn't be having with that, so I told him to buzz off. Those were the words I said, "Buzz off."

He and his gang nearly laughed themselves sick at that, and I would've shrugged it off like I had before if Connor hadn't opened his mouth and said, "So what's it like, living with a whore?"

We all got weaknesses.

I hauled off and punched him in the mouth and then leapt on him when he took a swing. We thrashed in the dirt for a good two, three minutes before being pried apart by the teachers and sent in to start class with the blood still on our faces. He didn't look at me for the rest of the day, 'cause he knew I'd won. I'd pay later, but I'd won.

And did I pay, just. Got shot the next day by a nutcase trying to poison our well, right through my shoulder where it hurt like hell. Erin killed that guy with a cleaver, but I was out of school for a week, during which Connor found a new place to sleep, so he had plenty of energy to come after me soon as I was back, after he ate his lunch, of course.

Some days, though, I feel like I'm still paying.

Mick picks up my book, flips a few pages. "I read this in high school. What's the essay topic?"

"Just a summary."

When he smiles, his gray eyes crinkle up at the corners. "No worries, then. You dictate, I'll write, and we'll bang this thing out in time for us to have a good night."

"Why?"

The word's out of my mouth before I have time to take it back, and now he's gonna make fun of me, gonna say he's helping me 'cause he's sick of watching me fuck up my homework, sick of my stupidity, tired of—

"Who cares who writes the words so long as they're your thoughts? Having help isn't cheating. If it was, I wouldn't be coaching you."

Admitting you can't do something ain't weakness. Erin can't help herself, and it shames her.

Oh. Oh shit.

When Connor said, "So what's it like, living with a whore?" I started a fight 'cause I didn't wanna say what was on the tip of my tongue, the words I knew would shut him up. Hitting wouldn't do it, 'cause everyone hit him, and he didn't care, no. The words I bit back was, "I dunno, Connor, how do you live with yourself?"

I never understood why I didn't say it. But maybe, maybe I knew something Connor didn't.

And maybe Mick knows it too.

He looks to me, not sarcastic, not mean, same as training in the afternoon. He don't insult me when I show my weaknesses, and he has that in common with exactly nobody else. "Ready?"

I nod, try to think about the book. Think about the beginning. And lo and behold, the words are there waiting for me, 'cause Mick's willing to listen.

36

TAYLOR

I stamp my feet to keep warm in the darkness, staring at the windows across the street until the yellow squares of light make my eyes burn. Mr. Petrowski said my job was to watch over Erin, and apparently being in the same room as her isn't a requirement. God, I'm so bored. Nobody does anything in Erin's place but drink and play cards or dominos or whatever. Standing out here's almost exactly the same as waiting tables in there, except inside has a heater.

Wish Joe would hurry up and get here so I can go off shift and get plastered. Tomorrow's my one day off Market duty, my one chance to sleep off a hangover. But no, I've got guard duty. Kill me. At least the girl Erin hired to replace me is good-looking. If I have to watch, I'd rather watch her than another guy.

"How's it going?" Ryan calls as he walks up with Joe.

"My nuts have crawled back inside for warmth."

Joe starts rolling one of his constant cigarettes. "That's why I smoke. You gotta sit down, relax. The time goes faster."

"You gotta take two thoughts and rub 'em together for warmth." Ryan laughs at his own joke. "How's the tattoo?"

I'd only just managed to forget about it. "Itching like hell, fuck you very much. I think it's infected or something."

"Nah, Joe here uses only the finest recycled needles."

"You're not supposed to—"

"Relax, Taylor, he's being an ass." Joe lights the cigarette. "Take your jacket off and gimme a look. Here, Ryan, be useful, hold up my lighter so we can see."

It's gotta be below freezing tonight, and my tattoo's on my arm, oh come on. Then again, I really don't think it's supposed to feel like this. I mean, I don't have any other tattoos, but when I roll up my sleeve, my skin's hot to the touch under the bandage.

Joe pokes the gauze. "You idiot, Burkes, I told you to take the bandage off no later than last night."

"Yeah, but it was seeping, so I put a clean one on."

"You gotta let it breathe." He starts to pick at the adhesive tape. "It's stuck down."

"What?"

"It's stuck. You left it on too long. You'll have to soak it off."

"My tattoo?" Oh shit.

Ryan's laughing again as Joe rolls his eyes. "The bandage. Calm your tits, it ain't that big a deal. Just soak it in hot water and don't be an idiot."

"That might be difficult for Burkes."

All three of us look up. Someone's standing on the street, watching us. No, two someones, and I'd recognize Flaherty's stance everywhere, so the other must be...

"Close your mouth, you'll catch flies."

Mick Perry. Aw, fuck.

"Piss off," I mutter. "It's a private conversation."

"Only you would be dumb enough to make working for Petrowski the second-worst decision of the week." With that, he turns and goes, taking Flaherty with him like a dog on a leash.

I hate him, I hate him, I hate him so much. Both of them, and from the look on Ryan's face, I'd guess he feels the same. He drags a finger across his throat. "You got any idea of the money I could earn?"

Joe shakes his head. "Yeah, if he didn't kill you first. I heard they pulled TJ Katowski out of a ditch half-drowned two days ago for trying that."

"Trying what?" I never hear anything.

"Trying to jump Flaherty. Apparently he had a lay bet on the Saint not fighting at all and tried to make it come true. Flaherty dunked him until he quit fighting back."

Ryan leans in. "I think TJ had the right idea. How much do you think I could make getting rid of that fucker? Thousand?"

Like Ryan could touch him. I mean, Ryan's big, and he's tough and shit, yeah, but it's like taking a dog to a bear fight. "Why don't you go find the boss and ask how much he'd pay for your ass if you did? C'mon already, let's *go*. I'm about to get hypothermia."

The look is too smug. "Knew you'd say that. You just keep watching that ass of yours, got it? And watch mine too. See you 'round, Joe, and don't fall asleep again."

"I won't, I won't."

We leave him to his guard duty and join the drunks swaying down the street away from the closing bar. A week ago, I was on the other side of the street, waving as they went. I was a waiter and a Market guard. Now I have a tattoo, a heart behind a cross in black ink, same as all Petrowski's guys. Because I am one of Petrowski's guys.

I need a drink bad tonight.

37

Erin

There's some big band playing at one of the clubs, everyone's been saying. A *good* band, with dancing music. Simon went with Mick, loosen him up, help with training—yeah, I bet, you slimeball—and Grace headed in the same direction soon as we finished cleanup. God, it's been so long since I been out at night.

And why can't I go out?

The pajamas in my hand pass through my fingers. Yeah, why can't I go out? No reason, that's why. What I'm wearing's fine, short skirt and a slinky top, they'll see me through. Not like I ain't been to clubs before. I don't need a nursemaid to take me neither. I can take care of myself. I can do this. Find my coat, pull on a scarf, and I'm good to go. Ain't like I won't be safe, ha.

Outside is dark, with heavy clouds above. A few snowflakes drift down to melt on the pavement, though it's not nearly cold enough for them to stick. I'm nearly at the park when the bushes rustle.

My gun's out and pointed quick as a wink. Stray cat, probably, or a possum, but better safe than sorry, right? They rustle again, actually shaking this time. Whatever's in there, it's bigger than a rodent. It's not bear season neither, and that only leaves one option.

"Show yourself! Whoever you are, on your feet, hands in the air. Now!" Pale fingers in the dark reach above a face I can just recognize. "...Connor Hall?" The very one. "The hell are you doing?"

"Nothing," he has the nerve to say.

"Don't you sass me, Connor," is the first thing out of my mouth, but I lower my gun. He towers over me like Simon does, six foot something, all dirty-brown hair and tattoos showing at his wrists where his jacket ain't long enough to cover. "Save the bravado, and for the last time, tell me what you're doing here or else."

"Or else what?"

Boys like Connor like to call bluffs. They think it'll make them look dangerous, without realizing it's not really that clever.

"Or else," I reply, as calmly as I can manage, "I yell, and whoever is following me tonight—and you know *he* always sends someone—will be here, and you, boy-o, will be a greasy smear in the dirt what ain't gonna fight next Saturday."

And I can do it. Oh, I can. Three months now *he's* been sending watchers. My little shadows, only they ain't little and they ain't so nice.

"So tell me, Connor, for old times' sake, just what you're doing out here tonight."

He spits to the side, nasty habit, and looks unimpressed. "Isn't that just cute. Well, as a matter of fact, I was waiting for someone. Not you."

"Business booming?" I can't stop the jab.

"Not that you care, but yes."

"Same as before, or you got off your knees?"

He smiles, and it's a ghastly look. Connor was cute as a kid, but his face has gone thin, his shoulders broader than seems possible. Cheekbones jut. "Don't worry, Erin. I wouldn't dream of couching on your turf."

"I wouldn't make fun if I were you. Pots and kettles." I watch him shaking his head. "What? You got something to say? Spit it out."

The smile's back, and there's an edge of disbelief to his voice. "You don't get it, Erin. You really don't, do you?"

"Get what?"

He waves his hands vaguely. "This fight. You don't get it. I'm going to kill Simon, and you're going to be out of cash, on your back just like before, only this time without all your bully-boys around."

"No," I say slowly. I can't believe he can't see it. "No. Things have changed, in case you hadn't noticed." My voice is barely even. One too many upsets lately, one too many loads of shit being flung my way. "I know what drugs you're running, and I don't care. You ain't gonna go back to being anybody's pretty boy, well, good for you, but you ain't the only one who can change their tune. So don't you go acting high and mighty on me, Connor Hall. Weren't but two months ago you were paying school fees in flesh. You ain't gonna kill Simon, and you ain't scaring me now."

Connor crosses his arms. "That's all you care about, though. Simon. Isn't it?"

"Is that what this is about?" My blood is rising. "That's why you hate Simon? I did wonder, because it seemed like you were friends a long time back, and now you all hate him. Is that why? Because I *care* about him?"

"No." His breathing's harsh, and five big steps forward put him square in front of me. I have to look up to see his face. "No, it isn't. I'm fighting for the purse. I didn't choose to be put up against Simon on the lists, but I'm gonna fight him. And then, after, when I've beaten him in front of that whole stadium, I'm gonna kill him."

I start to push him away, and he wraps his fingers around my wrist, squeezing hard. My lip curls. "Don't touch me."

"I'll do what I want."

I can feel his anger, biting against my flesh. "I don't care what you want. I said don't touch me."

"You'd like that, wouldn't you?" His teeth flash up close and personal. "Me just letting you go right now."

He stinks of peppermint and sweat, crushing my arm in his grip, and he wants to see weakness, see pain. I don't give him the satisfaction.

"Let me go, Connor Hall, or you'll regret it."

"You keep saying that," he whispers. "I'll regret it. You'll make me sorry. But here's me and you, and you aren't gonna fire that gun, that's what I think. Not at me." His eyes search mine, dirty hair brushes my face. "'Cause we're two of a kind, you and me. Two of a kind."

Footsteps crunch behind him, and Connor lets go to take a casual step back. A figure with the boxy shape of someone wearing a Market guard's riot vest stands there. There's a cigarette in his mouth and a rifle in his hands. Petrowski really does own this city. "Problem here?"

Connor smiles, smooth as butter. "No problem, just a friendly chat. We can't have those anymore?"

"Move along now. It's late."

Nobody moves, and Connor and I both realize in the same moment that I've got an escort home. No going out for me tonight. No going anywhere for me. The smile remains, but Connor's eyes are narrow, and he shakes his head at me.

"Well, Erin, it's been a lovely chat. You just remember what I said, though." He walks past, patting my shoulder like you'd pat a child, like you'd pat a dog. "Good to see you being *kept* safe."

His footsteps crunch all the way to the end of the street, though doubtless he'll be back later to wait for his latest deal. Sex to drugs, what a step-up in the world.

The man's still waiting. "Miss Livingston? This way."

I don't bother to reply. I don't need to. I can just walk and leave him to follow. I'm being kept safe whether I like it or not. Don't nobody need my consent.

38

Art

Chris grabs my arm soon as I'm out of the depot gates at six AM. What, is he setting up camp here or something? He's got his wheedling grin on, the one that gets under my skin and says he wants something, oh pretty please.

"Hey, Art, I gotta talk to you."

"Yeah? What about?"

His eyes dart everywhere. "About, uh, a bet what I made. The café down the road. I'll buy you breakfast."

I open my mouth, the word *no* forming on my lips, and his fingers dig into my bicep. "C'mon, Art, you skipped out last time. I owe you one. They do eggs and toast. Whaddya say?"

There's an edge of desperation to his voice under the usual ingratiating whine, and you know what, what the hell. "Throw in a coffee and I'm your man."

"Done and done." He lets go of me, thank God, and points up the street. "It's right up there."

I follow the poor bastard down the street and into a narrow alley between two shops. It's still dim down here, and the first inklings of wariness are crawling down my spine. Chris is twitching more than ever, swiveling his head to and fro. A moment later, he stops dead and raises a finger to his lips. There isn't a soul in sight, and evidently that's what he's been waiting for.

Leaning in, eyes bugging out, he whispers, "Art, I gotta tell you something. I'm so sorry." His voice is barely loud enough for me to hear. Fear's written all over his face, real fear, and flashing in his eyes. His words stumble over each other. "My mother, you know I take care of her, they said—well, I gotta do what they say for now, got a debt to pay. But I had to tell you. Knew you'd wanna know."

"Know what?" I ask, my own voice low. "Who's watching you?"

His eyes slide away. "It's Petrowski, you know how...how it is, you know, right? I borrowed to cover the odds, the odds I gave on that fight."

"The last fight?"

"Yeah, in the alley. I had someone bet Simon'd kill the other guy. They bet big, and I didn't think it would happen, so I gave good odds, but then Simon *did* actually kill him and—"

"How big?"

"Real big, like, I sold my *skin* big, Art. I swear I didn't think that'd happen, you know? Art, why you looking at me like that, Art?"

"You had someone bet that kind of money on something like that and you didn't *tell* me?" White-hot rage explodes in my mind, and there's Chris in front of me, pleading for me to shush, like I give a shit about that now. "That, right there, is proof the fight was fixed so he'd have to kill the other guy! That was a dead giveaway, and you didn't even think to tell me? How could you not get that?"

"I was stupid, okay? I was stupid and greedy, and look, I'm sorry, but you gotta listen to me, Art. Please. C'mon. I'm trying to make it up to you. If Petrowski knew I was telling you..."

"Telling me what?" I hiss. "You haven't said a damn thing yet!"

"I'm trying!"

Chris has to be the worst secret agent ever. I'm about ready to punch him in the face, and may just do it anyway. "Then say it already!"

He's twisting his fingers, working himself up to it. "You gotta promise to act normal, though, come to the café and not say where you got this. You gotta promise, Art."

"Okay, fine."

"I'm doing this as a friend, okay? I don't want trouble. I'm in enough of that already."

"Just tell me!"

"It's Erin." His hands flap. Useless idiot. "I know...I had to deliver a note, you see, couple days back, and I read it. I wasn't supposed to, and I think Simon read it too, but I had to do it, my mom...that is...the note..."

"Yes?"

He takes a deep breath. "I know when Erin's meeting him next. Petrowski. And where they'll meet."

My face goes numb. I can't feel my lips as they move. Shit. "Yeah?"

"Tuesday. Eden Boulevard. Two in the afternoon."

Fuck. "That's in two days."

"Yeah. Look, I'm sorry, but I had to. But I knew you'd want to know, knew you're real close to her, you know? You understand, right? Art?"

"Right."

He's actually clasping his hands. "I didn't have a choice. I had to do it, Art, believe me, if I had—"

"I said 'right,' Chris."

He tries to smile, still whispering. "Of course, of course you did. You know how it is, money, can't go back, gotta clear it up somehow."

"And that's all you've got for me?"

"Yeah, that's right. Sorry it ain't more. But now he's watching me, to make sure he gets his money, and that's why—"

I hold up a hand. Useless little rat. "I understand. Let's go to breakfast, then. We've been here long enough already."

"Yeah. Of course." He tries to smile. "And I'm buying."

"Thought you didn't have money?"

"I been washing dishes there this last week. They'll let me have a freebie."

We go to his little café, and I eat the breakfast, barely tasting it. My mind's going a million miles an hour. I *knew* Simon'd been set up.

We'd been watched, been had. Led to that alley and duped without us ever knowing it. That other boy thought he was being handed a prize, and really he was just up for the slaughter, for the glory of Saint Flaherty. I always carried that baseball bat and everybody knew it, but somebody got a good idea and knew exactly how to shove us in a corner and make Simon beat his way out of it. Big money on a kill with a boy who's never failed the mercy test before.

Never'd been tested that hard, though.

Christ, Jesus Christ. I thought I had it under control, thought Simon was immune from that sort of thing. Thought they'd ask me first. Thought someone would *care*. Wasn't I the biggest fucking idiot of them all?

I did this. I did this all, to Simon, to Erin, to all of them. I let them down. I'm the one to blame. I gave Simon a baseball bat and a kiss good-bye and made him an executioner.

At the park I wait for Simon to show up for training, rubbing my arms to keep warm. Where the hell is he?

There's a splash in the distance and an "Aha!" A minute later, Simon comes tramping through the leaves, holding what looks like a mason jar full of pond water.

"What's that?"

He looks at the jar, then at me, as if I'd be asking about anything else. "A frog."

"Why?"

"Got a science project. On frogs. I need to study it."

"I'm surprised you found one in winter."

"Yep."

You'd get more words out of the frog than out of Simon. I shrug. "Put it somewhere we won't trip over it, then. You warmed up?"

"Some."

"Well, let's get a move on, then."

We get down to work, my thoughts drifting away. This is what I like best: fighting, training Simon. This is what I do best. Let my mind cut free and my body take control. No thoughts, just the routine.

Simon dances in, then out again. I give him a jab and he blocks. A kick, he dodges. And then I pull my knife out of my pocket and hold it in front of me, the same way that nameless boy did two weeks ago.

Simon, for the first time in a long time, hesitates. He doesn't have his on him, I know that. It's over next to his frog bottle, right where I saw him leave it.

No baseball bat this time, no gun, no one to save him. Let's see what he does. Let's see how certain that other boy's death would've been if they'd fought without the bat. Could Simon have done it without killing him?

I stab in, going for the chest, same as I saw happen before. Simon evades it this time, different reflexes kicking in, keeping his eyes on mine, just like I've told him. Simon doesn't do insults, and he doesn't keep up banter, not in a fight. That's Connor's style, but Simon isn't fast enough for that. The wheels turn slow. Still, I'm not near arrogant enough to drop my guard. Simon is dangerous. Muscles are only the half of it.

"You don't have a bat this time," I say, switching my steps so I'm going counterclockwise now. "No knife. Best make a move before I make mine."

At that I leap forward, aiming toward the chest again. He sidesteps me and snaps out a kick. It hits my guts, and I feel that blow all the way to my spine, but there's no time to wonder about the bruises because I'm already back where I started, with my knife up.

But Simon isn't in front of me anymore. He's coming up and under. I slice down, feel my blade glance off his shoulder before his hands chop at my wrists, throwing them wide. The knife is still in my hand but only barely, and I'm trying to shove him off when he gets a hit straight to my throat.

I just manage to keep the knife bared in front of me, but I can't suck in air, can't breathe at all. Then his foot comes around like some kung fu master and knocks my knife across the clearing, near about taking my hand clean with it. I'm down. I'm down for the count, just like that. Disarmed, on my knees, the adrenaline pumping through my veins and screaming in my ears. I'm out of air, can't suck any in, black spots in front of my eyes, and Simon's grinning.

Goddammit. Goddammit. My neck. My wrist feels like it's on fire, and I swear I heard something snap. I swear to God I did, and Simon can do that just as easy as breathing, though that's not easy right now.

I gasp as air fills my lungs. The black spots retreat. Simon stands over me, blood dripping down his arm.

"Could you do that a month ago?" I gasp out between coughs.

"What?"

"Could you do that a month ago, Simon? In that last alley fight, when that boy pulled a knife. If I hadn't given you a bat, could you have done to him what you just did to me?"

He glances around wildly. "I...I don't know..."

"Think! Dammit, Simon, use your brain for once in your life! Could you have done that?" My breathing's getting easier, my voice louder. "Answer me."

Openmouthed silence, like a frozen rabbit, horror on every inch of his face. I can't stand it.

"Answer me! Now!"

"No!" He's breathing like a runner. "No, I couldn't've done it! I know your reach and I could get you, but I never seen that boy before. I didn't know what he could do, and I couldn't've done it! Not like that. I couldn't have."

His eyes are so wide, crystal blue in the morning light. He looks white as a sheet under the sweat and gore.

But he's telling the truth. Simon can't lie. He couldn't have disarmed that boy; I did the right thing when I gave him that bat. It was a killing, but it was not murder on my part.

My knees give out and I roll over, suddenly too tired to get up. Simon's by my side in an instant, turning me over. My wrist flops, and needle-pains shoot up my arm. Something's definitely wrong there. "Don't move my wrist."

He immediately picks it up, sending more pain radiating up my arm, but then he cradles it in his hands, muttering to himself and bending my fingers. I try to sit up, but Simon's right there pushing me down, dripping blood on my shirt.

"I think it's sprained," he finally says. "Not broken, but it's swelling up already. You oughta see a doctor. You wait here, Art, and I'll go get someone. Or can you walk?"

"Give me a second."

"Okay." Simon waits about two. "Why'd you ask me that? About if I could do that before?"

"Because." I swallow. "Because someone set you up to kill that boy. They knew I brought a baseball bat to fights. They knew our plan. And..." And this is hard to admit, harder than I'll ever say, to look in Simon's eyes and speak the words I don't know if he can bear to hear. "And I needed to know if there was another way. If I was wrong. If you never did need that baseball bat."

His mouth drops open a little bit, and something flashes across his face, rocks him back on his heels, the reel of an impact. With words, I think I've just done to him what it took a kick straight on target to do to me.

But no. Simon stands, holds his hand out, and pulls me up by my good wrist, though the world seems to sway a bit.

"I thought you said he's dead and I'm alive and in the end that's all that matters." He starts walking, towing me behind, talking to the trees ahead. "Don't matter who set up the match—I had to live. I didn't ask him to get in the way of that."

"But that's what I'm telling you, Simon. Someone bet big bucks on you killing the other guy. Someone knew you had a good chance—"

"So what."

"So what?"

"So what!" he snarls over his shoulder. "He brought the knife to the fight. He upped the ante. Don't bring a weapon you ain't prepared to use. I brought a baseball bat, and I used it. End of story."

"No," I cut in, "not end of story. You're missing the point. We were watched before and they're watching again. That fight was rigged, and more will be in the future, that's what I'm saying."

"No." He keeps towing me, faster now. "You were saying that you thought the death was on you, and how you're so damn excited it's not. You don't know how happy you've made me. Why don't you just grow a pair instead and stop trying to force-feed me more bullshit about being a man when you can't even manage it yourself!"

The bitterness in his voice is like a slap. This isn't like him. Not

Simon. "What has gotten into you? Listen up, I was saying it's still on *him*."

"Fine. Whatever."

His hand jitters on my wrist. "Not fine! You need to keep an eye out for what's going on around—"

Simon trips over a tree root and nearly goes flying, jerking me sideways. I crash into him, and for a moment our faces are only inches apart.

His breath smells of booze, sour and clear. My blood runs cold.

"Simon Flaherty, are you *drunk?*"

We stare at each other, him breathing hard, and now I'm positive. How did I miss it before? Under the pond water, he reeks of alcohol. His eyelashes flutter, and then he gives me the most defiant look I've ever seen from him, which means a lot more these days than it did a month ago.

"Yeah. I am."

I can't believe it. I cannot fucking believe it. Of all the people in the world, Simon ought to know better, and I pulled a knife on him and he beat me in *this* condition, of all the goddamned lucky son-of-a-bitch bastards...

I take a step back, yank my wrist from his grip. His eyes narrow. For the second time today, I'm so angry I can hear the roar in my ears.

"Go home, Simon. Go home, and when I see you again, you can put whatever idiotic ideas you had about being some fancy swank dueler under whatever rock they came from and actually take things seriously. This is not a game. I could've killed you today."

I walk past him, toward the street. If I stay, I'm gonna punch him and really break my wrist this time.

I'm ten feet away when I hear his reply. "No, you couldn't've. I beat you hands down, Art. I won. Don't you try to say I didn't." His voice is getting louder. "I won that fight fair and square, and I killed that boy, and I didn't kill you! I could've, but I didn't kill you, Art!"

He's running, chasing me, and now I'm running too, with him hollering right behind me. Something primal at the base of my spine goes *ping*, and fucking hell, I don't want to be caught right now. Oh hell, oh dammit.

Simon hits me like a ton of bricks, and we roll to a stop, agony shooting down my arm. The wind's knocked out of me. Simon's kneeling on the path bent double, tears dripping down his face. The world spins overhead.

"It felt like smashing a watermelon," he whispers. "His head."

I feel like I'm flying while lying still, and nothing makes a single bit of sense. Simon sobs, and I think I've got a broken rib, and there's two Simons in front of me, and now there's only one again.

"I just want to forget him. I don't ever want to think of him again. Not ever."

"Shh, shh," I say, like he's the one hurt and not me. "That's the booze talking. It's not real."

"It's always real. It's in my head, and I think about it all the time. It won't stop playing back. It's in my dreams, only it don't leave when I wake up."

"Shh, shh."

"And now you say it could have been avoided, but no, it couldn't have, 'cause it's in my head and I can't get it out, not ever, never ever..."

The boy who could kill me as easy as breathing sobs against my stomach as the world spins, and I think I might just lie here awhile. The pain in my wrist is the only thing that makes sense. Nothing else does anymore.

39

Erin

If I could choose a day to die, it'd be on a Sunday, just so I wouldn't have to live through another Monday night like tonight. I'm running on autopilot. When the stops jangling, I nearly jump out of my skin from the silence. Already?

Wipe the counters. Wash the dishes. Check the locks one last time. About scream when Simon's frog jumps in its jar, but if Grace notices I'm edgy, she don't say it, small favors. She's got thoughts of her own on her mind. She still ain't put away her curtains yet after three days, folded in the corner of the kitchen, and I ain't gonna make her.

I stay up late with a new bucket of paint in hand, touching up trim around the door what never got done since it was put in maybe six months ago. It's quiet work, soothing. I could do this all night. Pity that's not an option.

Wash up, store the can in the cellar. Go upstairs to brush my hair without looking in the mirror. Remember at the last minute that my boots are at the back door where I left them earlier, damn. Take a deep breath and walk down the stairs. One foot in front of the other, in time with my heartbeat. You're okay.

He's in the kitchen, sitting at the table, peeling potatoes by candlelight. No, no, why's he come here, I go there, we agreed—

He turns, and it's Simon.

Oh God, I can't do this. I can't *do* this, not right now, can't have another fight, can't say why I've gotta go, can't pretend I'm just up for a drink wearing my coat, Christ. Why? Why now? Why this time?

Because he read the damn note, of course. Read it, digested it, and figured it damn well out.

I keep walking straight past him. Undo the dead bolt and the chain, fumble with it in my cold fingers. Behind me, Simon doesn't move an inch, and maybe that's worse than an argument, him knowing and not even trying to stop it. Knowing and doing nothing, just like my mother did and Dr. Avery and every damn last one of them. Damn them all. Damn them fucking all.

"It's me, isn't it?"

I jump like I've been jumping all evening, chain falling to clack against the door. His voice is higher than his father's. Thank God for small favors, thank you, God, for every one.

"It's you what?" I do not need this right now. I do not need anything right now.

"I'm what you've got to lose."

I try to keep my voice steady, though it comes out thin. "What are you talking about, Simon? I couldn't lose you if I tried."

His face wavers in the candlelight like a monster's. "If you don't go to Petrowski tonight, I am what you have to lose. You can risk yourself, but you can't risk me. Because he told you."

"It's nothing to do with you, Simon." Arrows in my heart, pulled out one by one. My head spins. "Go back to bed."

He licks his fingers, almost delicately, and I can't take my eyes away. "No."

Then he pinches out the candle.

Instant darkness. Neon sparkles press against my eyes, and somewhere out there is Simon. My fingers scrabble at the locks, terror overwhelming everything but the need to go, run, *now*.

Iron arms squeeze the breath out of me. A hand crushes my mouth, big and rough, dry lips against my ear. "Don't scream, Erin. It's okay, I promise. It's okay."

That voice, that *voice*. Lifted off my feet, a door shouldered open.

I kick out wildly, my socked feet making no difference against him.

Simon's whispering as I try to scream. "Shh, shh, Erin, it's okay, don't struggle. It's okay. I'm putting you in the cellar and you can say I made you and it's the truth. Don't you see, Erin? Don't you see? It'll be okay."

Get an arm free, nails out, feel them catch on his stitched-up shoulder, hear him hiss. Running out of air from the hand on my lips, can't suck in right, can't make him let me go, and he's on the stair steps now.

"Erin, don't struggle. I can take care of myself. He won't kill me. He told you I'm not his heir anymore, but until his new kid is born, I ain't expendable yet, so just listen to me, please."

It's like he thinks he's talking sense or something. I make another wild kick, arch my back, feel it connect to soft tissue dead-on.

Simon folds like a straw man and I'm free, sliding down the last couple of steps on my side, gulping in air. Coughing comes from farther up the stairs, and for a moment I just listen to it, the cold seeping up from the concrete and through my bones. Oh God. Oh God. Why?

His voice echoes in the cellar, angry as I've ever heard it. "Why'd you do that?"

The adrenaline makes me shaky as I stand. I can still taste it on my tongue, the terror, the panic. My words tumble out all at once. "You mean the part where I stopped you from doing something so fucking stupid I don't got the words for it, or the part where you got what you deserved for trying it?"

"Erin—"

"You idiot! You moron, Simon!"

"Just listen—"

"You are not the only person in this house, Simon Flaherty!" I'm screaming and I don't care. I can't see straight I'm so mad. "You wanna tell Grace's family why Jeff Petrowski had her dragged down the street by her hair? You wanna watch them break her legs?"

"What are you talking about?"

I want to hit him so bad it hurts. "This is not a game! This is real! He will kill her and laugh, and then he'll lock me in some basement and tell you to be good unless you want him to start mailing you my fingers! He will do it! Don't you get it? Maybe he can't get you, Simon. Let's say, just for now, that he can't, and maybe he don't want to. But there's better ways to hurt me than killing you! There's better ways of hurting anybody!"

"But I thought—"

"You thought wrong!" In the dark I can just make out the stairs, and Simon hunched on them, rocking back and forth. "Get out of my way."

Lights turn on in the kitchen, silhouetting a single figure at the top. Grace don't say anything as I brush past and out the door, heart pounding as I run around the house and down the street, three blocks down and two over. Follow the road to the fork, turn, turn again to a building like any other, on a street with lamps so bright they hurt my eyes.

A door opens ahead of me, yellow light spilling on the asphalt. Silent men nod me up the stairs. Will my shame not be complete until everyone has seen my face tonight?

Jeff smiles at me. Simon never smiles anymore.

"Where's your shoes, Erin?"

I look down. This pair of socks is ruined. "Guess I forgot."

"Never mind that, sweetie. I'll get you something nicer than those old boots."

"I like my old boots."

"And you'll like what I give you."

He helps me slide the coat from my shoulders, every touch red-hot and screaming, a brand for all the world to see. Hands tighten on my wrists, and Simon would never do this to anyone, not like this, not in a room like this, stupid naïve Simon who ain't even figured out what the problem is yet.

"I've missed you, Erin," he whispers in my ear. Always the whispers, so intimate, making my skin crawl, but it's okay. I can deaden it out. I can deal with this. "Say you're all mine."

"I'm all yours," I murmur. An image rises in my mind unbidden, Simon's face by candlelight, trying to make me believe him.

"That's right, sweetie, you are." Vicious hands yank my chin and force me to look him in the eye. Blue without a soul, and I can't think of anything but this and him and every ounce of terror he ever conjured in my nightmares with those hands, those hands grabbing me in the dark just like Simon grabbed me just before now. Like father, like child, oh God.

"I own you."

40

TAYLOR

It's still early and I'm doing rounds at the Market, making sure everything is as it should be. Mostly I can figure that out by just glancing around. If nobody's shouting, it's probably fine. Familiar faces nod or wave or scowl. Nobody bothers me, though. That's what I like about being a guard, being invisible and the most visible, all at the same time.

Then coming through the crowd toward me I spot someone familiar. My successor, the black waitress from Erin's bar. Not that she has a clue who I am.

"Good morning." I nod to her and she nods back.

"Morning." Her eyes slide over me, already on the next stall...and then they snap back. "Hey. I know you. You're Taylor Burkes, right?"

She knows me? How does she know me?

"Um, yeah, I am."

"You used to work for Erin Livingston, right?"

Oh. That's how. "That's me." What does she want? "I guess that makes you Grace Farley."

"Correct." She has a nice smile, sexy. I've seen it before, but aimed at customers, not at me. "Hey, I got a question for you. If you don't mind, that is."

"Yeah, sure, sure. What about?"

She steps to the side, motions me over, and lowers her voice. "I know this might seem a bit...out of the blue, but you're the only one I can ask, seeing as you worked at the bar too. What I want to know is, did you ever feel unsafe there? Around the house, I mean."

"You mean because of Flaherty?"

"Well, yeah. Him having killed a man and all." She's really worried, I can tell.

Ha. I consider the question. "You mean, because he's unstable?"

She sucks in a breath between her teeth. "Is he? I mean..."

"Well..." I draw it out, savoring it. Two birds, meet one stone. I hate your fucking guts, Flaherty. "I'm a pretty big guy. He's not exactly what you'd call a threat for me, you know? But you're pretty slim—in a good way—but still. In your shoes, I might be a bit worried."

"You think?" I can see her turning it over. Then she smiles and cocks her head. "Hey, you might know. Where does Erin go at night?"

"What do you mean?"

"I probably shouldn't say, but I heard her go out late last night. Thought maybe you'd know if she was, like, secretly a werewolf or something."

I laugh out loud. "Witch, maybe, werewolf, no. But I could ask around, if you like."

Her face is cautious, but I can tell I've got her. "Could you? I mean, I'm sure it's nothing, but I'd rather not take any chances."

"Hey, you can trust me. I'll do it on the down-low. No one will know it was you asking." I squeeze her shoulder. "Catch me again next time you're at the Market, okay? I work mornings."

She twiddles her fingers and disappears into the crowd. I keep strolling, nodding to those I know. My week is looking up. Guard duty pays off at last.

Ryan's alone at the poker table in headquarters when I get in. "Taylor, got something for you."

"Yeah?"

"You'll like this." He grins. "Guess what happened last night?"

"Your ex-girlfriend forgave you?"

"Dick. No." He leans back on the stool, hands behind his head, smug as can be. "Erin went wandering and I followed her here, where the boss gave me a special task. Had to go wake up that shoe-shop lady at the Market and get a pair of tennis shoes in size seven and a half." He smirks.

I lean on the counter and scoff. "So what, you got a fetish now? Into sniffing feet?"

"You wish. No, I delivered them into the waiting hands of—oh, you're going to like this—none other than Erin Livingston herself."

"Wait. You don't mean...?"

"Oh, I do." He's got a wolf grin, Ryan. "Rustled out of her bed in the middle of the night for a booty call with Petrowski himself. Guess he felt the need to poke the kid in the eye."

"With no shoes?"

"Looks like she's going a bit cuh-razy, if you ask me. Boss sure knows how to pick 'em, don't he?"

I laugh with him, for more reasons than he knows. Question asked, answer received. Have I got news for Grace. Perfect, perfect. Yes, my week is looking up.

41

Art

Once upon a time, I'd walk into Erin's kitchen without knocking, but times have changed. I bang on the door with my good hand at lunchtime. The new girl, Grace, answers, wiping her hands on a dish towel and peering at me through the screen like I'm a kid asking for his friend to come out and play. "Is Erin around?"

"No, she's out."

Shit. "She say she'd be back soon?"

"No, sorry. Want me to tell her anything for you?"

I'm too late. Much too late. "Did she say where she went?"

"No, and I wouldn't tell you if she did." I catch her eye. There's steel behind that bland look. "Why do you want to know so much?"

"We're friends, Erin and I," I retort.

She doesn't rise to it. "That so? Then I'm sure you can guess where she's gone."

"Be easier if you told me."

"Wouldn't everything?"

So Erin's out. I know where she'll be at two o'clock, but at the moment she could be anywhere, at the Market, walking down Eden Boulevard... "Got a question for you, Gracie."

"Grace, not Gracie. What do you want now?"

"What are you doing?"

"Right now, I'm having my time wasted by you."

The door closes. I'm left on the steps, staring at the green paint.

Okay, so Grace isn't gonna be talked around, and Erin is God-knows-where. Great. Just great. I can search the town...

...or I can earn brownie points while I wait.

I knock on the door one last time. Grace ignores it. Knock again. The only answer is the sound of her starting a song.

Oh, hell with it. It's not locked.

There's a knife in my face before I've gone two steps in. It looks sharp, and considering who her father is, I'd bet money on it being the perfect weapon for carving her initials on my forehead. My hands are in the air instantly.

"What do you want?" If her voice were any more casual, I'd swear we were on the street just saying hello.

"I have time to kill," I hazard. "Got any work for me to do?"

Her hands don't waver. "Do you want paying for this work?"

"No, no, just something to do while I wait for Erin to get back. Just for an hour or two. Otherwise, I'll be sitting on the step outside, and what's the point in that?"

She considers this, and then the knife goes back in her pocket like it's never been out at all. "There's a bag of cured walnuts in the pantry that need shelling. The name of the game is to crack 'em without shattering 'em and get the meats out in big pieces. There's a hammer under the sink unless you know a better way. You got that?"

That works. Between me cracking nuts and her kneading dough, the kitchen is pretty loud but it's not bad work. Nice to hit something that doesn't yell at me to stop, if you know what I mean. Soothing. I've just about got the hang of it when Grace finally speaks up.

"So you knew Erin before? Like, when you was kids?"

"Well, sorta. I was friends with her brother, who, by the way, I don't suggest bringing up. Ever."

"I know what happened to him. My sister told me. What I'm asking is, what was she like back then? Personality-wise."

Erin as a kid seems to rise up before my eyes, unbidden and unwanted. Long hair loose, wearing half a friendship necklace to match the one worn by that other girl she ran around with, Abby Farley. I can picture Erin back then wearing shorts and leggings and cowboy boots, asking what me and Trey were doing a million times, asking us would we take her out with us to the skate park.

A hundred miles away, Grace is still talking. "Was she different?"

"Not much. I mean..." She laughed a lot. Smiled and whined and wheedled until she got her way, talking a million miles a minute. But her personality? The sigh feels like it comes from the bottom of my soul. "Look, if you know about her brother, you know that I'm about four years older than Erin. I don't remember her personality. She was just background noise. I only came to this house after the war 'cause I heard someone talking about an Erin living here and I wanted to see her ki—see her." Grace doesn't seem to have noticed. "We got to talking, and then I met Simon."

Simon, with those eyes. I nearly opened my mouth right then and there to ask Erin if this was her baby, when she cut me off and said, "I found him." That was when I knew that whatever happened to that pregnancy after I ran out of town, there was no kid now. Whatever she'd had was long gone.

There's a distant look in Grace's eyes and a faint frown between her eyebrows. "Why didn't she evacuate when everyone else did? Abby said she'd tell me when I was older, but of course..."

Abby Farley must have been her big sister, and from the way Grace is talking, I'd wager she didn't make it through the war. I lay my hammer down, lean against the table. Grace has stopped her work too. "What happened to Abby?"

"She went out to get supplies with my mama during a lull in the fighting, but a car blew up and they got separated. Erin tracked us down a week later. She'd found both Abby and my brother. His unit was in town, and he'd been stabbed. Erin was nursing him back to health. My sister too, but Abby hadn't made it. Someone scalped her." Her eyes are distant, lost in her own memories. "But I don't know why Erin stuck around. From what my sister said, I think she didn't have anywhere else to go. By the time she realized she should leave, it was probably too late, you know? We were supposed to go to relatives, but we didn't have time to get out in the end. And, I mean, it's a good thing we didn't go when everyone else did, 'cause of those bombs, but why didn't Erin leave with her family?"

I shift. "Look, you should ask Erin if you really want to know, though she won't tell much. She hasn't told me much, even."

Grace shrugs. "Tell me your guesses, then. I don't want to break your confidences or nothing, but I'm just trying to get my head around her a little better. She's told me some. But I just..." She trails off, her hands saying the rest. What Erin don't want to say doesn't get said. Silences are her specialty.

"Look. You gotta remember, her family, she didn't like them much. If you know about her brother, then I reckon you know why." I choose my words carefully for this next part. "I always gathered that her family left town, including her stepfather, and she refused to go. Guess she thought whatever happened here, she'd rather ride it out than keep with them."

"You mean she'd rather die than stay with those people."

Can't stop my head from jerking up. Grace merely looks thoughtful, examining something I can't see, like that's nothing at all to say.

And that's weird. That's a little bit weird.

How much do I know about Grace anyway? How much does Erin know about this girl? Her father we all know, but her? Turned up out of nowhere nice as you please, making bread like she owns the place. She's watching me out of the corner of her eye, watching me take a step back.

"If you're here to intercept her two o'clock appointment, it's come and gone. It was AM, not PM."

How the...? "How'd you know that?"

"Because," she states, perfect confidence in her voice, running through her veins so clear it shines out of her eyes, "you're in love with her. And you don't know what to do about it."

"What are you talking about?" My blood's turned to ice.

"You, Art Weber. I am talking about you."

Get it the fuck together. "Don't be stupid."

She pauses, thinks it over in that creepy way she's been doing. "That's something I don't get accused of much. Sorry if it seems sudden, but I figured you'd be wanting to know, being that you came here special and all."

"I am not in love..."

"About her appointment, I meant. And no, I don't know when the next one is."

Grace turns back to the kneading, flipping her braids back behind her shoulders. Like it's nothing at all and this is every day, and like I didn't...miss Erin.

AM, not PM. Last night. Two AM, when I was driving like the idiot I am, just worrying about being the front of the convoy, when back here, she was with him. With Petrowski. She went to him.

I don't say good-bye. I don't say a thing, just walk out the door and down the street. Did you think she gives a shit about you, Artie? Did you think anyone does?

42

Simon

I turn the corner coming home from school and hear arguing on the other side of the fence. Erin's pissed as hell, I can tell just from her voice.

"...quit if you were so inclined, but you seem to be enjoying yourself. Simon says you've got people in most afternoons just to see him spar so's you can brag after."

"It pays to advertise when..." That's Mick's voice. Whatever he says gets lost in the wind, and I take a few steps closer, listening hard, 'cause Erin don't tell me anything no more and Mick wouldn't be talking to her if it weren't about me. They hate each other like snakes eating each other's tails. Mick's halfway to the top of his lungs. "...he's not stupid!"

"Did I say he was?"

"No, you said he acts it," Mick snarls back. The wind snatches his words as brown leaves rattle past. "...because he worries about you!"

"Instead of asking me beforehand if maybe there was a *reason* I was having a baby instead of oops, gee, my brains just leaked out my ears during the night and I decided to throw my diaphragm in the garbage for giggles." I can just see between the slats as Erin shakes her head like she's trying to clear it. "Right. Yeah. Great idea."

Mick takes a step forward, crowding into her space the way she don't like. "Yeah, okay, it was stupid, but he was afraid for you. You didn't tell him anything, you just left him guessing. He was trying to make things better."

"He was letting his testosterone do the thinking for him, just like you do, Mick."

"What are you trying to say?" he hisses.

"I am saying you both think with your dicks, and don't pretend you don't." Erin turns on her heel to go back into the house.

Mick's a big guy, and he makes her stay, makes her listen with a hand on her shoulder. "That boy is scared to death that either he's going to die in a fight or spend all his days working for some bastard telling him to kill people. He is trying to do anything he can think of to make things better, because in his eyes, in his life, things couldn't get much worse right now. And instead of trying to help him, you're accusing me of thinking with my dick? You think *I* have ulterior motives?" He pushes her away. "You make me sick."

"Likewise. I take it back. You can leave Simon the hell alone, and if you ever come in my bar, you'd best be immune to rat poison. You're banned. Forever."

"Like I'd come back," Mick mutters as I open the gate.

His face is a picture. Shocked. Horrified. He didn't want me to hear that, no, didn't want me to hear what he said to Erin. What he told her about me, about what I said to him that I ain't told to nobody else 'cause it ain't nobody's business but mine, and he told her.

"You fucking jerk."

"Simon..."

"I trusted you! You shouldn't've told!"

He takes a step toward me, and I shove him back hard, go up the steps after Erin. She's just inside the screen door, hunched over with her face like a corpse. "Are you okay?"

"I'm fine." She rubs her shoulder where he grabbed it, though, and I can see the color on her collarbone.

"Don't lie to me," I say. Mick's watching through the screen door. He's still got that sick look on his face. He's in deep shit and he knows it.

"This is why she's worried," I tell him, because someone in this world has to understand. He's watching me as Erin opens her mouth to snap at me and I pull the collar of her sweater aside just enough to show the rainbow that I knew would be there, 'cause this morning when Grace patted her shoulder, she flinched.

Erin yanks herself away, her fingernails catching my skin, but not before Mick sees.

She's got a bruise as big as my fist, purple and black and green, with horrible red blotches. It wasn't Mick's doing—I know exactly whose fault it was—but he grabbed her shoulder where it would hurt her most, and I know he didn't mean to, but he needs to understand. I trusted him to understand, and I thought he did, but clearly he didn't.

He needs to know what's at stake here.

Erin's leaving the kitchen, head held high, back straight. Every day she walks that way. Mick's still struck dumb at the bottom of the back steps.

Right after my last fight, I dreamed of the boy I killed. Blood all over my face, so sticky that when looked in the mirror the next morning I could hardly believe it weren't really there, night after night. Blood running down my arms, filling my boots, staining that baseball bat what I couldn't drop no matter how hard I tried. Couldn't drop it, couldn't get my hands to let go, to work right, to do anything but swing and swing and never miss, not once, until the blood poured down the brick alley walls. *Smash* went Erin's head, *smash* went Art's head, *smash* went Connor's head and Mrs. Graham's and everyone's until their bodies was all I could see past the blood running down my face and in my eyes and mouth until I couldn't breathe, just choke and sob and say no, no...

About three weeks ago, Mick gave me a bottle out of that stash he sold Erin and told me a shot before bed was what I wanted. I haven't dreamed since. I don't intend to ever dream again.

I know what guilt feels like.

"Erin's right, I did something stupid," I tell him. "You don't need to blame her for what I done. But you might pardon her a few things. I don't know a better way to say it. She needs it. You don't have to live with her, and I do, but none of us have to live inside her head 'cept her. And she's scared." I catch his eye, try to make him understand. "Wouldn't you be?"

He understands some things, and him and Erin hating each other is something I won't ever be able to change. But Mick needs to understand this. He needs to know what I'm up against, and that if he's got my back, he's got hers, like it or not.

He squeezes his eyes shut. Nods. It's all I'm gonna get. He knows, and that's more than Art does.

43

Grace

I slice a piece of walnut bread for my breakfast and wash my face in the sink. There's coffee in a pot, black as walnut shells, hot as spent ammo. The oven's already been stoked, though only recently. "Did you get lard?" I ask Erin.

"Yeah, think it should be enough. It was delivered while you were up front last night."

"Okay, thanks."

That's my days here. Baking, baking, baking. I told her I could, and now I do. The back door opens, and Simon comes in muttering hello and dripping sweat. Erin points him to the tub behind the curtain she jury-rigged in the corner. He heads straight to it, and I can hear the slick sound of cloth being peeled from skin. A moment later, the back door opens again and in comes Art.

When he left yesterday, I wondered if he'd ever come back. He looked so lost, so helpless, and strong men like him don't like to be helpless. My mama did warn me, and I heed her, but sometimes caution's just not an option. You gotta spit in the wind and duck fast.

Erin doesn't look at him, but the way she picks up the knife and starts slicing a pumpkin tells me she knows who's here. "What d'you want, Art?"

"I just came to chat. Make sure we're all clear about what's happening at the tournament Saturday."

"Yeah, and what's that?"

He stands awkwardly, like he's waiting to be offered a seat. Erin still has her back to him. It's painful to witness, to say the least. "We don't have to worry about making weight for Friday, knives just have a ceremonial thing Saturday afternoon, but in the morning Simon needs to do his regular workout and have a big breakfast. Then he needs a light lunch around two o'clock, and a snack around five. Can you take care of all that?"

"No, Art, I ain't never fed a growing boy before." Ouch. "That all?"

"No." He leans in and pitches his voice low, but not low enough. "Can we talk somewhere else?"

"I'm busy."

He looks from me to the curtain that Simon's behind, then makes up his mind. "Erin, I've been thinking about things. About you. You need to get out of this town."

"Excuse me?" She speaks in her normal voice. "What do you mean, 'get out of this town'?"

"You know what I mean. Run away. Escape. Leave."

"Oh, right then, I'll just hop on the next convoy out. Great idea, Art."

"I'm serious, Erin." He looks it too. "Petrowski's gonna kill you at this rate. I know what he's doing to you. You have to get away from him."

"And how do you suggest I do that?"

"That's what I'm getting to. I've started making a couple inquiries, on the down-low, you know, to a couple guys I work with, and they think it might be possible to get out of Buchell without being noticed. Smugglers' trails."

Erin scowls at her work. "I didn't ask you to do that, Art, and I don't think it's safe that you're doing it. You just asking has probably put yourself and all your friends in danger, do you even realize that?"

Art snaps. "Goddammit, Erin! Will you stop being so pig-headed stupid and at least look at me when you shoot down my ideas? I'm trying to be helpful here! I'm trying to get you away from that guy so you can be safe and you should listen, unless this is your way of telling me you actually *like* sleeping with him—"

He stops himself. The room has gone deathly silent. Even Simon behind his curtain seems to have stopped breathing.

Erin turns on her heel and stands up straight. "What did you just say to me, Art Weber?"

He tries to back down. "I'm sorry. That came out wrong. I just mean...I mean..."

"For God's sake, just shut up, Art. Just shut up. You just open your mouth and let anything come out, don't you?"

"What? I—"

"Don't you come here and try to make more problems for me than you already have!" she screeches. "I don't want your attention, I don't want your advice, I don't want you in my fucking life anymore! Do I have to spell it? Get the fuck out already and leave me the fuck alone!"

I clutch my dish towel to my chest. Art actually tries to take a step toward her. Erin leans forward and shoves him back with both hands.

"Get out! Don't you try to touch me no more! I don't like it, and I don't like your schemes! Get out! Get the fuck out!"

"Erin!" Art opens the screen door but hangs onto the knob. He's not mad; he's astonished, like this is news to him. Like he's never seen that she don't like him, and even I knew that, and I only been here a couple of weeks, geez. "Whatever I did, I'm sorry. Okay? I'm just trying to make things better."

"I don't care what the fuck you think you're trying to do, Art, I really don't." She kicks the door so hard it flies out of his hand to bang against the side of the house. I wince. "Get off my property, and stay the fuck off. Just go. Okay? Can you do that?"

His expression has gone ugly and dark. "I don't know what the hell has happened to you, Erin. I don't get it. It's like you think you're being stalked by some sort of monster who's gonna leap at you from the shadows and you're taking it all out on me. Wake up! I'm not the bad guy—I'm trying to help you! So why you gotta scream at me every time I come by?"

Oh my lord, he doesn't get it, doesn't see it. He honest-to-God has no idea why she's angry. It blows my mind. How can he not? How can he be that dense?

The truth dawns in my mind, a dark stain spreading in a pool of water: he can't see that she hates him. He really isn't able to understand.

Simon comes out from behind the curtain, dressed in his school uniform. He stands behind Erin, a show of strength. Erin crosses her arms. Art looks to me, but I can't meet his eyes. He has no friends in this room.

"Fine! Be that way! Don't say I didn't try!" He jumps down the steps and runs out of the yard. The door closes in his wake.

The carving knife hits the cutting board so hard it sticks in half an inch. Simon catches Erin's hand as she reaches for the paring knife.

"Hey." It's all he says, in that quiet way he's got, the voice that he only ever uses with Erin. "Hey. It's okay. It's okay."

"He can't connect actions with consequences," I tell the room. My brain can't seem to get a grasp on this. "He can't do it. Can he?"

"No," says Simon, "not really."

"He must be nuts."

Erin presses her palms to the table, seeming to draw strength from the wood before picking up the bread knife and slicing the last of the walnut loaf. Looks like she's caught my dazed feeling. "I don't even know anymore. I really don't. It's like the person I knew was really a stranger for all those years. He's always been odd, but—I just don't know anymore. I can't stand him anymore. I just...can't."

Silence, long and thoughtful, pooling like a dammed stream.

Simon shifts. "I gotta get to school."

These words seem to pull Erin together. "Your lunch is next to your bag. Have a slice of walnut bread to take with you. Don't be causing trouble today, you hear?"

"Okay." He picks up his stuff, hesitates, then comes back and gives Erin a clumsy one-armed hug. "Hey. It'll be fine."

Then with a wave to me he's out the door and gone, leaving crumbs in his wake. Erin smiles, a crooked little thing. She don't get much practice using the real ones, I guess.

"Come on, then, Grace. Forget about him. Let's get things cooking."

44

TAYLOR

"Hey again!"

Grace finds me in the middle of my patrol rounds, near the same place that I saw her last time. "Hey yourself. How goes it?"

"Pretty good," she replies, smiling. She's got freckles on her cheeks. "You?"

"Not half-bad. Got a feeling my day just got better. Waitressing treating you okay?"

"I'm worked half to death cooking during the day, but that's nothing new. What's thirty men a night after my hungry family?" A delicate hand smooths back her hair to cover a sidelong look. "So. Hey. Got anything for me, by any chance?"

I play it off. "Well, not much. I mean, not much to tell, I guess."

She takes the hint. "Don't suppose fresh pumpkin bread would help your memory at all?"

"It just might..."

Grace laughs and pulls a loaf from her basket. "Well, asking around is hard work. So what'd you hear?"

I lower my voice, make sure no one's listening. Grace obligingly steps in a little closer. She smells like pumpkin and spice. "Okay, get this. Friend of a friend tells me Erin was at her stepdad's for the night on Monday. And I do mean *for* the night."

Her mouth drops open, and then she giggles. "That's just...yuck. Ugh, I don't even want to think about it. Why aren't they like, living together then, if they're having a baby?"

"You see," I draw it out, savor the taste, "I don't think she's exactly happy about it, if you get my drift. Heard she managed to arrive at his place without her shoes. Going a bit cray-zee." I twirl a finger around my ear. She just raises her eyebrows. "Anyway. Friend who was in the house at the time says Petrowski's super protective of her. Anyone caught causing problems for Erin is going to get a talking-to, and not the kind you walk away from smiling, either." I lay down my trump card. "Including Simon."

"Petrowski said that?"

"Specifically."

"Why?" Grace tips her head to the side. The curve of her neck is smooth and creamy-brown.

I lean down so that my lips are almost touching her ear. "Promise you won't tell a soul?"

"Okay."

"Cross your heart and hope to die?"

Her breath tickles my shoulder, and when she turns, her cheek bumps my chin. "Tell me."

I lower my voice to the tiniest breath. "He's Simon's father."

She gasps, leans back to stare at me in shock. "No shit?"

"Yeah. Dunno if you've ever seen Petrowski up close, but if you do, look at his eyes. Exactly the same."

I've rocked her world. Score for me. Knew that'd do the trick. "Wow. Just...wow."

"So." I smile, raise my eyebrows. "Got any free time coming up soon? Does Erin give nights off for a good girl?"

That sidelong look again, all eyelashes and gleam. "Dunno. Haven't asked for any yet."

"Well, if you do, I always know what's going on in this town. Maybe I could help you out."

She presses the pumpkin loaf into my hands, lingering a little longer than necessary. "Maybe I will. See you later, Taylor."

"Yeah. Later."

All that, for two minutes of asking? Talk about value for your money. And the bread is pretty good too.

45

Simon

One time, a long time ago, I think I was fourteen, Art said he'd teach me to shoot skeet. We went in the woods, him with his shotgun and me carrying the ammo, staying on a path, 'cause you don't wanna go straying 'round here, with the land mines and all. We found a clearing, and he reached in his bag and came out with these clay flowerpot-looking things. He showed me how to follow them with the muzzle, and then he tossed one in the air. I missed and it shattered on the ground. He tossed another. Another miss.

Finally I started hitting them, so Art threw them higher and higher. Then Art said, "Last one," and tossed something way up high in the air, higher than any of the others. And me, I shot it.

The explosion knocked me and him to the ground, and I couldn't hear right for a week. Don't know where he got that bomb, but it shattered the top of a tree near us and scorched my eyebrows off. The debris then triggered a mine about fifty yards away, and between the first explosion and the ones that followed, it took us ten minutes to stand up straight again.

I thought that Art had just made a mistake, a miscalculation. But then he grinned at me with blood all down his face and said, "Didn't think that'd happen!"

No, I reckon he didn't. 'Cause Art don't think ahead. Not then, not ever. Took me a long time to understand why that's a problem I can't afford no more.

Mick's waiting for me like he always does, timer out, with a couple pitchers of water on the folding table. I dump my bag, change into my shorts. Turn my knife over about ten times. It's freezing in here, but I don't feel cold today.

"I'm quitting Art. Quitting his training."

Mick sucks air between his teeth. He spent all yesterday avoiding my eyes, but now he looks, eyebrows together. "That's a big change, Simon."

"I know."

"You just decide this today, or been thinking about it for a while?"

"Since Sunday. He pulled a knife on me while I was unarmed. Said to try to disarm him, and that's when he sliced me on the shoulder. Look, okay, I know that's good practice, but you didn't see his face. Like he was gonna kill me for real." And if that idea had come into his head, maybe he would've.

Art don't think ahead.

"It's Wednesday, Simon. You have two more practices with him. You don't want to change your routine now."

I know that, does he think I don't? He's got some bullshit "grown-ups know better" expression on his face.

"Yeah, I know Art's extreme, but he's got you this far," Mick says.

"Grace says he's crazy."

"And Grace knows a lot about this?"

"Think she only met him last week."

He nods to himself, then catches my eye and holds it. He knows I'm telling the truth. He knows Art, knows what he's like.

"Art don't give a shit about me." I known it for months now, and I wanted so bad for it not to be true, pretended so hard. "He's always coming around the house, and every day he tries to get me to tell Erin to talk to him again, and I just don't want anything to do with it. I don't wanna be around him. I'm fucking sick to death of it."

Mick sighs. "Art likes her. He won't admit it, because he can't have her, but he does."

"I know that, I don't give a shit. I just wish he'd..." Give a crap about me. I used to think of Art as like an older brother, or...or...like a dad should be.

But he's not. He's not and he never has been and he don't care if

I'm pissed so long as I make him money.

Mick puts a hand on my shoulder, reassuring. "Look, I know Art's being an ass, but he's got you this far. Stick it out until Saturday at least, okay?" He cocks his head. "Or is something else on your mind?"

I shake my head, 'cause if I open my mouth, my voice is gonna break and it'll all just come out, and I can't do that. Can't say everything. Not to Mick. Don't matter if he and Art ain't friends, I just can't.

"Good man." Mick squeezes my shoulder, releases some of the tension. He's on my side. That's how I knew Art wasn't; the real thing shows every fake for what it is.

46

Erin

I feel like a leaf in the fall, crumbling around the edges. 'Bout to jump out of my own skin, I am. Caught Grace putting rags on the corners of the doors to muffle the slam 'cause she said she was tired of watching me flinch. Worth every penny, that girl.

Simon eats his dinner in the corner with his homework. On from frogs to history. He's trying in that way of his, plowing through the words, taking notes in his block hand so he don't have to read it again.

First rush in the front room is over, and I'm on my own as Grace pulls rolls from the oven. That was her idea, fresh bread. She thought it'd bring more customers in, and she was right. Not that the stuff I serve ain't fresh, as I've usually done it within a couple of days, but there's something about warm rolls and the scent of yeast in the air what makes everyone come back for seconds. Only been doing it a week and already it seems like we've got more people in. More women, that's for sure. There's six in here right now, and that's practically a record.

Simon disappears into the back at about half seven to fetch Grace out. The next rush will be just before nine. She comes in with the rolls in a basket, wafting their smell around. The door jingles and two men stomp in. Here we go again.

Scoop, pour, dish out, and hand over. Make change, count coins, smile and wave, just keep smiling. No time to think, so keep it coming.

It's not until half an hour on that I notice Simon never returned from the kitchen. Things up here have settled down; I guess I can spare a moment to see what's up. I leave Grace chatting with Darryl and head to the back with an empty jug in my hands. Needed more gin anyway. Need to know what my boy's up to. Push open the door and stride in, because I own the place.

There, sitting at *my* kitchen table, eating a bowl of *my* stew, is Connor Hall. What in God's name.

Simon stands upon my entrance, but Connor stays right where he is, his stare about burning holes in my back as I head downstairs. By the time I return from the cellar, Connor's alone, now drinking what looks like a pint of *my* beer.

I slam the jug of gin on the table. "What do you have to say for yourself?"

Connor eyes the jug, then looks to the ceiling.

"I came here to apologize," is what he finally chooses to say. "I shouldn't have said what I said the other night. It was out of line. You have your reasons for doing what you do, just as I have mine, and it wasn't my business to judge them, or you. I'm sorry."

Okay...

What on earth?

Connor's waiting for me to say something. "Are you drunk?" is all I can manage.

"No, it's sassafras. Simon's smarter than he looks, in that way at least."

"Don't you dig at him," I warn. "Not in my house. Not sitting at my table, eating my food. What do you really want, Connor? I've got people in the front room. Don't got time for none of your games."

"I wanted supper, what do you think? Wait, no, I wanted to sleep with the amazing Erin Livingston, she of a thousand orgasms! Not." I wait. Connor's at his nastiest when he's cornered. Apparently he's feeling trapped right now. "Having fun being pregnant?"

"Oh, yes, it's a blast." I smile at him, bright and brittle. "It's so much fun that you should join me and pretend to be the baby-daddy. Why don't we just set up house together and be one big happy family?"

"Only if I can beat my redheaded stepson." Connor spits something into his hand and drops it on the table. "You buy shitty meat, Erin."

"Good thing you're not paying, then. I'm sure Simon said it was free, or you wouldn't be here, am I right?"

"Of course."

I pick up the jug. Enough of this. "Finish your food already and get the hell out of my house."

I'm almost at the door when he gets in his parting shot. "Not your house."

I stop in my tracks, keeping my voice low. No need for the whole front room to hear. "What'd you say?"

"It's not your house," he repeats, eyes hard. "This whole street was rentals. Your stepdad's the only one who ever saved up enough to buy one. It's his house."

"And I'm the one been living here these past ten years. It's mine."

"Only because he lets you. I'm right, aren't I? No, don't answer, I already know. That's the truth."

"It's my house," I repeat. Does he get off on this or something?

"Why are you pregnant now?" he asks. "I don't mean why are you pregnant, I mean why are you pregnant this minute? He came back before the end of the war, right? Probably during the street fighting, yeah? Yeah, it must have been before the end, when I was stranded on the south end of town and the soldiers were flattening the factories in the west, 'cause that's when they put the mines in the hills. He helped them do it, I remember hearing about that. So why did he only come after you again now? Think about it."

Seeing as I ain't a necessary feature in this conversation, I make for the front room.

"I remember when your mom left."

Except, I can't move.

"Everyone was leaving except my family, the only ones stupid enough to stay on this street. And you, of course. Your mom and your stepdad had that horrible screaming match. She wanted him to force you to go and he wouldn't do it. But he grabbed your kid away and you started screaming. I remember that. I was just a kid, but I remember 'cause you were screaming he raped you and my mom dragged me inside and broke my toy tank when I wouldn't stop asking what that meant. 'Cause I didn't know back then."

The door is right there, and I can't walk through it and back out to the front. Can't do it. His voice bores into my skull.

"They left you to die and your mom and her kids never came back 'cause someone fucked up the coordinates and the traffic got carpet bombed two days later. And you thought it was over, didn't you? Half of Buchell dead in one strike. Everyone from this street. Except my family, though they caught it a couple years later." He pauses to think. "How long did it take you to figure out Simon was related to him? Or did you already know? Is that why you took him in? I don't really remember much about Jacob. Did Simon look like him?"

"Stop it."

"I always wondered that, ever since Simon told me who his dad is. Why'd you take him in?"

"Stop it now, Connor Hall."

"You must've been so happy hearing about that bombing, knowing your stepdad was dead. And then to find out that he wasn't after all, I bet that was awful—"

"Shut up. Shut up right now." I stride across the room to lean over the table and glare in his face. "What do you know? Nothing! You don't know anything about what he made me do—"

Connor laughs. "Oh, go on, Erin, tell me what about rape I don't know." We stare at each other, not breaking eye contact for a second. "You thought he was done with you, and then he showed up on your doorstep out of the blue. His other kids were dead, Simon finally deemed not fit to inherit the empire, so he came back to you with his demands and told you he needed a new son. Like I said, tell me when I start getting things wrong."

"What do you care?"

"I don't. I just like knowing. There's a difference."

The way he's watching me, the way no one watches me, watching just to watch. Is he lying? Probably. Everyone else is. Everyone has an agenda, something they want, and Connor's always been in it for himself and no one else.

If anyone could understand, though...

"Your kid was three, four years younger than me, so that'd have made you thirteen or fourteen when you had him."

"He told me if I made a noise, he'd tell my mom what I'd done and she'd throw me out." And for some reason, that had scared me. It's almost funny now.

"Personally, I'm surprised he only got you pregnant the once."

"I kept birth control in my locker at school. And when it shut down, I broke in and stole all the condoms. Don't you forget, you used to come to me for supplies."

"I didn't forget," he replies darkly.

He used to hide in my cellar when the airstrikes was bad, and later, when the scalpings started, he'd bring people to me for stitching.

Someone laughs in the other room. For a while, I'd forgotten that a world exists beyond the bones of the past. Some days, it don't seem to.

Connor drains his glass and grimaces. "Anyway, I should get going. Got work to do tonight. More shipments coming in. Business calls." He pushes his chair back, puts his hand on the doorknob, and then takes it back. "You should be flattered, you know."

"What do you mean?" Nothing nice ever comes from Connor.

"Petrowski must really think you're something special. I mean, what, you've raised three of his kids so far, if you include your half sisters, and Simon makes four? Going to be five, now, with the new baby. You must really be doing a great job. I mean, it's not exactly an accident, Simon living here, is it?"

He's already running down the path by the time I reach the door, laughing the whole way. I latch and lock it, closing my eyes and trying to get my shaking under control. Fucking Connor Hall. Fucking, fucking Connor Hall. Why did he have to... Why did he always have to...

Because Connor don't have anything to lose by doing it, not a damn thing in the world, and you can't hurt someone like that.

47

Buchell's awake by the time Simon and I finish up dawn practice, day shift on their way to work, night shift still making their way home. At least it's warmer this morning, back up in the fifties despite getting toward December. My boarding house isn't a long bike ride away, but more than once I've had my hair start freezing when I've rode sweaty. I need to dunk my head in a bucket.

Only, guess who's lounging on the porch but Taylor Burkes himself. I vaguely recognize the skinhead next to him as Ryan Jesser, who Simon beat up once. How time flies. What the hell do they want?

They stand as I march up the walk. "Morning, Art."

"Morning, faggots."

An arm shoots in front of me to block the path, fist at one end of it, Jesser on the other. "Manners, Art."

I don't think it's possible to roll my eyes further than I already am, but I give it my best shot. "Don't even try that. Get out of my way."

Taylor smiles, not a pleasant sight considering the state of dentistry around here. "Got a message for you, Art. Or maybe more a delivery than a message."

"That's nice."

Jesser blocks the way like a brick wall, and just about as intelligent. "Well, we say delivery. More like an invite."

"I'm busy."

"Mr. Petrowski thinks differently."

Their trump card shimmers in the air. I wonder if they know how still the world just went. I knew this day would come. Trey went down point-blank, and it was only Erin flinging herself at the gun that saved me from the same fate. She dove straight in front of it, knew he'd never hurt her. But me, well. He's not the sort to let go of a grudge, just let it simmer.

"Any particular reason he wants me?"

"Now, now, Art. Mr. Petrowski's a busy man. He's not gonna have time to tell us every detail of his day. I'm sure you'll find out why soon enough."

We face off on my boarding house steps, these two and me. No one so much as peers through a window or walks down the street. I am on my own. Word gets around fast in this town, and no one wants to piss off Petrowski.

"So that's the way of it." Their faces don't move, stuck in identical idiotic smirks. "You two come for me and tell me to go quietly, and I just go." To my death.

"Oh, you don't have to be quiet." Jesser shows teeth and pats his holster. "But bleeding sometimes offends, you know?"

I could try to escape, but there's two of them, and where would I go? Between a rock and a hard place, what do I choose? Either way is certain death.

I stretch, arch my back with my hands on my hips like I'm cracking my spine, but I'm really reaching for...

"Nah, Art, don't be like that." Jesser holds up a stun gun. "Just a friendly chat. You gonna come quietly, or are you gonna let us hurt you?"

Not the best one-liner I've ever heard, and I open my mouth to say so, but those little prongs are already arching through the air.

Electricity seizes up my veins. Everything hurts, and then it stops and I feel like I've run ten miles. I start to sit up, but the voltage hits me again, and all I see is a boot coming toward my head.

I open my eyes. My bones hurt, every muscle trembling. My mind is hazy. The fuck happened?

"Faster, Cooper! Faster!" someone yells.

Jesser. Taylor. Stun gun. Shit. How long have I been out, and where the fuck am I?

Country music blasts nearby. I'm being jolted back and forth, rolling across what feels like the plastic ridges of the bed of a truck. I was on the porch, now I'm where? I blink hard and turn my pounding head. It *is* a truck bed.

Jesser's face looms over mine, Taylor right next to him. "Hey, he's awake! Guys, Art's up!"

They laugh, and I try to sit up, but my hands and legs are bound together with what feels like zip ties cutting into my flesh. Shit fuck hell, oh this is so not good. Trees rush past overhead on one side of the road but not the other. We're on a ridge somewhere.

Jesser bangs his hand on the roof of the cab as the air blasts around us. "There's a corner coming up. Let's get this over with and get back to town. On three."

Taylor hauls at my shoulders, Jesser my knees, pulling me up until I can see the road flashing by under the tires four feet down. They're not...

They are. Oh shit. No, no, no, nonono. I try to struggle, but my muscles feel as strong as dough. They're gonna throw me, they're gonna fucking *throw* me out of the truck. "No! No, you can't!"

Jesser grins. "Mr. Petrowski has a message for you, Art."

"No! Stop it!"

"He says stop sniffing around his girl. Ready, Taylor?"

"No, please—"

I fly through the air. The sky is gray overhead, rain if I ever saw it. My last view of them is Jesser laughing and Taylor just staring, his mouth open, the stereo blaring in the background as the truck drives on. I fly high through the warm morning air, the wind whistling in my ears, and then fall down, down toward the slope below.

"And don't come back!"

48

Erin

Grace sells pies and bread at the Market on Thursdays, and I help her carry them down, piled high in a big tub between us, both of us hurrying before the clouds overhead actually dump the rain they've been threatening and ruin the whole lot. I'm swaying by the time we set our burdens down.

"D'you mind doing the shopping while I head back?" I find myself asking Grace.

"Yeah, sure, that's fine."

"Do you know what we need?"

"Course, got the list right here. I'll see you back in the kitchen, okay?" She peers at me. "You don't look so good. Are you okay?"

"Fine." I hold in a shiver. "I'll see you back there, right?"

"Right. See you there." She turns and goes, and it's all I can do not to make a beeline for the Market exit.

A truck waits there, black and rusty. It's waiting for me. Dammit.

There aren't a lot of cars around here, gas prices being what they are. Factory trucks going in and out of the depot, yeah, and there's a twice-weekly convoy out of the hills. People from out of town come in and park them on the south side of the Market. But this truck, I know this truck.

"You shouldn't walk alone, Erin. Lemme give you a ride," Chuck Farley offers.

"Since when do you drive around town?"

"I'm picking up supplies from the docks. Get in."

"I'm just on my way home."

"Looking like a thunderstorm in June?"

He leans over and pops the door open. After a moment, I climb in.

"Seat belt." He shifts into gear and starts down the road. It's warm inside, the heat up full blast. "What's got a burr under your saddle?"

"Just tired, that's all."

The streets 'round here used to all take cars, but even now some's got holes in them big enough to puncture a tire. He maneuvers through them with practice. "How's Grace getting on?"

"Fine. Fitting in real well."

"Is she? Good, good." He nods to himself and checks the mirrors. "Wasn't real sure about her going for that job, but glad to hear she's doing well."

"She's a hard worker."

"Oh, she's that alright."

The way he says that irks me. Like it don't mean nothing. "Innovative. Thinks up ideas and follows through."

Another nod. "She's good for that. Real flair for creative stuff. And Simon? How's he doing?"

"Still bad at the reading, but doing okay at science. Did a report on frogs earlier this week."

"Did he now? And Art, how's Art?"

I shrug. "Not on speaking terms with him these days, so you'll have to ask elsewhere."

He seems genuinely surprised at that. "Ain't you? Thought you two were doing well together."

"Not like we're married."

"No, that's true. You ain't."

Whatever he's hedging at, it's damn annoying. "We were never that way, and you know it."

"If you say so." He dodges a collapsed retention wall. No one to clean it up, no one to care. "And you're going to have a little one now, I hear?"

Hasn't everyone? "Guess so."

"You don't sound excited."

"I'm not."

"Why's that?"

"Didn't plan it this way."

"God has a plan for all of us."

"Then God can have this kid and leave me alone." The words are out before I can help myself, but Chuck only raises his eyebrows. "Anyway, it's gonna happen if I want it to or not. Not like I got a say."

I cross my arms and the scenery passes by. About three years back the dockyard barons came through and bulldozed this area to pull in trailers for the workers. Houses and bars, 'cause the river men like to do something on their days off, and what men like to do is pretty damn predictable on all counts.

We pull up next to a building, and Chuck quits the engine. "You wanna talk about it?"

"What do you think?"

"You don't have to snap at me."

"Sorry."

"I just wish you'd tell me if I could help."

"Is that part of God's plan too?"

Chuck sighs and coughs, old smoker what he is. "You helped my family way back, with Abby, with Evan. I'll do what I can to repay you. You know that, Erin. You name it and I will try."

"By sending your daughter to spy on me?" It's a shot in the dark, but the quick breath tells me I've hit bull's-eye. You son of a bitch. His gray eyes show alarm, and I've got him pinned, oh haven't I just. How dare he. "You sent Grace to spy on me, didn't you, 'cause I wasn't going to church no more."

"No."

"Yes, you did. You saw I needed help and said to her that it looked just right. Pay off your debt, and no one gets hurt."

"That weren't it and you know it." His voice thunders in that tiny space. "Now you stop trying to make enemies where you ain't got none, you hear me? I didn't tell Grace to go. She went all on her own 'cause her mama won't quit trying to turn her into Abby and she wanted some space. I am trying to help you, Erin. Will you stop biting my head off before I open my mouth?"

Nothing could make me feel smaller than I do now. Oh God, was I so desperate for someone to be angry at that I thought even the Farleys were conspiring against me? Have I sunk that low?

His words are quiet again, an echo of the previous roar. "Is there anything you need? Doctors? Rides? You name it. Me and Marissa, we owe you for what you done. You say the word and I'll do what I can, we both will. You just have to tell me."

The weight of that hangs around my neck, dragging me down, ever down. Owe and be owed, and all of us debtors, trespassing against those who have trespassed against us...

"How's Evan doing these days?" I ask just to have something to say. "He comes in sometimes, but we don't talk."

"He's here and there. Work's going well."

"Good. That's good."

"Says his arm aches when it rains, but otherwise it's fine."

A raindrop falls on the windshield. Evan's arm'll be aching now, after all these years. Infected bayonet wounds do that to a body, and worse. I couldn't do nothing for his head but put compresses on it, and Marissa said he was different after, but I saved his life, right? I saved it after he saw his sister and went crazy, and now that life is mine for the calling. One good turn repays another. I didn't have to save him, could've left him to rot in the summer heat, but I didn't. Not my friend, and not him.

Grace mentioned that he still screams at night. Different after the war. Always different. Healed, but still remembering with the rain. The drops turn into a downpour, but today I'm dry-eyed. For once.

I choose my words carefully. They cannot be unsaid. "I thank you for thinking of me. Your offer is kind, Chuck, I'm sure. But I think I'd best be going home now. I've stayed out too long as it is, and someone won't like it, if you know what I mean."

He leans over, a sudden move, hand like lead on my shoulder. "You saved my son from the scalpers. Ain't nothing too big in return."

Smile. Smile, Erin, say thank you, and get the hell out of there. You can do it. Ready, go. Now.

My face won't move. The smile won't come under the gaze of

those anxious eyes in a too-wrinkled face, like I'm some sort of angel of the battlefield, saving boys so selflessly. And now he's getting mixed up in my business, which only ever hurts people.

The words come from somewhere deep inside me, from my soul, if I have one. I don't have to think about them because they're already there, welling out of the dark, ready-made.

"I didn't save your boy to have you throw it in my face. I did it for Abby, 'cause she was my friend, 'cause this city didn't need another stinking corpse. If a debt is owed, then he can pay it to me, if he feels he has one to pay. But it ain't yours, and you can't claim it as such. If you really want to help, you'll not ask me again."

The look Chuck gives me now is long, and there is something there I don't understand. "Are you sure, Erin?"

"Don't ask me that. Just don't."

He nods to himself and takes my hands in his pale, rough ones. Scars on every knuckle, but still gentle with me. "I pray for you, Erin. Every night, you are in my prayers, right after my children. The Lord never gives us more than we can handle. Just you remember that, alright? You'll get through."

I leave without replying, lips sealed against everything I wish to God I could say to that as I flee back down the road home. The rain drips down my back, soaks through my coat and all the way to my bones, past the muscles and flesh until I'm nothing but numb.

49

TAYLOR

The head guard at the Market doesn't bat an eye at me coming in late. Being sent to run errands by my other boss actually works as an excuse. Mr. Petrowski really does run this town.

I spot Grace in the crowd as I start my rounds, a basket of groceries on her arm. Her hair's up today, except for one long braid tickling the back of her neck. I reach out and flick it.

"Hey!"

"Hey." I grin. "Your hair's coming down."

"Aww, is it already? It never stays up."

"You look good that way." Like she just shoved it in a bun after waking up wearing only the sheets, with that sexy smile she's giving me right now...

"Do not."

"No, you do. What're you here for this time?"

Grace shifts her bag, falling into step with me as the crowd starts pushing us along. "Not a lot. Just stuff for the bar tonight."

I throw up my hands in mock-sadness. "Too bad I'm banned. Course, you could always feed me at the back door."

"With the rest of the strays." If she flirted any louder, I think I'd have to wear earplugs. Not that I mind. "So, Taylor, what exactly do you do? If you don't mind my asking."

"Well, as you can tell, I'm a guard."

Her hair falls down even more as she shakes her head. "Yeah, I got that part. Kind of hard to miss, with the uniform and all."

"Hey, it's a good uniform."

"If you're into canvas vests." She laughs. "Is that all?"

"Nah, I work for Jeff Petrowski. Part of his inner circle, if you know what I mean."

"So you're an errand boy?"

"Well, I mean, sometimes. Hey, at least I don't have to listen to Erin's bitching all day."

She punches me in the arm lightly. "Maybe she bitched 'cause you didn't do the job as good as me."

Women. They're all friends. "Maybe she just thinks you're cute."

"Hah, yeah, that's it. Not my cooking at all; Erin's just got a thing for pretty girls. Right." We turn the corner and Grace is still there, smiling. "So running errands beats bartending."

"Yeah, well, it's a living. Ryan says I'll get to do more soon."

"Ryan?"

"Ryan Jesser, yeah. He's pretty chill, though not as cool as me, of course. In fact..." Isn't my luck just up today. I spot his leather jacket with a pair of crossbones stitched across the back. "There he is now. Hey, Ryan! Over here a sec!"

Ryan's on the other side of the square talking with Joe and Cooper and another guy I don't know well. I clasp forearms with Ryan and nod to the rest before putting my arm around Grace's waist. "Morning, all. This is Grace Farley. Grace, this is my crew."

Ryan smiles, showing those wolf-fangs of his, and holds out a hand. "You of relation to Chuck Farley?"

"My dad."

They shake hands. "Pleasure to meet you. Any friend of Taylor's is a friend of mine. And these are Joe, Cooper, and Miguel. We all work together."

"Oh, you do guard work too?" Grace asks brightly.

We all exchange a look. "Let's say we're in the business of surveillance," Cooper finally volunteers.

"Transportation," says Miguel.

"Persuasion," Joe snickers.

Ryan flips them off. "Enough from the peanut gallery already. What was it your girl wanted?"

My girl. "Don't know that she wants anything," I say before Grace can start speaking. "I think she just wants to hang out."

She glances at me but smiles. "Uh, yeah. I mean, that'd be pretty neat."

Neat? I knew I liked this girl for a reason. Ryan glances at me. "Hey, you know, Taylor, we usually get a block of seats for the fights. Think Grace here would want to come along?" He slings an arm around her shoulder. "You working then, Grace?"

"Don't know, I haven't asked. I know Erin goes, but maybe she'll want me to keep things open."

"Oh, do you work at Erin's?" What is Ryan getting at? He knows exactly where she works. "Well, you should ask. We always have a free seat or two. Don't we, boys?"

This isn't going how it was supposed to go. I don't want to take Grace to the fights. I want to ask her out somewhere nice. "Come on, Ryan, you can't just jump on her like that."

"Yeah, but she's Erin's girl. I want to know all about her."

I don't like how he says that, like he's mocking me. Grace swivels between the two of us. "What's Erin have to do with anything?"

"Oh, gossip, gossip." Ryan flashes his too-white teeth. "Guess that means you know Art Weber, right?"

Where's he going with this?

Grace thinks it over. "Medium-sized man, red hair and freckles?"

"That's the one."

"Simon's trainer, you mean?"

"Right on all counts. Heard he got fired, though."

"Huh?" That's news to her; it's written all over her face. "What do you mean?"

"Yeah, I didn't hear that," Miguel chimes in. "When'd that happen?"

"Oh, just this morning. He walked out of their training, and I don't think he's going back. Isn't that right, Burkes?"

I don't know what he's playing at, but it isn't funny. Don't call me goody two-shoes, but we aren't supposed to be talking about this, especially not in front of someone like her, and I don't want to be caught double-crossing. "You'd know more than I would, Ryan."

Miguel breaks the silence, running a hand through his frosted hair. "Yeah, but what happened? I thought those two were tight! I have money on Flaherty!"

Joe won't shut up sniggering, and you could scare mountain lions with Ryan's smile. "I wouldn't worry about that. Simple Simon's still as good a bet as he ever was. He's just on his own now."

"Except for Perry." We all look at Grace, standing there with her eyes big as plates. "He's still got Mick Perry to train him, even if Art quit."

Ryan's smile gets a little wider. "That's true, I guess he does. Better hope he stays away from Erin."

"What are you talking about?" There's a sharpness in Grace's voice I haven't heard before. "'Stays away from Erin'?"

Ryan leans in close, and I think if my fists clenched any harder, I'd start breaking knuckles. "You ever notice, darling, that Erin Livingston don't live in the same world as the rest of us?"

"Don't be ridiculous. Of course she does."

The fuck is he getting at? Because if it's what I think he is...

Without taking his eyes off her, Ryan snaps out, cool as you please, "Joe, where were you last night?"

He starts lighting a cigarette. "Watching Erin's place."

"When'd she go to bed?"

"Eleven fifteen."

"And when'd Grace here go?"

"About twelve, after doing the washing up with Simon."

"And Taylor, where were you yesterday afternoon?"

I know that we're still in the Market and there's people all around us, but they're staying away and we've got this corner to ourselves and I can feel the hairs on the back of my neck standing up. Grace's mouth is open, and Ryan isn't smiling anymore. He's whispering words that only she and I can hear.

"Take a guess, sweetie. You're something else, Grace Farley. Lived in this town all your life but don't seem to know how it works. I know who your family is, and I know that you've been chatting with Taylor here for the past few mornings. It's my job to know these things, and it's your job to listen right now. You go home and you tell

Erin that Art won't be bothering her anymore. And if she wants to know more, she knows exactly where to ask."

"And what if I want to know more?" White-knuckled fists; she's got balls, I'll give her that.

"Then you can walk across the street anytime and we'll work out a deal, just you and I. Payment in cash or ass, darling, and if you're good enough, maybe I'll even throw in a free ticket to the fights."

"You're disgusting."

"And you know where to find me."

He lets her go, and she looks ready to murder him. "You touch me again and I'll tell my brother Evan."

"Ain't scared of your crazy brother, sweetling. Now get back to the kitchen to go make some sandwiches, and don't forget to close your curtains at night!"

Grace shoves us both off, hawks a wad, and spits on Ryan's shirt with the force of a bullet.

He laughs, which is almost a pity because I'd take any excuse to pound the living shit out of him right now, any at all. Instead, he wipes the gob off with a hand and chuckles. "Kinky one, aren't you." Grace stalks away, head held high. "Don't think she likes me, do you?"

If I look at his greasy face for one more second, I'm liable to do something I'll regret. "Go fuck yourself, Jesser."

"Ooh, looks like I hurt someone's feelings," I hear behind me as I walk away. "Think she'll come by tonight, or I'll have to pay a visit? What do you think, Miguel? The cute ones are always bitches."

50

Grace

I make it into the house just as the rain hits. I don't think I'll ever get used to coming home to an unlocked door, but Erin said no one will touch this place, and I believe it after what that repulsive boy...

Doesn't live in the same world as the rest of us, does Erin.

Thumping dough is good for the body and soul. Hard kneading makes good bread, which is a relief, as otherwise I'd probably never get any. Goddamned stupid men and their goddamned stupid assumptions that I'm some goddamned stupid whore for them to get their goddamned kicks from.

We're watching you, oh yeah, I bet they just are, and loving every minute of it. Pervs. This whole town is watching this damn house. Can't go ten steps from the door before someone's pumping me for information about Simon, his techniques, his training, like I know anything about it.

Though I'd rather they hound me than bother Erin. She's all hollow eyes, jumping at loud noises, staying out of the kitchen when the food's cooking 'cause she about gets sick every time she gets too close.

In the evenings, when it gets noisy in the front room, I can see her true feelings. She asks all those men about their wives and mothers and children if they've got them, fixes all their little problems, dispenses advice like she cares, but she doesn't. Not really. And it shows when they start singing songs half an hour to closing and she laughs, but it's like she has to remember to bother first, smiling only with her mouth.

My mama always said that when you don't want to do something no more you should stop before it breaks the camel's back. Quit before it drags you down. That's why my mama started her café: she was sick and tired of housework. Course, she didn't ask me my opinion, but I can quit too, now can't I? Huh.

I leave the bread to rise and begin tidying up the front room. Simon's desk is getting grimy, so I wipe that down too. It rocks on uneven legs, the drawers tipping open. Just a little bit.

Hmm. No harm in looking. Not when I'm the only one here. Right?

Wouldn't help my argument if I added that I been dying to, would it? Ah, well. No harm, no foul. Erin's not home, so no one's watching me. Ugh, just ugh. Plus, if Taylor stops talking to me, I'm not getting answers any other way.

First drawer's pens and pencils, sharpener, paper clips. Even a stapler. Alrighty. Makes sense; he is in school after all. Second drawer sticks and won't come open. Third drawer has a box of bullets, small caliber, and a dead spider. I try the second drawer again, 'cause what you can't have is always greener. It seems to be stuck fast, though. I tug harder.

It finally pulls free in an explosion of paper, little bits and big pieces, flying through the air and drifting to the floor. Oh lord, what was I thinking? What if Erin comes home right now? What if someone sees I was spying on Simon's things and thinks I do this all the time?

They're a hodgepodge collection of old betting slips, receipts for prize money, and notes written on every color paper there is. Notes to Simon. Get 'em all, don't let a single one escape!

I read them without meaning to, words jumping from page to my mind without reason stopping them in between. I can almost hear the voices in the grimy papers, grease-stained and scribbled.

i i a lot of money off ur fite. just wanted 2 say THANK U! KEEP GOING!

Dont forget to tuck your chin! I almost cryd when you went down but you came back up, I knew you wud. Also, next time keep your elbows closer or theyll get hit. Good luck next time.

They're all that sort of thing, good-luck notes and encouragement and people saying how much they love watching him fight.

Except for one: *Meet me tonight after you close.*

Neat handwriting, pen, on a scrap of newspaper. Looks like Simon has a girl. Does Erin know? Does anyone?

I hear the footsteps just in time to close the drawer tightly and clutch my dust rag. The door next to me opens and I jump back. Nope, not anywhere near that desk, why do you ask? Just about to clean those tables, just like I was supposed to.

"Did the rain catch you?" The question dies on my lips. Erin's soaked to the skin. Already a puddle's forming under her feet, turning the floorboards dark. I don't know where she's looking, but it's not at me. "Erin...?"

For the first time in days, she doesn't startle. So slow it seems unnatural, she meets my eyes and then looks down at herself. "I'm cold."

It's like she's surprised to realize rain makes you wet. She starts to shiver.

I'm off in a flash, water on to boil, setting her on a chair and putting a brick in the firebox. Blankets, blankets, wool for preference, but anything warming will do. If I were a blanket, where would I hide?

I hesitate at the door to Erin's room. I've never been in there. No reason to, none at all. She keeps the door shut, and going in would be snooping in a way that somehow reading Simon's notes wasn't quite. Simon's a public figure, but Erin's more private than anyone I've ever known.

But she needs dry clothes.

It's not locked, her door, and that halfway surprises me. *Doesn't live in the same world.* Low bed, neatly made, pillowcases wearing thin to nothing. Plastic chair under the window and a closet in the corner where I find an old wool blanket. Lavender leaves fly everywhere when I shake it out. A quick rummage through a peeling chest of drawers reveals underwear, bras, and finally a pair of corduroy pants. There's an old sweater by the foot of the bed, and I snag that too.

Erin's shaking in front of the stove. I hold the dry clothing out in front of me. "You need to get changed. Get out of those clothes or you'll get sick."

Not a muscle twitches. She's staring at the flames like her life depends on it.

"You'll get sick," I repeat. "You have to get dry or you won't get warm. You can go behind the curtain if you want to." Nothing. I can hear her teeth chattering from here. "Erin. Erin!"

I wave a hand in front of her face, and that gets her attention. She's white as a sheet, hands like ice as I wrap the blanket around her legs. She barely protests, pushing me away with no strength.

"Come on, now. Don't be a child. If you're going to go out in the rain, you gotta get dry somehow." I sound like my mama, scolding her for being silly. Don't want to admit how much her blank face is scaring me. "Get a grip, Erin. You have to change."

"Don't have to." It's the first thing she's said since entering the kitchen, no louder than a whisper.

"Don't be stupid. Of course you do."

"No, I don't." Still won't look at me.

I undo an overall strap. "Yes, you darn well do."

"No, I don't!" She pushes me away, a wild look in her eyes. I stumble back as this madwoman snatches the blanket from the floor, backing up to the stove. "Don't tell me what to do!"

"What are you talking about? I'm telling you you'll catch your death if you don't change! Have you lost your mind?"

"Stop saying that!"

"No." Aha. Yes, I've seen this before, and now I know what to do. Time to take charge. "Go change your clothing right now or so help me I'll change it myself, whether you want me to or not." She backs away from my shouting. "You will change into the dry things I got for you and then drink a hot cup of coffee, and heaven help me if you argue. I don't want to hear a single word right now!"

One more step and she's in the corner. I yank Simon's wash

curtain across and toss her clothes over the top. There's towels back there already and she can use them. I'm not dealing with a tantrum.

Doesn't *live* in the same world.

I find a basin and start heating water. Bad as my brother, she's being. But she's not my brother, and I won't stand for it.

Soon as she's out and changed, I've got her feet in a basin and a blanket around her shoulders. Her hair drips on her lap, and I take a dry towel to it, then make coffee and get her to drink that too. Finally, I heat up yesterday's leftovers and stick a bowl of them in her hands.

I've finished the second kneading before she finally shifts and pulls the towel off her head. The coffee's gone, but she's yet to touch the stew.

"You going to eat that?" I ask. "You need your strength. When my cousin was pregnant, she was having a terrible time keeping things down, but the doctor said—"

"I know what to do. I don't need you to mother me." It's the first time that I've heard her anger directed at me.

"Well, la-ti-da, aren't we such a grown-up miss all the sudden." I can hardly believe I'm saying it, but if that's what it takes to bring her back, then, well, that's what it takes.

"Excuse me?" You could slice bricks with that voice.

"I'm not your nursemaid, Erin. I'm just trying to help 'cause I don't wanna run this place alone. You're not paying me enough for that."

"Hah." Such a tiny noise I'm not even sure I heard it. After a while the spoon clinks against the bowl. "You're not my babysitter."

"Lucky for you; I'd want higher wages."

She definitely laughs this time. "You're about the only one who doesn't want the job, I think."

"Am I?"

She goes back to her bowl, staring out the window while the rain pounds down. When I finally finish cleaning the front room, she's still where I left her, bowl cradled in her arms, fast asleep. Across the street, a man sitting doesn't move from his post on the rotting front porch. Only the flare of the lighter every once in a while shows that he hasn't also nodded off. He only arrived since Erin got home.

Screw you, Taylor and your jumped-up jerk friends, I don't need you for information. Screw all of you. I knew something was up since the day I got here, but this is the last straw. You want to tell Erin some big message? You damn well knock on the door and tell her yourself. I'm not your messenger girl. I won't ever sink that low.

51

I feel fried. The skin on my chest hurts like hell. Everything's stiff, even my eyelids. Christ, it's been a long time since I've felt like this. Like I ran twenty miles this morning and topped it off by falling off a cliff. Jesus.

I open my eyes. Everything's gray. Gray sky, gray trees stripped of all leaves. Is it dusk already? No, not yet, but getting well there. I shiver involuntarily. How long have I been lying here? And where is "here," anyway?

My head throbs, and I reach up to clutch it. My wrists are still bound together, and my temple's sticky. Brown clumps come away on my fingers. Blood? Dirt? Maybe both. I'm lying in the woods at the base of a ridge in the middle of fuck-all nowhere. Definitely both.

They threw me from a truck. Taylor, who I used to call my friend, who I got a job, threw me out at high speed to roll down a hill and die. What the hell? What's happened to my life? Why did those two come for me? What the everlasting fuck did I do to them?

I can feel that my knife is still in my boot, though, the idiots. Incompetent even when they're winning. My fingers can barely move, but if I strain real hard, I can just manage to slip my fingers between the leather and my sodden jeans until they brush metal. My bonds are just plastic zip ties; they snap on contact with the blade. Amateurs.

Blood rushes back into my hands and feet so fast that it hurts almost more than the rest of my bruises combined. Almost. Christ, I hurt all over. Maybe my head will fall off and leave me in peace. I clutch it with both hands, try to stop the spinning, suck in my stomach against the way it lurches when I sit up. No one's kicking me back down, at least. Anything broken? Don't think so. Maybe my wrist, or is that Sunday morning's sprain I'm still feeling?

I make it to my feet, an experience I'm not in a hurry to repeat. Rolling down the hill at twenty miles an hour wasn't the worst beating I've ever taken, but if anyone thinks it was a breeze, I suggest they try getting kicked in the balls repeatedly while being electrically shocked, because that's probably a good comparison. I'm lucky I don't have a fever or something, or my maybe I do and I can't feel it? Maybe that was their plan, a slow death. At least it didn't rain. I'd really have been fucked if it had.

I need to get back to town, but how? What direction is it even in? Let's see. I rolled downhill when I hit the ground, so that must mean the road is uphill, and if I can find the road, I can follow it...

Well, what the hell. If I can still walk, I'm going. Maybe that was just a warning, maybe they meant for me to survive. Just a little scare to tell me not to piss people off.

What the hell did I do so wrong, anyway?

I shove my hands in my jacket pockets—and touch paper. Hello, what's this? 'Cause it's not mine, I'll tell you that for sure. I read it.

Read it again. My jaw actually drops.

Oh hell no. Expelled from town? Are you kidding me? Are you joking? What is this, high school?

I'm going back if it's the last thing I ever do. Because fuck this.

52

Grace

The side door bangs, and I about jump out of my skin. I barricaded it, middle of the day though it is, 'cause Erin might live in a different world, but I sure don't.

"Erin, you there?" The voice is muffled, but definitely Simon. I unblock the door.

"She's upstairs having a nap. It's just me down here."

"Right. Just a sec." Simon drops something and dashes past me.

Mick comes in the door and closes it behind him. Meanwhile, I can hear Simon's footsteps slamming up the stairs, then slowing near the top. The plastic bag he dropped landed on my feet, spilling open a little. I pick up one of the handles, peering inside.

"Oh my lord!"

Mick Perry scoops the bag out of my hands. "Don't worry about it, Grace."

"Are those really...?"

Simon's back, skidding to a halt. "She's sleeping. She's fine. Are you okay, Grace?"

"No!" I point at the bag that Mick still holds. "Are those real?"

"Yeah?"

I squeeze my eyes shut. Lord, gimme strength. "Simon Flaherty, where the hell did you get scalps?"

He and Mick exchange a look. "Couple of guys shoved them in my hands when I got out of training."

Mick actually reaches into the bag and pulls out a braid of pink hair. "They're definitely Art's."

"Those are *Art's?*" My voice squeaks a little, and both turn to look at me. "I mean, he took scalps?"

"He didn't advertise it much after the fact, but yeah, he did." Mick drops it. "I remember when he took that one."

"Wait a minute." This has all gone surreal, stranger than fiction. "You did it too?"

"No. My unit was divided on that, actually. Art was in the 'for' group. Obviously."

"Why's Erin taking a nap?" Simon asks me.

"Got caught in the rain and I think she took cold. Why did someone give you Art's scalps?"

Simon's getting impatient. "Send a message. Did she say anything about today?"

"What—no, wait, Simon, what did you mean? Who gave them to you?"

"Dunno." He shrugs and looks from Mick to me. "That's the problem."

Mick ties the bag handles in a knot and tosses it on Simon's desk. It lands with a soft *whump* and the crinkle of plastic. Mentally, I cringe.

Simon continues, a dog with a bone. "Mick was in the shop, he didn't see. One of them was my size and was smoking. The other had blond hair."

"Male? Female?" I ask. "Facial hair? Defining features?"

The look he gives me is sullen as he crosses his arms. "Fine, one was an adult, and the other was Finnley Cooper. He's half a head shorter than me, and he had on a red sweatshirt."

Cooper, red sweatshirt, and an older guy who smoked.

Oh damn. Those jerks at the Market.

"They handed me the bag when I was walking home from training and said it was a present from Art. Said they were from Petrowski and love to Erin. That's why I thought..."

"A message," Mick mutters, then sniffs. "Is something burning?"

"Hell!"

Two of the saucepans are boiling over, and the egg timer dings just as I reach it. I don't have enough hands for this without Erin. Stir, move, turn the heat down, take it out, and let it cool. Half an hour to open and I ain't ready yet, not alone. Those two are gabbing away, no help from them. That's men for you.

"...do you think, Grace?"

"What?"

"You talked to Art. I know you did," Simon says. "What do you think it means?"

"The scalps? They did something to him, that seems obvious. But what?"

"Why is it obvious?" Simon asks.

"'Cause he's competition, isn't he?" Honestly, those two are staring like their brains leaked out. "Please tell me you've noticed the way Art watches Erin." Nope. "Oh come on, guys, wake up."

"I'm not saying he don't," Simon protests, "but she don't like him back. And anyway, who told Petrowski?"

"He told himself. This place is being watched. We're all being watched right now. Haven't you looked out the front window these past few days?" I try not to sound bitter. "They took him away, did something to him. I'm surprised they didn't give you a note, Simon."

Simon blinks at Mick, and Mick unties the bag. "He did."

"What's it say about Art? Does it say what they did? Where he is?" Simon says.

Mick scans it over, shaking his head. "No, it just says he's expelled from town."

"You mean, like, banned?" I ask.

Someone taps me on the shoulder. It's Erin, still in her pajamas and looking pissed. "The fuck do you mean, Art's banned?"

53

Erin

"Erin!" Grace jumps about a foot. The look on all their faces is priceless, surprise and guilt spread across them equally. "Did we wake you up? You feeling okay?"

"I'm fine."

Simon makes a snatch for the note, but Mick gives it to me. Cheap paper, with handwriting I recognize at the bottom. A picture of Art stares at me above the writing, mouth open, screaming something, what looks like a fight crowd in the background. He looks deranged, unhinged, dangerous. Maybe he is these days.

I crumple it up. "So Petrowski's finally decided to do something about him."

"You could say that," Mick replies. "Want a bag full of scalps?"

I focus on the plastic shopping bag that's appeared in front of me. "Get those out of my house right now."

He shuts his mouth, nods, and takes them out, door swinging shut behind him. Will miracles never cease.

Simon's eyes are intense, waiting for my next move. "What are we gonna do? Petrowski's taken Art."

"Petrowski himself, or his henchmen?"

"Oh shit." Grace claps her hand over her mouth, but too late, we all heard those two little words.

Simon zeroes in on her, dog with a bone. "What? What is it?"

"I know who took him." Her eyes are wide, darting between us.

"Who?" Simon urges.

"Taylor Burkes and his friend Ryan something."

The air hisses between Simon's teeth. "Jesser."

"Maybe, yeah. They were bragging about it at the Market this morning. Well, I mean, not saying it outright, but they were saying you had a fight with Art, so he wasn't coming back and—"

"Why were you talking to them?"

Simon's voice is staccato like gunshots, but Grace is already firing back. "'Cause they talked to me and I'm not so rude as to ignore that."

"Ain't rude when it's Burkes."

"Oh, is that so? Your enemy is my enemy? By what law?"

"By the fact that you're working here! He's scum!"

"You, Simon Flaherty, are not my boss, never have been, never will be. It's a damn free country and I will talk to who I please, and if you wanna go stomping around about something, why don't you go stomp on those two who are causing the problems!"

"They say anything else helpful?" I put in before they can really get going. Simon doesn't swallow bones, he chews them. This could go for hours if I let it.

"Not that I caught. I'm pretty certain that's what they were hinting at. Pretty pleased with themselves, you know?"

"I bet. Name of Jesser rings a bell." I focus on Simon. "Didn't you bounce a boy by that name pretty hard a while back?"

A sullen look. "Yeah."

"Too hard, maybe. He don't seem to like you much."

"I was protecting you."

"I got guns for that. Bouncing's to protect the business, not me." Ain't no venom in my rebuke, though, 'cause I understand, I do. I look around. Tables aren't set, food's not out, and lo and behold, it's ten 'til five. "Besides, I fail to see what Art going missing has to do with not getting things ready to go for here. Opening's soon."

Grace takes the cue and bustles off. I make to move when Simon finally gets his thought train into words.

"But Art..."

"Can take care of himself."

"But they'll kill him!" he bursts out, louder than I think he meant to.

I fix him a look, good and hard. There is a time for truth, and there is a time for honesty. Now is a time for the latter. "Art is a grown man. He should've known better than to go around doing the things he did. I tried to warn him, but he felt it worth the risk not to listen. Now he'll pay. That's what risk means. You win or you pay."

Simon's incensed. "How can you say that? So what if he's been weird lately? He's been around here forever, helping you, training me. How can you just abandon him like that?"

"And what do you want me to do, Simon? Tell him to come here, put him in the cellar, and feed him scraps in hopes that this'll all blow over? This house is watched, I am watched. *You're* watched by this entire damn town."

"Someone else could take..."

"Like who?"

"There's places—"

"Then Art knows them and will go there! And if you're smart," I add, "you won't try to find them."

He follows this thought like a puppy. "'Cause if I do, others will follow me."

"Bingo."

"So I can't do anything."

I pick up an abandoned dish towel and fold it. "Correction: you can do many things, but helping Art is not among them." I throw the crumpled letter in a trash can and push the hair out of my eyes. "Not the way you want to, anyway. Nobody can help him now but himself."

Simon's hand brushes my shoulder as he leans in. "Then I have a better solution: we can leave. He was right, we need to get out or Petrowski will kill both of us, and you know it. We can get on the next convoy out of this town and be gone. One leaves tonight. We can distract the watchers and get away. Escape."

Goose bumps rise on my arms at that word, a breath of fresh air down the back of my neck. "And just how would we distract them, Simon?"

"Well, if we ain't coming back..." He licks his lips. Nervous?

Apprehensive? "Torch this place with a bang, take a few potshots at anyone who tries to follow, and go. Convoys don't stick around when there's trouble. They'll leave quick, and if all goes well, they'll leave with us on it."

"Petrowski will close the town and have the roadblocks on high alert," I point out. Am I actually considering this? Have I lost my mind? "They're in his pocket."

"But he can't touch the convoys. Even he won't risk the bad side of the cartels up north. They cut this town off, he's finished, right? Be killing his own goose or whatever. So he can't do a thing once they're past the checkpoint at city limits and then we're home free. If not today, there's convoys every couple of days, we can leave anytime."

God, do I want to believe him. I want to run away and watch this town disappear into nothing. I want to be swallowed up by the darkness of the woods and never have to see this place again. Want it so bad it hurts. Simon's words whisper in my brain, and they sound like paradise. Escape. Go. Never come back. God, I can even see it in my mind's eye: striking a match and watching the bedrooms burn...

Something explodes deep in my mind, a bright light where it has been so dark for so long. It sounds so easy, just to leave.

"He'd kill us if he found us."

"Would that be worse?"

Our eyes meet, his washed of all color in this cold room. I open my mouth, but I can't answer that question because I know the answer and he knows it too, and when did he grow up so much? When did he start carrying my burdens?

"You two will need rifles, or something with a bigger clip. Otherwise, you'll run out of ammo first."

Simon whirls around and I meet Mick's eyes as he emerges from the shadows by the kitchen. Don't matter how much he heard, I guess. He ain't the tattling type.

"Anyway," Mick continues steady, "you need tickets to ride the convoys, and they're damn expensive. You can't buy them in advance, or he'll know. And what are you going to do when you get out? Where are you going to go?"

Mick's right. God, I know he's right, even.

Simon's shoulders hunch. "We could do lots of things. We'll tell people we're siblings."

"You don't look a thing alike."

"Engaged."

"And then?"

"I got hands, don't I?" Simon mutters. "I'll find something. We'll find something."

Mick's eyes slide back to me, unreadable.

Simon's barely audible now. It'd never work, only I don't want to admit that yet and neither does he. Because... "Just think about it, okay? We don't have to go tonight, but we could. We can." He pushes open the door to the kitchen, letting in the rattle of cutlery and clunking pans.

I fight to put the bite back in my voice. "You done standing there, Mick, or am I gonna have to start charging rent?"

He tips his head sideways, studying me. "Are you going to think about it, then?"

What does he care? I don't trust Mick, don't trust his motives. He don't like me, so why would he help? Because helping me will help Simon? "Maybe."

"Petrowski will come after you."

"I know that."

"A couple shots at his boys won't be enough for you to get away. You'd have to take out half the town to make it stick."

"How do you know?"

"Because..." He trails off, staring over my shoulder, horrified. "Holy fuck. He's here. Right now. On the sidewalk out front, Petrowski's here."

What? No.

Him.

No. No fucking way.

The clock strikes five, and I ain't ready yet, we ain't ready, ain't nothing ready for this. Oh God, how could it be?

He's here.

The rag twists through my fingers, pinching enough to let me breathe. Thinking time's over. Move or die, my voice a hiss between my teeth. "Get Grace up front to open the door. Whatever she's doing in the back can wait, and for Christ's sake, Mick, get Simon out of here. Out the back. Don't let him see. For anyone's sake, don't let Simon see or know who's here. I gotta get changed. I'm not ready for this."

Mick ducks a nod. I don't hang around before I'm back up the stairs, my bones aching with every step, panic rising in my throat.

Escape. *Escape.* It wouldn't work, of course. Jeff would hunt me down and drag me back and kill Simon and me both and laugh the whole time, I know he would.

But would it be worse than what's happening now? That's the thing, see. I don't even know anymore.

He's here.

54

Simon

Mick's got my backpack in one hand, my shirt collar in the other.

"The hell is this for?" I ask him.

"Emergency training."

"I got homework."

"You ain't going to school tomorrow." He finally drops my collar and locks the gate behind us. But soon as that's done, he's shoving me along again.

I try again. "Erin won't like that."

"She won't care, trust me."

"Why?"

"Why won't she, or why trust me?"

I hate it when people play mind games, and Mick don't usually do it, but there's something he ain't telling me. Maybe Erin told him to get out and he's taking me as revenge, or maybe those scalps spooked him as much as they did me.

"Do you think my idea will work?" I ask.

"For Erin?"

"Yeah. You heard it."

He looks left and right, and I get the picture. "Talk about it later."

"After training?"

"Yeah. You're staying the night, seeing as you're not going to school anyway and I have to run your morning workout. I've got a spare bed you can use."

"Don't Kaylla sleep there?"

"Jesus, no. She's got a husband somewhere."

"She's married?"

"Please don't tell me you think she's my girlfriend."

"Do you think Art will try to find me?"

We're onto the street at last, heading toward his place in the twilight, and Mick finally stops shoving me, though he sticks close. "Honestly? Yes. That's why we left by the back. We'll lie low until tomorrow."

"But the note said he'd been warned to stay away. So why would he bring me into it?"

"Because the punishment for not getting caught is nothing at all, and if you understand that, you understand Art. He never does expect to fail. Look, forget him. He won't be watching the fight, there's no way. Not with how things stand now."

Shit. Art's been to all my fights, and as pissed as I was with him, him not being there hits me in the gut. He should be. He trained me. Even if after Saturday I don't see him ever again, he should be there for that one.

"Simon? You okay?"

"I'm fine." I kick a rock, and it hits a rotting fence post. Then I kick the fence post. It falls over in slow motion, and I wish I could stand there and kick every last one of them. Nothing is right and nothing is fair, but I thought Art would at least still be at my fight. "He's been to all of them, ever since I started fighting official. No, before that, when he put me in a couple street matches without telling Erin. He's seen them all. The ones that count, anyway."

"Are there some that don't?" Mick's eyes are too sharp, watching me, always watching, always looking. He gets me, and sometimes he gets too much.

"Not like he came to school and watched me fight on the playground."

"That happen a lot?"

"Enough."

"Recently?"

"Not since I was fourteen. When they started making us pay tuition, the principal said if I fought again, I'd be expelled. And Erin said she'd whoop my ass if that happened."

"Not that she could." Mick snorts, and he's not wrong, she couldn't have, but I knew what she meant. She meant "don't you dare fuck this up." The school didn't have no money from the government, 'cause Petrowski kept killing their officials every time they came to town, so Erin was paying out the nose to keep me in class, and she was doing something she hated to earn that money, so if I fucked up, it'd mean I didn't care about her. And I did. And there weren't no more fights after that.

But not because I was trying, no, but because there just *weren't*. Of the boys staying on, only Connor was left of his gang, and maybe the principal told him the same thing he'd told me. Maybe it was just too much trouble without an audience. But that was that and we didn't fight. Don't.

Not at school, anyway.

Every once in a while, Connor and I'd do it out in secret at the old playground. Just the two of us, no weapons, see who's better. Not often. Maybe every month or so. He'd tell me when and I'd show up, big dumb ox that I am. Usually neither of us won.

Haven't done that in months, though. Not since I wiped the mats with his face in the ring in August. He didn't like that, no, he didn't.

But now we're gonna try it again, the same old tired fight, only this time we've got shiny knives, see, gonna cut each other up. Just a little, just enough. No punches, no kicks, no wrestling in the dirt until we're hot and tired and sick from exhaustion, not this time.

This time, this fight, it's for real.

You don't get much more real than this.

Mick's shop looms out of the darkness, tinted windows and that stupid sign he keeps up, like anyone really believes this is a pawnshop, yeah, right. He opens the door for me, and I head in to where Art won't find me. Won't no one find me. Except Petrowski, of course, 'cause he finds everybody eventually.

55

Grace

Our first customer of the night is the one man I never thought I'd be serving here. Stew for him, a healthy-sized serving, and a glass of the expensive stuff. Only the best, yessir, the very same. Petrowski's elbows stick out as he goes at his dinner with spoon and fork. His hair is black-turning-gray, shining in our fancy electric lights.

Erin's lights. Not ours.

The regulars trickle in, each of them double-taking at the door. I serve them as usual while keeping an eye on the man at the bar. The man of the hour. Customers chew and mutter, the snap of cards the loudest sound here. No one raises their voice as I try to keep up with too many orders, because Erin's yet to come down from wherever she disappeared to. Maybe she went to sleep again. Maybe she's sick from being in the rain. Maybe she can't face the music and is leaving me to do it for her, because I really appreciate that, don'tcha know.

Whine whine whine. Shut up, brain.

Nathaniel Greene catches my wrist as I go past. "She here tonight?" he whispers.

I shake my head and whisper back, "Dunno."

It takes him a moment to find the right words. "Wouldn't blame her."

"I'm sure she knows."

Returning to the bar, I find Petrowski holding up his glass. I pour him another measure with the greatest of care. Is he going to pay? Is this going to be okay by Erin? Even so, I'd rather be on the good side of him and apologize to her later. He's got heavy knuckles, the kind my daddy says are the sign of a fighter. Been busted too many times to look nice, see? And that nose's been broken once or twice, by the look of it. He's yet to say a word beyond ordering food. Silent and watchful, like father, like son. Wish I hadn't thought that. Gives me the willies to think of them as flesh and blood.

What's seen cannot be unseen, though. On my next run back to the bar, he's wiping his mouth on a napkin, wrinkling his nose. Same nose as Simon, same eyebrows, jawline. Hair's night to day, though.

Erin's kid's going to have black hair, same as both of them, though the eyes are anybody's guess whether they'll be brown or blue. Both of them are rather sallow, but hers probably 'cause her father was Asian. Or maybe native? Looks it anyway, at least. She's got those slanted eyes like they sometimes do. And Petrowski, well, he's got Simon's eyes, or vice versa.

The first wave's in, and it looks like I have a second to breathe. I gotta find Erin. The real rush is going to start soon, and I don't care to tackle that alone. Don't really want to be doing any of this alone, truth be told, 'cause Petrowski's watching me, there's a couple of men across the street watching me, and everyone else in that bar's glaring out of the corner of their eyes. This is stupid going on ridiculous, but I don't got much choice.

First chance I see, I run upstairs to knock on her door.

"Erin, you in there?" No answer. "We're getting full up downstairs, and I'll be needing a hand in a minute. I can keep track of Petrowski if you like. He's drinking the good stuff. It's not a trouble for me to keep his glass full, but they need you down there. Everyone's asking about you."

The door swings open, revealing Erin's pale features. "You said *he's* drinking?"

He. She doesn't ever call him by name, does she? Just says *he* with that twist of her lips that says there's only one *he* she'll ever refer to.

"On his second glass."

"Fuck." She pulls her sweater closer, shrinking back for a hair's breath of a moment. "Right. I'm coming. Sorry. Just collecting my thoughts."

"That's fine."

"I'll take care of him."

"It's no trouble—"

"It will be. Trust me." I can nearly see that smile snap in place as she hurries past. As if I needed a reminder: Erin's a professional.

The bar turns toward her as she enters, flowers in the sunshine. Petrowski stands like a monster emerging from the forest. His smile is so cold I swear to God my own heart nearly freezes seeing him tracing Erin. Possessive like you wouldn't believe.

"Erin, I just dropped by because I heard your cooking had improved. I see the rumor's true."

She sweeps through the room to tuck herself behind the bar. "Then you'd best thank Grace here. She's been taking a turn at the griddle these last few nights."

"I did wonder when you learned to use anything but a frying pan." He laughs like he just told a joke or something. A couple of men join him under their breath, which is odd because that wasn't funny at all. It was rude and condescending.

Erin laughs too. "Oh, I couldn't do that. No one'd get enough fat for their daily vitamins if I did."

"And how's our prizefighter? How's Simon doing?"

Our. I'm staring, but it's hard to stop.

"His homework, if he knows what's good for him. That's his job here."

"A regular scholar." Another laugh. My jaw is clenched. Work it loose, calm down. Pour another glass of beer and hurry it up already. "He'll be venturing out among the unschooled tonight?"

Erin picks up the bottle and tops his glass, smooth as butter. "Not with that book report due, sorry. You finished that bowl? Have another."

The bell over the door jingles, and I nearly drop the mug I'm holding. Chatter begins to start up again here and there, louder than before. Nathaniel scoots his chair so his back is exactly to Petrowski, and another man does the same, a little bit at a time. No one can seem to forget who's in their midst; even in the middle of rush, no of them take the seat next to him. Erin leans against the bar the whole time, jawing away, looking for all the world like there's nowhere she'd rather be. For me is left the rest of the room. Wait and serve, yes and no, of course, coming up, here's your change and have a good night, we'll be seeing you now, y'hear?

Then Darryl Hensley scoots his chair back at the wrong moment, and the stack of plates I'm carrying go flying through the air. They hit the floor with a crash loud enough to wake the dead, shards everywhere, sticky with the remains of dinner, me on my hands and knees in the middle of the mess. Silence descends. Waiting, watching silence.

From the bar, clearly audible, comes a single word. "Idiot."

Darryl's face goes red, a slow coloring from the neck up. "I'm sorry. I didn't see you there."

"It's fine." I smile and try to mean it, picking myself up. "Don't worry about it."

Erin's already hurrying toward me with the wash bucket. Petrowski's hand shoots out and clamps around her wrist. "Leave it."

"I was just gonna pick up the—"

"Leave it, I said. She was clumsy. That's what's the matter with you, Erin. You're too soft."

Under the smile, Erin's got that rabbit look I see whenever she thinks I'm not looking, only now she's got it in front of everyone, totally visible. She's panicking inside, doesn't know where to go, what to do, and he's still got her arm like he's any right to it. Everyone's staring at them and something's gotta give.

"But I—"

I take the bucket out of her hand. "It's fine. Don't you worry about a thing, Erin. I got it. We'll soon get this place cleaned up."

Darryl stands. "I'll pay for it, it was my fault."

Credit to me, my smile never wavers. "We'll talk about it later. Let me just take care of this first and we'll sort it out."

I busy myself on the floor, but something's changed in the air, the atmosphere; it's gone low and deep. A grim-faced woman starts to stand, but the man next to her pulls her down, whispering in her ear.

Me, I'm on the floor piling shards in a bucket, a shrill clatter that just makes things worse.

Petrowski pushes his chair back and all eyes are on him, the air taut as wires. You wouldn't find a better audience at a theater.

"You'll come upstairs with me, Erin?"

"Now, you know I got a business to run here." She makes a go at chuckling, but it falls flat. She has to know we're watching. God, she has to know.

"Seems they've been managing without you tonight. They can manage a little more."

Erin keeps polishing a glass like she's been doing all evening. "I'd hate to impose on Grace any more than I already have. It's not her job to run things alone."

"You're the owner, aren't you?" He raps his fingers on the bar. "Make it her job."

His boots thump across the floor and all the way up the stairs. We can all hear the door closing at the top because the place has gone silent.

"Erin..." Nathaniel makes a move, and his tablemates catch him just in time.

"Shut up!" someone hisses.

"Erin, please listen—"

A hand clamps over his mouth, and Nathaniel's friends start dragging him for the door, him struggling all the while. When it clicks behind him, we all turn back to Erin, she who's the ringmaster of this stage.

She looks so tired, mask slipping away for the second time tonight, second time ever, maybe. Do they ever see her sad or unhappy here? Does she ever show them that side of her, or has she always played it too close for that?

Someone else tries. "Erin, if there's anything we can do..."

Erin pushes a strand of hair out of her eyes, and something flashes in them. "Yeah, there is." We all hold our breaths. "You can leave."

Shocked silence, then, "What?"

"Go home. Get out."

A muttering sweeps across the room. "Erin, it's not that—"

Her voice creaks. "I said get out." She takes off her apron and throws it on the floor. No smiles now, just empty eyes and so much shame it hurts to see. I'm holding my breath, waiting for the cracks to appear, because she's surely falling apart. Can't anyone see she's coming to pieces?

I stand. "You don't have to—"

She loses it. "I said get out. All of you. Get. Out!" She snatches a full glass from the bar and hurls it at the wall before pointing a finger at me. "You too. Out! Now! Get out!"

Then she flees, her footsteps pounding on the stairs.

"Anxious to see him much?" someone mutters.

A dark hand tugs at my elbow. Seth Williams, stone-faced, steers me to the door. The rest follow, leaving plates and cups and the taste of resentment behind. The freezing night hits my bare forearms and I turn back. "Wait, the door, I gotta lock it at least."

"No, you don't." Seth tows me down the street by my elbow. "You really don't."

"I need a coat or something."

"You're fine."

"It's freezing! I do need one."

Seth spins me around by the shoulders, shakes me hard enough to make my teeth rattle. "No, Grace, you don't. Because we going somewhere else." He raises his voice. "We all going somewhere else."

"What if someone else comes and tries to eat there?"

"Then they'll see it empty and go. It's Erin's place, Jesus, they won't stick around. Or Simon will tell them what happened." He glares into the distance. Right, no one knows that Simon's gone to Mick's. "Anyway, I'll take you wherever you going. You don't wanna be out here alone, good girl like you."

"I'll go find Simon."

Seth sets his jaw. "You can't be going back there. I known Erin a long time and, trust me, ain't never seen her that way."

"Of course not," a woman hisses. "You saw the way he treated her, ordering her around like that."

"So why'd she go up with him?" someone else retorts. "Tell me that."

I try again. "She's trapped, don't you see? Simon knows it, and you know Simon."

"Do we? He killed a man in cold blood. I didn't think he had it in him, but he did. Goes to show." Seth pats my arm. He *pities* me. "Now, where you going? I'll take you there."

And I swear, my brain says "my daddy's workshop," but my mouth when it opens says, "I ain't going anywhere. I need my coat."

56

TAYLOR

I knew the minute I saw Mr. Petrowski go in Erin's place that it wasn't going to end well. Sure enough, they all come streaming out a little past eight, sulking away to better watering holes where no one's screwing their favorite fantasy upstairs.

Only two of them stick around, Grace and another dude, arguing on the sidewalk ten feet in front of me. They probably don't even know I'm here what with heavy clouds covering the moon. Their voices rise until I can hear them loud and clear. Apparently, she thinks they should go back in the bar.

"Lemme get this straight," the man says. "You think Petrowski told Erin he'll do something to Simon if she don't put out?"

"I don't think. I know," Grace retorts.

The man isn't taking any of her shit. "You got proof?"

"I heard her. And you saw."

"I saw him saying he was going upstairs and her following him. Didn't see any force there."

"Are you kidding? He's holding Simon hostage against her. She don't do what Petrowski says, her stepbrother gets it."

"Simon's a big boy. He can take care of himself, just give him a baseball bat," the man replies. Most true thing I've heard all night. "Anyway, for all his faults, I don't see Petrowski as the type to bump off his own son."

"He killed his stepson. Murdered him in cold blood. My sister told me. He'd..."

They both look to the sky. The rain's starting up again. Grace spreads her arms, then they both sprint for the nearest shelter—the porch I'm standing watch on. "Evening."

Grace jumps about ten feet and swivels. "Taylor Burkes? Don't do that! I about had a heart attack."

The man peers at me, flashing a lighter to illuminate all our faces. He's one of the regulars, a black guy in his thirties or so, Seth something. I should've recognized him by his accent.

"Oh, it's you." His lips curl up, and then the lighter goes out and he turns his back. "Grace, you might be right, but I don't understand what you wanting me to do about it. She ain't asked me for help. Far as I heard, she ain't asked nobody."

"Course not, she's terrified! And why wouldn't she be? He's got her watched every hour of the day and night by the creepiest pack of crackers I ever met." Grace glances in my direction. "No offense, Taylor; I'm talking about Ryan Jesser and them from this morning."

I don't know how to take that, so I shake my head and shift my radio on my belt. "It's just a job."

"Find another," she snaps. "Oh, and while we're at it, you can tell Ryan that if I see him again, I'm packing heat. I don't want him near me awake, and I really don't want him watching me sleep. I feel unsafe enough as it is."

That was just low. "What are you implying?"

"I'm not implying anything. I'm saying he's the type, and that's why he's working for Petrowski."

"And just what's that supposed to mean?" I demand.

"Isn't it obvious? You say no and the both of them hear what they wanna hear. Don't they, Seth?"

Seth has his arms crossed, a square figure in what little light there is. "I ain't saying nothing against Jesser and nothing against Petrowski. They're nothing to do with me. If Erin don't like what's happening—"

"She speaks up and finds Simon missing half his fingers. Or me." She states that like it's a fact, and enough is enough.

"That's not what we do—don't exaggerate. We watch, so what? She should be grateful to have the best security in town."

"I'll remind you of that the next time you find me standing outside your bath," Seth shoots back. "Shut up, Burkes."

But I can't let this disrespect pass, not even from Grace. That was one of the things Ryan was on about, how Petrowski doesn't tolerate stuff like this and neither can we. "He's the one keeping the feds from flattening this town. If you've got a problem, why don't you go move to Scioto with the rest of the traitors."

"Sounds good; leastways I'd have electricity there." I can all but hear Grace roll her eyes. "C'mon, Taylor, you didn't like Ryan talking to me any more than I did. I saw your face. You knew exactly what he wanted from me, and don't pretend, given half a chance, he wouldn't take it."

She's not wrong; I was ready to lay him out flat for that but was too afraid of what Petrowski'd do to me if I did.

Does Flaherty feel that way? Too scared to stop what he knows is happening?

My earpiece crackles. Speak of the devil, it's Ryan, his voice tinny in my ear where no one but me can hear. "Taylor, you know you've been leaning on the speaker button for the last five minutes, right? You're draining the battery."

"Oh shit, sorry. Uh." Crap, has he been listening? "Didn't mean to."

"Just quit it, ain't good for the radio. Anyway, if you wanna collect on that dogfight bet, get your ass up to headquarters in the next fifteen minutes. Bookie's here paying out."

And I need that money. "But I'm guarding."

"I'll spell you. I'm in the area anyway."

"Thanks, man, I owe you." I holster my radio, making sure not to hit the button this time before turning back to the other two. "Look, you'd both better clear out. I've gotta run, and Ryan's gonna be watching this place."

I can feel Grace's eyes on me, anything but nice. "Your boss got a thing for people watching him do it, is that it?"

Yeah, why are we still guarding her? He's in there. Grace isn't wrong.

Has she ever been wrong?

Fuck it. "I dunno. I'll be back in half an hour, argue with me then."

Grace stomps down the steps into the rain without another word, Seth a silent shadow following behind her.

I head down the street, and Ryan passes me at the corner.

"Quiet night?" he asks.

"Oh, yeah. Hey, thanks, man. I owe you one. That's my rent money I bet."

He punches me on the shoulder too hard. "No trouble at all, my man. No trouble at all. Actually, you might have made my night."

57

Grace

The rain picks up, pouring down the back of my neck as I search for another shelter. The house two doors down is all but a foundation, but an ancient bus stop sits in front of it. Seth and I huddle under the cracked plastic overhang, and I start to shiver. I really did need that coat.

After a moment, Seth drapes his jacket over my shoulders. He's been quiet since we left the porch, but he seems to have put the facts together now. "What I don't understand is what you want me to do about Petrowski. Because according to you, there's nothing I can do."

"Of course there is," I say to him. How can he be so slow? There's everything to be done. "We can tell other people. Let Erin know she has our support, that we're here for her. She thinks no one in the world gives a care about her, and so far, she's been right."

"The other guys would never believe me. *I* barely believe it."

"Why?" I demand. "You just saw it."

"No, I didn't." Seth turns his back on me. "All I saw was the guy who Erin *admits* fathered her kid come in for a drink, be a dick, and go up to her bedroom. For all we know, he's giving her a foot massage." He throws his hands in the air, takes a few steps into the downpour, then comes back. "Look. Grace. I believe you. But there ain't three people in this town who wasn't there tonight who's gonna do the same, and that's being generous."

How can he not see it? How can he not understand how scared

she is right now? Can't he see her hands shake when she picks up the gin pitcher? Doesn't he get that her smiles aren't real?

No, he doesn't. Because he's never seen the real ones. She's too scared to show him. And maybe it's because she knew they'd react just like this.

After all, nobody believed my brother would hit me, either. Nobody in the world, not even my mama. She saw it with her own eyes and said, "He's just playing too rough, don't pick fights with him." But Jesus knew and so did I, and He made my daddy come home early one evening to see my brother in the middle of one of his tirades.

And now He's called me here to stop what's going on in that house just down the street. With Seth Williams's help or not.

I face him, shoulders back, chin up. "Fine. You know what? Go home, Seth. Go home and sleep well. I don't need your help. I will help Erin, because you are too busy watching your own back to even think of covering hers." I yank off his jacket, thrust it out. I've had it to here with pigheadedly stupid adults who won't see what's in front of their own noses. "Go home, Seth. I don't need you."

His hand closes around his jacket, and it's like a light going on. Fury floods his face. The true cards are out. "You stupid girl. I told you I believe you. What more do you want? Me to die on some street corner to protect what ain't even mine? She ain't my family, she ain't my woman."

"You fought a war, didn't you? Tell me, do you own this town? Because I don't and neither does my brother, so don't you call me stupid. You're the one who doesn't have any loyalty."

Seth puts on his jacket, every word clipped. "You know what, Grace? You're right. I don't have any loyalty—to you. Loyalty's earned, and you ain't done it. Go get your coat or stay here and freeze, I don't care. I'm not gonna stick around to be insulted."

And just like that, he walks off and leaves me here with the rain dripping down my neck. The coward.

Cowards, all of them, sitting there and watching. They love her so much, but they won't lift a finger for her. Love, my ass. To hell with them. I don't need anyone to believe me; I know the truth and so does Jesus, as the pastor says. I still believe those words, even if he didn't believe me.

Rage keeps my face warm, but a gust of wind reminds me that I'm still wearing my work clothes, a tank top and jeans, not exactly made for facing the elements. My braids are heavy, and my fingers are going numb. I need a coat, a frikkin coat, and it's fifty feet away in Erin's kitchen.

To hell with Seth. I can get in there and out again without Petrowski ever figuring out I'm there. After all, he thinks Simon's home, doesn't he? A door opening and closing won't surprise him. Doubt he'll even notice if he's doing what I think he's doing. If I had a gun, I could creep up there and blow his brains out right now.

Yeah, and then Ryan Jesser would be first on the scene.

A shiver goes down my spine, goose bumps rising up on my skin as wind blows rain down my back. I don't stand a chance. Erin's right, Petrowski'd drag me down the road by my hair. He'd rip my scalp off.

On the porch across the street, a lighter flares. Taylor? It goes on again as I approach. No, Ryan, definitely Ryan. Asshole. Him and Petrowski, they deserve each other.

I turn my back on him, ears pricked as I head around the side of the house to the gate. The latch, slick with rain, slips in my numb fingers. My jaw hurts from clenching my teeth so hard as the wind picks up, making the bare branches dance. God, I'm so cold right now. Come on, open, open already. I just want my stupid coat. Stupid Seth, stupid gate—

A lighter flares next to my hands. "Need some help, sweetie?"

Ryan. I didn't even hear him come up over the wind. Didn't hear him at all.

Play it off, just play it off. Turn and smile. The gate knocks against its latch as I back into it, still shut tight against me.

He's grinning at me, all teeth and glittering eyes, and I can't smile no more. Oh God, I shouldn't be here alone with him half a foot away, standing over me, closing off my escape. Oh lord. Oh lord, I've made a mistake.

Ryan leans in close enough I can feel the warmth of his breath on my face. "I heard what you said to Taylor about me."

Run.

He bear-hugs me against him, hand over my mouth. Oh God, *this is how it happens.* Hot breath in my face, too dark to see anything, and he's squeezing the life out of me. Oh God, oh Jesus, I can't breathe...

So fight.

He's holding my face against his, but my arms are free. My fingers find my pocket, touch my knife, the knife what my daddy gave me, and I know what to do. The hilt is solid and smooth in my hand. Ryan's trying to grab my wrist, but it's slick with rain and I can feel the button on the side of my knife. *This is how it happens.* I press it down, no time to think—

My knife plunges into his chest like so much meat. Ryan's arms loosen.

I can't believe that worked, I can't believe it. He's staring at me in shock, but I can't stop, not now, not this time. *You're not going to rape me.* My arm jerks the knife back, and I stab him again right in the stomach this time. Pull it out and do it again and again and again until his fingers uncurl from my shirt as he makes a bubbling, wheezing sound.

I step back, watch him tremble like the Tower of Babel, and then fall with a sickening crack as his head meets a concrete block, the handle of my jackknife still sticking out of his chest.

He's not going anywhere. I am safe. I am safe. This is how it happens, but not to me.

Ryan's still now, and the only sound is the rain hitting the grass once again. I reach up to wipe the water out of my face. My hands are sticky. Wet. Warm. I'm warm all over now. I just killed a man, but I swear that's the only thing that feels different. Oh my lord.

Something moves in the darkness. Someone else is here.

The knife is back in my hand before I knew I was moving, held out like they do in the ring. Maybe I don't know how to dance like they do, but I did it before and I can do it again.

"Grace?" Someone's five feet away, hands out and moving careful. "Grace, is that you? It's me, Art."

He slows when he sees the body, looking from it to me. Ryan's white shirt has turned dark with blood where I stabbed him.

My stomach suddenly rolls. Stabbed him. I stabbed Ryan. To death.

Oh my lord, what have I done? Jesus, savior, what have I done?

Art takes me by the forearms and shakes me hard. "Come on, Grace, snap out of it. What the hell happened?"

"Huh?"

The rain is coming down hard, but I swear I can hear Ryan gurgle, a sick, sucking sound. He's still alive. Oh Jesus. Is that better or worse than him being dead? Art's talking, but I can't hear what he says. He lets me go and turns to examine Ryan.

"He came after me." I grab Art's collar, pull him close, peer into his eyes. I can't see much out here, but I can tell that it really is him. It really is Art holding me, prying the knife from my hands. He has to believe me.

He presses his hands to my cheeks, and the warmth seeps through, jolting me back. "Did you stab him, Grace?"

"Yes. It's Ryan Jesser. He's not dead yet." Why did I say yet? Oh my lord.

"Jesser attacked you? Yeah, yeah, I can see that. I see it. Okay. It's okay, Grace." He pulls me in so tight, then pushes me out to arm's length. I can't make out the expression on his face, but his voice is calm. "You're a good girl. I won't ask why you're out here. I'm sure there's a reason."

Is there? Is there anymore? Was there ever? Did Ryan's fingers just twitch?

Art gives me a shove, gently, so gently, then folds my knife. My head spins. Does he really believe me? Just like that?

Art shoos me away like you would a chicken, a child, a frightened animal too dumb to run, and that's me, staring at Ryan with the blood blooming dark roses on his shirt. Art's flicking my knife open and closed, my old knife what my daddy gave me years ago and I carry every single day.

"Go on, Gracie girl. Art's gonna finish the job for you."

No, Ryan isn't dead. Yet.

Art unlocks the gate, disappears into the house, and returns with the shirt Erin was wearing when she got caught in the rain earlier, the one I left to dry in the kitchen. It's clean. No blood. He turns his back and I change into it, ball up the old shirt, shove it in my pocket, and pray my jeans are dark enough that nothing shows. Not in this light, anyway.

"I got this. Go home, Grace, and burn the clothing you're wearing, do you understand? Don't tell anyone what happened. Find an alibi. I'll make him disappear. No one will know it was you."

"Thou shalt not kill."

"Jesus forgives, but the law doesn't. Pray on it, and you'll be fine." Art squeezes my hands. "Now go get that alibi."

Alibi.

Alibi.

Jesus will forgive me, but a rope around my neck won't. They don't believe Erin's getting raped, and if they won't believe her, why would anybody in this town believe me? No one believed me about my brother, not my mama, not my daddy, and I wasn't guilty then of nothing but being a little sister. Maybe Ryan just wanted to give me a hug. Maybe I shouldn't have provoked him.

I walk across the street. Taylor isn't back yet, so I wait on the porch while somewhere in the pitch-black rain, Art makes a man disappear.

But Jesus saw.

Taylor doesn't return for what seems like ages, until I'm shivering uncontrollably in my sodden jeans, huddled in a corner of the porch. "Hey."

He jumps about a foot. "Grace! What are you doing here? Where's Ryan?"

"He went to get something, I think," I say, and it's true. "Look, Taylor." Jesus, forgive me, but I've been practicing what I'm about to say for what feels like hours. "I don't have a place to go tonight, 'cause I'm not going back in Erin's place. I don't suppose you get off shift soon?"

Taylor's silent for a moment too long. Was I right, or does he suspect something?

"I'm sorry for what I said before," I add, and that's true too. Oh, so true.

Taylor scrambles to sound cool. "I'm off in half an hour. Want to, uh, I mean, I've got a spare pillow if you want to borrow it. Yeah?"

"Could I? You're a lifesaver." I try to pull myself to my feet, but my legs have gone numb. He's there in a moment, tugging me up to lean against his arm. It's almost hot, even through his coat. I'm so cold, so cold I can't do anything but clutch it for the heat, thoughts murky. Is this why Erin was in the rain earlier, to numb the feelings she doesn't want to have anymore? Did it work? Did she feel forgiven for her sins? "You're the best, Taylor."

His other arm goes around my shoulders. "I try. But that's weird Ryan hasn't come back. That's not like him."

From where we're standing, the only thing we can see is the front of Erin's house. Can't see the gate I tried to go through, or the path where Ryan's lying. Taylor could have come back on shift while Ryan was attacking me and not noticed a thing. And now Ryan's paying for it; there's no sign of Art.

I let my forehead rest against Taylor's chest, feel his heartbeat speed up to match mine as I open my mouth to start lying just like I'll be doing forever and ever and ever. "Yeah, weird."

58

Simon

From the day I showed up in Erin's backyard, I ain't spent more than a handful of nights away. Couple times I been out late, or early, or both at the same time, but not gone really. "Hey. Mick."

"Yeah?"

"You got...?" There's gotta be a better way of putting this than "You got some liquor I can drink? 'Cause I get nightmares if I don't," only I can't think of anything. "You got a bottle of comfort I can borrow? Mine's at home."

Oh God, I can't look at him, I feel so stupid. He knows exactly why I want it; it must be written all over my face. He pushes himself away from the table and rummages around in a cupboard. "Here."

It's a dusty bottle, two-thirds full of clear liquid. "What is it?"

"Rum. Doesn't taste like whiskey."

Well, that's something, anyway. My fingers close around the bottle, but it's a moment before he lets go. It don't weigh much, but it seems to drag my arm down with gratitude. "Thanks."

"Don't mention it. I'll show you your room."

He leads me upstairs to a door straight off the top. It's narrow and painted dark, with nothing but a bed and a chest of drawers. "Used to be my youngest brother's. You need anything, I'm just down the hall. I don't get up that early, but I'll make an effort tomorrow."

We stand there for a moment, then he shrugs, taps the bottle of rum with a fingernail, and heads down the hall. I close the door behind me and lock it for good measure before turning off the lights and climbing under the covers.

This bed's wider than mine at home, and longer. My feet don't hang off the end, which is weird. I'm dead tired, but my eyes stay wide open, an unfamiliar ceiling above. It's got shapes, his ceiling; it's not flat. Like whoever made it didn't really know what they was doing with the plaster and just slopped it around. It's weird.

God, the fuck was that look Mick gave me? Same look he's been giving me since I told him I'd never kissed a girl, though now half the town thinks I've kissed Erin even though she's gonna have my half brother or sister, which is plain fucking weird. I don't think Mick was thinking about that, though. When he gives me that look, it's like he's trying to make up his mind about something. Been trying to make up his mind for a month now, I guess. Wish he'd hurry up about it, whatever it is. I'm sick of mysteries.

I take a sip of the rum. It don't burn too much, though it tastes about like gasoline, oily and strong. Take another, keep the shudder down this time, and it's a little better. Maybe third time's the charm.

I bet I could make it all the way empty and not feel a thing, 'cause I'm big and that's what counts—that's what all the men in the front room say. Not that I've tested that out, really, even if I did drink last Saturday at the Calico. But all I drank was what Mick called dirty beers, which tasted strong but didn't do that much until I'd had a few, and then the world got tippy and slurry. Then I tackled Art and it got much clearer.

Maybe that was when I knew I couldn't keep training with him. Or was it sooner, as far back as when...when I killed that other guy in the fight? Maybe. Art trained me and taught me, but it weren't me he cared about, was it? Erin, always Erin, everyone cares about Erin. I care about Erin. And Art don't care about me one bit. Not beyond the money he can make 'cause I'm good at beating up whoever they put in front of me. And what does that make me?

Okay, now the bottle's half-empty. Two-thirds minus one-half is...a lot. Uh. Didn't mean to do that.

What do I do now?

Sleep it off, right, yeah, wait, no. Take a leak first.

I find my way out the back door toward the outhouse. It's raining steady, no moon tonight. Everything's pitch-black, and I can't seem to find my way in the dark. Before I know it, I'm at the front door instead. Totally turned around.

Or maybe I don't want to find the outhouse and then go back to that bed and sleep all night like a good little boy. Maybe I'm tired of that. Maybe I'm fucking well sick of it. Some days I just feel that way, tired of being good. Tired of being Saint Flaherty.

It's times like this I go to the old park. And who knows, on a night like this when can't nobody see nothing, maybe I'll find someone waiting for me.

Just maybe.

59

You know how hard it is to carry a body through this town in the middle of the night without anybody seeing you?

Not very, it turns out. In case anyone was wondering. Borrow a wheelbarrow and away I go. It's a good night to be alive, unlike some people.

God, the night patrols are laughably easy to avoid. Stay off the main roads to their territory and they don't give a shit. Same with getting back into town, just avoid the checkpoints and go through the woods and nobody cares, because who would bother to smuggle stuff in on foot? Hardly worth the trouble, considering the land mines, though I know how to avoid them well enough. No, no one knows I'm here except Grace, and she'll never tell. I can dump the body without a fear in the world.

Splash in the river the remains of Ryan Jesser go, probably with some weird bruising, but so much the better. When he turns up, if he turns up, it'll be that much harder to suspect Grace. I'm in trouble anyway, aren't I? Might as well take advantage. Petrowski may not realize it, but he's given me something valuable. A tool, a gift if you will: perfect freedom. I can do anything I want right now and it doesn't matter so long as no one sees me.

Now I'm hiding out in that abandoned house across the road from Erin's, 'cause Petrowski's boys never venture past the hole in the living room floor to see that the kitchen's still in good shape. The lights are off at Erin's place, her and Simon asleep in their beds, and hopefully Grace as well. Lucky I was there. Lucky I arrived when I did. God knows why she was out there, why he was with her. Does it matter? Ryan Jesser won't be missed.

Well, he'll be missed eventually, just not mourned.

Grace is a funny one. I like that girl. She got Jesser good. He'd have died from his wounds anyway, and good riddance. I was fucking pissed at Petrowski before, but I'm thoughtful now. The perfect gift, yeah. No one could have helped her tonight but me. Like it was meant to be.

I got time right now, time I never had. Time to think clearly. I was mad at Erin before, but I was getting worked up over the wrong things. She's in a bad position, I have to remember that. And maybe I should have made myself clearer sooner, let her know I was there for her in so many words, rather than trusting she'd get it.

Though she should've gotten it.

I'm gonna get Erin out of this town, and Simon. Grace can come too if she's worried about what happened tonight. I like her. She's spunky. She's got something, that girl. But mostly Erin will be out from under Petrowski's nose, and I'll be the hero. I've been tied to this town, this job, for way too long. Tied by nothing but assumptions and stupid human fear. Now? Now I got a license to do what I want.

Freedom's just another word for nothing left to lose. Well, now I'm free, and fuck me if I'm gonna lose this game. Your move, Petrowski.

60

Erin

For the first time since my mom died, I cook Jeff Petrowski breakfast. Eggs and bacon, and toast. It couldn't be any more cheesy if I tried. He eats it at my clean kitchen table. Rest of the kitchen is a mess, but this bit is pristine. Cleaned it myself in the early hours when I couldn't sleep. He eats, kisses me on the cheek, and gets up to leave. "I'll be seeing you tomorrow, sweetie."

Last night's drinks are waiting in the front room, all those half-eaten plates of food. I can feel them still sitting there, abandoned. One for every person who now knows what I am, what I do. A glass for every one.

Does it even matter?

The weather is foggy, clinging and close. It feels like I'm the only one in the world. Grace didn't come back last night. Hasn't come back yet. Will she ever return, or did my sins drive her away for good?

I drift from room to room, touching the walls with my fingertips. I feel like I'm floating. No Simon to tether me down. I've got him taken care of, if you can believe it, by Mick Perry, of all people. But Mick will be good to him. For whatever reason he can find in his sick heart, he will.

Is time passing? Surely it is, but I can't feel it. The windows are wrapped in soft white and I'm all alone. Maybe I've floated away.

Someone knocks on the door. I drag it open, an inch at a time. I've only got my robe on, not that it matters for Taylor Burkes. "Yeah?"

"Is Grace here?"

Figures. "No."

"Will she be back soon?"

"I doubt it."

He looks so uncomfortable I almost feel sorry for him. Almost.

"Can you give these to her, then? She left them at my place last night." He holds out a rolled up pair of socks, light purple and damp.

I should ask, but I just don't want to care right now. "Fine. I will."

"Um. Thanks." He stares at me like I'm supposed to say something to that. "What happened to your face?"

I shut the door in his. Or I try to, but he's put his foot in it, pushing until I open up again.

"No, seriously," he says, "what happened?"

"What do you think?" I don't want to talk right now, him staring at me like a zoo animal.

"Hey. Mr. Petrowski's going to be pissed." For the life of me, I cannot shut this damn door. "There are guards out here for a reason. Does he know?"

I can't think of a thing to say except, "Yes. He does. Go away."

"Besides, Grace said that he was..." He figures it out. His mouth drops open. It'd be funny, but it's not. It's not that hard to know what dots he's connected if I can guess what Grace said, which I'd bet you anything was something along the lines of, "She's sleeping with Petrowski tonight, so can I stay over, pretty pretty please with sugar on top?"

And then Taylor asks, "Does Flaherty know?"

I can't breathe. "No. Taylor, tell me, where'd Grace say she was going this morning? What'd she say?"

He snaps to attention. "Home. I thought she meant..."

"She meant her dad's place, then. Go there. Tell her to find Simon. He can't come home right now."

"But why?"

"You know why." I meet his eyes. Everything is clear now. I can see it all, in my mind, laid in a path in front of me. Taylor might be working for the other side, but he's the only chance I've got. "After she talks to him, she's to come here, keep this place running as usual. Simon can't see me right now. Do you have that?"

"Yes, but—"

"Then go. Now."

He backs away, still hesitating.

"Please."

Yes, everything is in focus now. I know exactly what I need to do, the road ahead laid out clear as day. I don't know where it goes, but it's going and I'm on it. This, this I can do. If it's all gonna collapse anyway, I might as well take the chance. I can escape, or I can die trying, but either way, it can't be worse than this morning.

But before we leave town, I've errands to run, starting with Grace's dad.

Chuck Farley takes one look at me and sits me at the table with an ice pack on my cheek.

"Has Grace been here?" I ask.

"She ran out about half an hour back."

"Good. She'll run my place tonight. She'll be fine."

He waits for me to continue, leaning against the kitchen counter, watching carefully. Well, he's a right to be careful. Times are dangerous.

"You said you wanted to help me," I say, and pause. "How did you mean?"

"How do you need help?"

I rub my jaw, staying away from the tender spots. "I need out of this town."

He don't comment on that because he don't need to. My face tells the whole story, don't it just? Don't nobody need to ask what happened when it's stamped in purple and blue.

"Tonight?" he asks.

"Tomorrow, after Simon's fight, when the convoy leaves town." They always leave late after tournaments, because the drivers like to watch.

"Simon's going too?"

I nod. Oh yes. "He can probably get out on his own, but he wants to go with me and I won't stop him. It's probably for the best. But I need to know what kind of help you're offering."

Chuck finally sits down, taking my small hands in his big ones.

"You saved my son, Erin. You brought my daughter home. I owe you, and their mother would say the same. I am offering whatever I can do. You know that."

I move my hands out of reach, twining the fingers together again and again. Look down, 'cause it's better than looking at his face. Gotta face the truth. Gotta be straight now. Won't have another chance. "But see, Chuck, that's the thing. You don't owe me for that."

"I know you couldn't save Abby, but you saved Evan. He'd've died without you."

"But that's the thing. That's why I always said there weren't no debt, that it was up to him." If I'm gonna do this, if I'm gonna have help, I'm gonna have it honestly. That's what I realized. "The night I found Abby..."

"What about it?" There's an edge there that weren't there before, like he's heard the dark tidings, and he don't like what he's thinking. I keep going.

"I did save Evan, I promise you that. But I was there to save him...because I was the one who stabbed him." The silence gapes. "He tried to scalp me."

I need help, and I don't know what Chuck is thinking. If he says no, then it serves me right. I'll find another way. But I can't lie to him and get it. I can't be a sinner no more.

"He was in the army." Chuck's voice creaks. I've hurt him, I'm sure. God, I hurt everyone.

"So were most who were doing that. I...I don't know who got Abby, but he came for me. Maybe he thought I'd done it. He weren't right in the head, I know that."

Ages pass, a decade at least, until Chuck looks up from whatever spot on the table he's been staring at. "He always was different after."

"You've mentioned that."

"But maybe it wasn't the hit to the head like we thought. Maybe he was wrong long before then." He takes a deep breath. "There's a trail in the woods what's pretty well hidden. It'll get you around the checkpoints. But if you're still being followed, it's not hidden enough."

It takes me a moment to answer. "Don't worry about that part. I can give them the slip if you'll torch my place, make a distraction. I've got casks in the cellar that'll go sky-high. All you gotta do is stack some firewood and set a fuse."

"Sky-high. I can do that. That all?"

It's now or never. "No. I need something else."

"What? Money, gear?" Chuck's sizing me up. "A car?"

"Yeah. A car. And someone to drive it." Will he get it, or do I have to say it? "Grace. I need Grace's help. I trust her."

"You can't have her."

"I'm not asking permission. She's her own woman."

"No."

"You said anything."

He takes a deep breath, stands up sudden-like. "I know, but not her. Not my baby girl. I'll get you your car with a driver and draw you a map for the trail. I'll buy your convoy tickets. And then, that's it. We're even; I can't help you any more. And you don't get Grace."

"What if she wants to leave town?"

"Then she can go, but not with you. It's too dangerous, and she's my baby. Bad enough she's in your house to begin with." I am a sinner, and he knows it, looking anywhere but at me. "Where are you going now?"

I'm no longer welcome here, and I understand that. "To take care of things."

"Fine. I'll get everything to you before tomorrow noon. It'll all be arranged."

I stand. "We'll be on our way as soon as the fights end tomorrow night. More specific than that I can't say."

"Then don't."

I'm half out the door when he turns to face me again. "The Lord bless and keep you, Erin. I'll pray for you."

It's as much as I'll ever get, and more than I deserve for lying all these years, and lying still. "And you, Chuck."

61

Simon

First thing I hear in the morning is voices in Mick's shop. The door's just closing by the time I get down there. "That sounded like Grace."

Mick's busy with his back to me. "It was. She just had a message from Erin telling you to stay put because she'll be sending some clothes around later. Hey, can you go into the storeroom and grab two cases of the ammo in the boxes marked number five? I've got an order for them today."

Someone knocks again and he shoos me away, 'cause people ain't supposed to know I'm here. If they know, Art might find out and come here. I go into the storeroom and start pulling open boxes as Mick opens the front door.

Connor's voice comes down the hall. Because of course. Jesus, make my day better, why don't you. "I heard Simon's holed up in here for the day. Making a man out of him before I slit his belly?"

Shit. Mick's voice drifts back here, cold and drawling. "I don't know why you think having sex makes anyone a man. Being living proof against that and all."

"Is that a yes, then?"

"Get out."

"Patience, Mick. Did you know there's a reward out to anyone who keeps Saint Flaherty from making it to his fight tomorrow?"

"Where is this going?"

"How much would you pay to keep his location a secret?"

"Not very much," Mick retorts, and he sounds about three seconds from something drastic. "In fact, I think I'd pay nothing at all."

Something slams into the door, a body hitting hard, and I'm sprinting into the room before I can think.

Mick's got Connor in a choke hold, his back to me. Connor's still struggling, but then he spots me and goes real still as Mick hisses into his ear, "Don't you even fucking try it or I'll—"

Connor's eyes find mine. He smiles. "You'll what, fuckface? Be sure to use small words or Simple Simon won't understand."

Oh fuck no.

Mick closes his eyes for the briefest moment, then looks at me, not pissed, no; resigned. Connor was trying to get me out here, and I just screwed this up. Simple Simon.

Mick drops his arms and Connor steps to the side, dusting himself down. Making a show of it, just to piss off Mick. "That's more like it. I got a deal for you, Simon. And you'll like this." Bet I won't. "There's another fight next Wednesday, same alley you painted the wall with last time. They want to see you and me have it out like we used to. No weapons, just strength and speed the way it should be. They'll pay you to be there, win or lose."

"How much?" I ask.

"How much do you want?"

Mick's shaking his head, but I already know the drill. "Art said they only offer that when they think you won't be alive to claim it. So how about no."

Ain't no honesty in Connor. "Come on, Simon. Don't be a wimp. How about it, Mick? A good old fight, line your pockets."

"Simon makes his own calls."

There's a pause as Connor switches tracks, like changing CDs. "Want to know where Grace slept last night?"

"Was it in her bed?" I ask, knowing the answer. He just wants under my skin.

"It was in someone's bed."

"Good for her."

"It was in Taylor Burkes's bed."

Yeah, right. "That's nice."

"That's 'cause Erin kicked everyone out of the bar."

"And why'd she do that? Lemme guess," I say. "'Cause Jeff Petrowski himself came in and ordered her to."

Connor throws back his head and laughs, wiping a pretend tear from his eye. "Oh, Simon, Simon, Simon. They said he must've been the first customer in last night. Erin kicked everyone out and went and fucked him upstairs, and all along you were here, sucking Mick's little dick? Oh, this is beautiful. Just purely beautiful."

I keep my voice steady best I can, but I'm watching Mick, who's glaring at Connor like all he wants to do is kill him. "You're full of shit," I say.

"He must've got there, what, five minutes after opening? When did you leave last night, Simon? You couldn't have been there for that, or we'd be visiting you in the morgue."

Something's nagging at the back of my skull. Mick said we needed to go, he had plans real sudden, even though we were in the middle of stuff, just after opening time. Out the back door, out of sight.

"You're full of shit, Connor," I repeat, but I see it in Mick's face.

"Did I hit a nerve?" Connor snickers. "Is Saint Simon pissed at being the last to know? Because it's all true. I don't lie to you, Simon. You're too dumb to sort lies from the truth."

I lunge for him. Mick grabs me around the middle, holds me back as Connor dashes out the door, laughing the whole way when all I want to do is put my fist in his face until that sniggering is gone, and I'm gonna *kill* Mick for stopping me.

He kicks me in the side so hard I double over wheezing, sinking to the floor. Fuck, that hurt. Fuck, I hate him, I hate him. He lied to me last night to keep me from protecting her, and I bet she told him to do it, even. Petrowski was there, and there weren't nothing I could do to help her 'cause she wouldn't let me. She sent me away.

Mick's down on the floor with me, hands on my shoulders, trying to look me in the eye. "Simon, don't listen to Connor."

"He don't lie. Not to me."

"He's an asshole and you know it." God, the way he says it, and I *know* what he's really thinking and I don't fucking *want* to anymore.

"Petrowski was at the bar last night."

"I found out this morning. Grace came by and told me." He's still lying, lying.

"You fucking knew it last night. You knew and you didn't tell me! You should've! You should've told me!"

I shove him off but he comes back, holding my arms, holding me in place. "Yes, okay! I should've told you, but I also knew there's a bounty on your head! Simon, Petrowski didn't go there for Erin; he was there to keep you from making it to your fight by provoking you into an attack, because that's all the excuse he needs to get you out of his way forever, and I couldn't..." He stumbles over the word, holding back whatever it is he really wants to say, just like he's been holding back for days, now, for weeks. He reaches up to touch my cheek, that look on his face like I saw last night. "I couldn't, Simon. I just couldn't."

My adrenaline's going so hard I can hear it in my ears, my senses singing, and I know why he looks at me that way. I've known for so long but told myself I didn't. I can nearly smell it, clear as day. I know where I seen that look before and know what it is, and Mick never tells the truth unless he has to and he's still not telling it now and there's nothing I can do about it.

Unless I make him tell it.

I touch his jaw, feel the stubble slide under my fingertips as his eyes find my lips.

I don't know who leans forward. I don't know why, the whys of this. The whys of anything. I'm kissing Mick on the floor of his shop, and all I can think is that I was right.

62

Grace

I feel raw, turned inside out. My head is pounding. I've got a sore throat, runny nose, and I can't shake this chill that keeps coming and going. If this keeps up, I won't be able to run the bar tonight.

I'm alone right now in Erin's big old house, and I wish I weren't. I wish so much I weren't. I killed Ryan Jesser. I *killed* Ryan Jesser. No, don't think about it. Just concentrate on what needs done before tonight. Cooking, yes, I need to cook. But first I need to lay my head on the table for just a minute...

It's nearly dark. A blanket's around my shoulders. I must've fallen asleep. What time is it?

The side door opens and closes. I'm bolt upright reaching for my knife, but I don't have it because...oh my lord.

"Grace, it's me. Where are you?"

Erin. Erin's here, oh good. "In the kitchen," I croak, and cough. How long have I been asleep?

Erin flicks on the light. She's got a basket on her arm, and her black eye looks, if anything, worse.

"You okay?" She lays a cool hand on my forehead. "You feel hot. What're you still doing down here?"

"Fell asleep," I mumble. "Look, Erin, I'm sorry I left you last night."

"Don't matter," she says shortly. There's cuts around the bruise. He hit her hard, really hard.

"I brought you some ice, but you weren't here and it melted. Taylor said you were hurting."

Erin starts unloading her basket. It's full of vegetables and some sausages. She managed to get it all pre-cut somewhere.

"I cleaned up the front room earlier," I add. "It's ready to go. I just hadn't gotten to the food yet."

"Don't worry about it, you just rest up. We got a big day tomorrow."

I'm so near to bursting, wish I could tell her everything. Wish I could tell her why I was with Taylor, why I was in the rain, why everything. "Where you been all day?"

"Out. Getting things sorted. Your dad wants you to come by later, but don't worry about it if you're sick."

"Oh." I try to focus. "Any news around town? Anything happen today?"

"No. Why? Should there have been?"

Yes. I want to scream the word. Yes, yes, yes, there should have been. I killed a man! I stabbed him, and I don't know what Art did after I left. What was I thinking last night? How could I have left it to Art? What was Art thinking?

Erin's looking at me funny, and I press my lips together. I didn't say that last bit out loud. I'm sure I didn't. My head feels funny. Jesus, have mercy on my soul.

"Grace, you ever think about...leaving town?"

"Like on the run?" I blurt out.

"No, like, well, yeah, okay. Quiet-like. Not taking much more than money and just going."

"I guess," I come up with. "Sometimes. Doesn't everyone? You?"

"Yeah. Yeah, I do." She pauses to think. "Ever think you might really go? Like, soon?"

Ha. "Been thinking about it a lot today, yeah. Yeah."

"Really? Okay. Well. That's good." She seems to actually see me again, though how she can see anything through that eye I don't know. "You're sick, Grace. Go rest upstairs. I'll take care of stuff tonight. You just rest."

I make it to my room, snuggle into my comforter, and close my eyes. Thrust the image of Ryan into the back of my mind, deep where I can't see it. Instead, I think about when I was a kid, when I thought it'd be so great to have a job. To do something real, be grown up like Abby and Evan.

What a fool I was. The bell over the door jingles, and the sound of it soothes me to sleep. Things carry on.

63

TAYLOR

I'm on watch tonight, which is a total pain in the ass because it was supposed to be Ryan, but no one's seen him. I ran by his ex-girlfriend's place, but she told Cooper and me to fuck off, and seeing as I'm the new guy, guess who got stuck? I'm not sure what's the point of being on watch tonight. It's seven o'clock, and a total of three guys have gone in the bar. I guess after last night's tantrum, the regulars decided they'd rather drink elsewhere.

Another guy's coming up the street, and that makes four, whoopty doo. Mother of God, I'm cold.

"Taylor Burkes, hey man, good to see you!" The guy turns out to be Chris Hopkins. He strides over and claps me on the back.

"Hey, Chris, thought you didn't have any money."

"Yeah, well, that dogfight did me well. What are you doing here? Weren't you on watch last night?"

"The other guy fucked off and I got lucky." You so owe me, Ryan.

"They better give you a raise, then." He laughs and smacks my back again. Suck-up little shit, but Chris is fun to hang out with. He always knows what's going on. "So hey, heard a body turned up a couple miles down the river. One of the barges spotted it floating. Had its face all broken up and about twenty stab wounds. The boat hands thought it was some smuggler getting on someone's bad side. Nasty, huh?"

"Whatever. That's what happens when deals go bad. That's why I stay out of it. You wouldn't catch me dead double-crossing, you know?"

"Yeah."

"I mean, I'm at the Market every morning. I was there last month when someone gunned down a guy right in the middle of the veg lane for skimming off some dealer's profits, which just, like, blows my mind. Come on! You do that, you get what you asked for."

"I hear you. You wouldn't catch me crossing the big guys, no way." He elbows me. "So anyway, back to my story, it doesn't end there. Turns out after they get this guy on their boat, they think to themselves, hey, maybe he's still got money on him. And, I mean, what're the odds that whoever did a number on his face left anything, but the river guys started checking his clothes. And it turned out this guy was one of Petrowski's inner circle, 'cause he had one of those heart-and-cross tattoos. You know?"

I point to my own shoulder, where my tattoo throbs under my jacket. It's still tender, but at least it's not infected anymore. "Yeah, I know."

He gives me the side eye. "Right. Uh. Anyway. So—and I got this from a buddy of mine who was there at the time—he says Petrowski went crazy. Total nutso. 'Cause he knew exactly who it was because of the tattoo, like, right away, even though the face was all nasty. Which I guess means it wasn't an inside job or they'd've known to take off the tattoo, you know?"

Shit, I guess. "Who was it, then? Who was killed?"

"Wolf's head tattoo was all I heard."

Swallow. "Wait. Say again. What was the tattoo?"

"A wolf's head."

"A snarling wolf, with black fur?"

Chris snaps his fingers. "Yeah! That's the one. You don't mean...oh shit." His face falls big-time. "Oh shit, Taylor, sorry. You knew him?"

Knew. I knew Ryan, knew that tattoo. Right on his shoulder for everyone to see, 'cause he loved showing it off. It's a punch to the gut so hard I actually clutch my stomach. "Yeah," I say, and repeat it, "Yeah, that's Ryan's tat. I just saw him last night. He's the one who didn't show up today."

"Holy crap, Ryan? Ryan Jesser? I'm so sorry, man. I didn't know, I just heard about the tattoo."

I swallow. "Yeah. No. I know, it's fine. I just..." Take a deep breath, clear my throat. Do it again because the first time didn't stick. "What did Mr. Petrowski do when he knew it was Ryan? You were saying something."

Chris nods, trying to get his train of thought back. And me, I feel like I've been hit by a ton of bricks. I saw him last night. Saw him go on guard. God, maybe I was the last one to see him before he died.

Except I couldn't have been. He didn't die by himself. Stabbed. *Murdered*. Shit.

I scrub my eyes with the palm of my hand while Chris continues. "Petrowski, right. He went, well, kinda crazy, busted the jaw of the guy who told him and started saying it was Art Weber who did it, who killed this guy. 'Cause Art, like, got driven out of town or something and was out for revenge, which I mean, like, I don't know if I believe, 'cause I know Art, but then again, I mean, I know Art..."

Yeah, Art. Even before I fell out with him, I knew he had a temper. And yesterday morning we threw him into the woods. Shit, I almost forgot about that, what with Grace and, like, Grace.

But it makes sense. Ryan and I hurt Art, and Art got Ryan back. It makes sense, in a twisted sort of way. Revenge. And if that means...

"Then what'd the boss do?" I gotta ask it, gotta know.

"Well, that's the whole thing, nearly. He gave a bunch of orders and stormed out, and now there's a big notice going out tonight for information on the murder. My buddy told me all about it. Anyone who knows what happened, there's a reward. He's pretty determined."

"I bet."

And I do. Oh shit, I do. Murdered, Ryan. Last night. I told him thanks for the favor, he said something like it wasn't any trouble, that I'd "made his night," whatever that meant. By the time I got back, he was gone. I didn't even wonder where he'd gone because Grace was there too, shivering and wet, saying she couldn't go in the house and would I let her come over?

And where was Ryan right then? Already dead? Did someone

jump him in the dark? God, it could've been me if I hadn't had to go collect on that bet. I was *right there*.

"Taylor?"

"What?"

"Are you okay?"

"What?" Ryan's dead, is all I can think. "Look, I need to be alone right now. I'll catch you around, okay?"

He's relieved, I can tell. "Yeah, right, take all the time you need. Sorry to be the bearer of bad news and all that. You'll be at the fights?"

"Wouldn't miss 'em."

He heads back down the street, and I try to think again. Grace, yeah, Grace. She'd been shy at first and said she wanted to dry her clothes but didn't want me to see, so I gave her an old shirt of mine and turned my back. Then next thing I knew, she was pressed up against me telling me she was all dressed now, in my T-shirt and nothing else.

Time to think of something else.

Art survived his fall and killed Ryan 'cause Ryan fucked him up. And where does that leave me?

Next.

Mary, Mother of God.

64

Erin

Ain't had the bar this empty since we had a snowstorm a couple years back and almost no one could get in 'cause there was ice and wind and a fire downtown to boot. No snow tonight, though. Darkness and clouds, and it's cold but it's not that cold. I'm almost glad Grace is upstairs sick and not down here to see this because it's a disgrace, it is.

Nathaniel's not here, neither is Darryl nor Seth. Or Liz or Tybert or Ephraim or Zalenski or Adam or Jerome or any of them. Only three men are in tonight, and they're from out of town. Even they look confused. I serve and I chat and I laugh it off, saying Simon's not here, they must've all gone off with him for a bit, he's growing up, don'tcha know? They shake their heads, and my stomach shrinks into a hard ball. I know why they ain't here. I know.

By seven thirty, they've got a dominos game going at a table and I can nip off to check on Grace. Flu season already, I guess. I push open the door to her room, poke my head inside. She's sound asleep, chest rising and falling, eyelids twitching like crazy. I make to close the door.

"Who's there?" Grace rasps. Not asleep after all.

"It's me, Erin. You okay there, Grace?"

Her eyes close, and she sinks back on her pillow. "I'm fine. I just—" A cough racks her body, doubles her over, hacking and hacking with a wet, sucking sound. "Just sick. That's all."

"That didn't sound so good."

"I'm fine," she whispers. "Just a cold."

It's more than that. She's sweating in this chilly room, fingers clutching the covers. "Looks like the flu. You throw up at all?"

"No."

"A chill, then. I don't really know, I ain't much of a doctor," I admit. "It sounds bad. Want me to send for your dad?"

"Don't bother him." She coughs again, only a little.

"Your mom, then."

"No!" Grace's hand flutters up, as if to stop me. "Don't wanna talk to her. She'd just be all 'I told you so.'"

"About what?"

"About bad things happening..." For a moment, she looks like she's gonna cry.

"Getting sick can happen anywhere, even my mom knew that." She shakes her head, though. Something's going on. I crouch by her pillow, try to get my face level with hers. "Look. I got people downstairs and you need someone with you. Who can I get, if not those two?"

"Don't care. Not them."

Fingers clutch mine, squeeze tight. Her eyes drift shut as her breathing evens out. She's asleep, or something like it. Perfectly fine yesterday, I'd swear to it, and look at her now. I should call a doctor, that's what I should do, only who'd come out at night?

At least I can keep her warm. I go to my room, tug the quilt off the bed, and spread it over her. That'll keep the chills at bay. Sweat out a fever, that's the way to go. Get her better.

One thing's certain, though: she's not driving anywhere tomorrow. No way. Not even a chance of that. When one door closes, a window breaks and there's broken glass everywhere. Dammit. She was the only one I trusted to help us, unless Chuck's willing to do it himself. I can put the date off, or I can drive us. I don't know how really, but it can't be that hard. Turn a key and press the gas. I managed it once or twice in the war, and I can manage it now. Maybe. Probably.

A bell rings downstairs.

I'm back down to the bar as fast as I can. The domino game is paused mid-play, and someone's leaning against my counter like a bad penny.

"What d'you want, Connor?"

He's had a haircut, will wonders never cease. Found a nice pair of jeans somewhere, too, and a decent shave for the peachfuzz that he's begun to sprout. If you could call a smile oily, you'd be describing his. "Lonely tonight, Erin?"

"Not really," I lie. "Been a busy day." I wave my hand at the players in the corner, and they go back to their game. I lower my voice. "Seriously, Connor, do you want something?"

His voice matches mine. "Thought you'd want to hear the news: Art's twice wanted. Murder and attempted rape."

My breath catches. "You're joking. Who?"

"Ryan Jesser and you." He's attempting casual and nowhere near it. "I'm sure you can figure out which is which."

This is ridiculous. This cannot be real. "Are you kidding me?"

"Cross my heart, hope to die."

"Why are you telling me this, Connor?"

He examines his fingernails almost delicately. One of them's bruised black. "Guess I just like you, Erin. You've been like a big sister to me, times."

"This from the boy who spits on his family grave."

His eyes narrow, the nice act dropping a shade further. "Low blow from the former whore."

"You keep using that word," I remark, "like no one can throw it at you."

Now we're on our usual footing. It's comforting, in a way. "I came here to tell you something important. You'll want to know it."

"Then spit it out already."

"Mick Perry"—he smiles—"is in love with Simon. You should have seen the sparks fly when I made a few harmless remarks earlier."

Well. "So? Is that all you've got?"

"Thought that was about your worst fear."

"Simon's a big boy, he'll figure it out. If I was afraid of homos, I'd've stopped talking to you long ago."

"Cute." Connor can never stand being wrong for long. He's

pissed I stole his thunder, so he'll want to get even fast, and the hurry will make him sloppy. "Then here's what else I had to tell you: I saw Art Weber tonight, about two streets over. Heading here if I'm not mistaken, sneaking through the bushes. And you know the penalties for helping criminals."

Same punishment for both. I lean my elbows on the bar. "Yeah, I do. And do you know the penalties for being an asshole?"

He draws a breath to say something snarky, and then I hear it, just barely: a floorboard overhead, creaking.

That ain't Grace getting up, no way.

I meet Connor's eyes. "Don't you dare touch anything," I hiss. "Don't you dare."

Smile at the men in the corner still clicking away, take the stairs nearly two at a time. Her door is open, shit shit, and...

Yes. Art's sitting next to her bed, stroking her hair back, glass of water in his other hand. I'd know those eyes anywhere—in the dark, in the night, from the bottom of the deepest well. Staring at me across the room, they are memory itself.

Terror clenches in my gut just as hard as the day my son was taken and I cried for a mercy I knew didn't exist. Art's gonna get us all killed, every one of us.

Connor bumps into my back, hands clutching my shoulders, strong fingers digging in. I can feel him opening his mouth, breath streaming past my ear. "Call the guards outside. Turn him in."

Grace's eyes open, blinking in confusion. She looks up, sees Art. Connor's fingers press too hard.

"Is it okay?" Grace croaks to Art. I don't dare move. "Is he really dead?"

He? He who?

Only one dead person I know of, and that's Ryan Jesser, and Grace couldn't know about him yet, because she's been inside all day. After all, I only just found out a minute ago about this and the only way she could've known...

"I took care of it," Art murmurs. "No one's coming for you."

She mutters something and turns over, coughing that horrible cough, not noticing me at the door. Art's eyes are steady on mine as he stands up and walks across the room, daring me to say something, but I know what I heard, and if what I heard was right...

The door shuts in my face.

My fingers clutch Connor's wrist, not that he's moved. "We're going downstairs. Don't you dare call anyone. I want more info."

"I want paying," he says.

"I'll pay. Tell me everything you know." I'm back downstairs in the front room reaching for the cash box before he has time to speak. "I want to know everything. *Everything*. And for the love of God, don't call anyone, or we'll all hang."

65

Simon

Mr. Farley comes by Mick's place just after dinner, packet of paper in his hands: convoy itinerary, map of the town, map of the surrounding minefields, and a schedule for when we'll meet our ride. All of it's handwritten, all of it enough to get me or him killed if the wrong person finds any of them.

"Erin says you can come home in the morning," he says.

Home. Won't be home for much longer. "Thanks."

"If I don't see you again, stay safe."

I meet Mr. Farley's eyes. He's worried. He should be. I sure as hell am. "I'll try."

He heads into the night, and I return to Mick's kitchen. He's sitting at the table with a pack of cards, but his eyes watch the papers in my hands.

"Me and Erin, we're gonna leave tomorrow," I say. *Leave.* The word tastes sharp, like licking a battery. "Don't wanna say too much, but yeah. You heard me talking to her yesterday, right?"

He's gone guarded. "Yeah."

"Well, that's what we're doing."

How do I say this next part? Could've said it this morning just fine, yesterday okay, but now? After what happened?

Don't think, just do. I'm better at one than the other.

"You wanna come with us?"

Mick's eyebrows shoot up, and I can see his mouth dropping open and the word *no* in his eyes, and that's not fair. I won't let that happen before I can say why.

"Not because of today. Because..." I don't know what the fuck I'm doing. Because I feel like a kid against Petrowski and I know he can squash me like a bug, but I think I'm just big enough to make him not want to, too much of a legend to be got over quickly. It'd make people mad if I died, and we gotta leave while I still have that protection. "It's gonna be hard. And we need someone who knows what they're doing."

"So what you're saying is, you want me along because I'm a big baddy too, and if someone comes after you, I have enough guns to blow them to hell and back."

Yes. No. Not like that, no, not that way. Mick's voice is flat and his face is too, true feelings hidden with his indifferent mask that he uses when he's lying. I've pissed him off, I can see that well. But I don't know how to un-piss him, 'cause it's not like what he said wasn't true, only *not like that*.

Maybe my internal fight shows on my face, 'cause he softens a fraction. "Simon. I have a business here, you know that as well as anyone. I have stock, got money sunk in, people who depend on me. I, of all people, cannot up and leave at a whim."

"I know." My voice cracks.

"If that's all you want me there for, I can't help. Maybe give you supplies, okay, but I gotta stay on the good side of Buchell and Petrowski, same as anyone else. I need the Market too."

It was stupid of me to ask, stupid to think there was anything in this for him but the money what makes this town spin round. Maybe his looks at me were all in my head too. Maybe this morning was just too much tension or my fault or who knows the fuck what.

He's still going. "And what would I do when I got out? I've got something set here, and I don't see—"

"Okay, okay, I get it. I shouldn't've asked. Fine." That just sounded angry. "Sorry. I just wondered."

"Why?"

"Because." 'Cause we train every day, and you actually listen to my problems and don't tell me to just suck them up, but now you sound like Art. Grow up. Be practical. Don't you understand, Simon?

No, I don't. I really don't.

This morning was a mistake. This whole thing is a mistake. This is stupid, this is wrong. I'm wrong. I always am. Everything would have been simpler. Everything would have been better if I'd just kept my mouth shut.

Only, then I'd never have known. You gotta ask if you wanna know.

"Because what?" Mick asks.

"'Cause I thought you might, okay? But you don't want to. That's fine. Are we done now?"

He's giving me that same look, where he's trying to hide that he likes me and I'm sick to death of this bullshit thing where he sits there thinking that and then says he won't come with us. I'm so fucking tired of two-faced liars. First Art, and now Mick. Is there anyone around me who don't just wanna use me up for everything they can take? That ain't fair of me to say, and I don't care, I don't want to care anymore. I wish I didn't care about anything anymore.

"Simon? Where you going?"

If I open my mouth, this will all come out, so best I keep walking through the house and out the door, grabbing my coat along the way. It's cold out, cloudy again. The temperature's dropped something sharpish with the sunset. As I watch, a single snowflake floats down from the sky.

Now that I'm out, where do I go? Where do I go tomorrow, when we leave Buchell? Where do I know of? What's out there? Mountains on one side, flat on the other. North there's big lakes, south there's swamps. There's Scioto City and North Zion and Cattleton and New River Port and who knows where else.

Erin's place'll be in full swing, and I can't face that right now. Nobody I wanna see downtown, or for ten miles around for that matter. My feet take me to the old park instead, where the chains on the swings are rusted but I can sit and think for a while. I find the trail to them, feel my way along, like I'm the only person left in the world.

Only I ain't, 'cause someone else is there already. Wasn't sure he'd come.

"Connor?"

"Who else?"

I might be mad, but I ain't stupid. He shouldn't be here. *I* shouldn't be here. It hits me like a hammer. Like a bride on her wedding day, you don't meet your opponent beforehand. It messes things up. But I still came, didn't I?

Connor pulls out a lighter and starts flicking it. "Mick not everything you wished he was?" I don't say nothing and he laughs. "Please. It's not hard to guess."

"I don't know what you're talking about."

"You're so transparent, Simon." He leans back, stares up at the snow that's falling faster now. "I'm so sick of hearing about your problems. I can't take three steps without something coming up about you. Simon Flaherty, Simon Flaherty, yada yada yada. You know what? Let's not talk about you tonight. Let's talk about me."

He glances over to where I'm still standing. I can't see his face, it's too dark for that, more's the pity. My knife is still on Mick's table. "You, Simon, sicken me. You have everything going. You have the warm bed, the love and attention, you have someone holding your goddamned hand as you do your homework every night. And yet here you are, moping around because Mick Perry isn't as good a fuck as you thought he'd be."

"What?" Of all the things I thought he'd say.

"Oh, he's tall and handsome, but he's not good enough for the great Simon Flaherty. Life isn't a fairy tale, and that breaks your little heart."

I cross my arms. "What the hell are you talking about? You keep going on about this, and I haven't a clue."

"Please. It's obvious. That jerk'd do anything for you."

Not anything. "You're talking out your ass. Don't—"

"Don't tell me what to say or not say, Flaherty." Connor shoots to his feet to stalk toward me. "You of all people, don't you dare tell me anything."

I step back. "The hell is your problem? You're not supposed to be here, even! We're not supposed to see each other!"

"Why? Your boyfriend jealous?" He's so close I can finally make out his features. "Mick tell you I'd say something mean? Is that it,

Simon? Suddenly I'm not good enough to talk to Saint Flaherty's noble personage?"

"Fuck off, Connor. You're the one who's jealous."

"Jealous? Christ, I can't imagine why." He leans over and spits. "Erin would do anything for you. Anyone in this town would. But not for me."

It's true. I know it's true. "I don't ask for it."

"You don't have to. Everyone else does the dirty work for you."

Is that what he really thinks? Is it really true? I don't know anymore.

"I came here because I had news for you, but you know what? You can suck my dick if you want it. I'll see you tomorrow, and then you better watch your back because I'm done watching you walk on water. You can get beat, and then you can learn to live like the rest of us."

I grab hold of his bicep as he shoulders past. It flexes under my fingers. "And how exactly," I grit out, "is that? You mean not being followed around? You mean letting my dad run my life, as well as this town? You mean bending over and taking it in the ass 'cause that's what everyone else is doing?"

"You don't know anything about it."

"You don't know anything about this! He's hurting Erin 'cause of me!" The words scream out of my mouth before I have time to stop them. And it's true. Oh God, it's true, and I knew it the moment I realized it was Petrowski. It's all my fucking fault. "He wanted a new kid because his other son ain't fucking good enough! I told him I'd never join up, so he needed himself a new kid and Erin was right there and now look what's happened. Just look at it!"

God, I've been wanting to say that for so long. Been bursting to say it. I hate my dad so much. I hated him before and I fucking hate him more now, and it kills me what I done to Erin and I can't undo or take it back 'cause I wasn't smart enough, tough enough, *good* enough.

Connor smiles. He always smiles when I start yelling, and I got steam coming out of my ears just about. Fuck him, though. Just fuck him.

"You know what I like about you, Simon?"

"What."

"You're the one person who does what I want." Snow is collecting in his hair and on his hoodie, melting on my hot neck. "I can play you like a drum."

He leans over as if to whisper in my ear. I'm waiting for the catch, watching him come closer. I don't know what I'm doing that he wants me to until I realize exactly what he's got planned. I can see it, laid out in front of me.

Our lips meet. I let go of his shoulder, and he steps in closer, hand on my neck, squeezing hard. My hands are on his hips, and this isn't nice, no, but it's good. I press harder and he presses back. If I bite down, if I scream in frustration, this will keep going 'cause this is what I need, what he needs—someone to hate and despise and take it all out on. I won't betray him, and he can feel what he wants to feel, 'cause so can I, and it works 'cause he is my secret and I am his and neither of us will ever, ever tell. Not ever.

I wasn't lying when I told Mick I'd never kissed a girl, 'cause I ain't. But I was fourteen when I finally figured out why Connor Hall wouldn't leave me alone. Took me two fights in the park weeds before I realized I wanted him too.

He bites my ear and it hurts and that's good too. He can take it, and I'll take it back, and I want it 'cause no one else would. Ain't Saint Flaherty around him, no, I'm not. Just Simon. Just me.

Tomorrow we'll duel. Tomorrow I'll leave. Tonight, tonight it feels like the end of the world, and this is all I have: one last time with him.

66

Grace

Erin's side gate rattles against my fingers, and suddenly there's someone behind me. I can just make out his features in the dark.

"Need some help, sweetie?"

Ryan. He's grinning at me, all teeth and glittering eyes. I can't move.

"I heard what you said to Taylor about me."

He bear-hugs me against him, hand over my mouth, hot breath in my face, too dark to see anything, and I can't breathe...

Something strikes my head. Pain sears across my skull. Can't move, can't get my knife or get away, and I squeeze my eyes shut only to open them again...

It's dark. I'm lying down. My head hurts so bad. I'm not outside, no, I'm in a dark room. I try to look around, but it feels like I'm being smothered under heavy weights.

"Shh, shh. Settle down," someone whispers.

"Who is it?"

"It's me, Grace, it's Art. I'm here to take care of you for the night."

Is that true, or will he stab me too? Or will I stab him?

"Is Ryan coming for me?"

"No, don't worry about him. He's not coming for you." Water drips, and a cool cloth touches my forehead. I feel like I'm boiling and freezing all at the same time. "He's dead, I saw to that."

"I killed him?" My voice comes out tiny.

"No, I did. And then I threw him in the river. He won't come for you again, I promise."

I shiver, and then I can't stop shivering. It's so cold in here. "But I saw him. He...he's coming for me, I know it."

"That was just a dream. You're sick, Grace."

The cloth disappears from my forehead. Water splashes lightly. Or is it blood? Is he bathing my forehead in blood?

I try to sit up, but the blankets are too heavy. Is there blood on my face? Are my clothes stained red?

"I shouldn't have killed him."

"Did you have a choice?" Art asks.

"I could've let him do it." My head spins. "Only I wouldn't have been letting him 'cause he wasn't asking, he'd just have done it. But I didn't want to kill him. I didn't want to, Art, but Jesus is going to hate me now."

"Shh, Grace, you're okay, you're okay. I'm putting the cloth back on your head. You've got quite a fever, so just settle down." Art wipes my cheeks. "You rest. I'll watch over you. Ryan won't come in here, I promise, and Jesus doesn't hate you for doing what you had to do. That'd be pretty unfair of him."

"None of it's fair. I didn't want to kill him."

"Sometimes we don't get good choices." He lays the cloth on my forehead, and the coolness trickles down my face. Calloused fingers stroke my cheek. "It's okay to wish you hadn't done it. But me, I'm glad you did. You made the world a better place, and why would Jesus object to that?"

Art sighs. His chair creaks.

Taylor's holding my hand again, standing next to my bed. "That's Ryan Jesser. I work with him. He's pretty chill, though not as cool as me, of course. In fact, there he is now. Hey, Ryan! Over here a sec!" Ryan steps forward. "Morning, Ryan. This is Grace Farley. She'll be murdering you later tonight."

I try to cry out as Ryan shakes my hand and smiles, but he won't let go of my fingers, holding them too tight. Someone touches my face and begins to hum "Amazing Grace." Both boys fade away and I begin to fall...asleep...

67

Erin

Simon's sitting at the kitchen table when I get up at dawn, twiddling his thumbs and looking sleep-rumpled. He nods when he sees me, and I raise my eyebrows back.

"Got your message from Mr. Farley," he says. "I'm gonna pack up this morning."

I put on a pot of water to boil and take a seat myself, fold my hands in front of me. It feels oddly formal, like we're interviewing each other. "We've got a bump in the road, Simon. You hear about Art yet?"

"Something new?"

I don't know how much this'll affect him, so I just come out and say it. "Ryan Jesser is dead. Art's being charged with murdering him. He's also got a charge for attempted rape. Of me."

His head jerks up in surprise. "Wait, what?"

"Don't ask me, I've nothing to do with it." The irony. "I only heard it last night from Connor Hall, of all people. Which brings me to the bump."

He smoothes his expression back to normal. My bet is that won't last for long. "Yeah?"

"Art is upstairs in Grace's bedroom. She's sick and he snuck in, and I don't dare tell anyone besides you." I narrow my eyes, try to see his thoughts. I'm not even gonna touch on what she was mumbling last night. "You, me, and Connor Hall, the little shit, are the only ones who know this, and it's gonna stay that way. You and I have a lot to do today."

"Yeah, I know," he says. "How sick is Grace?"

"She's out for the count today."

"Right. Okay." He thinks it over. "We gotta act like we always act, not give ourselves away. You want I should do my homework or something like that?"

School. There's one thing he won't miss. "Maybe later. This morning go do your training and jogging, same as always."

I don't think Simon could look more uncomfortable if he tried. "Mick and I agreed I didn't need to practice this morning."

"Then go stretch and drink coffee, I don't care. Do your run. But you're going over there and you're taking these with you."

I reach over and pick up the bundle of papers I put together last night. The house deed from the fireproof safe, yellowed and brittle at the edges, and a bill of sale what I drew up, furnishings and land included. Everything I own, to Mick Perry. Sell for cheap. For cash.

Oh God, we're really doing this. That is, if I can keep my feet on the ground and my head on straight.

"You take these over and try to get him to sign. I left the price blank, but I know what kind of cash he keeps there in that safe of his. Don't go lower than that last number. Think you can do it?"

"Yes." No waffling, no wondering.

I don't want to know if Connor was right about Mick having a thing for him. Gift horses and all that.

"Alrighty. If you can get any small arms or ammo in the deal, that'll do as well. We'll try and join the convoy the first stop down the road."

Simon swallows all this and takes his time digesting, eyes following thoughts only he can see. My heart is beating fast already, and neither of us mentions my eye. Small, small favors. We don't need to talk about the whys, only the hows.

"I gotta be at the stadium by four o'clock for weigh-in. Thing starts up at five, but I'm not fighting until last, maybe seven thirty, eight or so?" Simon thinks about this for a moment. "I gotta eat around two."

"Yeah, I know that. I'll kill a chicken for it." I shrug. "Might as well. Chuck Farley's in charge of blowing this place sky-high. I don't know what the after-fight will be like, but you'll hear the explosion no matter what. And then you just meet me at the car. Got it? Meantime, I gotta start work on the pie shells for Monday, and you can crack that bag of walnuts after you get back from Mick's."

"But we ain't gonna—"

"What we gotta do is pretend. Like you said." I shake my hair out of my eyes and stand up. "Tell yourself we'll be here tomorrow until you believe it. Then you'll act normal and no one will suspect. Trust me. Once you lie to yourself, the rest of the world is easy."

His chair scrapes against the floor, arms wrap around my shoulders tight. Just for a moment, a hint of a moment, I let myself sink back in their comfort because I'm so scared right now that if I think of what we're gonna do, what we're trying to do, what we're gonna die trying to do, I don't think I can move an inch. We're gonna die and I know it, gonna be taken and killed and we ain't ever gonna leave this town, but I can't stay, not like this, not anymore. I gotta do something, if only to say that for once I tried. I tried to live.

Simon squeezes my shoulders and kisses me on the cheek. Then he's out the door with the papers in a string bag, and here I am, in my kitchen, on the last day of my life.

Oh wait. I'll be here tomorrow too. Mustn't forget to tell myself that.

68

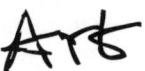

Erin's retucking Grace's covers when I wake up. How I managed to sleep in this chair is anyone's guess. It's wooden and rock-hard, but I hadn't slept in, what, thirty-six hours? Something like that.

"Her fever broke in the night," I whisper as I stretch. "She was pretty restless but finally started sleeping soundly around three, after you went to bed."

"That's good." Erin's got a bundle of towels wrapped around a hot brick, which she slips under the quilt. "Do me a favor. If she starts thrashing around, take that back out. Don't want her injuring herself."

"Sure." I wait for her to ask about me, about Grace, about anything. She settles herself on the windowsill, leaning against the curtains. Once she's comfy, she'll start on it. Erin's so predictable sometimes.

"What are you doing here, Art?"

Now's not the time to fob her off on anything smart-ass. She looks exhausted, and it hurts to see her that way.

"I had to make sure Grace was okay."

She nods, says nothing, but I can hear the unspoken question.

"I had to tell her...something."

Erin waits. Words fail me. For what seems like the first time in my life, I don't know what to say. I thought about it and thought about it and thought some more, of everything I could tell Erin to make this right and make her understand, but I just don't know anymore.

"Last night," Erin says when I don't continue, "Grace said something about someone being dead. Who did she mean?"

I meet her eyes. "You know who. I'm sure you've heard."

"Jesser."

"He wasn't supposed to be found so soon." The statement hangs in the air, heavy and accusatory. It says too much, and it doesn't say enough. "I mean, he was supposed to be found, just not yesterday. A few days from now, maybe."

"When his body was totally unidentifiable?"

I can't tell if she's angry or not. It's like we're two people who've never met before but have heard a lot about the other anyway. Strangers who know too much.

"And how," she finally asks, sounding more weary than ever, "did Grace know about it? Did she see it?"

"She did it. Not the whole of it. But she got him in the lung."

Erin raises fingers to her temples in a wince. "Why? Why did Grace do it? I assume you were there. But for God's sake, why?"

"He came after her," I say simply. Silence greets this, sucking the words out of me. "I just cleaned up after, tried to disguise things a little. Cut up his face a bit, 'cause women don't usually do that, you know? Saw it on TV a long time ago. And then I put the body in the river 'cause I didn't know where else he could go that would disguise things so quick, and Grace didn't know that part 'cause I told her to run and find an alibi."

I shut up rambling. Must be the sleep deprivation getting to me. I've always been stupid when I'm tired. I just wish Erin would say something. All she does is listen and judge, and I feel like her eyes have never been so dark.

"You'll be happy to hear she found an alibi," she says finally. "Taylor Burkes will vouch for her whereabouts that night. I will vouch that there's no blood on her clothes. She's safe. And now you're wanted twice over."

"I heard."

Damned if you do, damned if you don't.

"Erin, you gotta get out of this town. You gotta go. I'll take you, or

Simon will, but you need to get out. Petrowski's coming after me to get to you. I'm a threat to Petrowski, and he knows it. He knows you listen to me, or you did once. He wants you here to stay, and he's not gonna stop until he destroys everyone who might keep you from him."

"And if I go, then what? Think it through, Art. Who helps Grace? Who takes care of Simon? Who protects them?" She's not even angry, and that hurts. Like I don't even rate anger. "You always do this, Art. You never think."

"Don't say that. I have. I really have. I found a path and—"

"Listen to yourself!" she cries, louder than she meant to, and claps a hand over her mouth. "Listen to yourself. Don't you get it? I can't go. I'm sorry, Art, but I really can't."

I could cry with frustration. "But you have to. Grace—she was trying to get those idiots who go to your bar to do something, to help you, and they wouldn't even do that. That's why she was waiting in front of your house, that's why Jesser came after her! For you! All for you!"

Erin's hunched up in a ball, small like a child, knees drawn to her chin. It'd be better if she was angry, but there's none of that anymore. There's just pain whispering in her voice and the way her fingers clutch at her feet.

"I didn't want that," she says. "I didn't want any of this. I wanted—"

Downstairs, the back door opens and shuts. I bolt up, but Erin rubs her face. "That'll be Simon coming in from training."

But it's far too early for that; it's not even close to eight. Footsteps cross the floor and start up the stairs.

They're coming for me.

I'm up in my socked feet sliding on the wooden floors, pushing off the walls and down the stairs because, Christ, I was right, I was so right. There's two big guys coming up the stairs for me.

"Art?"

It's Seth Williams and Nathaniel Greene. They seize my shoulders, and we all stare at each other. Not Petrowski's boys. Shit. I know them, and they know me, and I know who they do not work for.

"What the hell are you doing here?" Seth demands.

"I could ask you the same."

"We need to talk to Erin," Nathaniel says. "Is she here?"

We're standing at the bottom of the stairs with the front door window in plain view. Out that window, across the street, sudden rapid movement. Someone's talking into a radio and pointing.

They can see us. Me. They see me.

Fucker.

"I gotta go!" I try to run, but Seth's still got my arms, my sleeves. I'm tangled all up.

"What...? Art!"

"Let me go! They're coming!"

"What are you *doing*?"

"Art!"

Shouting. Shouting outside, someone running up the walk toward me. Nathaniel and Seth look bewildered, unable to see what's nearly on top of us.

"They're coming for me!"

The front door crashes open, and two men lurch in with weapons drawn. "On the floor! Everyone on the floor!"

One of them leaps at me, and I can't even run. I'm pinned to the stairs without even being able to resist, damned by those two stupid fuckers. God fucking dammit.

"You have the right to remain silent or we'll kick your fucking head in." Handcuffed and kicked, I'm dragged upright by our very own Market Authority. "We're arresting you for the murder of..."

Their words run together, meaningless garbage. I am caught and I am done for.

There's more of them swarming the property, running up the stairs, running at Erin and Grace, handcuffing Seth and Nathaniel as I'm being pushed out the door and down the steps. Away from them.

Goddammit, this isn't fucking fair! Why'd Nathaniel and Seth have to go and do that for? Why couldn't they see what I was there to do, to help Erin? Why couldn't they just let me be?

And now they're in that house and the authorities will say they helped me. Even though it's not Erin's or Grace's fault. They'll say they helped me, and Petrowski doesn't even need a fucking excuse now, does he? Christ.

I thought I was free before. I thought I had nothing to lose, but turns out I was wrong. So wrong, dead wrong. I didn't have my life to lose; my life here's already gone. No, I had their lives in my hands, and I just fucking lost them.

69

Erin

Nathaniel won't look at me, and Seth won't quit staring. We're all of us sitting around Grace's bed, and a man with a machine gun is leaning against the door. It's surreal. This used to be my room where I slept with my son. The guys have never been in here before, and they're taking it in with wide eyes, not sure what to make of it. Grace slept through it all somehow. I heard Simon outside half an hour ago asking what was happening, but so far the only thing we've been told is that we're under arrest. They radioed headquarters, and apparently we're waiting for orders. Or something.

Someone knocks on the door, and the guard opens it without taking his eyes off us. Taylor Burkes comes in. His eyes flick to Grace before landing on me. "Erin Livingston's wanted by the boss. The rest can stay here."

I stand up, and Seth does too, looking nervous as hell. "Erin, I just wanted to say—"

"Save it."

"No, I wanted to say, I get it. Grace tried to tell me. But I get it now." His mouth is earnest, shoulders squared.

"Get what?"

"Hurry up!" the guard barks. "Don't keep the boss waiting."

I walk out the door. It doesn't matter. None of it matters now. Escape was a dream, nothing more.

There's a car waiting outside, a real car, not a truck. Taylor opens the back door for me and we pull away. I look back at the house as we go. Will Simon go through with the plan anyway? Is this the last time I'll ever see my place? The peeling white paint, the straggly bushes along the front, the dead leaves trampled into the sidewalk. It's been my home all my life. Will it be ashes by tomorrow?

"We're here."

I look up. This isn't headquarters; this just a house in the middle of town. A hairdresser. I know the woman. She showed me how to get rid of Simon's lice when he first showed up. Why are we here?

"Come on, Erin."

Taylor takes my elbow and helps me out, ushers me up the concrete steps and down the walk to the front porch. The woman who owns it opens the door.

"Erin needs her hair done up," Taylor says. "Do you have an open appointment?"

She purses her lips, looks from him to me and back again. "I suppose. But what is this about?"

"A fancy occasion. Mr. Petrowski's money."

The magic words open the screen door. I'm in a chair, a cloth draped over me, my braid undone and being combed out down my back. There's a radio on. Taylor leans against the wall, and I can just make out a man outside the door holding a rifle. Has the woman noticed yet?

"This any particular occasion?" she asks Taylor, not me.

"Just nice."

She rubs my hair between her fingers. "Mm, don't think it'll curl, not with hair like yours, but we'll see what we can do. Was one of your parents Chinese, hon?"

It takes an hour for her to do my hair, a long hour in which I avoid looking in the big mirror in front of me. My eye's as dark as it was yesterday, with a weird green tinge along the edges. There's cuts around it, and another on my chin. My lip's gone down in swelling, but the bruise on my cheekbone is a shadow that can't be ignored. Raising my left arm higher than my shoulder makes me dizzy. I'm being killed by inches, but now my hair looks pretty.

At the end, the hairdresser shakes a can of something and tells me to close my eyes. When she finishes spraying, I am covered in glitter.

I have never worn glitter before. I've never had my hair done at a salon before. Never looked like this before. I haven't eaten today, but I feel close to puking.

"Well," she says, meeting my eyes in the mirror. Her face is apprehensive. "I think that's as formal as it gets."

Taylor leads me back to the car, and I'm leaning on him now. Don't care who sees I'm weak, don't care, don't care. Escape was only ever a dream, and my feet tread heavily now. Gravity drags me down. I slump on my side as soon as I hit the seat only for Taylor to pull me back up.

"Your hair. Can't mess it up."

Whatever. He sits next to me, holding my forearm, holding me up. I close my eyes for a moment.

"Are you alright?"

I don't bother to answer. Taylor shakes my shoulder lightly, taps my cheek with his finger. "Erin?" The car starts to move, and we sway with it. He tries again. "Erin? Are you asleep?"

From behind my eyelids, I can sense the buildings pass, shadows flicking over my face. Taylor leans in, stubby fingers tucking a loose strand of hair behind my ear as he whispers, "Erin, do you know what's happening? Did he tell you? Seriously, are you okay? You don't look good."

A finger touches my bruised eye and I flinch.

"Oh! Sorry."

My eyes fly open, and I turn just in time to see Simon as the car flashes past him. I twist in my seat, trying to see out the back. Trying to tell him with my face to keep going, to save himself, to not worry about me. I'm a goner and I know it, and if he has any sense, he'll go through with the plan and get out and never look back, not ever, not once. It's not worth it for him to stay. I'm not worth his life. Tears are streaming down my face, and Taylor's trying to tug me back around, but I won't move, no.

I watch him until we turn the corner, and then I don't want to sit down because I know as soon as I do, it'll be over, and Simon will be gone. My boy, my boy who I raised and loved and tried so hard for, he will be gone. Forever.

70

Simon

The guard at the front door's been stonewalling my attempts to get info for the past five minutes. Won't give me nothing, not even so much as "Erin's okay" or "We'll know later."

"Can you at least tell me where Erin went?"

"No."

"Can I go inside and talk to Grace?"

"No."

"She's sick. Is she doing better?"

"I don't know."

"God," a voice drawls, "he sounds almost as smart as you, Simon."

It's Connor, here to make my day better. Fuck off.

"What's up, Simon? Mommy's gone shopping and you're getting lonely?" He smiles, and if he comes much closer, I think I might start today's fight a few hours early.

The guard at least seems to be aware that Connor shouldn't be here. "Piss off, you. This is none of your business."

"Oh, but it is," Connor replies. "Simon making an idiot of himself is always my business. The fact that you're here just makes it better."

The guard's eyes are flickering like crazy, which just makes Connor smile more.

"I said piss off. I mean it. Scram."

"And fuck you too. But you should know what little Simon here isn't telling the adults."

Come on, Connor, do what the man says and piss off.

"Mr. Chuck Farley himself is on his way here," Connor announces. "He just found out what's happened to his little princess, and he's fit to be tied. Battle stations, if you will."

Actually, Mr. Farley knew an hour ago when I told him. If he's on his way here, that means he's got the tickets in hand 'cause he knows Grace is okay. No one's gonna touch her, 'cause no one wants to annoy him. Being Buchell's only knife maker is the best insurance in the world; the town loves him.

Connor's not finished with me. "Anyway, I'm just here to drop off your homework from yesterday, because apparently God forbid we let Simple Simon miss a day of schoolwork, lest all the things you've managed to learn just shrivel up and fall out your ears in its absence." He thrusts a folder at me. I snatch it away. "We learned a new theorem. If you have any questions, you know where to find me. Have fun failing math."

"Screw you." Never have I wished I was more good at comebacks than now. Or anytime that I have to be around Connor, really. Nothing makes him happier than yanking my chain, and nothing makes me wanna punch him more. "Is that all you came here for?"

"Mrs. Malone said good luck, and I agreed. You'll need all the luck you can get. The rest of us have a little something known as 'skill.'"

"Are you done being catty, or you gonna bitch about your period now?" the guard says. Glad I'm not the only person wishing I could drop Connor in the river. "I ain't gonna tell neither of you nothing, so get out before I call backup. Both of you!"

Connor shrugs and I scowl. We get about ten steps down the walk when the guard calls out, "And good luck in the match, Flaherty! I got money on you!"

Connor sticks his middle finger up in the air. I open the file, see what's inside. Not like I'm gonna go back to school, and ain't that a weird thought, but I can do homework if it makes me look like normal and keeps me from going nuts while I wait. I'll learn the theorem or whatever.

The paper inside is blank. I turn it over. There's nothing written here. No theorem, nothing. What the hell?

Wait a sec. Connor didn't go to school yesterday, either. So why is he...?

He's already disappeared between a couple of houses, but what were his words when he gave me the folder? *"You know where to find me."*

Oh shit, I hate when he does crap in code. I break into a run for the park.

Connor walks into the clearing looking cool as a cucumber. "You got here fast."

Sweat trickles down my back, cold and sticky, that folder still clutched in my hands like it's life itself.

I thrust it at his face. "What do you want? Why did you give me this?"

"Why do you think I want anything?"

"'Cause you wouldn't've bothered if you didn't want something. You want me to forfeit the match, is that it?"

"I don't need you to forfeit, because I will beat you outright," Connor hisses. "But I wanted to let you know that I know you're planning to run out of town. You and Erin both." My heart stops. "You are, aren't you?"

How does he know? How the fucking hell does he know? "We're not."

"Don't lie to me."

"I'm not."

He steps forward so we're nose-to-nose, facing off. Connor takes a deep breath. His eyes are blank, dead like they get when Principal Miles comes in the room to tell him tuition's due. "Yes, you are, and I'm coming too. Or I'll kill you."

Was that a threat, or a warning?

"You're coming?" I repeat blankly.

"Yes."

"Why?"

"Why do you think?"

I can't think. "But you scheduled a rematch for Wednesday already."

"Who cares about that!" It busts out of him like a tank shell, half screaming from his mouth. "Who cares about that fucking fight, or this one, or the next one! There's always gonna be a next one! And you're always gonna be someone's golden fucking boy, and I am gonna be the goddamned queer whore! Everyone in this town knows who I am and what I've done, and I'm so fucking sick of being treated like the scum of the earth while you walk on water. I'm good at school, I could go to fucking college in Scioto if I could get the money, but no! I'm stuck in fucking backwater Buchell, and what do people say to me? *Oh*, you fight with *Simon*, you go to school with *Simon*, isn't he so *great*! But not me, because I sucked dicks to survive! And here's me working my ass off pushing this and delivering that until I'm so fucking up to my eyeballs in it that I can't even see straight and it's still not enough money for living, let alone school, and I want out! Out of this town, out of this life! OUT!"

I stare at him standing there panting, ten kinds of rage coming off him in waves. I never knew. I looked at him and I hated him, but I never knew. I mean, I knew he didn't like being a whore, yeah, but the drugs, like, that was his thing. He always had a smirk on his face. Like, that was what he did. But all along, this? I didn't know. Been so wrapped up in my own problems. Never saw past my nose.

"I'm sorry," I say, 'cause I don't know what else to say. Ain't I been blind.

He turns away, brown eyes avoiding mine. "Don't apologize. You don't fucking do it, okay? It's the rest of the town. It's everyone. Even the teachers, saying shit like they're thinking, 'Oh, you could go to college, but...cum dumpsters like you don't do that.' I'm so sick of it. It's everyone but you, and I fucking hate you so much."

"Erin's coming," is all I can think of to say. "This is for her, not me."

"That's obvious."

"Is it?"

"Trust me." His smile is all teeth, no mercy. "That's why you need me. I know where she is right now, and I know what they're planning tonight."

"Is he with her? Is Petrowski with Erin right now?"

"No. Not now." The way he says it also says I ain't gonna like the answer. Connor's got a way with words; just hearing them makes you wanna smack him. "He won't see her now because, tell me, Simon, riddle me this: What event aren't a man and a woman supposed to see each other before? It starts with *w* and ends in *edding*."

I turn and punch the swing set as Connor laughs, long and low.

71

TAYLOR

Mr. Petrowski told me to help Erin, and I am damn well going to do my job, though right now what she seems to need help with is keeping it together. Between the hairdresser and the woman who does makeup, she's nearly fallen over half a dozen times. She's got her eyes closed, won't even open them when I say her name. Something's seriously wrong here. Ever since she freaked out in the backseat of the car after the hairdresser's, maybe even before. The lights are on, but nobody's even close to home, and it's getting eerie.

When we get out of the car at the dressmaker's shop, I don't bother to let go of her, just keep an arm around her waist. I knock on the door as quick as I can. "Come on, wake up," I hiss in her ear as we wait. "If you need a doctor, you gotta say. Otherwise, we gotta do this."

She opens her eyes, dull and flat. Then she seems to pull herself together, and just in time. When the door opens, she almost looks halfway normal. At least she's not crying anymore. It took ages for her to stop, and then the makeup woman wouldn't shut up about it, kept going on saying, "Is she okay?" and "What's wrong?" as if Erin was going to talk. Because she wasn't. Not that I've got a fucking clue.

The dressmaker's front room is done up with mirrors and a ritzy stool. Erin steps up on it, and the woman fusses around her, taking measurements and nodding to herself. "And now let's just get this dress on. Out you go, young man! No men in here, not in my dress studio. It'll be just a few minutes and you wait out there." She points outside.

Well, it's not like I'm worried about Erin doing a runner, not in the state she's in. I sit on the concrete steps next to Joe, who's been driving. He's starting on a roll-up when his radio crackles to life. "Joe, this is Cooper, you read me?"

"Loud and clear."

"Location?"

"At the dressmaker's. She's putting it on now."

"When will she be finished?"

Joe and I look at each other. How long can putting on a dress take? "Ten minutes? Does that sound right?"

"Roger. Radio when you leave."

"Gotcha."

"Over and out."

Joe puts his radio down and rolls his eyes. I roll mine back. Some guys just can't figure out that saying shit like that makes you sound like a royal douche.

A shriek splits the air in the dressmaker's. I'm on my feet and throwing open the door before I can even blink.

The dressmaker's holding up a white gown like she's warding off evil spirits as she cowers by the curtains. Erin stands in the middle of the room clutching a shirt to her chest. She looks around wildly, spies me, and bolts for the door behind her.

I leap, my fingers catching on the fabric of her shirt. It comes away in my hands—because she's not wearing it—and now I'm holding the shirt and Erin's clutching at her naked chest still screaming her head off.

"What is that for? What is that dress for!" she screeches.

"Erin, it's okay, calm down."

"I'm not wearing that!"

"Erin, please, just calm down for a second."

"No! You can't make me! Get it away from me! Get it away. *Don't touch me!*"

I snatch my hand back. I was just trying to touch her shoulder, that's all, I promise, and now she's hunched up like I just backhanded her. There's horrible bruises on her arms like someone held her down. I'm staring and I know it, and she's gulping back dry sobs, gasping like she's running a marathon. I can count her ribs, one, two, three, see her hip bones jutting out above her jeans. And she's supposed to be pregnant, looking like that?

I hold my hands up, drop her shirt, and turn my back. Joe's standing at the door with his mouth open, and I gesture for him to do the same. Dressmaker's exactly where I left her, looking shocked. Behind me, the sound of Erin's breathing is subsiding as she dresses.

When I turn around, she's still hunched over, arms across her chest as if it's still on display.

"Erin, are you okay?" I ask her.

"No. No, I am not." She points a shaking finger across the room. "What the hell is that thing for?"

"It's a dress," I say. "A wedding dress. For your wedding."

"My wedding."

"Today."

"My *wedding*."

Has no one told her? Mary, Mother of God.

"What did you think all this was for? The hair, the makeup, the car?" I throw open my arms and she flinches back. "Your wedding to Mr. Petrowski."

"And when did you hear about this...wedding?" she asks.

"This morning. He announced that he proposed the night before last. And you said yes," I add.

This looks like news to her. "He asked me to marry him and I said yes. And now this is my wedding dress?"

The dressmaker finally steps forward. "He...he came by here last week. Picked it out from my stock. I spent yesterday retailoring it. It should fit alright..."

Erin's glare would stop anyone in their tracks. "And when is this wedding gonna take place?"

"Tonight," I answer. "After the fights. After Flaherty wins. Or Hall. Whatever."

"They're gonna have a bunch of men fight, and then there's gonna be a wedding. Is that it? That's all the fun there is planned?"

Her voice is flat, makes me feel like I'm stupid.

"No," I say, 'cause my mouth won't seem to shut up. "They're going to hang Art Weber tomorrow afternoon."

Her face goes white, and I never seen anyone do that before. White as that dress, all in a moment.

"What?" she whispers. "Why?"

"For attacking you. Petrowski walked in and fought him off...and then he proposed...and you said yes..."

The story's a total lie. I know it, and she knows it, but who else saw Erin that morning, when we knew Art wasn't anywhere near that house and she had that face that'd been used like a punching bag, like something you do to a dog, not a human being, let alone a woman? Not like that, anyway. And he did it. Petrowski did it, and I believe that with all my heart because that man is terrifying. He would do that and then have the balls to say someone else did because it was convenient. Because Art's got a thing for Erin, and even if she don't care two figs for him, she might've once and he can't suffer a rival to live, now can he? Not when it comes to the apple of his eye, bruises and all.

"And that, right there, is my dress."

I didn't think Erin could make me feel any more like shit, but I was wrong. "Yeah. That's it."

"You want me to get married to my stepfather the day before Art's hanging. Wearing white."

Mary, Mother of God, when she puts it that way. "Yes."

"No." She pulls her elbows in tight, purses her lips, and stalks toward the door. "Not on your life."

"Erin! One minute," I toss that over my shoulder before following her. "Erin, it's not like that. You're not wearing the dress for the hanging, you're just..." She's got her hands over her ears.

The radio's crackling on the walk where Joe left it. All I can make out are the words, "Attention! Attention!" I scoop it up, still staring at Erin as she begins walking down the sidewalk away from the car.

A frantic voice crackles over the waves. "All men report! Art Weber has escaped from headquarters! He is armed with a semiautomatic assault rifle and is not to be approached directly.

Capture dead or alive! Attention! Attention! All men report!"

Erin looks behind her and starts sprinting, one last bid for freedom. Joe starts running after her. He's gaining, but she jumps a fence and it could be a while before he can get her back without messing up her hair or makeup. And you know, I should help him, but right now...

I will follow my original orders and help Erin. In this case, I'm protecting her from Mr. Petrowski, because I don't want to see what he'll do if she doesn't show up in a dress tonight, not to me, not to her.

The dressmaker's sitting in a chair having what looks like quiet hysterics. I pull out the wad of cash Mr. Petrowski gave me.

"We still need a dress." I thrust out the money, easily what she makes in a month, and smile without meaning it. "Do you have any other colors? I don't think she likes white."

72

That little café where Chris has been washing dishes is easy enough to reach by back alleys. A storeroom with a small window comes in handy right now, bless my old sergeant for teaching us all this trick, and I'm inside in a trice. I can hear people eating in the front, so it's still busy, which means Chris should be...

"Fancy seeing you here."

He doesn't quite drop the plate he's holding, but it's a near miss. Good.

"Art." He's shaking in his shoes. "Whole town's looking for you. What are you doing here?"

"Came to see you, of course."

His worst fears have been confirmed. "If this is about that last fight—"

"No. No, Chris, it's not about the last fight. It's about this one. You know every way in and out of the stadium, right?"

"Yeah, but—"

"So how do I get in that no one else knows about?"

"You can't!" He looks around wildly, apparently convinced that this answer is gonna get him murdered. "There's no secret way in or out, not that no one knows about. If you're lucky, they've gotten the old steam tunnels cleaned out and open again, but I don't know why they would've because..."

Steam tunnels. Forgot about those, and they go everywhere.

Perfect. I can get in and no one will see me. I've gotta stop this wedding. They were all snickering about it in headquarters, and I'm not gonna let it happen, no way.

"...Farley's daughter got brought in around an hour ago."

"What?" I'm tuned in again. "Repeat that."

"We heard that you'd escaped when a couple local guys came by to bring Chuck Farley's daughter in to stay here for a bit."

"Why would Grace be here?" I ask dumbly.

"Because this is her mother's café."

Huh? How did I not notice this? Have I been that out of the loop lately?

Change of plans. "I want to see her."

"Marissa?"

"Who?"

"Marissa Farley, she's the one who owns the café."

"No, not her. Grace. I want to see Grace. Take me to her," I order.

"Art, I'm busy. I'm working—"

"Not a request, Chris. Want me to tell the world you're in Petrowski's pocket these days?"

He opens his mouth, and I hold up my stolen rifle. That seems to get the point across. He shrinks and sulks and opens the door next to him. "She's upstairs somewhere. I don't know where exactly, it's not like I go up there."

"That's fine. Thanks, Chris, I owe you one."

"If you get caught..."

I ignore his pleading and go upstairs to a dark hallway with closed doors. Gotta find Grace, check on how she's doing. The first door's locked. Second door opens into some sort of linen closet. Third door is a bathroom, dusty in the remains of twilight. The last door opens into darkness. Gotcha.

She's sleeping, braids fanned around her head on the pillow. Her skin is waxy, chest rising and falling under a mound of crocheted blankets. Not dead, but not totally recovered. I place a wrist on her forehead, another on mine, and it's cool enough. Just a twenty-four-hour bug. She'll be okay.

Thank God. I'm glad for that, at least.

It's funny, I didn't know that I cared until just now, but I do, because there's something about this girl, even-keeled and straight-edged, something that speaks to me. I press her fingers between my hands, hold them to my forehead, try to think clearly through this dizzy relief. Here is one I have saved. Here is one who will not die because of me. I fucked up big, but I helped her.

Grace stirs, eyes fluttering open.

"Art?" She looks happy to see me.

"I'm here, Grace. You're okay now," I whisper. "Don't worry. You're not under arrest."

"But you...my mama said you were going to be hanged. She said. Is this a dream?"

"Not a dream, I promise." I pull the covers up a little, smooth them down. The least I can do. The very least. "No one's gonna hang me tomorrow. No one knows I'm here." Except Chris, who I'll take care of. "I don't know if I'll be able to see you again, but I just wanted to make sure you had your alibi fixed. You got your story?"

She nods.

"You told anyone yet?"

She shakes her head so hard her braids tangle around her head. Good. No one's spotted that she was anywhere near yet. Very good. "Well, whatever it is—don't tell me what it is—add this: You thought you heard something, but it was so windy you figured it was just the tree branches. But it spooked you, so you hurried away. That's your last resort. Don't tell them unless they ask. Okay?"

What a thing to say to her. No one's gonna ask, but if they do, if they ever think to, she'll be well covered. She'll be safe.

"Alright. I will."

"I know you will. You'll be fine." Girl like that, she could keep her head in any firefight. I'm not worried, somehow. Not about this. "I gotta go. You just hang in tight. And don't worry about me."

Fingers wrap around my wrist. "What're you going to do?"

"Gonna get in the stadium. Gonna right all the wrongs. Got nothing to lose, you know?" I try to smile, but it comes out wrong. "I'll take the steam tunnels."

"The what?"

"Tunnels. All under the really old part of town, good for getting around unseen. The stadium was part of the old junior high school, you know?"

Grace frowns. "Why don't you just wear a disguise?"

"It's not as simple as that. The tunnels—"

"I don't see why not. I got a box full of stuff in the closet." She sits up, pushes down the blankets, and stands, putting a hand out to steady herself. "My mama used to do theater when I was a kid. We've got everything."

"I doubt you've got..."

She opens a closet, pulls out a big plastic tub. Clothing goes everywhere. A pink skirt, some weird hat, a...

Priest robe.

Wedding.

Hey, I've got an idea.

I pick it up and shake it out. Should fit okay, okay enough, anyway. "A nice shirt under, maybe a wig..."

"Not a wig." She pulls out a smaller box, opening to reveal jars of makeup. "Wigs are too easy to lose. But glasses and a beard ought to do it just fine, and my mama's got a razor somewhere..."

Grace grins in the dim light, and I find myself smiling back. We're a good team, she and I. And this, well, it's so crazy an idea, it just might work.

73

Simon

Weigh-in flashes by, the numbers ticking past on the scale as everyone waits, newspaper camera flashing. At 188 pounds, six foot three inches, I've grown again, growing up all the time. Connor's on the scale next, 183 pounds, six foot four, and if we was still in bare-knuckle, we'd be in different classes, but we ain't.

When our numbers are on the boards, they put us face-to-face like we're gonna kiss and hope that we'll put on a show, glare at each other and talk trash for everyone to get pumped about. Connor does, he always does. I don't, and I never do. That's why I'm Saint Flaherty.

Then it's into the locker room what they divide with sawhorses to keep us all apart, and there we sit. They keep you away from whoever you gonna fight. Totally different sides of the room. They don't want you to start early. Like dogs chained up, see? But I don't wanna fight in here 'cause there's no audience in the locker room. If no one sees a thing happen, it never did. I want this seen. I want everyone to see me win so they'll listen to what I got to say.

Not time to warm up yet. Not time to do anything but wait, and no one can tell you what it's like waiting for a fight. No one in the world. If they say they can, they're lying. Only way you can know is to live it, though I doubt you'd want to do that twice. I ain't bragging, but it's not exactly great.

There's this feel in the air, like thread pulled tight, like someone's put a scarf around your neck and knotted it up too much. You ain't strangling yet, but you might. You might. And the air, greasy thick and too hot, with a buzz in your ears as your mind turns in on itself, searching for all the answers to the questions that keep you up late at night, only it's not night now, it's day, and there's no sleep to escape to. There's just you and the fight.

Mick sits next to me, looking anywhere but at me. He ain't looked at me since the weigh-in. I fucked it up last night, and now he's mad. Well, fine. Be mad. I'll win this fight and leave this town and fuck you. The plan's moving and you said no, you didn't wanna come, so you're not a part of it, and if you don't like that, then you gotta speak up.

Are my teachers in the stands? Are the kids from school? The people in the Market, and the woman from the library who explained to me how to find books and check them out and keeps my library card for me 'cause she knows I lose it on my own? If I get hit, will they cheer? Will they clap if Saint Flaherty breaks Connor's nose? Will they listen to what Simple Simon has to say?

Twenty minutes to the first fight, then another couple hours of sitting here wondering. I start pacing and no one stops me. Two hours to the end of the world and counting.

74

TAYLOR

Half an hour ago, the corridor was full of footsteps, all the last-minute arrangements getting made, but now the board is set and the players are getting ready, and it's just Erin and me in this dingy room. I play solitaire to pass the time while she sleeps on a ratty sofa. Outside these four walls, the stadium pulses with energy. The radio will tell me when it's time for us to go to our seats.

A door slams down the hall, someone walks a few steps. Another door opens, though quietly this time, closes again. And another. Another. Someone's...searching for something?

The door to our room opens and I stand, putting myself between whoever and my charge. That's my job, the meat-shield.

It's Grace's bodyguard from two nights ago.

"This is a private room. State your business or leave."

Seth rolls his eyes heavenward. "Cool your heels, Burkes. I've been looking for Erin. I need a word with her."

I cross my arms to hide my confusion. "Yeah, what of it?"

"Can I talk to Erin or not?"

A rustle of silky fabric from the sofa says she's awake. "Seth? What are you doing here?"

He shoulders past me, striding over to kneel next to her. "Erin? You okay? I've been looking for you..."

He whispers something to her, and they're glancing at me. Alright, I can take a hint. Whatever. There's only one door to the room; after all, it's not like she can run away again. I roll my eyes.

"You have two minutes," I say before I step in the hallway and close the door behind me.

A cloth presses down across my nose and mouth. I gasp and start to fall.

75

Erin

"What have you done with Taylor?" I heard the thumps, and I ain't stupid or drugged. "The hell you playing at, Seth? What have you done?"

"Put him to sleep." He's grim, determined. "Time to get you out of here."

Like hell. "Where to?"

"Not sure yet."

"Then I ain't going."

"What?" Seth looks totally baffled. They're dragging Taylor's body somewhere, I can hear them. Do they think I can't?

I set my jaw. "If you don't know where you're taking me, I ain't going. It's safer here."

"Because you *do* want to marry Jeff Petrowski."

I fix him with the look I use when someone's getting a little too friendly at the bar. "No."

Seth throws his hands in the air. "Then let's go! Look, Grace explained everything to me—well, not everything, but enough, and I get it. You need our help and here it is. Nathaniel and Darryl'll be back any second. You got anything else to wear?"

I been stitched into this gown, navy blue and shiny like something my brother's prom date wore. In another life, maybe I would've worn it too. No virginal white for this bride. Anyway, it's not got a zipper. There wasn't time.

"No."

"Dammit." He paces for a few seconds, then looks at me. Really looks at me. "Why won't you come?"

Finally. "If I leave this room, half the county's coming after me," I explain. "I stay here, I'm safe. Not that it's your beeswax."

"And safe but married to him is better than unsafe and single?"

"Didn't say that. I leave, what do you do with me? How'd you get out of custody, anyway?" I ask just to distract him.

"They let us go once Farley got there." Seth crosses his arms. "Grace said...she said you were trapped in this, but you have to understand, none of us knew this, alright? We didn't know. You didn't seem in any trouble or say anything. You looked the same as you always did every night. So how was we to know you needed help?"

"I don't."

"You do." He straightens his shoulders like the hero he ain't. "And do you have any idea what'll be happening to me or Nathaniel or Darryl if we get caught?" The hall door opens, the two aforementioned men trooping in. "I'm sure you can guess. But you've been there for us, one time or another, and so now we are here for you." It sounds rehearsed. Seth takes a deep breath, cools his anger. "So why won't you come?"

"Wait, she won't come?" This from Nathaniel, who looks alarmed. "Erin, what? Why not?"

Darryl turns to the other two, his voice low. "Clearly they've given her something to make her docile so they could go through with all this. I say we just get her out of here and wait for it to wear off."

"She doesn't look drugged. She says she just doesn't want to go."

"Why the hell not?"

They look at me as one. Somewhere in the building a loudspeaker crackles to life and music begins pounding through it. Ten minutes to fight time.

I stand. Let them sort it as they will, 'cause apparently I'm not needed in this conversation. "If you'll excuse me, I gotta head."

"Where?"

"Where else? My box. Taylor said they've done one up for me so's

306

I could watch in style. Get a good view of Simon."

They trail along like ducklings, not quite willing to touch me. Their little Magdalen, everybody's precious whore, that's me. I'm only in trouble if they try to take fate into their own hands.

Nathaniel catches up to me. "Erin, if you go into that box, then you have to marry Petrowski. Is that what you want?"

"Since when does anybody care what I want?" There's a tiara in my hair and dainty heeled shoes on my feet what hurt like hell but look oh-so-good. "And that includes you. I don't need your pity, and I don't need your help. I don't know what Grace told you, but me, I can take care of myself." I smooth the dress, take a deep breath through the stiff fabric. I know what I'm gonna do. I got the idea from something Connor said ages ago, about us being two of a kind. He wants the whole stadium to see him beat Simon. Well, I want them all to hear what I gotta say about Petrowski. Out in the daylights, or stage lights, or whatever it is I'm gonna get. "Now, you can come with me, as my guests in the good seats, or you can fuck off. I don't care which."

"Erin—"

"And you can shut up while you're at it." I meet their gazes one by one. "Come on. Best seats in the house, on me. I'll tell everyone you're my honor guard. Since when do I give away anything this good for free?"

Seth glares, Darryl has his mouth open, and Nathaniel looks hurt. That one twinges, just a little. I never set out to hurt no one. Not even these three idiots.

Nathaniel shakes his head, more bewildered than anything else. "Alright. Fine. Fine, then. And you don't want us to do anything?"

"No." I start walking, then reach out and squeeze his hand. "You done enough."

I can smell the crowd before I see them, hear the noise echoing. When we walk into that box, every eye is on me and my escort, the ones who stuck by, just as bad but better than nothing. Everyone in Buchell is watching, and everyone can see that I do not enter surrounded by Petrowski's men.

Well, everyone but two people. The son will get it. The father...?

Two minutes to go, and I've got the safest seat in town, every eye on me, now don't I just. Finally.

76

TAYLOR

I wake up with a pounding headache. It feels like my brain's about to come through my skull. What the hell happened back there? My mouth tastes like an old penny, and my arms and legs are cramped. Everything's dark except a line of bright light near my eyes.

Am I in a box? No, not a box. I try to stand up, and something long and wooden attacks me. I grapple for a moment only to find it's a mop. A closet. I'm in a closet. The line is the bottom of the door. My groping hands find the doorknob, and out I spill into an empty hallway.

I was supposed to be guarding Erin, and dammit if I didn't fuck that up. I start jogging.

"Taylor? Taylor, stop! Wait!" Chris Hopkins runs down the hall toward me wearing what looks like a long white apron under his coat.

"Chris? What are you doing here?" The pounding music cuts off suddenly, so a fight must've begun. But how long have they been going? That's the question.

"No time to explain!" He bends double, panting for air. Sweat's trickling down his face. "Taylor, you gotta help me! Art Weber turned up at the café I work at looking for Grace Farley. He was crazy, Taylor. You should've seen it!"

I blink. "What the hell, man."

"But that's not the worst of it. He went up to talk to Grace, and I went to the back room to get my coat, only I could hear everything they were saying. And...and..." He stops to cough, and I grind my teeth. Come on, Chris! "And, he said something about your friend Jesser, how Grace Farley was trapped by him and that's why Art killed him, and that he was gonna disguise himself as a priest and come interrupt things. I don't know, Taylor, it all seems crazy, but I swear...I swear..."

Grace was trapped by Ryan? Chris keeps talking, hanging onto my arm now. "When I left, he was still up there with Grace. He's got a rifle with him, and he just looks crazy, crazy I tell you! I was half-afraid he was gonna kill me and kill Grace and then shoot the whole place up just for the hell of it, 'cause Art's always been kinda nuts, but now he's totally flipped."

"You did the right thing, Chris." I do my best to sound authoritative. "Thanks for telling me. Now, listen carefully. I want you to keep going down this hallway until you reach the doors to the box seats. Tell Mr. Petrowski what you just told me. Okay? And in the meantime, tell him I went to question Grace Farley on the exact details. Can you do that?"

Chris looks even more alarmed. "Talk to Petrowski? Me?"

"You'll be fine, Chris. He'll take care of you. Our priority is to stop Art. He's killed one man, and he'll kill again. We have to protect everyone from him. Can you do that?" He nods, less than certain. I reach out and squeeze his shoulder, just like Petrowski does when he gives an order. "Good man. I know you will. Go quick, now!"

Chris skitters off with one last glance at me, off to spread the alert. And me? Yeah, question the witness. More like get the hell out of Art's way. He's coming here to the stadium to fuck shit up and kill me, I can feel it. Sweat's already trickling down my back at the thought. He won't bother Erin, no, he's got a thing for her, and we're all protecting her, but no one's protecting me. Ryan was first, I'm next.

If Art's coming here, I'm getting the fuck out.

77

Grace

Someone knocks on my bedroom door just as I'm drifting off to sleep. I pull my covers up to my chin. I thought everyone already went to the fights, but maybe they left someone to keep an eye on me.

"Who is it?"

A male voice answers. "It's me, Taylor." Then the door opens and he walks right in.

I shrink back, only I try to make it look like I'm not cowering, really, honest, I'm not hiding anything. It's dark in here, the sun's just gone down. Maybe he can't see me. Maybe he can't see my face. Maybe, please?

I don't want to see Taylor. Of all things in this world, I do not want to see Taylor Burkes.

Jesus, please believe me, I regret everything, only I don't, because if I hadn't...but I did.

He takes another step in. "Sorry, I didn't mean to startle you. No one's downstairs, so I let myself inside. Hope you don't mind."

"No, no, I don't mind." I lick my dry lips. "What're you doing here? Thought you'd be at the fight, same as everyone else."

"No. I mean, I was, but I knew you'd been feeling bad, so I came over to check."

I laugh. It comes out slightly hysterical. "You're missing the fight of the century to see me? That's awful sweet." Is this guy for serious?

All at once he comes over and sits on the edge of my bed.

"Actually, it's more than that, really. I heard—that is, someone told me—that Art Weber came here. Came up to talk to you specifically, just a bit ago."

"You did?" Chris. Chris must've run off and told. Wasn't he the one who let Art in? The rat. "Yeah. Yeah, he did. I mean, I guess I should've called for someone, but how could I?"

"Yeah, of course. I understand. And he didn't...say anything?"

"Say anything?" I repeat. "Like what?"

"Like, oh I don't know, like he was going to disrupt the fights or go kill someone. Something like that."

I rush to assure him. "No, no. Nothing like that. He wanted to go see the fights, but I don't think he was going to mess them up." Just the wedding afterward, only please don't ask me about that.

"Right, right." Taylor pauses, running a hand over my quilt and touching my arm almost by accident. "That's good to hear. Only, I heard something about a priest's disguise...?"

Think fast. "Yeah. Yeah, he wanted to disguise himself as a priest because no one would ever guess it was him, and he wanted to know if I had anything he could borrow. Like a costume. And, well, I mean, I had to help him 'cause...'cause..."

"Because he threatened you?"

What? Oh right, dangerous criminal. "Yeah. Threatened me." My throat is parched, and my hands are sweating, shaking as I fumble for my empty water glass. "Taylor, I been sick, so can I ask you a favor? Can you fill up my glass and jug, please?"

He leaps to his feet. "Yeah, course. Course I can. You got a tap downstairs?"

"That's right, in the kitchen."

"I'll be right back."

I lean back against the pillows, watch him go, then close my eyes. Try to slow my heartbeat. Oh my lord. You're okay, Grace, you're okay. Taylor likes you. He's not going to hurt you. You're okay. Art won't blame you for this. You're fine.

Why did I go to Taylor the other night? Why did I have to like him when I was just supposed to be using him for information? He's the enemy, he's one of Petrowski's, the perfect alibi, but if he finds out what I did to Ryan...

What happened to all the easy choices?

Erin was talking yesterday about leaving town. God, but I'd love to go right now.

A radio crackles downstairs, and I about jump out of my skin. Keep it together, Taylor always carries a radio, all the Market boys do. That's all. You can hear him climbing the stairs, girl, he's coming back. Now keep it together, okay? Close your eyes. Play it off that you're sicker than you are.

Taylor's talking to someone, but I can't make out the words coming through the speaker, even when I strain my ears. I open my eyes. Is it just me, or does his face look sweaty? His eyes are definitely big. He's...surprised?

I take my water glass from his outstretched hand with a thanks. No response. "Are you alright?"

Taylor twitches. "Yes. No. I'm fine. I...it's that...I just got a call." He takes a deep breath. "They want you at the stadium. Mr. Petrowski wants you at the stadium."

We stare at each other. I bet I look scared, but so does he. Why would he be scared?

"Me?"

"They want you." The bomb drops. "They want you for murdering Ryan Jesser two nights ago."

Oh my God. Oh my God, this can't be happening. I was just thinking, what if he found out? This can't be for real. Can it?

"Do you believe them?"

Pause. Taylor looks away. "Yeah, I do."

My alibi falls to ashes around me. "He was going to rape me." Taylor says nothing. I have to convince him, I have to. "Taylor, you know him, you heard what I said earlier, you know what he's like. He came out to get me, and I had to do something or he'd have gotten me, and a knife was all I had. It was dark, and he had me trapped and nobody was out there, nobody to help me, so I had to, don't you see? You gotta believe me, Taylor!"

I stop, holding back tears. They didn't believe Erin. Why the hell would he believe me? Please, please, just believe me.

Taylor meets my eyes square. "I do."

Oh my God. Oh thank God, thank you, Jesus.

"Can you walk, Grace?" He looks grim.

"What?"

He opens a dresser drawer and begins rooting around. "I believe you, Grace, I really do, but we still gotta go. We've been ordered, and you don't disobey those, believe me." He stops for a moment to stare at the wall. If I didn't know better, I'd say he's as terrified as I am. "Not Mr. Petrowski, you don't."

78

Erin

Safety is an illusion that nothing bad will happen; you have to feel it in your bones, because it don't exist anywhere else. Nothing's safe. Not really.

I can't run in this dress, can barely walk in the shoes someone strapped me into. They cut into my ankles, rub the top of my feet, pretty sure I'm bleeding there somewhere. I'm on a seat like a throne in a place where I shouldn't be. All those factory barons and their fancy wives sit in these boxes, and they don't talk to me, the barmaid, the girl who ain't got the sort of face you show off right now. I feel so...disjointed.

Married. Wedding. Is there anyone who objects? Speak now or forever die inside.

Nathaniel's been whispering in my ear for the last half hour, something about signing with my left hand and giving the wrong middle name, as if that will fool anyone, like this is some unfortunate event and not a fucking spiraling disaster that's long out of control. We're not in Kansas, I don't have a fairy godmother. This is the real life because fantasy is no longer an option.

Three bare-knuckle fights go down, first one is quick, second one is three rounds of bloodbath, and third is a fair fight to the finish. Now we're into the duels as the crowd is moving past tipsy to all-out drunk. They scream for blood as the boards change over.

Knife duels go two rounds of seven minutes. The first one of the night is over before it starts, a sudden attack sending a jet of blood spurting dark across the mats. The paramedics close in like swarming ants, but the crowd ain't satisfied, no, not yet. They want more, more death, more pain, more violence. They're staying for the wedding after, they're staying for it all, and if I would've worn white, it would've soaked up that crimson like the fed's battle flag.

Second duel begins ten minutes later, two skinny men like dancers on the balls of their feet, graceful as snakes, with fangs just as sharp, as the bell rings. And after this...

Fight number six will end the night, ages sixteen and sixteen. They've done it with fists, now let's make 'em do it again, but better. Simon and Connor, dueling it out in the battle of the decade.

79

TAYLOR

As soon as we're in Petrowski's box, Joe and Cooper bind Grace's hands, strips of plastic around her wrists so tight they nearly cut her. I watch as they do it. Let it happen.

Gotta play by the rules or watch my own self get murdered instead. Mr. Petrowski can do it. Will. It was all fun and games throwing Art out of a truck, only now I'm the one being held to the fire, and it's not funny anymore, blessed Mary.

Maybe it was never funny at all. Maybe it was all nervous laughter.

Petrowski's watching the fights. I stand behind him in guard position, hands clasped behind my back, ready for anything. The break before the final match has just begun when he crooks a finger at me.

"Yessir?"

Petrowski doesn't even look at my face. "Look over there. Way up, near the top."

He points with his little finger, not to the mats below, but to the stands. I squint and peer over the lights at the shadowed faces.

"Near the top, sir?"

"See the one in the priest getup? Bald guy with a mustache."

I've got a sinking feeling in my stomach. "Yessir."

"Art Weber. Go take care of him."

Take care of him. Me.

I do believe in spooks, but I have to pry my jaws apart to answer. "Yessir."

My eyes meet Grace's as I head to the door, and she breaks into a struggle. "Where are you going? You can't just leave me here!"

I can. I really can. I can let them tie you up and toss you to the wolves and bet on your survival. Erin's in the next box over surrounded by her friends, and she's wearing shoes she can't run in and a dress that makes it hard for her to breathe, and I watched that too. I watched over it all. I've watched everything. No, worse, I've *helped*. And now they're hurting Grace. Am I going to help them with that too? Am I going to take care of her?

I stop, turn back. "Sir?"

"What is it, Burkes?"

"How long will Grace be here?"

"Not...long. Not once you finish your errand. For now, she stays with me."

Finish my errand. Stays with me. It's like the words are rattling back and forth in my head, around and around and around. One leads to the other.

Grace said Simon was being used against Erin. And now Grace is being used against me. Oh Mother of God. I can't meet her eyes. "Yessir."

She was right, she was so right, and I've been so stupid. Yeah, he'll make me hurt her. He'll make me do anything he fucking wants. So, so very stupid.

Back to the corridors, with their electric lights and concrete floors and my footsteps echoing ahead of me. I know what he does to traitors and rogues, I believe every story. Art won't get away with what he's done, and now that Petrowski knows that Grace was part of it, neither will she. If Erin tries to escape tonight, he'll take out Flaherty, son or not, and probably me, for that matter. I'm her guard. I can't let anything happen to Erin.

Can I let something happen to Grace?

I find the maintenance stairs to the top of the stands. They're right next to a small room where a shaking Chris is picking the lock on a gunmetal gray door. Chris Hopkins, bookie, dishwasher, loser.

Sneak.

He told on Grace, he told Petrowski, and now Grace is at the mercy of that monster who's going to take her out back to shoot her just so he won't get blood on the carpet.

The door pops open. I grab the handle before Chris can go in.

"When you finish following whatever orders you got"—I smile at him as his face goes even whiter—"you wait right here, Chris. Boss's orders. You got it?"

Our radios crackle to life at the same time. "Are you in place?"

I don't take my eyes off Chris as I unholster my gun. Looks like I'm just tying into the main plan. And of course Chris is part of it. Of course. "Almost there."

"Hurry up," comes the call. "The fight'll start any second."

Maybe I've never been a hero, but maybe I know what Grace was talking about that night. Maybe I get it. Maybe I know why she cares—because you have to care, because if Petrowski will do it to Erin, he'll sure as hell do it to anyone in this town. Me, Grace, Flaherty, Joe, doesn't matter who we are if we get in his way. I can die now, or I can die later. Would the wait be worth it?

Some things are worth absolutely anything.

I climb the back stairs all the way to the top, spot my target a few rows down. Time to do this.

80

Simon

Someone got stabbed on the mats. They don't say, but I know it. Fights got paused too long, there was too much noise. They don't tell us maybe 'cause they don't want us getting ideas or something, but it's obvious, really. I can feel it in my hands, naked without the gauze I've always worn to fight but don't need for knives.

A bell rings. Plenty of hubbub and noise, shouts, cheers, it's all blurring together. Connor's trainer, Tom Keats, is eating something, moving his jaw like a cow. Connor's stretching while I bounce on the balls of my feet, warming up. Need to get warm. Come on, come on.

There's four people left in here, maybe four people left in this whole entire world. I catch Connor's eye, hold his look. Us next.

The door opens. Is it that time already?

"Flaherty and Hall, you're on deck!"

Yeah, it's already. Now or never, and it's gonna be tonight.

I walk down the dark tunnel ahead of Connor, toward the light. My feet seem to swing themselves, one foot, then another, into the brightness.

The roar nearly knocks me off my feet as people lose their fucking minds. I almost stop, but Mick's hand is there on the small of my back pushing me on, forward march. No stopping a barge once it's on the river. Mick's arm is around my shoulders as he points to something way up high. A box. A box, and a woman in a blue dress waving like to die. Erin, yeah, and...is that Seth? Darryl? All of them from the front room, together and cheering for me, 'cause I can do this, I gotta do this.

Mick squeezes my shoulders, leans in until his lips almost brush my ear to shout, "Just like in practice, Simon. Just like you always do. Kick his ass." One extra squeeze. "I know you can." Then he slides the jacket off my shoulders, fingers brushing like hot wire until I'm left in my blue shorts, all but naked in front of the whole world. My whole world.

"SAINT FLAHERTY! SAINT FLAHERTY!"

Saint Flaherty. That's me. The cheer's sweeping through the stands like a plague, louder and louder, but now there's another chant under that. "HALL! HALL! HALL! HALL!"

The official runs his hands over my shoulders, arms, and ears, checking the tape across my knuckles. No gauze, no gloves, just tape, cup, and mouth guard as my only protections. There's no grease on my face or arms, no needle marks, nothing. Just me and my knife.

Mick unsheathes it, gives it one last polish on a bright white cloth he brought along just for doing that, and hands it over. I'm not sure the screaming could get louder, but I swear to God it just did.

Whatever happens next, it's gonna be a good match.

All I can hear is our names. All I can see is the gleam of that blade, reflecting a thousand and one faces, a million hopes, but only two dreams.

Me or him, at last. That's all this is, Simon Saint Flaherty versus Able Connor Hall in the fight of the year.

I duck under the ropes and climb onto the mats to better see the box where Erin's still screaming my name. I touch my fingers to my lips, a final kiss for her, 'cause I never got to hear her say good luck before this fight. Every fight, but not this one. Across from me, Connor's crossing himself, 'cause that'll make a difference, any of this will make a difference. It's the end of the world, and I'll die in front of five thousand people.

And then I'll be born again.

The ref's waving us toward the center. I flip my mouth guard around, stride forward. Catch one last look from Mick.

And now it's Connor and me facing up, me and him, yeah, him and me, just like always. The ref's shouting, and I can't hear what he's saying, but I don't need to. I know how to do this. I *know*. Here, I am king.

Connor smiles, a real smile, just for me. I adjust my grip on my knife. We stand in position. Ready or not, here I come.

A bell rings.

I grin.

81

Like poetry, that's how a knife fight looks. Like something beautiful in the middle of all the world's ugly. If you do it right, anyway.

It's being done right today.

They circle, sizing up each other. They know each other's reach in the normal way, but it's amazing what three inches of steel will change, and that's the beauty of it.

I'm holding my breath, clutching the bench. The stadium's gone so quiet I can hear their footsteps on the mats all the way up here. Couldn't have stayed locked away if I'd wanted to. This is where it is. It. Everything.

Simon lunges, fist out, quicker than a boy of his build looks like he should be able to go. Connor dances back, ducks, sideswipes. Simon spins out of the way, then kicks out, connecting with Connor's thigh. Connor staggers and swipes, but just as quickly they're both ten feet apart, back in position, Simon in dark blue shorts, Connor in light, and who decided that?

Come on, kiddo, you can do it. Fuck him up.

Connor goes for a backhand swipe. Simon catches his forearms and they grapple for a moment, fingers scrabbling at soft wrists, then break apart. No time to breathe, though, 'cause Simon's back at it, coming in high, leaving his side vulnerable. Connor goes all out, up and under with a reach that's an inch longer, but Simon slips past at the last moment.

Connor hits the mats hard, knife sliding away before coming to a stop two feet out of his reach. Simon's on him in an instant, attaboy, pinning his legs, but Connor's got Simon's wrists, forcing his own knife toward his chest, closer, closer. Simon swivels, comes around, and just like that they're apart again, on their feet, and Connor has his knife back, dammit. If my heart beat any harder, I think it'd explode.

This, this is fighting. This is what it's all about. This is everything we've trained for, everything I could've hoped. It's going to be close, but Simon's gonna win. I can feel it.

I know it.

They're breathing heavy, but the round still has four minutes. Three have passed. Come on, kiddo, come on.

"Get him, Simon!"

That from the boxes, followed by a ragged cheer that dies down just as quickly. They're squared off, weapons in position, and the feeling's turned from electric to thunderous. You can almost taste the copper blood scent in your mouth.

They move at the same time, head-on, in and out. First, Connor backs Simon in a corner, and just as quick they're on the other side and Simon's at the advantage. Back and forth they slash, trading blocks until suddenly with thirty seconds on the clock they go down in a tangle of limbs. This is it, the do-or-die moment. Come on, Simon.

Everything plunges into blackness as the lights cut out.

All we're left with is the afterimage of those pale arms moving too fast to stop, thrusting down. Oh fucking hell no, Simon...

A thud from the mat, and a sound like a knife plunging into something soft.

"NO!"

One voice, male, from the center of the ring, and I can't tell who from. Oh God. I can't tell who from as Erin's voice splits the air with, "SIMON!"

I'm on my feet. No no no, this isn't what you think it is, *no*, he's okay. Not Simon, it couldn't be, nothing's happened, it's not Simon, it's not him, my boy like my little brother, it's not him, please, don't let it be him.

The barrel of a gun presses against the back of my head. Recognize the feeling anywhere.

"Time's up, Art."

A hand drops on my shoulder, heavy and hard. My stomach drops through the floor.

No. This can't be real. It can't be Taylor. They wouldn't send Taylor. We were friends once.

My heart stops and then starts again. No, this is real. People are moving around us, people talking, running, but in this darkness, I am all alone. The gun weighs against my skull as an arm wraps around my neck, holding me there, cutting off all air. Cold steel doesn't lie. My heart's beating like crazy, my hands just went numb, and there is no way to escape from this gun, is there?

No, there isn't. Simon's dead, and I'm trapped. Game over.

Breath tickles my ear. "Sorry, Art, but I'm not dying today."

82

Erin

Two gunshots ring out from high up, one after the other. Screaming from everywhere. I claw my way out of my seat, gotta get out of this box, get to the ring, to Simon, but someone's snagged the back of my dress, holding me in the box, pulling me to the ground.

Just as suddenly, muscular arms haul me to my feet. The lights are still off, people panicking everywhere. "Let's get out of here!"

"Darryl?"

"No, it's Seth."

Nathaniel's voice now. "We need to go before Petrowski gets over here!"

My feet tangle. "I can't, these stupid shoes! They're heels. I can't walk."

Hands grip my ankles and rip off the shoes, plastic snapping against my skin. Cool air rushes in from the open door of the box.

Another gunshot blasts through the air. Time to scarper, Darryl on one side, Nathaniel on the other, into the hall that's lit by emergency lights. They turn the teaming bodies into green nightmares, half running, half falling, being jostled by the people pouring out of the exits pushing and shoving, stepping on my bare feet until they're bloody and bruised until just as suddenly we're spat onto the street outside where the crowd spreads out, exclaiming.

Two more gunshots come from somewhere behind, and the crowd surges. I fall to my knees, but the guys keep going, and I'm being dragged by my arms as people step over and around me, but we can't stop or we'll be crushed, stampeded.

Darryl yanks us down behind a bench, and the crowd breaks around us like the waters of a flood, a shrieking mass. My skirts are shredded, legs bloody underneath, but I'm alive. We're alive, all four of us. Nathaniel helps me to my feet.

Machine-gun fire rips the night a dozen yards away. I don't know what the fuck is happening, and the last thing I saw in the stadium was Connor's knife plunging up. If Simon's dead...

Simon's not dead, and we ain't gonna die here tonight, either. We have to get out of here. I sink my fingernails into Seth's wrists, and we're off down an alley, feet pounding the pavement to the rhythm of my thoughts: Simon's not dead, we're not dead, Simon's not dead, we won't die tonight.

We will survive this. Ten more blocks. We survived a war, and this will not kill us. Seven more, come on, boys, you can make it, my lungs burning hot. I will not die of the dark. I will not die because of this. I will *live*.

We're two blocks away when I smell the smoke.

No, no way. It's too early.

I break away from the others, flat out sprint with all I've got left. An explosion rocks the street under me, and I keep on until I round the corner and see it for myself.

My house is in flames, red hot climbing up the walls and beginning to break through the roof as the smoke boils out. Windows blow out one by one, popping like gunfire.

Holy shit.

It's one thing to dream it every night of my life and another to see it. It really is.

Oh my God. My God. All my sins.

Tears drop down my face and land on my chest, and I didn't even know I was crying. Don't even know why. My shoulders begin to shake, and I want to laugh, scream, and dance in the ashes raining down from the sky. This is what I wanted. This is what we planned. So why am I crying? The hell is wrong with me?

It's burning. It's burning and it's gone. My home. My house. My life.

And it don't matter, 'cause Simon's dead. I saw it.

Seth is staring, mouth open, and Nathaniel reaches out toward me. "Erin, I'm so sorry..."

I shake my head, wipe my tears, keep down the bubble that's growing in my throat. There's small explosions coming from the front room now. The bottles, it'll be the bottles of liquor boiling until they pop, and ain't nobody here to see it but us.

Well, not quite.

Down the street, the door of a truck opens. Chuck Farley gets out, jogs over, closer and closer, his back to the fire so I can't see his face. Every bit of blood seems to have leaked out of my body, and my legs are throbbing where the pavement scraped them, feet red-raw agony. I wish could just die right now. All my work, and I burned it to the ground as sure as if I'd lit the match myself. I'm a fool. A fool and an idiot, and I dragged him into it.

Chuck's panting with exertion. "Sorry I started so early, but I laid the fuse too short. How'd the fight go? Who won?"

I can't speak, so Seth does it for me. "Power failure at the stadium and then someone opened fire. It was a stampede."

A siren goes off in the distance. The sky? No, war's over. A fire truck, or something like it.

Chuck pulls himself together, his face a nasty shade of white. "That so? I've got your bag in my truck, Erin. Went in and got your stuff earlier. These three coming along?"

Nathaniel, Darryl, Seth, they came for me, came to rescue me, even though it was stupid and misguided and could've got them all killed. They did that. It didn't matter in the end, but they did it.

And if I keep standing with them, they'll die for it. It ain't over yet. Can't cry, or I'll never stop. Come on, girl, lock him away with Jacob. Lock it all away. Close your eyes, and pretend it don't matter.

Swallow.

Speak.

"No, they ain't coming. They've done enough."

Seth steps back as realization breaks across his face, resentment and astonishment all together. "You...you really did have it planned. You planned to get out all along."

No. I planned to tell the world what he'd done to me, out there on those mats with everyone watching. I planned to die so Simon could get away. But instead—hush. Head up. Shoulders back.

Nathaniel tries to take my hand. "Your house, Erin..."

It hurts to say it, literally hurts my throat. "Let it burn." Chuck puts his hand on my arm. "Go home, you guys. Go now, and go quick, and good luck. I'm getting out of here, and you should too. Show ain't over yet."

There's a cold place in my heart where I can't think no more. Can't deal with this no more. I'm going, I'm going and Simon is dead. My boy, dead, just like my son, just the same. Jeff always wins. Always.

Chuck leads me to his truck. I don't look back.

83

TAYLOR

I turn the stadium lights back on after finishing up business. The place is empty. Refs are gone, everyone's gone. Flaherty and Hall aren't there, but there's a long streak of blood across the mats, no telling from who. I swallow to calm my nerves. No one is here to watch me head down the stairs to the floor.

No. Wait. Someone's crawling out from under the platform to come to his feet. Tall guy with a leather jacket and a military haircut. Mick Perry. Must've hid there when the panic broke out, and now he's glancing around to see if he's alone.

He isn't.

"Freeze!" I call down. His hands go up instantly. I never pegged him for dumb.

I reach the floor just as Petrowski himself comes out of the locker room, swinging a heavy flashlight by his side. "Well, Mick. This is fortunate."

"Is it?"

"Just the man who can help me most. Well done, Taylor. You've been a good investment."

"Thank you, sir."

I stand at attention next to the ring, waiting as Petrowski turns to our captive. "Where did Simon and Connor go?"

Mick scowls right back. "How should I know? After the lights went out—"

"You didn't see. I understand. Then perhaps you'll know where they're going?"

"Home? I really have no idea, sorry."

"Hmm. I see." My eyes follow Petrowski's gaze to the top of the stands. A team of four men are dragging Art's body down the stairs, only Mick doesn't know whose body it is yet. "That's unfortunate. I was under the impression that you and Simon were quite, hmm, close."

"Are you implying something?"

"Implying what?" Petrowski sounds reasonable. He isn't. "Come on, Mick. Simon's planning something. You know it. I know it. The boy's transparent as water. Why don't we stop him before he gets carried away and does something foolish?"

"Does something to Erin, you mean?" Mick's watching the men, watching the body, wondering who it is. I can see it on his face.

Petrowski smacks the flashlight on his hand, bringing attention front and center. "I don't think that's your business. Besides, Mick, Erin's no friend of yours."

"Course not. You should know plenty about that."

They come down the last few stairs until they're level with us. One of them reaches down and tugs the false mustache. It comes away in his hands. It wasn't a bad disguise, but it wasn't enough. Mick's mouth falls open, and he starts to step forward.

"Hands in the air if you know what's good for you," Petrowski orders, and it's a voice that's made for obeying. Mick stops in his tracks, but he can't keep his eyes off the body. "Art Weber didn't cooperate, let's put it that way. So let's see if you're smarter than that. What is Simon planning?"

"I told you, I don't know."

Petrowski slams the flashlight down on Mick's left shoulder. Something cracks. He doesn't quite cry out, but sweat breaks out on his face as his arm falls to his side, the other clutching it. There's no sound but the breaths he draws between his teeth and the smack of that flashlight hitting the flesh of Petrowski's palm as he smiles.

Petrowski never smiles unless someone's going to die. "Let's try this again. What are Simon and Erin planning? Both of them are gone, and you've been right in the thick of it."

Mick's watching that flashlight, lip twitching, but still not backing down. "I don't know. Erin hates me, she'd never tell me a damn thing, and if you got spies enough to watch her all the time, then you should know that."

Petrowski wallops him in the stomach. "You think I'm stupid? The truth, Mick Perry. I will have it."

"Why?" Mick's trying to be brave, which is pretty fucking stupid right now, but I get it, I really do. Because sometimes you have to. You have to stand up; you'll die either way. "I'm a business man. I trained Simon for the money. I don't know a damn thing about what that kid gets up to in his spare time, and I sure as hell don't know a thing about his redneck foster mother—"

The flashlight swings between Mick's legs, and every guy flinches at the sound he makes as he drops to his knees. Only Petrowski doesn't move. He likes causing pain, and he likes knowing that we know it. "Let's try this one more time, Perry. Last chance. What is Simon planning? I'll do it again."

No answer, no answer from Mick as Petrowski lifts an enormous boot and brings it down on a finger with the sound of a snapping twig.

That does it. Mick whimpers, swallows, closes his eyes. "Fire, a fire."

"That's more like it. Where?"

"Her house. Distraction."

"And after the fire?" Petrowski prompts, resting the flashlight on the back of Mick's neck.

"The river. A friend's going to take them across."

"A friend? That friend wouldn't be a member of the Farley family, now would they?" Petrowski looks to me, nods. "Bring her in."

And that's my cue. Time for me to be a good dog, go into the locker room, and bring in Grace from where he left her.

She's got a bloody lip she didn't have twenty minutes ago, and there's blood around her wrists from where she's struggled with the zip ties. Joe stands behind her, blank as always. I nod to him, and he nods back, then turns to go.

My stomach lurches. "Wait."

"Yeah?"

I hold my hand out for his gun, pointing to my empty holster. "Lost it in the blackout. Loan me yours."

"You gotta carry extras." He pulls a pistol from the front of his cargo pants and hands it over, warm in my palm, then he leaves.

And I can't believe it worked. I meet Grace's eyes. It's now, or it's never.

It's gonna be now.

Petrowski's alone except for Mick, watching for us, waiting. I shove Grace down on the floor in front of him and wait, ever the good guard, ever the yes-man.

"Hey!" The yell echoes down from high up the stadium. "Somebody shot Chris Hopkins!"

All eyes turn upward as sweat breaks out on my forehead. I edge backward, behind Grace. Bend my knees slightly, so no one can see, no one but Grace and Mick. Cut the plastic band around her wrists just like I promised.

I didn't lose my gun tonight.

She's flexing her fingers, and a thrill goes down my spine. We can do this. We will do this.

I slip Joe's pistol from my sock and place it in Grace's hands, put my hand on my holster where my own waits. No, I won't be dying tonight, but somebody else will.

84

Simon

We make it out a side door and down a back street straight for the hills. No time to hide, no reason to, with half the town running with us. Our bags thump my back. I've got the tickets, and Erin'll meet us there. We'll be gone tonight. Forever. The plan's working perfectly.

Except for one part. Oh God, oh shit.

By the time we hit the trees, I'm holding Connor up, arm around his waist 'cause he's stumbling a lot. The towel around his hand is turning dark in a way that scares me more than I really want to think about, but we just gotta follow the path and find the turnoff and he'll be okay. He'll be just fine.

"Hold on," Connor grunts, and I slow to a walk. He slides down, out of my grip, sucking his breath in through his teeth.

"Is it still bleeding?"

"Dunno. Probably."

I kneel, unwrap the towel around his hand. Don't know how much we'll be able to see in the moonlight, but probably we can tell if it's stopped bleeding, right?

The first knuckle of his left middle finger is cut clean off by the sharpest steel, polished up just for me. Bone gleams.

I lean over and puke on a patch of dead weeds.

He's got it wrapped back up when I look again. "No," I say, "it ain't stopped."

Connor don't say nothing. His eyes are closed, oh God. Is this the part where I panic yet? 'Cause I don't want to panic, and I'm trying not to panic, but this ain't exactly in the plan. None of this is in the plan. We're following the plan sorta kinda, but it's cold and we don't have coats, just these stupid tracksuit jackets, and I don't have no fucking clue where Erin is or Mick or anyone, really.

Light flashes on the tree trunks, throwing shadows like crazy-long prison bars. Headlights pull up at the base of the trail and the engine idles. Oh shit, that might be a patrol. We've got about seven seconds to get down and get still before they get out.

Connor doesn't open his eyes when I pick him up, doesn't move as I half run, half crouch behind a boulder next to the path. I cradle him in my lap, though he's as big as I am, and pull the collar of his jacket aside enough to press my ear against his heart 'cause he ain't protesting and the only reason he wouldn't complain about me carrying him is...

Still beating. Right. Of course.

The truck door opens, then clicks shut. Someone's coming up the path. Erin? A guard?

Never know unless I look.

Connor opens his eyes, squeezes them shut again, and tries to sit up. I shove him back down, finger to my lips, and try to peer over the boulder. No dice. Fuck.

With a smirk that's more than half grimace, 'cause I bet he's hurting like anything right about now, Connor levers himself up until the top of his head just clears the rock. Then he's down just as fast, his hand over my mouth. Good news, it ain't.

Leaves crunch, then comes the scrape of boots on stone. A flashlight beam sweeps around the trees, casting us in deeper dark.

There's a small click of the flashlight going off and another click I can't identify.

Bullets rip into the woods around us, back and forth, hitting stones and trees until I've like to gone deaf. Fucking hell, what do they know? Someone wants us dead, someone's banking on us hiding in these weeds, and if we move even an inch, we're finished, both of us.

Another sweep, louder than the first, and I wish I could remember how to say a Hail Mary.

A hundred yards away, a land mine detonates. Then another next to it, and another behind it. Holy shit, they're all triggering in a line but heading away from us, not toward us, thank God. I peel Connor's hand off my face so I can breathe, nearly crush it in my fingers.

Headlights sweep through the trees again. Our guy's legged it. The roar of the land mines stops echoing. I bit my lip so hard it's bleeding all down my chin.

Connor's tugging my hand. "Come on, come on. Let's go."

"Why?"

"Because someone tipped us off. They came here, didn't they?"

I wipe my mouth on the back of my hand, try to shake the ringing from my ears. "Connor, you feeling okay? A couple minutes ago you sorta seemed to…"

"I'm fine. Let's go."

Right, okay. I don't believe him, but we can't linger neither, 'cause he's right—Petrowski's after us.

We stumble on, eyes peeled for the boulder that's been cleft in two by a tree. That's what the map said we was looking for. Not that I can see much, but every last rock's getting a going over, and I hope we don't miss it in the dark. What if we do? Will we ever make it out? Will we be stuck in the minefield forever?

There it is, just like the map said. Right there, the big boulder.

"It's got mines all around the sides," I tell Connor. "Mr. Farley said they was bouncing betties. That's why no one bothers it; we gotta go over the top."

It's about seven feet high. We both stare at it for a long minute.

"You go first, then pull me up," he says.

"You okay?"

"I'm fine. Stand on my back." He kneels down in the leaf litter, bending over until he's turned himself into a human step stool. Probably been in that position a million times, waiting to be stepped all over by a hundred different men. Jesus, fuck my brain sometimes.

"You gonna hurry up, or you waiting for the sun to rise? What, Simple Simon can't climb in the dark?"

Ten seconds later I'm up and Connor is reaching for me. I haul him over and jump down on the other side. Reach back, let him slide into my arms. He's hurting something bad, 'cause he ain't never let me help him with anything before, and this is so bad. If anyone's out there watching us, please, please help us, anyone at all, 'cause I'm so sorry, Connor.

Didn't mean to cut your finger off, though I know you'd have done the same to me. Didn't mean to win like that, didn't mean to hurt you that bad...

I set him down as gentle as I can. Almost in slow motion, he stumbles backward a couple steps. He's tired and hurt, and it's been a long night already, and it won't be getting no shorter. His foot crunches something under wet leaves.

Click.

I hit the ground before Connor even moves and grab his ankle, yank hard, get him down now now *now*...

The night explodes.

85

Grace

Petrowski's goons all run out of the arena toward the body they've found, leaving Art on the floor just a few feet away. Poor Art, who was only trying to help me, help Erin, help everyone but doing it all wrong, hurting them all instead.

But he's not the one who's to blame for tonight. No, not just tonight. Everything.

Soon the only ones left are me, Mick, and Taylor. And, of course, Petrowski, staring impassively at the corpse in front of him, back to us, 'cause we aren't even human to him. I hate him, no, I *abominate* him. He's the one who started all this. He's the reason Art's dead and Simon was fighting and Erin was hurting so bad it near killed me to see it.

He's the reason I had to kill Ryan. He was the boss, and he said women were worthless. Ryan learned the lessons straight from the top, and I can see that now. Art was right, I did the world a favor the other night.

I feel the weight of the gun as it thunks into my palm behind my back. Remember what Taylor said in the locker room: "I get it now."

I don't even stand up, 'cause I'm too close to miss. Petrowski and Ryan have that much in common, and so much more. Swing my arms around and up, finger on the trigger...

Crack.

The recoil shudders through my body like the taste of something bitter. Petrowski falls to the ground face-first. He never even saw what hit him.

Me. It was me. I hit him for every fucking thing this man ever did. Everything he would've done if he'd had the chance. It scared me to death to kill Ryan. God, I about died 'cause I killed Ryan, but this, this? Not an ounce of guilt, not a shred of it. Jesus, I do not feel guilty, and if you don't understand, then take me to heaven and I'll explain it.

We're free.

Mick struggles to his feet, cradling his arm, and Taylor's already shoving me forward. "Go, Grace. I'll cover for you, both of you, just go!"

I take two steps, turn back. Take Taylor's hand in mine. "Come with me."

"Don't worry about me, babe. I'll find you after." He squeezes my fingers and pulls away, a little wistful. "I made a mess, but I'm fixing it now. I promise. So don't you die tonight."

I believe him. Somehow, I really do. Mick takes off, and I follow, running into the night to safety, and it's a safer world than it's ever been before.

86

Erin

"Where are we going?" I ask.

"The path. You'll see. Where's Simon?"

"Not coming."

"I'll take you down it, then. There's a car waiting there. Don't know if you'll like the driver, but you'll just have to get on."

Buchell's lone fire truck speeds past. Too late for that. More machine-gun fire in the distance, another direction this time, maybe the hills? The town's gone crazy. Just crazy. It sounds like a total war, but I'm getting out.

At last we're into the woods, ground cold as charity as I change into clean clothes, wincing every time they touch my battered legs. They're beginning to ache, but I can't let that stop me now. Keep it down, go numb, it's only pain. Only pain.

Chuck leads me down a rough path what seems to go forever. Half a mile? A mile? I don't know how far we walk, up the hill until we're high enough to see a bit of the town below, see the stadium lit back up, cars burning in the parking lot, and a fire that's gotta be my place on the other side of town. The depot on the edge gleams brighter than anything else. My last view of Buchell is total chaos.

Over a boulder we clamber, down the other side to stumble through the dark woods into a stream. I'm so cold my teeth chatter, so cold I can barely stand it, wading through knee-high water with Chuck's hot hand in mine. My cuts sting, needles singing through my veins, and my teeth are chattering as we reach the far bank.

I freeze. Someone's muttering nearby.

"C'mon, come on, you can do it, come on, *please*." A branch snaps, and dry bushes rustle. Chuck and I stay still, water running over our calves.

"You gotta move, you gotta. Come on."

Lord in heaven, I know that voice. My stomach lurches. It's Simon.

I stumble up the embankment, and there on the ground, right there, I can see his red hair glinting in the moonlight.

"What...?"

My boy. My precious boy, precious, stupid boy. I seize him in my arms and I can't stop crying and feeling his face to check that he's all in one piece. He's really here. He's really alive. I never thought he'd make it, but now...

"Erin? Oh thank God, Erin, you have to help us, you have to!"

Us?

Simon's clutching my arms, pleading. "Connor got fucked up in the fight, and then some mines went off and he's got shrapnel in his leg and I carried him here but he won't let me no more, says it hurts too much."

Chuck pulls out a flashlight and shines it on the tangled shape on the ground. Lo and behold, it's Connor Hall, clutching his leg, face twisted in pain. Blood's smeared all down his legs and Simon's too. The hell is going on here?

Simon kneels by his side, stroking his hair. "Come on, Connor, it's okay, you'll be okay. You're coming with us, you'll be fine."

The night is too cold. We're all shivering, Connor most of all. Chuck pulls bandages from nowhere, and all I can think is, Why is Connor here at all?

Oh come on, you know why.

I join them on the ground, fishing Simon's fighting knife out of his pocket and slitting Connor's shorts up the leg to reach the wound better. It's a dark spot on the pale skin of his upper thigh, nearly at his privates, ragged around the edges. Chuck moves the light over it.

Then he moves it farther up Connor's hip.

Right there, right for us to see, is the reason Connor be here, can't come with us. Not ever, no way.

You know, I never thought I'd see the day, and that was pretty stupid of me because we all knew what Connor was, didn't we? I saw his pain, didn't I? I knew it, I'd been there, hadn't I just? Connor's sold himself to every devil in town, don'tcha know? Don't everyone know? Don't we even listen to ourselves? He did deals and got fucked by every last bastard in hopes that one of them wasn't a devil after all, but no, them's all devils, and Connor was tricked and duped and hung out to dry by all of them, including me, and that's why he can't come, Simon, he just can't.

He's got a tattoo just like all Petrowski's men have, except instead of on his arm or neck where everyone in town would see it, Connor's hidden his away on his hip where no one would look these days. Heart and cross and a crown of thorns, inked black on clean flesh.

Did he think that would save him?

Simon covers the tattoo with his hand, hiding it from our prying eyes. "He wants out." His voice is low, pleading. "He bought his own ticket and he asked if he could come and I said yes. So he is. He wants it as bad as you do."

I can't hear anything but the sound of the stream rushing through the night and Connor's ragged breathing. There's no one here but us. Chuck looks to me. Simon looks at Connor. Connor opens his eyes and focuses on Chuck.

So much pain there, all his sins. "You're Grace Farley's dad, right?"

Chuck's on instant alert. "That's right."

"You better go back to town right quick."

"Why?"

"'Cause I told Petrowski that she killed Ryan Jesser." No. No, Connor, no you didn't, say you didn't do that. Connor meets my eyes. "I wanted out of this town so bad, and we needed a distraction. I wanted it so bad."

Right in front of me, for the first time I ever seen, Connor Hall starts to cry.

Chuck makes a move, and I seize his wrist. "Go. Go help Grace. I'll take care of things here, but you go find Grace. Help her. We'll be fine."

"If they've hurt her—" Chuck pulls me into a tight hug, whiskers brushing my hair as he pushes his flashlight into my hands. "Godspeed, Erin."

Then he's splashing across the stream, sound fading in the distance. Our last protector is gone, and there's just us, me and Simon and Connor, and what can I do?

87

TAYLOR

I kneel next to Petrowski, take his pulse. Nothing. No, wait. Sluggish, faint, but still there. I turn him over. He glares up at me with hateful eyes. Yeah, well, you can hate me, because I fucking well hate you too.

His breathing is shallow, the bleeding steady. I don't try to stop it. Why should I?

There's a bit of finger on the floor nearby. I pick it up, hold it in front of Petrowski's eyes.

"See this? You see this? You told Connor to kill Simon when the lights cut, but he didn't. And if Flaherty had been the one to make it out, you'd have had him executed for murder. It was perfect, but they didn't do it. They didn't follow your plans. This is all you got." I place it on his chest on the pool of seeping blood. "Grace said that she didn't kill Ryan, that Art was the one who did the actual deed. She felt horrible, though. I could tell. Well, hope she doesn't feel bad about this, 'cause you deserve it."

I take out my knife, hold it up where he can see it.

"This is for you." I slash my botched tattoo straight across. It hurts like fire, and like fire, it makes me clean. The blood flows out bright red, covering up what never should have been there. "You tried to make me into a monster like you. You damn well nearly succeeded. But I'm better than that."

I pluck his radio off his belt. He makes a feeble swipe at me, but I step back. No one's going to stop me now, no way. I grin and press the button. One last thing to do before I get out of this town.

"Attention! Attention! This is Taylor Burkes speaking on behalf of Mr. Petrowski. Call off the search and pull all units in. I repeat, pull all units in! Over and out."

Then I level my gun at his forehead. One more bullet to end it all.

88

Erin

Connor's still watching me through dead eyes as I reach out to touch the tattoo, trace it with my fingertips. Heart and cross and a special little symbol of his own choosing, just like all the rest.

But he isn't them. He's Connor, and everyone knows what Connor is.

"Do you hate me, Erin?" he whispers.

Can't answer that.

"You'd have done it too, if it'd have got you away from him sooner. You'd have turned Grace in."

I tug his shorts back over his tattoo again, smooth them down.

He's not wrong. I would have done anything if I thought it would have worked. Anything.

"You can come," I say.

We slow his bleeding. The leg needs stitches, but there's no time, so we pour the antiseptic from Simon's bag over it, wind a bandage, and pray the blood won't seep through too quick. It's not enough. It'll have to do. Simon puts Connor on his back, and we keep on hiking until we reach the road, just a gravel lane, no wider than it needs to be.

The car's on time, a quiet-running SUV, hoods over the headlights and tinted windows to beat all. The driver's face is covered, but he climbs out to help us get Connor in the trunk.

"I'll cover you in blankets now," he explains. The voice is familiar.

"Evan Farley?" I ask.

"That's right." He turns away. "Gotta pay my debts."

We all lie in the back and pull blankets over ourselves. Evan's about to close the hatch when crackling static fills the air.

A tiny voice squawks, "Connor, come in. Connor, are you there? Are you alive?" We all look at Connor. He reaches into his jacket to pull out a radio. The voice continues. "We're pulling back to headquarters. Did you kill Flaherty? I repeat, did you kill Flaherty?"

"Do your own dirty work."

He flings it out of the car into the woods and collapses back into our waiting arms.

Evan slams the hatch and starts the engine. In the dark, a hand finds mine and squeezes, once, twice. Slowly, surely, we pull away into the darkness beyond.

Acknowledgments

First and foremost I would like to thank Mark for believing in me and pushing me to publish. Without your support, I would've abandoned this endeavor long ago. Without your patient ear, I would've gone crazy from not having anyone to tell all my plots to.

Thank you to my alpha reader Ro for your unflagging encouragement. Your willingness not only to read and reread my work but also to brainstorm new ideas and characters has led me to write worlds I would otherwise never have known.

Thank you to my family for listening to me wax poetic over fictional people, and my friends for the same. To Laura, for reading this book back when it still had fifty thousand extra words and then again when it was much lighter.

A big thank you to my copyeditor, Jennifer Zaczek of Cypress Editing, for keeping me to the straight and narrow even as I drowned you in apostrophes. This book would not be half so polished without your patient efforts.

A thank you to all the indie authors who have gone before me and offered not only your knowledge of what you did well but also your warnings from previous failures. You keep me heading in the right direction.

Thank you to all my Twitter friends, too numerous to name, and the folks of #1lineWed, who read my lines and told me you'd love to read more. You have no idea how much your interest has kept me going.

About the Author

S. Hunter Nisbet is a long-time resident of Appalachia, director of theater, and writer of dark tales. You can read more about Hunter at www.shunternisbet.com.

You are encouraged to leave a review of this work online, so that others will hopefully discover and enjoy it.

Please enjoy an excerpt from *Saint Flaherty* Book 2!

1

Connor

The darkness eats my eyes, little teeth tearing into my flesh. Sleep, I wish I could sleep. Just lay my head down and pray the lord my soul to keep.

Not gonna happen.

The breathing on the pillow next to mine stutters and stops. I close my eyes and send up my own little prayer. The empty syringe tumbles out of his hand. Well. Not quite empty. How much left, exactly?

A snore erupts. Time to go.

I don't bother trying to dress in the dark, the hallway is good enough. Management doesn't like us doing that, but the fuck do they know? Two minutes later, I'm down the stairs and onto the street outside. The night is cold enough I've got my coat on, but spring is coming, of that I'm certain. I take a deep breath, draw the smells of the city into my lungs, wet pavement and garbage can rot and the remainders of rain. This is the life I chose. Or the place, at any rate.

My eyes itch with tiredness, but I'm a long ways from home. Seventeen city blocks, to be precise. I knew that when I got my place, did it on purpose. When I'm done for the night, this walk gives me time to settle my thoughts and order them.

I need that time. This time.

A car slows down as it passes, then speeds up again. I flip it off as it goes.

Scioto City is where I live, where I belong, this hive of humans in their concrete boxes. I walk these streets and I own them.

Or do they own me?

Some days, it all feels the same.

THE MERCY OF MEN, coming summer 2016

Printed in Great Britain
by Amazon